All rights reserved. All characters appearing in this work are fictitious. Any resemblance to real persons, living or dead is purely coincidental.

No part of this publication may be reproduced, distributed, or transmitted in any form or by any means, including photocopying, recording, or other electronic or mechanical methods, either now known or unknown, without the written permission of the publisher, except in the case of brief quotations embodied in critical reviews and certain other noncommercial uses permitted by copyright law. For permission requests, write to the publisher, "Attention: Permissions Coordinator", at the address below.

Grey Wolfe Publishing, LLC
PO Box 1088
Birmingham, Michigan 48009
www.GreyWolfePublishing.com

© 2015 Jamie Kincaid
Published by Grey Wolfe Publishing, LLC
www.GreyWolfePublishing.com
All Rights Reserved

ISBN: 978-1628280807
Library of Congress Control Number: 2015935169

Kismet
Book One Of The Kismet Series

Jamie Kincaid

Jamie Kincaid

Kismet
Book One Of The Kismet Series

Jamie Kincaid

Jamie Kincaid

Dedication

I would like to thank my husband, David and my three beautiful children, Jacob, Joe and Julia for their love, support and belief in me at all times, it means more than you'll ever know and to my faithful companion, Shiner who is always by my side when I write.

To my sister, Pam... your lil' sis finally did it! And to my mom and dad who are looking down at me and are always with me, thank you for being the best parents a girl could ever ask for, I'll always be "your girl." Live life with no regrets!

I love you, guys!

And to my beloved hometown of Spencer, West Virginia and to all who call this place their own like I do... this is for you... there is no place like home!

Liam and Jenny... they are in each and every one of us, believe in fate, true love, kismet... pickles, wild horses, silly jokes, sweet tea, endless talks, endless nights, drives to nowhere, heart and soul, you n me, always here, always and forever, destiny 831.

Prologue

      My mom used to say to me that things always happen for a reason. There's no use worrying about something that's out of your control. We may not understand it in the beginning, but if we give it time things have a way of becoming clearer and working themselves out. It's not always up to us to understand but just to accept things for what they are. I never took much heart to what Mom used to say. I was a kid and thought I knew it all, but Mom got it. She hit the nail on the head when she told me those sayings, and not until he came into my life did I realize how much Mom's little sayings rang true, especially for me.

The world is a funny place, and things do happen for a reason. There are many unforeseen elements in our lives that we don't pay attention to that can shape our future without us realizing it. Everyday decisions we make can play such a key and vital role in our lives. There are many signs along the way to alert us, to guide us, and paying attention to them is our job. We may not realize the signs for what they are and mistake them for something else, and circumstances beyond our control can intercept and change our path. They are there for a reason if we only take the time to consider them. The signs can be different for everyone: a feeling, a memory, or even a spiritual being that forewarns us of upcoming events, good or bad. For me, the sign was a number. A number that until my senior year in high school I thought was nothing more than a mere digit. But that was before October 11th, before he came into my life.

Liam Larson, just the sound of his name ran shivers up and down my spine, but that wasn't always the case. As a matter of fact, I used to detest the mere mention of his name. Liam was nothing more than a super jock at our school, who thought he was God's gift to every girl old enough to know who he was. He was the all-star tight end for our football team, the Spencer Yellow Jackets, and the thought and desire of every girl fifteen years or older within a three county radius. Not that I cared, but it was hard to ignore his devastatingly good looks even if I did want to. When Liam walked into a room, all eyes turned in his direction. He was easily six foot three with curly dirty blonde hair that fell right above his shoulders. He kept it back most of the time in a tight ponytail, and during football season he would have his "#11" shaved into the back of his head, it was a trend he started that caught on rapidly with the rest of the football team. His eyes were blue, but not your ordinary blue. No, Liam's eyes were transparent, a crystal-blue, like pool water; and when you would look at them I swear they danced with the same motion that happens when silent water has been abruptly interrupted by the splash of an unwanted visitor.

Liam ran with the popular kids, and I never was one to go for that crowd. Liam might as well have been the president of the United States, and I wouldn't have cared. Going unnoticed was much more my style, and one I wasn't ready to relinquish. But mind you, I had great friends. There was Brenda Benson: she had everything, beauty, and brains. She was tall with a model's figure and chestnut brown hair that she curled to frame her face. Frannie Downing was more my height, (five foot four on a good day) with coal, black hair that she wore in a very smart bob below her chin. Her favorite piece of clothing was her brother's ratty old football sweats and even in them she looked good, although she never thought so, but the rest of us knew better. All you had to do was watch how the guys in the school would stare at her when she would walk by, always looking but never approaching. Shauna Stewart was the bubbly one out of our bunch. She hadn't a care in the world and didn't think any of us should either. Then there's Missy Garrett. She was smart as a whip, and it was apparent that she came from a family of doctors. Her brain never stopped working, and she always had a book in her hand. She wore glasses, and her straight, metallic black hair that framed her face made her already look like a doctor; all she needed was the white coat and stethoscope.

  Then last but definitely not least, Kendra Bishop, my dearest and closest friend in the world. If there were ever two peas in a pod, it would be the two of us. We became friends when our moms put us both into the Bumble Bees Majorette Marching Group when we were five years old, but it wasn't until we entered high school that we became inseparable as best friends. We did everything together; you name it and we did it. Kendra and I could talk on the phone for hours and not say anything. Most of the time, we would just be listening to each other's music. She was my confidante, and I was hers. We were crazy and always had fun. If I was feeling down and out, all I had to do was call Kendra and the party began. Definitely my go-to girl, we could depend on each other more than the other girls. The two of us shared our innermost secrets with each other (especially if the subject was boys) and always—and I mean always—had each other's back.

Chapter One
Chance Encounter

It was Friday night, which in Spencer meant high school football. Most people spent their entire lives in the area. If you were a boy, you either played for the beloved Yellow Jackets or you marched in the almighty Blue & Gold Marching Band. Spencer was a tiny town that lived and breathed for its Friday night lights. We were facing our arch rivals, the Walton Tigers. I was a majorette; my third year on the squad.

We had just finished our half-time show when I saw him. We came off of the field, and I had forgotten to pick up one of my batons. The crowd was in a complete state of hysteria, chanting and roaring as the anticipation grew. In a matter of moments, the Spencer High Yellow Jackets would be thundering into the stadium, If I wanted to retrieve my baton, I would have to act quickly or it would end up crumpled and mangled under the football team's cleats. The rest of the band was already off of the field. Where was it? I didn't understand it. I pretty much stayed between the forty-five and fifty yard line the entire time I did my routine. I murmured to myself, but my baton was nowhere in sight.

The noise from the crowd intensified. I looked into the bleachers, and all I saw was a sea of blue and gold bowing and rising in perfect unison to produce the rippling effect of an awesome wave. The fans were on their feet. They were stomping and clapping in time to the beat of twin brothers, Marty and Mike Skinner's drumbeats... bop diddy bob, stomp, stomp, stomp, bop diddy bop, stomp, stomp, stomp. I quickly turned around, the clock on the scoreboard was counting down from 14, 13, 12 11... 11 seconds to go I was panicking.

"Where's my damn baton?"

"Get off the field, dawg! The team is coming."

I knew exactly who was talking to me. There's only one person who calls me dawg. I glanced up to Kendra to give her a "don't you think I realize that" look when suddenly she yelled, "Watch Out!" But it was too late. I heard the stampede. But before I could react I was trampled by the Mighty Blue and Gold. The second half had begun. My head was spinning from left to right, I couldn't tell if I was still standing or if I was on the ground. The roar of the crowd was muffled by the sound of football players chanting "beat the Tigers, beat the Tigers." They were all around me. I couldn't tell what was going on, and I felt dizzy from the commotion. I had to get out of the way, but where was out of the way?

All around me were football players who for some reason had no idea that there was a majorette on the ground beneath them. "Can't they see me? What's the matter with them?" It seemed like hours were ticking by, but in reality it had been a mere few seconds since I had fallen down. Then out of that sea of blue and gold came a hand, reaching down to me as if the heavens above had opened up and were reaching for me. Suddenly there was nothing around me; all the noise was gone as if someone had pushed the mute button on a remote control. I could see the players all around me; I could tell that they were still chanting, but I could not hear them. They were a blur. The only thing in focus was his hand, and in slow motion out of the craziness from above, I reached up and placed my dirt covered hand into his, my savior, or so I thought.

"Here, let me help you," he said, and with an instant he had lifted me to my feet. The noise returned along with the chaotic revelry and in an instant I knew where I was, about four feet in on the football field near the fifty yard line. The chanting from the stands was as loud as ever, and the chanting on the field was even louder. I looked to my right to thank my savior when he spoke again.

"You better get off the field unless you plan on playing." Then he turned away.

The first thing I noticed was his eyes. They were the bluest blue I had ever seen, with an unusual twinkle. When caught by the stadium lights they flickered with different shades of color. They were mesmerizing. The second thing I noticed though was his tone. The heaven part was right because he thought he was God's gift to women, but in reality he was nothing more than an egotistical moron; a football jock with a tone to his voice that made me want to vomit. In that instant, I utterly loathed him.

"Uggh!" I looked down at my uniform; my once beautiful velvet, cadet blue skirt with gold trim was streaked with green grass stains and dirt, and I still did not have my baton. Time was up. I couldn't look anymore, and both teams were already on the field to begin the second half. Mr. God's Gift had left as quickly as he came. Thank, God! I stomped off the field more pissed off than ever. Not only had I embarrassed myself to the tenth degree, but Mr. God's Gift to women had made me feel even worse by thinking he was doing me a favor by stepping in to save me, HA! I didn't need his or anybody else's help, I was fine. I knew exactly what had happened and I would have been up and out of there on my own accord if he hadn't felt like he had to show off for his adoring fans and peers. "Ahhhhhh! What a jerk! Who does he think he is anyway? Did he think it was funny that the poor little majorette was on the ground? I hate you, number eleven; I hope you drop the ball!" I turned from him, secretly hoping that nobody had heard my outburst. As I said, football ruled Spencer, and a fumble wouldn't go over very well, especially if it happened after I said it.

Once on the sidelines, I threw my remaining baton on the ground with such force that when it hit the ground, it bounced back up and knocked the Gatorade cups off the bench. There had to be at least a hundred of them. *Great,* I thought, with wounded sarcasm. Thankfully nobody witnessed my second airhead act; the blue and gold fans were too wrapped up watching Mr. God's Gift run for a ninety yard touchdown. As everyone screamed "Go eleven!"

I exuberantly screamed, "I hope you fumble!" forgetting my throat was still reeling from the pain from my first outburst. That'll show him. I'm sure it was my ego that was more bruised and battered than my body and quite possibly why I blurted out the fumble, but he really irked me, and I had no idea why. He never had before.

"Really, Jen?" Cody Hodge, the football team's water boy had heard me say everything. I just looked at him in horror. Without saying another word to me, he started picking up all the Gatorade cups. I began to feel more and more like the moron, knowing it was his job to keep the cups ready for the team.

"Here, let me help you with that."

"Nah, that's okay. I got it, anyway I think you better get back with the rest of the majorettes."

I looked back to see the rest of my squad along with the cheerleaders forming a single line to do the touchdown dance, number eleven had done it again.

"Oh, you're right. Sorry Cody! I really have to join them. I'd help otherwise. I'm really sorry I knocked them over. It was an accident."

"Did he really make you that mad?"

"Who?"

"Liam," Cody replied.

"No," I said, as if I didn't realize it was him that I was penning my frustration on. "I'm just upset because I can't find my other baton."

"Well, I'll keep an eye out for it if you want?"

"No, that's okay. I'll just wait till after the game is over. It's no big deal. I'm sure it's got to be here somewhere. It's probably destroyed anyway, but thanks." I smiled apologetically and turned around while he received dirty looks from the team wondering what had happened to all the cups.

After the line dance, I sat down next to Kendra. For some reason, the antics caused from me losing my baton had drained me. I was exhausted from the ordeal and also thirsty as hell. I just wanted to get away, even if it meant just going to the concession stand. "Let's go get something to drink."

"Nah," she replied, "I'm not thirsty right now. Anyway, I don't think you can leave."

"Huh?" She was looking straight ahead; Mr. God's Gift was walking straight towards us, looking right at me with those beautiful, magnetic blue eyes. Oh My God! I thought to myself.

I stared as he approached me, hypnotized by his eyes. The palms of my hands had become suddenly sweaty. His right hand reaching out to me.

"Here, I think this is yours."

I looked down, my mangled baton was in his hand. "Oh, thanks." I glumly looked at what was once a perfectly good baton. The one rubber tip was completely torn off and the blue and gold tape that wrapped the shaft was now ripped into shreds dangling in pieces. My face must have said it all.

"Sorry, looks like it got destroyed when we entered the field."

"Yea, ya think?" I scowled. I was surprised by my tone, wondering why I suddenly ripped into him. Apparently he was trying to do a nice gesture, and I just tore into him.

"Well, here."

He handed it to me as if he didn't even notice my blatant sarcasm towards him. I reached out to grab what was left of the baton; my sweaty hand accidentally touching his when he placed it in mine. A shiver went up my arm. I contributed it to the cold weather but in the back of my mind I knew it was because our hands had just touched, and again, I didn't understand why.

Nothing about Liam had ever been attractive to me. *Why do I now feel this sudden rush over such a simple act?* In trying to compose myself over the premature attitude of being rude, I looked at him and realized he was still staring at me. Our eyes locked into each other's for what seemed like minutes. I looked away, feeling my face becoming flushed. I realized our hands were still holding the baton. I immediately reacted and flinched my hand back taking the baton with me. His hand dropped and as he walked away I watched him go back to his bench where Coach Green was waiting for him.

"What was that about?" Kendra had watched everything.

"What do you mean?" I acted clueless.

"What do you mean, what do I mean?" she replied as if I missed the whole thing. "He couldn't stop staring at you! It was as if I wasn't even here. What happened on the field when you got trampled? Did I miss something? I even told him 'nice touchdown, Liam' and he didn't even say a word to me or look in my direction. It was as if you were the only one here, Jenny!"

"You said nice touchdown to him? When did you say that? And even more importantly, why did you say that? Don't you think his ego is big enough without you inflating it even more?"

"Well, you both need your ears checked, and he was staring at you whether you think so or not."

"Whatever," I replied. "Why would Liam Larson want anything to do with me? He had to look at me, he was handing me my baton! That's it." I took my baton and started walking toward the concession stand for something to drink. Realizing I had just been a complete jerk to Kendra, I turned around to apologize. Glancing down at the bleachers, I noticed Liam was looking in my direction. He quickly turned around when our eyes met. I didn't put much thought into it until I saw Liam look back at me again and gave me a wink and what I thought was a smile. He totally took me off guard. *Was that for me? It couldn't have been. It had to be for someone else. Yeah, that's it.* Anyway Shanna Smith, his on-again-off-again cheerleader girlfriend was right in front of him as she cheered her little heart out, and she was making quite sure that she stayed in Liam's sight. Feeling somewhat disappointed that the gesture wasn't for me, I tried to dismiss it and once again made my way to the packed concession stand even though by that time, I wasn't even thirsty anymore.

"What are you getting?" Brenda and Frannie asked me as they came up from behind.

"Oh, hey guys... ummmm, I don't think I'm getting anything," I said as I looked at the menu.

"Well, are you going to tell us what that was all about?"

"Huh?"

Brenda spoke first, "Liam Larson, you goofball, we all saw it, are you going to talk or do we have to drag it out of you?"

"Oh that, that was nothing. You saw what happened to me. I left my baton on the ground, and he was just returning it to me. That's all." The one thing about having a group of friends: they never miss a trick when it came to boys.

"That's all, huh?" Frannie said, giggling to herself. Brenda and her exchanged smirkish glances towards one other.

"Yeah, that was it. Why is everybody thinking there is something more to it? He just handed me my baton. That's it, done, nothing more." I looked at them both, hoping the subject would be dropped and wishing they would mind their own business.

"What can I get you, Jenny?"

I had made it to the front of the line without realizing it, thank God for Mrs. Hawthorne's interruption. Mrs. Hawthorne waited for my reply, "Oh, sorry Mrs. Hawthorne, I meant to get out. I was just talking and didn't realize I was still standing in line."

"That's okay, hon, do you want something anyway since you're here? I'd hate for you to change your mind and then have to stand back in this line." Mrs. Hawthorne was the wife of Mr. Hawthorne, our band director. She always took it upon herself to make sure that there was nothing that the band members, majorettes, or flag corps ever needed. Mr. Hawthorne and his wife were in their early forties and never had children, so during football season as well as other times they had become our extended parents, adopting all ninety-five of us. I looked back and saw that the line had grown easily to over twenty or thirty people, so as not to hurt her feelings, I went ahead and ordered a bottle of water. It would feel good on my throat, it still stung from my screaming episode towards Mr. God's Gift. Handing her my money, Brenda, Frannie, and I walked down to the bleachers where the band sat. On our way, I ran into Mom and Dad.

"Nice job, honey. Hi Brenda, Hi Frannie."

"Hello, Mr. and Mrs. King," they both chimed together.

"Jenny, do you want us to take your stuff so you don't have to lug it home with you after the game?"

"Yeah, Mom, I'll go get it." My parents came to all of my performances, besides my sister, they were my biggest fans and never missed an opportunity to watch me twirl. But after half time they were always ready to go home. I often felt that they painstakingly endured the first half of the games just so they could watch me at halftime. Dad loved football, watched it every Sunday, especially if the Dallas Cowboys were playing, but I really felt that he could have cared less about the Spencer football team. He was probably one of the only people in Spencer who didn't. His only thoughts, as well as Mom's, was that their daughter was twirling. Football just happened to be going on at the same time. I handed them my batons, keeping the only good one I had left.

"What in the world happened to this one?" Mom exclaimed.

"Oh, I dropped it and the football team trampled on it." Obviously they didn't see what had happened on the field, so the most direct to the point answer was the best. Besides, Mom and

Dad didn't need to know about the whole Liam incident and how infuriated he made me feel.

"Well, we're going to head on home. You looked beautiful out there, Jen."

"Thanks, Dad."

"Tell your families hi from us," Mom said looking at Brenda and Frannie.

"We will," they chimed together.

"Come over some time, I always have apple cake on hand."

"Yum," Brenda answered.

"Definitely," Frannie replied.

My mom was known throughout the county for her baking skills, apple cakes being her specialty, and all of my friends absolutely loved them.

"Don't forget I'm going to Lougini's, after the game!"

"Do you need any money?"

"No Mom, I still have the ten bucks you gave me before the game. I'm good."

"Okay then, we love you and keep safe. You did a great job tonight."

"Love you too," Dad said as he hugged me slipping a twenty dollar bill into my left hand.

"Thanks, Dad," I whispered back to him. "Love you too."

By now the fourth quarter was almost over, I took my seat with the rest of the majorettes. There were four minutes and sixteen seconds remaining in the game. I finalized my plans with Brenda and Frannie and told them that Kendra, Missy, and I would meet them at Lougini's. Missy was in the band with Kendra and me so she would go with us. I sat down in the front bleachers next to the other majorettes, Linda, the head majorette gave me the evil eye as if to say "where have you been?" After halftime we only have the third quarter to walk around and do what we want, me, returning so late only meant she highly disapproved of my actions. She took her role as "head" majorette seriously, something I'm sure I would pay for at the next practice.

The Yellow Jackets were up by three points. It looked like another victory was in the bag for the team. The Tigers had the ball, but it was fourth down and eleven yards to go. There was no way they were going to pull off a first down. Most of the crowd in the stands was beginning to rise and gather their belongings for the trip back to the parking lot, even Cody Hodge was packing up the remaining cups and Gatorade coolers. In the twenty-year history that the Yellow Jackets and Tigers had competed against each other, the Tigers had never won, so, most people weren't expecting anything different from tonight's game. Both teams came out of their huddle. Johnny Bryant was the Tiger's quarterback and their number eleven.

"Hut, hut," he yelled.

The Tiger's center snapped the ball to Bryant. Bryant stepped backwards, his right hand went back in position to throw the ball. Seconds ticked off of the clock. There were less than three minutes and seventeen seconds left to go; and then, as if in slow motion, like the parting of the Red Sea, Johnny Bryant saw an opening right down the middle of the Yellow Jacket line. Instead of throwing the ball, he ran. Without hesitation, he started running, taking the Yellow Jackets by surprise. Forty, thirty-five, thirty, twenty-five yard line. He was still running. The Tiger fans were on their feet going crazy. Anyone who was about to leave stopped what they were doing and watched in disbelief at what Bryant was doing. "Go Johnny!" was all you could hear echoing from the visitor's stands. He was now on the twenty yard line and still running strong. Parker Duncan was on his tail, but Johnny seemed to be two steps ahead of him. He was on the fifteen yard line. The screaming from both sides of the stands was deafening. The Yellow Jacket fans couldn't believe what they were witnessing and neither could the Tiger fans. Touchdown Tigers!

But before the referee could even blow the whistle, I began to hear the whispers. Someone was hurt on the field. All you could see were blue and gold and green and white (Tigers colors), no one could make out who was hurt and what team he was on. Dr. Garrett, Missy's dad, rushed from the stands down to the field, making his way to the huddle where all the players were on bended knees. This was an act of respect for the injured player.

"It's Liam," Kendra said in a subdued voice.

"What?" I said. "How can you tell?" Without having a chance to answer I saw his jersey, number eleven, lying on the ground, not moving. "Oh my God," I whispered to myself.

The medics were now on the field with Dr. Garrett, and in the distance you could already hear the sirens. Liam was hurt. The crowd became quiet; you could've heard a pin drop in the stadium. Everybody sat back down in their seats waiting for number eleven to get back up on his own accord. It looked like the beginning of the game instead of the end, and the only thing I could hear besides the sirens was my own heart beating, and the screams now coming from Liam. He was squirming in pain. "It's okay, shake it off, get up." I kept repeating to myself in a murmured voice. "Get up, what could be wrong, why isn't he getting up?" Injuries were common with football players; it's something they just dealt with: broken noses, broken fingers, you just wrapped them up and sent them back out on the field to play. So why wasn't he getting up? Why wasn't Dr. Garrett wrapping his hand, or ankle? It didn't make any sense.

"Did you see what happened?"

I looked at Kendra, but she just shook her head no. To my right, I could hear Shanna Smith crying and the other cheerleaders trying to console her; obviously their relationship was "on" again. Just then, the ambulance arrived on the field. Pete Garrett, (Missy's uncle), got out and went to the side of the ambulance, along with his assistant, Kay carrying a stretcher. *Were Liam's injuries that bad?* The players backed away, making way for Pete to enter with the stretcher. You could see the coach along with his assistants and Dr. Garrett talking to Liam. Dr. Garrett had removed his helmet. He wasn't moving, but it did look like he was talking. One of the trainers was behind Liam crouched in a kneeling position holding Liam's head. Dr. Garrett waved to Pete to bring the stretcher closer. It took all six of them to put Liam carefully on the stretcher, lift him up, and start carrying him to the ambulance. The crowd went wild, standing and clapping feverishly, yelling "We love you, Liam!" Liam's best friend, Parker Duncan walked alongside the stretcher, giving him much needed support.

I sat there, waiting to breathe. I'd seen players get hurt before, but for some reason I was grief-stricken. Aside from tonight, I didn't think Liam and I had even exchanged glances, much less words to each other. Now I felt like I couldn't breathe until I knew what was wrong with him. *And why? Why do I even care? Of course, I didn't want anyone to be hurt, but why do I have this ache inside me, wondering if Liam will be okay?*

Before he went out of sight, I saw Liam turn his head towards the crowd. The fans went wild again. He definitely was the all-American boy and the one the fans adored. I could have sworn he looked right at me and gave me that same wink and smile from earlier. But Shanna was still right below me, I was sure it was for her. There's no way it was intended for me. He was probably looking for familiar faces in the crowd, and I definitely did not meet that criteria. Pete and Kay carefully lifted Liam into the ambulance; he gave the crowd a "thumbs up" and the crowd roared again as the ambulance doors closed. A hush fell over the crowd as the ambulance drove away.

Parker Duncan, who you could tell was still shaken from Liam's injury, ran back to the sidelines. There still was a game to play with a minute and forty-six seconds left on the clock. The hope of winning the game seemed pretty much obsolete. The Tigers kicker, Rick Morehead entered the field, the kick was up and the ball was good, spiraling to the left of the Yellow Jackets goal posts, inching its way in. The referee held both his hands up in unison, a minute thirty-seven left to go, could this game never end? Coach Green frantically huddled his team together, and you could see the urgency on his face. Parker and the rest of the team huddled around him, hanging on every word the coach said. They broke the huddle, the fans were on their feet again, and Kendra and I stood up, watching in anticipation and hoping for a miracle. "Do it for Liam!" a voice from the crowd yelled.

Parker crouched into position. "Hut, Hut," he yelled. The center snapped the ball and Parker took two steps backward. His right arm in position to throw the ball. It brought to mind a mment of déjà vu of Johnny Bryant. You could see him looking for an open player, he moved to the right, then the left as the clock ticked down. Fifty-six seconds left. The fans were on their feet waiting for Parker to do the impossible. He was becoming desperate, running back and forth, but no one was open… and then, Bam! He went down, sacked. The crowd knew, we all knew, the final seconds ticked off the clock; the Tigers had beaten the mighty Yellow Jackets, fourteen to ten. With helmet off, Parker Duncan walked off the field, with his head hanging. Liam getting hurt had affected Parker and the whole team. After Liam's injury, no one could keep their minds on the game, especially the team. The game was over as soon as Liam left the field. The crowd didn't move, still standing as if waiting for something to happen, but nothing did. In the distance, you could barely hear the siren of Liam's ambulance.

The Tigers had won the game, ending a twenty year losing streak. Their fans were delirious. The screaming was deafening as they greeted the team with a violent enthusiasm. The Walton Tiger crowd stormed the field as they soaked in the victory that Johnny Bryant had brought them.

On the sidelines, the Tiger's Coach Lee walked over and shook Coach Green's hand. You could see him mouth "nice game," and then as he ran back to his team, three of the Tiger players doused him with a cooler of Gatorade. Nice game indeed... for them.

The mood was different on our side. It was sobering. The team was leaving the field, all thirty-two players (minus one) hanging their heads, no one looking up, especially Parker Duncan.

"I feel bad for him," Kendra said.

"Me too."

Although I didn't know him from Adam, you couldn't help but feel some sympathy for what him. Kelli Hanson, Parker's girlfriend, and Yellow Jacket cheerleader ran to him, her brown ponytail flitting from side to side. She gave him a huge hug, but he wasn't in the mood. Rejected, she walked back to the sidelines next to Shanna Smith hanging her head too.

Turning around, I picked up my baton; how funny it looked to me. I reflected on the events that had happened over the past two quarters. Not only did I make a fool out of myself by being trampled by the team, but I also let Liam Larson get to me in a way I was still trying to comprehend. He spoke to me, not much, but enough that it bothered me, and then he got hurt. I thought I was mad at him for embarrassing me on the field, but when he spoke I felt this angst inside me that I couldn't explain.

"Are you ready?" Kendra was waiting for me to move.

"Oh yeah, sorry."

As we walked up the steps, I glanced into the bleachers. Most of the Yellow Jacket fans had already left. The fans that remained were still in shock. You could hear them asking about Liam and the worry in their voices. The usual banter that goes on during and after a game was gone. Nobody wanted to talk and if they did their thoughts were on the humiliating defeat against the Tigers and... of course, Liam Larson. Everyone listlessly gathered their belongings and headed out of the stadium. One thing's certain, no one would forget tonight's events. Everyone was thinking about Liam, including me.

Chapter Two
Lougini's

    The drive to Lougini's was silent. Kendra, Missy and I still weren't in the mood for talking. To be honest, the thought of going home sounded very appealing to me. Shinedown was playing in the background, and Kendra was mouthing the words, but I wasn't listening. Friday night at Lougini's had become a ritual for us girls as well as half of Spencer. It's where everyone went after the game. We pulled into the parking lot, I could tell all the regular crowd was here. Parker Duncan's lime-green Ford truck was there as well as a number of other football players' vehicles. It looked like Lougini's was putting on a truck show instead of serving pizza. The boys of Spencer loved their trucks, almost as much as they loved their football. The one noticeable missing vehicle was Liam Larson's black Ford pickup truck. It was still sitting in the high school parking lot.

Kendra was maneuvering her mom's van into a spot right in front of Lougini's. "I hate driving this boat. How is it on your side, Jen?"

"Fine, you've got plenty of room."

Kendra had been driving for almost two years and still wasn't sure of herself when it came to parking.

"Finally!" She groaned as she put the van into park.

Getting out, Missy and I both noticed how crooked she had parked but didn't have the heart to tell her. Inside, the usual noise was quite evident with half of the team from both sides there.

"Do you see them?"

"Nah," Kendra replied, "I don't see them anywhere, just the usual crowd: football players and cheerleaders."

Finally, I noticed at the far end of the restaurant, Brenda's hand waving frantically back and forth, motioning us to come.

"Over here guys," she bellowed.

We edged our way to the front of the line and walked past the disgruntled group of people who were wondering why we were being seated before them.

"When did you guys get here?"

"About fifteen minutes ago, we pulled in right before the team came in."

"Thank, God," Kendra said. "We didn't think we were going to get a seat."

A very agitated waitress placed six menus in front of us.

"Are you guys ready to order now?"

"I'm not. Why don't we just put our drink order in first? Six Cokes please."

The annoyed waitress rolled her eyes and abruptly walked away.

"What'd you guys think of the game?" Frannie asked.

"It was awful, I can't believe we lost to Walton! The first time ever!" Missy said.

Three tables down from us you could hear the exuberant applause as Johnny Bryant entered. His team had gathered in the back corner, and they were waiting for their hero. Johnny walked past our table, high-fiving his friends as he went. He was handed a drink, and the clinking of glasses could be heard throughout the restaurant. He was being toasted for his job well done.

"Missy, have you heard from your dad? Any word on how Liam is?" Kendra asked.

"I probably won't know anything until tomorrow. Dad's on call tonight at the hospital."

"I hope he's doing okay, don't you, Jenny?" Kendra looked at me with an ulterior look in her eyes.

"Uh, yeah, of course, I hope he's fine."

Her glare was noticeable, as well as the rest of the group's. I tried to ignore their stares and show no emotion by fidgeting with my silverware. One polite gesture from Liam and they have me marrying the guy and having his children. The slamming of six glasses hitting the table was a welcome distraction.

"Thank you," relieved to see our waitress had showed up at the exact time I needed her to.

"Are you guys ready to order?" We looked at each other. None of us had even looked at a menu.

"Ummm, no," I said.

"I'm not really hungry," Kendra said. "I don't think we're going to get anything, but thanks."

With a disgruntled scoff, the waitress took our menus and huffed off.

"Hey girls, hi Frannie," Steve Conner said in a sing-song manner as he and his best friend, Drew Metz, joined our table. Steve Conner had held a crush on Frannie for over a year, and not until recently did Frannie even acknowledge that he was alive.

"What's up?" Drew asked.

"Not much," Brenda said.

Steve and Drew squeezed their way into our table as Steve gravitated towards Frannie's side.

"A bunch of us are headed over to Drew's to listen to music, you girls wanna come?" He was looking straight at Frannie as if the invitation was meant for her alone. Kendra and I both kicked each other under the table (a sign that we weren't interested).

"Sure, sounds like fun." Brenda had answered for all of us.

Frannie gave her the evil eye and also politely agreed to go.

I think we're going to pass," I said as Kendra nodded in agreement.

"Yeah Steve, not tonight, but maybe next time."

"Well, okay, but you guys are going miss out," Steve said.

"We'll take our chances."

Kendra and I were getting ready to leave when all of a sudden a roar of applause was heard throughout Lougini's. I figured the rest of Johnny Bryant's posse had shown up to join the Walton celebration, when I saw him, Liam Larson walking through the door. My jaw dropped.

"Oh my God, it's Liam," I said, not realizing I was talking out loud.

"Yeah," Kendra said, grabbing my arm and forcing me to sit back down. Apparently I had become frozen in a half-seated, half-standing position. He walked in greeting his fans as though he had just won the primary of a major election. Half of the restaurant got up to greet him. I looked at him, checking him out from head to toe. Nothing seemed to be wrong with him. Then I noticed the crutches, his right leg was in a cast, one of the soft ones that have the Velcro that straps around the leg. He also had a large gauze bandage on the side of his head that was covered by his wavy, long hair. He limped in, trying to maneuver himself through the sea of fans all wanting a part of him. Shanna Smith was the first to wedge herself to him. She jumped on him, almost knocking him down. Apparently, not caring at all that he was hurt. She wrapped her arms around his neck, squealing in delight as she gave him quick kisses all over his face. He wasn't amused. He gently but forcibly pushed her away, making it quite clear he wasn't interested. Nevertheless, she didn't leave his side, ignoring his gesture and holding onto him as if her life depended on it, clearly sending a message to everyone that he belonged to her. Parker Duncan was the next to get to him. He took his right hand and slapped Liam's left hand as a gesture to say "what's up man, glad to see you." He then half hugged him with his free arm as they walked in together. I glanced over my back to see which way they went, when in my horror I realized they were coming towards us. I instinctively sank down into my seat hoping he wouldn't see me.

"Look who's headed our way," Kendra said.

"Who?" I said, pretending to be oblivious to the situation.

"Liam, dawg! Looks like they're coming our way."

"Great" I murmured, wishing we had already left the restaurant. To avoid eye contact, I concentrated on my drink and gulped it down voraciously as if I had never had a Coke in my life. Kendra, on the other hand, decided to keep an eye on Liam, making sure our whole table knew just what he was doing.

"Oh no, he didn't," Kendra said excitedly.

"What?"

"Liam just pushed Shanna away."

"What'd she do?" I asked with bated breath, realizing I was more curious than I thought.

"Well, right now she's walking away from Liam and going to the table with the rest of the cheerleaders. She looks like she's about ready to cry or get mad, it's hard to say, but her face is a lovely shade of red."

An overwhelming feeling of triumph came over me. For some reason, the fact that Shanna had been dumped by Liam made me feel really good inside, justification if you will. I continued to stay low in my seat as I softly chuckled at the thought of Shanna when I suddenly noticed all eyes staring right at me. Liam and Parker were walking our way; I held my breath as I prayed to God that they kept on walking. My eyes stayed focused on the empty Coke glass in front of me. To my relief, both of them walked by without even a nod in our direction.

"Whew, that was close," I murmured to myself as my heart rate slowly descended back to normal.

Johnny Bryant stood up as Liam approached him, with one hand balancing himself on the crutches, Liam and Johnny both slapped each other's hand in the same manner that Liam and Parker had done moments earlier. Although you couldn't hear them, you could tell that they were being cordial to each other.

"You're staring," Frannie informed me.

"What? No, I'm not. I'm just watching like everybody else. It's not every day you see players from the Tigers and Yellow Jackets exchange pleasantries. Besides, I think everyone is surprised to see Liam walk in when the last time we saw him he was being carried out on a stretcher," I said matter of factly.

"Yeah, if you say so," the girls were giggling, and I felt my face turning red.

"Enough," I thought. "Kendra, I'm ready to go."

"I'm not."

I rolled my eyes, knowing exactly what she was doing. Steve and Drew were still sitting with us having brought their pizza to our tables. I hadn't noticed since Liam walked in that the girls decided to partake in their dinner. I reluctantly sighed, knowing full well that my wishes to leave right now were in vain.

Giving in to defeat, I grabbed a slice of pizza and joined the rest of the group as we devoured the pepperoni pie. For a while, the conversation at our table consisted of the normal chit-chat and of course Steve trying to sweet talk his way with Frannie. The group had agreed to meet up at Steve's house to listen to music except for Kendra and me, who both decided to cruise Spencer for a while before calling it a night. I had become absorbed in the conversations at our table and forgotten all about Liam being a few feet away from me until Kendra reminded me.

"Ouch! What was that for?" I asked as I tried to rub some circulation back into my arm where Kendra had so rudely squeezed it.

Kendra's eyes did not meet mine; they were focused straight ahead at the object that was coming towards us. Before I had time to react, I felt the presence of someone standing in front of me. The whole table grew silent, all of them focusing in my direction. I slowly turned my head to see what all the fuss was about when I noticed a set of crutches directly in front of me. It was Liam.

"Hi," he said, showing off a magnificent smile.

A normal girl's reaction would be to respond with a "hi" back, but in my case nothing came out of my mouth until Kendra kicked me under the table with her foot. "Hi," I said as I quickly gave Kendra a grimacing look for the kick.

"I just wanted to make sure you were okay?"

"Huh?" I was confused.

"From earlier, at halftime."

"Oh that, yeah, I'm fine." I tried to act coy about the whole matter.

"Are you sure? I couldn't really ask you during the game." He was insistent.

"Yeah, I don't understand. Why do you care anyway? You're the one who got hurt?" He looked down at his leg.

"Yeah, well I'm okay. Just some strained tendons, nothing that a little TLC won't cure," he said with a crooked smile.

"Oh, okay, well... ummm I'm fine... really. You don't need to worry. It was nothing; thanks for asking though."

The whole table was glued to Liam and me, waiting for our next response to one another. I tried desperately not to look at him, but it was impossible. I could feel the stare from his ice-blue eyes penetrating my very inner being. I sheepishly looked at him. His eyes were mesmerizing, even bluer than I remembered. I felt as if they were inviting me in, to take a look inside Liam's soul and find my destiny. I quickly looked away again, grabbing my empty glass and gulping what little melted ice was in it. He continued staring, and so did the rest of the table, waiting for me to speak as if I held the answers to the world's problems. The awkward and uncomfortable silence continued because I didn't know what he wanted or what to say. I squirmed in my seat to make myself look busy as I ignored the constant stares from Liam and the group.

"Yeah, you definitely look fine," he finally said with the same crooked smile.

What nerve, I thought to myself. *Who does he think he is? Is this a sympathy gesture to see how the poor little majorette was doing? Why did he even care?* I became even more infuriated with him, realizing I was nothing more than an opportunity for him to show off in front of my friends, as well as his. I glared at him, my body seething with anger.

"If that's it, you should probably get back to your adoring fans," I said with a sarcasm which took me by surprise.

"See ya later then." I didn't answer him back. Crutches in tow, he hobbled away like a wounded puppy.

Hopefully my rude remark had left an impression on him, I thought. There was no reason for him to give me the time of day. He had plenty of friends to keep him high on his pedestal; showing his pity for me was definitely unnecessary. I had showed him, I thought, but as I watched him walk away, head hung low, I questioned my intent. Maybe he was being sincere. He definitely wasn't reacting with the showy banter I thought he would among his friends. As a matter of fact, he was doing quite the opposite. Instead of engaging in the camaraderie of his friends, he just stood there quietly, trying to seem interested in the ongoing conversation as he occasionally glanced my way. But Liam has a girlfriend, and I was not in his group of friends. My first instinct was right, I thought, he was amusing me and his friends by trying to play the hero, even on crutches. I grabbed my purse and threw my share of the food bill on the table.

"I'll wait for you outside, Kendra. Bye guys." I turned in a hurry and heard Kendra fumbling to find her keys as she caught up to me.

I couldn't get out of there fast enough when turning the corner, THUD! I ran into none other than the one person I was trying to avoid. I knocked him down, his crutches falling to the side. "Uggh," I groaned, pulling my hair out of my face. I realized I was laying on top of Liam, our face inches from each other. We were so close I could feel his heartbeat (or was it mine?). I groaned again, his one crutch had fallen on my ankle bone, causing an excruciating painful and throbbing sensation.

"Well, hello there. Missed me already?"

My initial reaction was to ask if he was okay, but after his cocky remark I decided wholeheartedly against it.

"No! You were just in my way." I was so mad I almost cried and if it wouldn't have caused me even more embarrassment I would have, not because of him, but because my ankle was throbbing. I tried to free myself from his hold, but he wasn't letting go. I couldn't move, he had grabbed me around my waist and was holding on tight.

"Do you mind?" I said sharply.

"Not at all," he said with that same cocky confidence as he held me in a death grip.

"Are you okay?" he asked.

"I fell on you, and you are asking if I'm okay? Why are you always so worried about me?" He hesitated before answering, our eyes locked into a deep, penetrating stare.

"I don't know, I guess I just am."

"Well, don't be. As I told you before, I'm fine, fine then and fine now." I could feel the eyes of every person in Lougini's on us. "So if you're done, would you kindly release your hands from around my waist so I can get up!"

"If you're sure that's what you want, Jenny?"

It was the first time he had said my name. I didn't even know he knew my name. I hesitated, "yes, that's what I want!" He winked, and from behind me I could feel myself being pulled from behind, Liam's grip slowly letting go. It was Parker Duncan.

"Thanks, Parker."

"Don't mention it." Then he reached down and helped Liam to his feet, making sure Liam was able to get his balance.

"Here," Parker said, "don't forget this." My purse was in his hand. As I grabbed it, I heard the tinkling of change falling to the ground. Parker and Liam both bent down to help me pick it up. "Here you go," Parker said as he handed me some quarters and a $20 bill.

"Don't forget this," Liam interrupted. He placed in my hand a penny and a dime gently, closing my hand with both of his. His hands felt rough, and I could feel the dry, calloused skin against mine. Then tenderly he squeezed his hands against mine, before finally letting go. Time seemed to be standing still when all of sudden there were at least four other people standing next to us; all ready to help Liam with his crutches. Everyone wanting a piece of him, except me. The attention was on him, and I made my escape. Kendra was beside me now, her eyes bug-eyed, wondering if she really saw what had just gone down. A crowd had surrounded us, and trying not to feel intimidated or embarrassed, I motioned to Kendra for us to leave. The door couldn't have been close enough. All I wanted to do was to get the hell out of there, and before I could even take two steps I felt someone pulling me backward. I tried to pull free, but the pull was too strong.

"What now?!" I said in a bullish manner thinking that it was Kendra's hand pulling on me. I jerked my head around to find Liam again. I just couldn't seem to get away from him, no matter how hard I tried. He pulled me close to him, bringing my face to his. What utter nerve! I could feel his breath on my face as he spoke.

"Hey, I didn't mean anything back there," he whispered softly. "I really was concerned, you know, that's all."

I looked at him, realizing he was talking to me, but it wasn't registering. All I saw were his blue eyes. I tried unsuccessfully to pull myself free, but he had full control. I tried to focus, to gain control of my senses. My stomach felt weird and tense, and I didn't know what to say. I wanted to rationalize everything, but I couldn't. Time stood still every time I was near him. I didn't even know if I could speak. In a frail attempt, the word "okay" came out. I wasn't even sure if I said it or not. *And why did I say "okay"? How stupid it sounded coming from me.* I started to turn again. He clutched my jacket, and I could tell he was doing all he could not to lose his balance. He was unbelievably strong and resisting him was pointless. The more I pulled away the more he pulled me in, holding me tighter than before. I got the impression that what he wanted he got, and the word "no" didn't exist in his vocabulary unless it was to his advantage. He came forward, and he smelled so good, just like the outdoors: fresh and clean. Then, without hesitating he leaned into me, his lips barely passing mine as he touched my right ear.

He whispered, "Oh, by the way, just thought you should know that I didn't fumble the football tonight like you had hoped."

My head jerked back. He had heard me! I was in shock. I stood there in his strong grip, my knees buckling beneath me. He brushed my cheek as he faced me, expressing more with his eyes than he had by talking. I was in a trance, a statue frozen there, locked in his grip, unable to move. Then as quickly as he had grabbed me, he released me, his arms sliding down careening the contours of my waist as they found their way back to his side. With another smile, he turned and walked away.

I stood there waiting to breathe. Then a light bulb went on in my head and I realized what was happening. He wasn't being nice; he was being a chauvinistic pig, a showoff jerk, as usual. At that second, I hated him more than I thought I could possibly hate anyone! I was repulsed by his very presence. I watched him in disgust as he went back to his table, everyone clamoring to be near him. *How pathetic! I have to get out of here before I explode.* The rest of our crew walked up to Kendra and me, and I felt like the whole world was watching me. Steve Conner looked at me with sympathetic eyes.

"Hey, why don't you guys come on over to my house, maybe listening to some music will help take your mind off of things?"

"I don't know, Steve."

"Come on, all of your friends are gonna be there."

I looked at Kendra. "Might as well, Jen."

"Yeah, I guess, the night could only get better, it definitely couldn't get any worse. Sure, Steve, thanks. We'll follow you there."

I glanced over at Liam's table. Shanna was sitting next to him caressing his shoulder. They deserved each other, even if he wasn't paying her any attention. She just sat there like a trophy. I walked out of the restaurant with Kendra.

"Let's get the hell out of here," I said without giving Kendra the chance to respond.

"Are you okay? " She finally asked, but I wasn't in the mood to answer.

"Yes," I said quietly.

"Are you sure?"

"I told you yes, now just drop it!" I snapped at her without realizing I was taking my frustrations out on her.

Her head went backward and her arms up. "Sorry, Jenny, I didn't mean to upset you!" But it was too late. I was upset; not at her but at Liam Larson, Mr. Number Eleven, the biggest jerk in the world, who just happened to have the bluest eyes I had ever seen. Kendra apologized again as we got into her van. I should have been the one apologizing.

"Jenny, I really didn't mean to upset you; I was just trying to make sure you were alright, that's all. But you have to admit you two put on quite a show in there!"

"I put on a show? Don't you think it was all him?"

"I think he likes you."

I looked at her. "What, did you just say?"

"I think he likes you, Jenny. Why else would he go to all that trouble to talk to you?"

"He just wanted to know if I was alright from falling down at halftime."

"Well, that's what he said, but I think it was his excuse to talk to you. You've never talked to him before, and he's never talked to you either. Then all of a sudden he helps you up off the ground at the football game and he can't seem to get to you fast enough here, even though he's on crutches! If that's not sending you a message, I don't know what is!"

I stared at her. She did have a point, but why? I've never even gave him the slightest notion that I was interested in him, and I've never noticed him trying to talk to me before tonight. We ran in different circles. I rarely saw him aside from a couple of classes we had together, and I didn't even think he knew my name until tonight. *Did he really like me? Was he interested? And if he wasn't, what was tonight all about?*

We were still sitting in the van, waiting for the rest of our group to come out. The windows of Lougini's were smudged with the fingerprints of small children, but I could still see inside and I could see Liam, and Liam could see me.

Chapter Three
The Nemesis

The next day was Saturday, sleep-in day. I laid in bed looking out my window. My clock read 10:11am. My thoughts kept slipping back to last night. Yesterday at this time, everything in my life was normal: my friends, school, band, being a majorette, Mom, Dad, everything. Then he entered the picture. *Why did he have to be the one to help me last night? Why couldn't it have been someone else, someone who seemingly didn't care? Why was he bothering with me, and what was Lougini's all about?* It was driving me crazy, and I couldn't think straight. I pulled my covers over my head. *I could stay here all day, maybe that's what I should do,* I thought. *I'll just sleep the day away and forget everything.* Then, hearing the noises from outside, I pulled the covers off my head and looked out my window to the left. It looked like it was going to be a beautiful day. It was still warm enough at night that I could open my window, and a slight breeze moved my light blue curtains back and forth. It was too beautiful to waste it in bed sulking. *But, honestly, I wasn't really sulking, was I? Liam did *seem interested in me, didn't he? Or was he just being cruel? But he wouldn't do that, would he? And if he would, why me?* I groaned and pulled the pillow over my face. Too many questions and no answers for them. Then I thought, *there was Shanna. What about Shanna?* They were definitely a couple, or at least had been for most of our high school years. They've had more break-ups than most but always got back together. *I'm sure that's what this was, I was just a distraction after one of their fights,* I thought. I was wasting my time even thinking that Liam might be interested in me. But then again, he seemed pretty adamant about her leaving him alone last night. I needed more information. I needed to find out if they were still an item. I jolted out of bed and headed for the shower.

"Good morning, hon."

"Morning, Dad."

"You slept in late."

"Yeah, I guess I did. I didn't sleep well last night."

"Why, sweetie?" Mom came in through the back door, carrying a bag of groceries. It was nice having your own supermarket in your back yard.

"What?" I replied.

"I heard you tell Dad you didn't sleep well last night. Why not?"

"Oh, it's nothing, you know, just one of those restless nights, I guess." I didn't dare tell them about Liam, not yet at least.

"So, what did you and the girls end up doing after the game?"

"Oh, you know the usual, we went to Lougini's and then Steve Conner invited us over to his house to listen to some music."

"Did you have fun?"

"Yeah, it was okay."

"Steve Conner is such a nice boy," Mom said, sweetly.

"Yeah, well I think he has a crush on Frannie."

"Oh, how does Frannie feel about him?" Mom asked. Mom was notorious for having a thousand questions when it came to me and my friends.

"Umm... I'm not sure. She hasn't really told me, but it seemed like she had a good time last night."

"Oh, that's good to hear."

I was ready for this conversation to be over, the last thing I wanted to do was to talk about relationships.

"I think I'm going to call Kendra."

"Okay, hon. Don't forget, Dad and I are going to be at Kendra's house tonight to play cards with her parents. If you girls have plans, you can drop us off and use our car."

My parents had been playing cards with Kendra Bishop's parents since we were in 5th grade.

"Thanks, Mom, I think I'll do that since we used her car last night." With a hug from both, Mom and Dad left. Saturdays were the day they did deliveries for the store, and they would be gone most of the day, leaving me free and on my own.

I grabbed a glass of orange juice when my cell rang.

"Hello? Hey Kendra."

"Hey dawg, so... what do you think about last night?" She never was one to beat around the bush.

"Hi, and how are you this morning, Jenny?" I said sarcastically.

"Sorry, I just couldn't get last night off my mind, so I was sure you were feeling the same." She was right about that.

"I don't know I've been racking my brain over it. Why would he act that way towards me, especially with Shanna there? I'm clueless."

"Well, it's like I told you, I think he likes you."

"You don't know that, that's just you making an eager assumption."

"Whatever, but Missy called me earlier, and after we left Steve's, you and Liam were the talk of the hour."

"So! That doesn't mean he likes me."

"Everyone agrees though."

Then I had a revelation. "Kendra, what if he just did that to make Shanna jealous? What if he was just playing me to get back at her for something?"

"You can't be serious, you're way off base. If he and Shanna are having problems like they always do why would he include you in on it? I really don't think he would go to all that trouble if he wanted to dump her or whatever. He would just do it. He wouldn't have to put on a show for you to do it."

"I guess that makes sense, but I just don't get him. I'm not going to let him ruin my weekend though. It's over, and I'm glad."

"I have a feeling it's not, Jenny. I still think he wants something from you. Like I keep saying; he likes you. You should be so lucky; he's one of the hottest guys in town, and he seems to want you!"

I felt a smile coming across my face just thinking about the idea. Maybe he did like me. I sighed.

"Well, if that's the case, he's going to have to come after me. I'm not chasing him. I'm sure he thinks he can get any girl he wants. It's not going to be that way with me."

"Don't be so fickle, Jenny. You know you think he's cute, even if you are mad at him for last night."

"I'm done talking about him, Kendra. Hey, Mom said I could have the car tonight. You want me to pick you up, and we can go do something?"

"Sure."

"Okay, Mom and Dad are playing cards at your house at six-thirty. I'll drop them off, and we can go then."

"Great, see ya then. Bye."

I hung up, smiling from ear to ear. The thought of Liam liking me was starting to agree with me. But I knew I had to be careful. The last thing I wanted was to be made a fool of, especially by him. Saturday night in Spencer was cruising night. Friday night was reserved for football, so Saturday was open for all those with their driver's license to let loose and enjoy the weekend. Saturday night was also date night in Spencer, something that hadn't applied to me or Kendra for quite some time. Most Saturdays we spent together either cruising the main drag of Spencer, or hooking up with the rest of the girls to go to a movie or something. There wasn't anything good playing at the Robey Theatre, and rumor had it that Frannie was out on her first date with Steve. Brenda,

Shauna, and Missy all had their own plans, so Kendra and I decided to cruise the strip, listening to our favorite songs. Avenged Sevenfold had become a particular favorite of ours and we had nearly worn out their latest CD.

"What do you want to do? We've already used half a tank of gas going from one end of town to the other."

"We could find Frannie and Steve and see how their date is going?"

"What? No way am I going to go spy on them. Anyway, I think he took her to Charleston to the movies."

If you couldn't find anything to do in Spencer, Charleston always was the second alternative. We were becoming desperate. The idea of spying on one of our girlfriends while they were on a date was pitiful and we knew it.

"I'm thirsty. Let's get something to drink."

We pulled into the local convenient store. Behind me, I could hear some kids talking, but I didn't pay any attention to them.

"Jenny, did you see who was outside?"

"No, who?"

"It's Shanna and Kelli."

I didn't turn around. We went straight back to the coolers and grabbed a couple of sweet Cokes. Shanna and Kelli walked in and came towards us.

"Jenny, can I talk to you for a minute?" I looked over at Kendra. She shrugged her shoulders as if to say she didn't know what she wanted either.

"Umm, sure. I'll be right there."

Shanna and Kelli waited in the corner next to the newspaper stand. I wondered why she and Liam weren't together tonight; it was Saturday. She looked like she could be on a date though. She was dressed to kill: tight jeans, white cami with a hot pink tank top over it, suede thigh high boots, and, of course, her blonde hair was perfectly curled and in place. She was waiting patiently for me as I paid for my drink. I wondered again what she wanted. I was sure it had to do with last night. I walked over to them as Kendra motioned that she would meet me outside. Shanna and Kelli were standing side by side, arms folded. I felt I was on trial, and Shanna and Kelli were my judge and jury.

"What's up, Shanna? Hi Kelli."

"Hello," she mumbled back.

I looked at Shanna, her pink, lip-glossed lips were pursed together.

"Jenny, I just thought I should tell you that Liam belongs to me. I don't know what last night was all about, but rest assured we're still dating, and whatever he was doing with you was nothing."

"First of all, Shanna, I didn't think there was anything going on anyway. And secondly if there were, it wouldn't be any of your business, and from what I hear you two are done. He dumped you."

"It is too my business!" she shouted back at me, her index finger in my face. Kelli was standing rigid, ready to strike at me as well, waiting for Shanna's signal. I didn't back down.

"Get your freakin' finger out of my face, Shanna. You've got this all wrong. He approached me; I did not, let me repeat, did not approach him."

"I saw you two at the football game," she screamed.

"Are you kidding?" You're jealous of me because he handed me my baton? You've got more problems than worrying about me and Liam."

"That was just the beginning; you went to Lougini's in hopes to see him, Jenny!"

"What? You're crazy, Shanna. First of all, I went to Lougini's to hang with my friends, not to see Liam. And second, I don't think anyone in their right mind thought he would show up after getting hurt at the game! And believe me, the last thing I wanted was to see him when he did show up. If you noticed, which I'm sure you did, he came over to my table!"

"Well, you definitely made yourself friendly to him when you landed on top of him. That was convenient!"

I was fuming at this point. "Listen, Shanna, I was leaving and he just happened to be in my way. I'm not finishing this infantile conversation with you. I am not after your precious little Liam, and I would appreciate it if from now on if you would stay the hell away from me!"

I was so mad that I threw my Coke down. The impact busted it open, and it sprayed all its contents on Shanna and Kelli's legs, making a nice stain on Shanna's suede boots.

"Ugggggh! You're gonna pay for this, Jenny!"

"I'm really scared, Shanna." I turned around and walked outside. Kendra was waiting on the curb, and her mouth was wide open again.

"What was that about?"

"Nothing!" Kendra knew better. We both got in my car. Shanna and Kelli came after us. She ran to my window.

"Listen, I don't know what went down last night, but it better not happen again, and you stay the hell away from Liam, got it?"

I pulled out, screeching my wheels as I left the parking lot. I could see Shanna and Kelli in my rearview mirror, standing there making lovely hand gestures in my direction as I drove away.

I drove through town without saying a word. I couldn't believe what had happened. This was all his fault, I kept thinking. I didn't approach him. I never led him on, and now I was being threatened by his arm candy!

"Are you going to tell me what that was all about?" For a minute, I had forgotten Kendra was even with me. It also seemed that within the past twenty-four hours I had done a lot of explaining to her.

I looked over at her. "I don't know, Kendra. I'm as confused over this as you are. Apparently, Shanna thinks there's something going on between me and Liam. Go figure!"

"Well, he did kind of give that impression, Jen," she said cautiously, knowing in my fragile state of mind I could rip into her too if she said the wrong thing to me.

"Look, you know as well as I do, that there isn't anything going on between us. This was all just a huge misunderstanding!"

"I know, but I don't think that's what everyone else is thinking."

I didn't respond. Instead, I continued driving until we were back at Kendra's house. It was only eleven-thirty, but I was ready to just go home.

The rest of the weekend was uneventful. On Sunday, my parents and I took a trip to Charleston to do some shopping. The homecoming dance was in a few weeks, and I needed to buy a dress. The girls and I had decided that we would all go together and had made a pact that if we were asked by a boy that we would turn them down. I was glad to be out of town and to concentrate on something besides what had happened the past couple of days. Shopping was a great outlet. It always, and I mean always, helped take my mind off things.

Dad had dropped Mom and I off at the mall and we went straight to my favorite dress shop, Just Beautiful. You could tell that homecoming was soon. The store was packed with eager teenage girls looking for their perfect dress. I tried on about three dresses before deciding to go with a long, cream-colored one with spaghetti straps; very pretty but not over the top either. I had a pair of silver shoes from a wedding that I had been in over the summer that I knew would also go well with the dress. Mom was happy. Along with the dress, she bought me a crystal necklace to match.

As we were leaving, we ran into Frannie and her mom.

"Hey, Frannie."

"Hi, Jenny, what are you doing here?"

"I just picked out my dress for homecoming."

"That's why we're here." Frannie seemed to be happier than usual.

"What's up, you seem to have a little more pep in your voice today? Do you have something to tell me?"

"Well, yes," she hesitated.

"Spit it out then," with the events of this past weekend, my patience was strained.

"I'm not going to the dance with you and the girls."

"Why? What do you mean?"

"Steve asked me, and I said yes."

"Okay, I know you went out with him last night, but what happened?"

"He took me to the movies, and we had a great time. He is sooooo nice. I don't know why I didn't see it before. Anyway, on the way home, he brought up the dance and asked me if I would like to go with him, and I said yes!" I suddenly felt like a wallflower.

"That's great, Frannie. I'm really happy for you." Frannie looked down at my garment bag.

"Can I see your dress?"

"Of course." I pulled back the bag to reveal part of the dress.

"Ooooh, very nice, I love it. Well, I better get in there if I want to find anything."

"Good luck," I glanced back at the store. "It's crazy in there."

We both laughed. I could tell she wanted to ask me something else. Her eyes shifted back and forth.

"Hey, Jen, what's going on between you and Liam?" I knew it was coming.

"Nothing, nothing at all. Honestly, I think he was just being a show off the other night. He's still with Shanna. I'll probably never talk to him again."

"Well, you two were definitely the talk of the town over the weekend."

"I heard, but really, there's nothing to it."

"If you say so. Well, see you tomorrow at school."

"Okay, see you tomorrow, bye, Mrs. Downing."

We hugged while our moms waved to each other.

"Let me know what you pick out. I can't wait to see it!"

"Did I hear Frannie say she had a date for homecoming?" Mom asked.

"Yeah, she's going with Steve Conner. He asked her last night."

"Oh, I thought you girls were going together?"

"I did too, but she had a better offer."

"Well, honey, don't worry. There's still plenty of time before the dance, maybe someone will ask you."

"Maybe, Mom, but I think I'm still going to go with the girls. Besides Frannie, no one else has a date. Anyway, I'm happy for her. It's no big deal, really." Although, inside I was a little jealous. Of course every girl wants a date for homecoming, me included.

Chapter Four
Intentions

    I awoke Monday morning feeling like the whole weekend was a complete and utter disaster. I was ready to forget everything and leave it behind me. The upcoming week was going to be particularly busy for me, and I needed to have a clear head if I was going to get through it. I couldn't afford any idiotic distractions. Not only did I have an extra hour of majorette practice every day after school to prepare for the Black Walnut and Majorette Festival that began this week, but I also had some major midterms coming up. I was happy for the diversion; I had been spending too much time thinking about the false possibility that Liam Larson actually took an interest in me. Lucky for me, I only had two classes with him, 4th period study hall and 6th period Senior English. Half the time, he didn't even show up for either class. The coach usually got the boys out of study hall so they could study films of previous games, and English, well, Liam seemed to pass even if he wasn't there. Mrs. White, the English teacher, had a thing for the football boys and always excused them from being late or missing class. All they had to do was say how nice she looked and they got away with murder. It was blatantly obvious, but something nobody ever challenged.

The morning dragged on. It seemed forever before lunch and it was still only 3rd period. After Mrs. Harris' Social Studies class, I walked to study hall in hopes of finishing my English paper on To Kill A Mockingbird. Shauna caught me off guard.

"Hey girl, whatcha doin'?" Her bubbly personality was in rare form today.

"Oh, nothing. I'm on my way to study hall. I have to finish my paper on *To Kill A Mockingbird*, I'm hoping to turn it in early."

"What's the rush?" Shauna, being the ever happy-go-lucky person that she was, also never understood why homework should be completed early.

"Where are you headed off to?" I asked, in hopes to direct the attention to her instead of why I shouldn't finish my paper.

"I've got Geometry." Her mood was exuberant.

"Why are you so excited about math class?"

"Didn't you hear?" she said, like I should already know.

"Hear what?"

"I got invited to the homecoming dance!"

Shauna was bouncing from side to side. She could hardly contain her enthusiasm.

I tried to act excited for her, but I felt somewhat jealous. "Congrats, girl! When did this happen, and who are you going with?"

"Paul Hartford asked me last night!" She looked like the cat who just swallowed the canary. She was beaming!

"Really? I didn't even know you guys liked each other."

"We talk a lot during band, and he showed up at Steve's after you and Kendra left, and well... we kinda hooked up!"

"Awesome Shauna, I'm really happy for you." It was a pathetic attempt to sound convincing.

"Yeah, thanks, Jen. Anyway, everything happened so fast. He asked for my phone number Friday, and then out of the blue, I get a call from him last night, and that's when it happened. Mom's going to take me to Charleston tonight so I can get my dress. He wants to know my color so he can match his suit and order me a corsage." Shauna was beside herself, talking a mile a minute and grinning from ear to ear.

"Jen, did you hear Frannie is going with Steve?"

"Yeah, I saw her yesterday in Charleston. Mom and I picked out my dress."

"Oh, that's great! Well gotta go before the bell rings. Oh, by the way, Brenda is going with Drew, and Missy got asked by Eric Manns!"

"What?" I thought we were all going to go together and now everybody seemed to have a date except for me, and hopefully Kendra. I definitely didn't want to be the only one going to the dance by myself. I just wouldn't go. As Shauna bounced off, I started feeling very depressed. The bell rang, and I rushed to study hall with no intention of finishing my paper.

Study hall was in the auditorium, a huge room that was used for all the concerts, as well as the plays put on by the different classes. There were easily three hundred seats in the room, plenty of space to lose myself until lunchtime. Finding a chair half-way down the middle on the far right side next to the exit door, I slumped into my seat and felt sorry for myself. I pulled out my English paper and stared at it blankly. I looked around the sporadically filled auditorium. Half of study hall seemed to be missing, including him. I didn't notice him anywhere, and I breathed a sigh of relief. At least I wouldn't be distracted by him today. *Looks like the coach got him out of class again.* I realized my paper was not going to finish itself, so I grudgingly began to read and edit the rough draft. *At least I could finish this and then write the final copy tonight. I could still turn it in tomorrow and be ahead of the game.* The paper actually wasn't due until Thursday. *Bonus points for me.*

    I absorbed myself in my paper, when I heard the commotion. A bunch of the football players stormed through the far door, laughing and talking loud as if they had forgotten that study hall was going on. They received a seriously dirty look from Mr. Buford, the study hall monitor, and Physics teacher. They were being obnoxiously loud and didn't seem to care. My heart jumped, wondering if Liam was with them. There had to be at least fifteen of them, and they were passing through to get to the exit door, a shortcut that led to the annex building where they reviewed the football tapes. I looked down at my paper, trying not to pay any attention to them as they swaggered past. *How lucky for me that I picked this seat.* I slumped lower into my seat, bringing my book and paper closer to me. As they walked by, I heard one of the guys call out his name. My heart pounded faster. Keeping my eyes glued to my paper, there was no way I was going to look up. I could see the exit door opening, and I breathed a sigh of relief, in a few moments they would be through the door, and I would avoid another confrontation. I didn't even know why I cared. It wasn't like there was anything between us, but my heart raced as the group of boys came closer to me.

    The impending moment when he passed me scared me more than waking up on the day of an exam that I hadn't studied for. I glanced up to see if they were gone. All of them were except for Liam. He was standing in the doorway, staring at me. His smile was gorgeous. I looked away quickly, hoping he didn't notice that I saw him. I became immobilized as I waited patiently for him to leave, but he didn't do that. Instead, he just stood in the doorway. *Why didn't he leave? Maybe someone was holding the door open for him, but he should have moved on by now. Maybe his crutches were being a problem for him? That's it.* I kept staring down at my paper, hoping for the exit door to close, and finally, after what seemed like hours, it did.

It took the rest of study hall for my heart to stop racing and my palms to stop sweating. Thankfully, there were no more interruptions, and the rest of study hall went by un-phased. I re-wrote my English paper and even started reading the first chapter of the next assigned book. How boring my life seemed. Finally, the bell rang. If you had Mr. Buford for study hall, you had to wait for his signal before you could leave the room. He would raise his hand in the air, and with a slight flip of his wrist, he would say "Carry on." That was his way of dismissing us. It seemed ridiculous, but if you didn't wait for it, he was known to hand out detentions for ignoring the signal. On his cue, I ran out of the auditorium making a bee-line to my locker, wildly throwing my books into it. I headed to the lunch room where I caught up with Kendra and Brenda, who were already in line.

"Hey, what's up girl?" Brenda asked.

"Not much. I finished my English paper re-write in study hall. How 'bout you guys?"

"Not, much. School's been pretty boring today. I thought I was going to fall asleep in History," Kendra said.

"Brenda, I heard you're going to the homecoming dance with Drew Metz?"

"I am. Can you believe it? He asked me Friday night at Steve's house."

"We must have missed a really good party after we left," I said looking straight at Kendra. "Looks like it's just you and me dawg."

"What do you mean?"

"Everyone has a date now to the dance except us."

"Are you kidding? You mean Missy and Shauna too?"

"Yeah, that's how I knew about Brenda. I saw Shauna in the hallway this morning and she gave me the scoop. Missy got asked by Eric Manns, and Shauna is going with Paul Hartford."

"Paul Hartford? The trombone player?" Kendra asked, not believing me.

"Yeah, he showed up at Steve's after we left. She said they started talking and before she knew it, he asked for her phone number. He called her last night to ask her to the dance."

"Wow, I guess we did miss the party," Kendra said in a somber tone.

"Well, at least we have each other," I said pitifully to Kendra.

"I guess."

By the time school ended, I was drained. The weekend antics had finally caught up with me, and it didn't help that I hadn't slept well Sunday night. With the festival coming up, Linda had us learning a whole new routine for Saturday's performance. I didn't want to stay after school to learn it but knew I had to if I wanted to do well on Saturday. Our band was known for its Black Walnut Festival performance, and Mr. Hawthorne was not about to let the town down. We actually had been practicing the new routines for a couple of weeks, but this was crunch week. No excuses would be accepted.

I grabbed my batons from my locker and headed down the hill. The band practiced to one side of the football field, still allowing most of the field open for the football players to carry on their drills and practice. The flag corps, which Kendra was in, and the majorettes practiced farther down, next to the goal posts. I arrived, batons in hand and Linda and the other majorettes were already there. I received the "look" from Linda, reminding me of Friday night when I came back late from halftime. I ignored her and said hi to the girls. There were four majorettes: senior and head majorette, Linda Nelson, Allison Masters, junior and first-time majorette, Amber Linney, the only sophomore on the squad and myself, the other senior. Mr. Hawthorne blew his final warning whistle, and all members of the band, flag corps, and majorette squad were to be on the field.

Once practice began, Linda lightened up on me; thankfully she didn't hold a grudge long. She was a great majorette and her intentions were always meant for the well-being of our squad. Besides, we had been together since we were both sophomores. She knew how dedicated I was to our squad. I noticed Mr. Hawthorne had the flag corps doing a routine that would be highlighting a drum solo of Marty and Mike. Kendra hated that. Kendra said they had been acting like they were placed on this Earth just to entertain us with their drumming ability. By the time five o'clock rolled around, I was beyond exhausted. We had gone through our routine twenty times and all I could think about was going home and plopping on my bed. It was an unusually warm day for October and felt more like the middle of August. So a nice, hot shower was also in my plans. Like Mr. Buford, Mr. Hawthorne would not let you leave practice until he blew his final whistle. *What was it with men and their whistles,* I wondered. I looked down at my watch, it was six minutes after five. Mr. Hawthorne finally released us with a blow of his whistle, and everyone scattered in a hundred different directions except for the percussion and flag corps. It looked like they were going to have to stay and practice longer. Something that I'm sure Marty and Mike had to do with.

    I waved to Kendra, and she waved back frowning. I could feel her pain. It looked like the football players were still practicing too, I found myself looking for Liam, but I didn't see him. *He probably had been excused because of his injury.* I grabbed my stuff and started walking home. I was still in the vicinity of the school when the traffic started passing. Most of it was from the band, but I could tell football was over too because there had to have been six or seven big trucks that roared by me as the boys whooped and hollered. Half the team owned their own trucks, so it wasn't unusual to see so many at one time. I continued walking, twirling my baton in my hand, waving to my friends as they drove past me.

    Suddenly, I noticed the sound of a truck engine; it was almost like a humming noise. I wondered why it wasn't passing. Instead, it seemed to run idle as I walked. I turned around to see what was going on, only to find it was Liam. There was no mistaking his black Ford pick-up truck. It was large and shiny, with silver chrome outlining the sides of it. A blue and gold football decal in his window with his number eleven on it was also a dead giveaway. I quickly turned back and increased the speed of my walk. He didn't pass me; instead he stayed behind me as I continued on, allowing oncoming traffic to go around him. I kept walking, looking forward with blinders on. The engine revved making my heart skip a beat. I took a deep breath. "What is he doing?" Before I had time to consider, he quickly drove past me and pulled over, cutting me off. I glared at him, and he just smiled. I turned away, going in a different direction; he backed up forcing me to stop.

    "What do you want?"

In a sweet, melancholy tone he asked if I wanted a ride.

"What?" *The audacity,* I thought. "No, I do not want a ride." I turned away trying to get around his truck. He backed up some more. I looked around to see if anyone saw us. The back of his truck was practically sticking out into the road, definitely causing a problem if another car drove by. I took another deep breath and tried going in a different direction, this time he pulled the truck forward.

"Do you mind?" I was livid and totally annoyed by his actions.

"Not at all," he calmly replied.

My only other option was to turn back towards the school and take a different direction home. When Liam saw me do this, he put the truck in park and jumped out, a major feat I thought, considering his leg was still in a cast.

"Jenny, wait up."

I kept walking, wondering to myself why he was doing this and why he was going to all this trouble. *Why couldn't he just leave me alone?* I was surprised that he caught up with me so fast, knowing his walking ability had been impaired. He pulled me backward, forcing me to face him.

"Liam, I told you I don't need a ride. I don't know what you're doing, but please leave me alone."

His blue eyes looked genuinely hurt as he stared at me. "Jenny, I just wanted to apologize for Friday night."

"Apologize? For what?"

"I could tell you weren't too happy with me at Lougini's, and it definitely wasn't what I was meaning to do, so I just wanted to say I was sorry."

"So, you cutting me off like you did just was just your way of getting my attention so you could apologize to me?"

"Yes, and to offer you a ride home."

"Well, you are persistent, I'll give you that." He looked like he had just gotten out of the shower. His wavy, dirty blonde hair was hanging down still damp and out of its ponytail, which was looking very nice on him. I could feel myself staring. It was so easy to do with him. "Thanks, apology accepted, but I'm really close to home. There's no need for the ride." He looked disappointed. I couldn't believe what I was about to say. "But, if you're sure it's not out of your way, okay, as long as it's no trouble." His eyes lit up and he smiled a beautiful, crooked smile.

"Great! No trouble at all."

He motioned me to his truck. He opened the passenger side door for me, holding it open as I started to step up into it. His truck was huge, reminding me of the monster trucks I'd seen on TV. Thank God for the step or I would have felt pretty stupid trying to gracefully sit myself inside his cab. Before I could get in, I felt his hands on my waist. Without hesitation or effort, he gently lifted me into my seat.

"Thanks," I said shyly.

"You're welcome." He quickly hobbled around to his side and jumped in. "Okay, let's go."

"Don't you want to know where I live?"

"I already do."

"You do? How's that?"

"I've seen you go home lots of times."

"Oh." I felt embarrassed for some reason. Before he could even put his truck into drive, we were both startled by the sound of a loud horn honking behind us. All I could think was that his truck was sticking out in the road and that someone must be pretty pissed off with him for parking so erratically. We both turned to see who it was. It was none other than Liam's partners in crime, Parker Duncan and Tony Williams. There was no mistaking Parker's lime green pick-up truck. Both of them were yelling and laughing and making gestures apparently meant for only Liam alone to see.

"Oh my, God," I whispered to myself as I slumped down into my seat. Liam started honking back and laughing. "Please get me out of here," I continued to whisper under my breath.

Liam turned back to me, placing his hand on my left knee, a bold move. "Sorry about them."

Trying to act like it didn't bother me, "Oh, don't worry, it's okay."

Parker pulled his truck around to Liam, Parker and Tony both gave the "thumbs up" sign and drove off. I wondered what they meant. As they pulled away, we could still hear Parker honking the horn. Liam looked at me. I was staring at his hand on my knee. Without saying a word, he removed it slowly, but not before he gently squeezed it.

"So," I said to break the mood from what just happened, "you know where I live?"

"Yes, I do."

The clock read 5:33 p.m.; Mom and Dad were sure to be wondering where I was. I noticed that Liam had no problem driving with his cast. Only he could do that, I thought to myself. He pulled up to my driveway, and Mom was sitting on the porch swing. She got up instantly when she saw the truck.

"Is that your mom?" he asked.

"Yes, she's probably wondering where I've been. I forgot to tell her that practice would run late today."

"Well, I better let you go then; I don't want to get you into trouble."

I smiled. "Don't worry, I won't be, but thanks."

"Anytime, Jenny." I just looked at him. His response sounded like an open invitation.

I stared at him again. The sound of Mom's voice broke me from my trance. I grabbed my stuff and opened the door as Mom was walking down the steps. I knew I wouldn't be able to get out of this without introducing her to him.

"Hi, Jenny," she said as she looked straight at Liam.

"Mom, this is Liam Larson. He was nice enough to give me a ride home since practice ran over."

"Oh, nice to meet you, Liam."

"Hi, Mrs. King, nice to meet you too." He was looking at me, and I felt more awkward than ever. "Well," he said, "better go. See you at school, Jenny, bye, Mrs. King."

"Good-bye, Liam."

He pulled away. I watched him back out as he gave me a wink. I turned to Mom. *Thankfully that's over,* I thought to myself, *pretty painless.*

"He seems nice, Jen."

"Yeah, he's okay."

"Is he in the band. I don't seem to recall his name?"

I looked at her dumbfounded. My parents had to be the only two people in the entire town who did not know Liam Larson.

"No, Mom, he's a football player."

"Liam? Oh, is he the boy who got hurt at Friday's game?"

"How did you know about that, you and Dad left before that happened?"

"Missy's mom told me about it over the weekend."

"Yeah, he's the one."

"Looks like he's okay. That's good."

"He's fine. So, what's for dinner? I'm starving!" Actually, I wasn't, but I was hoping to change the subject.

"Meatloaf."

"Yum." I started up the steps.

"Jenny?"

"Yeah, Mom?"

"He's really cute."

I paused, looking down the street to where I last saw his truck. I was smiling from ear to ear.

"He's alright."

The next day, Dad let me drive one of the delivery trucks to school. I got the impression that Mom had told him about Liam. Dad was very protective and I'm sure he wanted to make sure that I didn't need to rely on a football player for a ride home. The morning dragged on as usual, by the time I got to fourth period study hall, I was ready to leave. It was only Tuesday, and the weekend seemed so far away. I took my usual seat near the exit sign and found myself thinking that I could make a quick escape and no one would even know I left. But then I wasn't one to ditch class, even study hall, so no use wasting my time on planning my escape route. I looked around and didn't see Liam. I was a little disappointed and a little relieved all at the same time. *Hopefully, we could at least be civil towards one another. It was nice of him to go out of his way yesterday to apologize to me and to give me a ride home, but that was it.* I was positive of it.

Study hall was almost over, and Mr. Buford was absent today, so Mrs. Allen, a teacher's aide, was filling in for him. She didn't own a whistle, so when the bell rang, nobody waited for her signal to leave. I went to my locker, thinking I would skip lunch. It was mystery meat Tuesday, and it just didn't seem appetizing. Besides, Kendra was going to the dentist during lunch, and the rest of the girls were sitting with their new love interests. I definitely didn't want to sit with them while they talked about the dance. I decided to go out and sit on the bleachers. It was another beautiful and unusually warm day for October, and I could take my book and soak in some much-needed sun.

I was by myself, or so I thought. I headed out the door and found a place on top of the cliff near the band room. I grabbed my book and sat down. Before I could even read the first page, Liam sat down next to me so close that I felt myself moving over to make room for him. He scooted closer. The more I moved over the more he moved in on me.

I gave him an uneasy glare. "Do you mind?" I asked, but he didn't answer.

"What'cha reading?"

"Umm, *Moby Dick*."

"Ahhh, Mrs. White's assignment," he said.

He was in my class, but I couldn't remember the last time I saw him there, so I was surprised he even knew what the homework assignment was.

"Yeah, it's the book we have to read after we're done with *To Kill A Mockingbird*."

"You're done with your paper already?"

I looked embarrassed. Most people wait until the night before the assignment was due before even starting it, not me though. No, I start on them as soon as they are assigned.

"Yeah, almost. I finished my rough draft. I just have to copy it."

There was an awkward silence. He was looking at me with those fiercely blue eyes of his. His hair was pulled back in a ponytail today and we were sitting so close that I could see his face clearly. He definitely had some scars, battle wounds I'm sure, from playing football. I looked away, trying not to stare, wondering where Shanna was. They usually spent their lunch break together.

"Is there anything I can do for you, Liam?" I was still wondering why he was sitting here.

"No, I just thought I would say hi." I could tell that there was more to this. He looked away from me, pulling at some grass and playing with it.

"Where's Shanna?"

"I don't know; don't really care."

"What's that about," I thought. He looked at me again, this time coming closer.

"We're not together anymore, actually we haven't been for a long time."

"Really? It sure looked like you two were together at Lougini's on Friday night. She couldn't keep her hands off of you."

"Well, she's trying to hold onto something that isn't there, that hasn't been there for a long, long time."

I thought about my run-in with her at the convenient store on Saturday night, her threat for me to stay away from him. I turned away, watching the kids mingling around. I saw Shauna, Brenda, Missy and Frannie all sitting together talking, making plans for the dance.

"Jen?"

"Yeah?" I replied. He was silent, pausing as though he was collecting his inner-most thoughts.

"Jen, I heard you had a talk with Shanna over the weekend?"

"Yeah, I did, how did you know that?" My curiosity was aroused.

"Well, you know that kind of stuff gets around, plus it's a small town."

"If you're worried about what I said, don't be. I straightened things out with her. I made sure she understood that you were just helping me at the game and that was all there was to it, even at Lougini's. I guess she thought there was more to us than there really was."

Liam was looking down, playing with the same blade of grass. "Jenny..."

Just then, the bell rang meaning lunch was over, interrupting his thought. He looked upset and annoyed that he didn't have enough time to finish what he wanted to say to me. My next class was Spanish, and it was on the opposite end of where I was now.

"Liam, I'm sorry, I've got to go, I have Spanish now, and it's a long walk from here."

"That's okay, I understand. Can I talk to you later?"

"Umm... sure," I replied as I tried to figure out what he meant. He stood up and for the first time since he came over I notice that he didn't have his crutches with him.

"Hey, where are your crutches?"

"I left them at home. I don't need them. They were more of a nuisance than anything, besides my leg feels a lot better. I'm supposed to be cleared this Thursday by Dr. Garrett to play in Friday's game."

"That's great. I'm sure the coach will be happy."

"I guess."

I could tell he would rather be talking about something else instead of the idle chit chat we were making. I started to get up, and he instinctively took my arm and helped me.

"Thanks," I said.

"You're welcome, like I said yesterday, anytime."

He smiled at me. His eyes were magnetic and I had to catch myself to make sure I wasn't staring again.

"Well, I'll see you later, Liam."

"You promise?"

I was taken aback by his response, not quite understanding what he meant by that.

"Yeah, sure, I promise." The second warning bell rang. "Oh shoot, I'm going to be late. Sorry, I really gotta go. Bye." I walked quickly away. Hmm, that was very interesting, I thought as I ran to class, excited about what had happened. As I turned the corner, I glanced back towards where we were talking and to no surprise to me, Liam was still standing there watching me as I disappeared into the building.

Chapter Five
Confessions of a Madman

I didn't see Liam the rest of the day. A thunderstorm rolled in and all practices scheduled for after school were canceled. I was relieved. I knew my routine by heart and it would be nice having an afternoon with nothing to do. I drove to Kendra's house, assuming she would be home from the dentist. She was the only one I trusted when it came to discussing boys. As I pulled into her driveway, the closed garage door told me that she still wasn't home. With a sigh, I drove home, my cue that I should be working on my paper.

On Wednesday morning, the rain still pounded the pavement in sheets. Mom and Dad were going out of town, so they drove me to school. Dropping me off at the rear entrance, we bid farewell.

"Love ya, Jen."

"Love you too."

I took my finished report and placed it under my jacket to keep it dry. I was glad to be free of the worry. Besides, even if it wasn't the greatest paper on *To Kill A Mockingbird*, hopefully, the extra points of turning it in early would guarantee me a decent grade. By third period, Social Studies, the rain was coming down harder than ever before. It was depressing. Nothing was worse than the festival being in town and it being completely wet, not to mention having to march in it. As I entered Mrs. Harris' room for Social Studies, to my relief, I saw Mr. Buford standing behind her desk. She was absent today which meant a double study hall. As soon as the final bell rang, he instructed the class to move over to the auditorium across the hall, where he told us that we could do homework or read quietly.

I found my usual seat near the exit sign and seriously considered using my escape route this time. But instead I took out *Moby Dick* and began to read. *I might as well put this time to good use,* I decided. Before I knew it, I was on chapter six and the bell rang for 4th period. At least I didn't have to get up. It was time for my second study hall. I slumped back down into my seat and continued the plight of *Moby Dick* and the perils of Captain Ahab and Ishmael. Being that it was 4th period, I wondered if I would see Liam. *Probably not.* Just like English, he'll probably skip out of study hall as usual. I absorbed myself into my book. It wasn't my favorite read, but I had definitely read worse. I started to re-adjust myself in my seat when he whispered in my ear.

"Having fun?"

I took a breath while my heart skipped a beat. I felt the temperature in the room rise. My heart began palpitating. The middle of my palms became sweaty making my hands stick to the pages of my book. I couldn't believe the effect he was having on me. *Two words from him could make me feel like this?* This was utterly crazy. I turned to look at him. He was sitting right behind me wearing his usual, gorgeous, crooked smile. His hair was pulled back in its signature ponytail, and his blue eyes caught the light from the room making them appear lighter than normal.

"Hi, Jenny."

"Hi. Where did you come from?"

"Through the back door, I thought we could pick up where we left off yesterday if you don't mind?" He seemed nervous.

"Sure," I said hesitantly. "Did I do something wrong, Liam?"

"No, why would you ask that?"

"I don't know. I guess I'm just trying to figure out what you want from me. What is this all about? I mean, normally we don't even speak to each other, and now you're actually taking time out so we can talk. It's just not what you usually do, that's all."

He shifted in his seat, edging himself closer to me and positioning himself as if he was getting ready to tell me a secret that was meant for my ears only. I found myself leaning in to hear him better.

"Jenny, remember yesterday when you told me that you had talked to Shanna over the weekend?"

"Yeah, why?"

"You said that you had told Shanna that Friday night meant nothing to you," he paused, "that there was nothing going on between us."

"That's right. Wasn't that okay?" He was staring at the exit door. I repeated, "Wasn't that okay?"

"Jenny."

I could tell he wanted to tell me something, but for some reason he was having trouble doing so.

"Yes, Liam, what?"

He glanced away again, looking out the window next to the exit sign. Maybe he was thinking of an escape too, but then I noticed his left leg was still in the soft cast, he wouldn't be able to pull it off.

I tried to break the silence. "What, Liam, please just tell me."

"Jenny, I'm sorry you said that to her."

"What do you mean?" He was now looking down at his arms which were crossed over the back of my seat. "Sorry, Liam, I don't think I understand what you're getting at. Honestly, I just told her the truth. There isn't anything going on between us, right? I mean what happened over the weekend was nothing." He looked at me, and his demeanor changed. His blue eyes were telling me something totally different. He grabbed my right hand, placing it inside both of his. His gesture was so bold, but for some reason I didn't seem to care. His hands felt warm, rough, and calloused but nice around mine. My hands were sweaty, and I hoped he wouldn't be able to tell.

"Jen." Hesitating even more, he stuttered my name again. "Jen, I really hope you didn't mean that."

"Mean what?" I asked, trying to get it out of him.

He took a deep breath. "I really hope you didn't mean that there wasn't anything between us." He leaned a little further into me, closing the gap between us even more, inching himself to me, keeping my hand in his, not worried that someone might notice the body language between us, much less that we might catch the attention of Mr. Buford. I felt all weird and funny inside, an indescribable feeling that I couldn't ignore or much less want to ignore. "I really hope that there is something between us, Jenny."

He leaned back slowly, waiting for my reaction. I sat there, looking at him, feeling numb, not knowing what to say.

"I don't understand. What about you and Shanna?" I still wasn't convinced that their relationship was totally over.

"I told you, it's over between us."

"She definitely gave me the impression that you two were still together."

"That's Shanna for you, but trust me, it's over."

I looked down at my book. I couldn't even remember what the story was about anymore. I felt uncomfortable, and he was just looking at me.

"I really don't think I should be talking to you, Liam."

"Is it because of Shanna? Jen, I could care less what she thinks."

I looked at him, wanting to believe him, but still questioning his intent. "Liam, how do I know that you're not just on the rebound, that you're just looking for a good time 'til you and Shanna work things out? I'm not going to get into the middle of something like that. It would be humiliating, and I would be the laughing stock of this entire school. I just can't do it."

He looked crushed. "I can't believe you would think that of me."

"I don't know you, Liam. I don't know who you really are or what you might think or do."

He sat back in his chair, releasing his grip from my hand. He took his hands and ran them through his hair, pulling his ponytail out in frustration.

"Liam, I'm sorry. You have got to understand where I'm coming from. This came out of left field for me. I mean, we barely know each other, and now you're offering me rides home, sitting with me at lunch, and confessing to me that you hope there can be more between us? It's a lot to process." I turned around in my chair and faced the stage.

"Jen, please wait. Look at me. I don't know what to say. This didn't exactly go as I had planned. All I can say is that I'm speaking from my heart. You don't know how I've wrestled with this." I turned to face him, curious about what he meant. He was much closer to me than I expected, his face inches from mine. "You can think whatever you want. I'm not on the rebound. I'm not trying to play a game with you. I'm trying to tell you that I like you. I'm crazy about you actually, and it has taken me weeks for me to get my nerve up to even talk to you." My jaw dropped to the floor. "I mean, I don't know what I mean anymore. Yes, I do. I like you, plain and simple. I have for a really long time." I sat there dumbfounded, just watching him, not believing this was actually happening.

"You know, I left Lougini's despising the very ground you walk on."

"I understand. Friday night was a mess." He gently squeezed my hand in his. His felt sweaty too, or maybe it was my sweat that I was feeling. "I know you were upset with me on Friday. That's why I wanted, no needed, to apologize to you. That's why I stopped you on your way home from practice. I couldn't stand the thought of you being mad or hating me. If I thought you hated me..." His voice hesitated.

"Liam, but we don't really even know each other. How can you feel this way when you don't even know me?" I was grasping at straws, trying to make sense out of all of this.

"Please, you have to believe me, I wasn't trying to embarrass you or anything. This is real for me, very real. Why do you think I showed up at Lougini's on Friday after I got hurt? I should've just gone home."

"You mean you were there for me?"

"Yes! I've seen you there a hundred times. I know you go there every Friday night with your friends. I needed to see you. I needed to be there. I knew you would be there."

"Half the school goes there on Friday, Liam."

"Yeah, but I didn't want to see half of the school, just you. Look, Jenny, I'm not expecting you to tell me you feel the same way about me, but I hope someday you can, but I needed to tell you now. I couldn't wait any longer. You don't know what it's been like for me to feel this way and have you not know. I'm not trying to pressure you into anything, but I do want you to know how much I like you. It's just you, nobody else, so don't worry that I'm doing this because I'm on the rebound from Shanna. I'm not. Take all the time you need to think about what I've told you. I can wait, just ask my friends. I've already been waiting for months."

"Your friends know about this?" I was stunned and shocked.

"Of course. I needed to talk to somebody about you, and it's not like I've told the whole school, just Parker and Tony, my buddies, that's all. Jenny, it's been unbearable for me at times, when I see you, I'm sure people have caught me staring at you. I pass you in the hallway and I find myself walking in your direction. It's all I can do not to pick you up and take you away from here just so I can be near you. I've watched you at practice, hoping you might notice me. It's been insane for me."

I was in shock, trying to take everything in that he was saying to me, not really believing that this was happening.

"I know it's a lot for you to take in, but I've never been more sincere in my whole life. Jenny, please just think about what I've said. Give me a chance. I'll do whatever it takes to make you believe me, I promise. And as far as who you think I am, maybe from things you've heard about me, they're not true. I'm not that type of guy to hurt a girl, to hurt you like that."

I couldn't speak, much less breathe. All I could do was stare at him.

"You know when you fell down at the game. I saw my chance, and even though you acted like you didn't want anything to do with me, I still felt different. That's why I brought you your baton. Actually, Cody found it, but I asked him if I could give it to you. It was my chance to talk to you. I didn't care that you didn't seem to want anything to do with me. It made me that much more determined to try. I had to try, Jenny, and that's why I'm here right now."

Was this guy for real? Was he really serious, or was I listening to the confessions of a madman? I had to think clearly. It seemed so surreal that Liam was telling me all this. I almost felt violated knowing he felt this way for me for so long without me knowing anything about it. He continued with his confession.

"And, when I got hurt I kept looking for you in the crowd. Didn't you see me look for you?"

"That was for me? You know I did see you, but Shanna was standing in front of me, and I thought it was for her. I never dreamed you were looking at me."

"Well, it was for you." He pulled my hair to the side. "I sometimes sit in class just staring at you."

When you make it to class, I thought to myself.

"The entire time I was being carted off to the hospital and the whole time I was there, all I could think about was getting to Lougini's so I could see you. I didn't care how hurt I was; I was determined to be there that night. I knew you would be there." I sat there in disbelief.

"Jen, you don't have to say anything. I know you weren't expecting this. I understand it's a lot to take in; hell, I'm surprised I said as much as I have. I've been a nervous wreck all day just thinking about this conversation with you."

"Liam, I..."

"Jen," he stopped me. "Just think about it. Like I said, I'm not asking anything of you. No pressure, but I'm tired of watching you from the sidelines. I want to get to know you a lot better. If you decide you want nothing to do with me, I'll understand. I won't be happy about it, but I'll leave you alone." He smiled, almost intuitively knowing that I wouldn't want him to leave me alone. When the bell rang, I stumbled getting up, almost dropping my books in the process. My hand was still in his, and he grabbed my arm pulling me to him. "Can I call you tonight?" I looked at him questionably. "Please."

Hesitantly, I replied. "I... I... um, sure... I have majorette practice after school and won't be home 'til after five."

"Great, I have football anyway. I'll call you when I get home, say seven?"

"Okay."

I started to leave when he pulled me back again. His touch was forceful but gentle. He brought his face down to meet mine. It looked like he was going to kiss me. I held my breath. I never felt so nervous. Wondering if I should try to pull away, wondering if anyone was watching us, his lips were millimeters from mine. I thought how forward his advances were. He barely knew me, but he seemed so sure of himself, as if he knew I wouldn't refuse him.

"I'm going to need your phone number." He backed away, barely though, enabling me to speak.

"Oh, yeah, I guess that would help." I opened my eyes, not realizing that I had closed them. "Liam?"

"Yes, Jenny?"

I was trying to clear my head and decided not to say anything. "Nothing, Liam." I took out a sheet of paper and wrote down my number. He took it from me, looked at it for a minute and then crumpled the paper and threw it away.

"Hey, why did you do that?" I asked feeling somewhat slighted.

"I don't need it."

"Huh?"

He leaned towards me again. "I've got it memorized."

"You do, do you? What is it then?"

"777-1111," he said coolly.

"I'm impressed by your talent."

"It's one of many," he said smiling as if there was more to that comment than he was letting on. The final bell for lunch rang.

"Well gotta go," I said.

"Me too," he replied. "Jenny?" his voice was soft, but sincere, "Thanks."

"Thanks for what?"

"Thanks for now, for this. I've told you the truth and I just hope you can find it in you to believe me 'cause I'm really crazy about you."

He leaned into me grabbing my right pinky. *Here comes the kiss,* I thought. *Should I let him kiss me so soon?* Our faces were touching nose to nose practically, and I could smell his minty breath, then he whispered. "Bye." His breath felt warm as it passed by me. I breathed it in and sighing as he gazed at me. He straightened up, and I watched him walk away. I never noticed how tall he was, with a lean muscular build, not beefy but just right. His white t-shirt fit him well, showing off his tan, chiseled arms. My eyes went down to his jeans. They were worn and the bottoms were frayed but they did accentuate a very nice butt, a very nice butt indeed. I was still watching him when he turned around and winked at me, as if he knew I would still be standing there. He gestured with his left hand that he would call me and mouthed "I'll talk to you tonight." Another wink and he was gone. I walked to lunch with the same gait that Shauna has on a daily basis.

The lunchroom was full by the time I arrived. The clock read 11:18, only twenty minutes to get in line, grab my food, pay for it, find Kendra, eat, and tell her what just happened to me. Not nearly enough time, I thought. I decided that I wasn't that hungry. I grabbed a bottle of water and a bag of chips and started scoping the cafeteria for Kendra. I could hardly contain myself from smiling. I'm sure I looked pretty silly standing there in the lunchroom with a big smile on my face, just grinning from ear to ear. Kendra was over in the far corner. I was happy to see she was saving me a spot and that she was alone. I couldn't wait to tell her about Liam, but I wasn't ready for the rest of the girls to know. I ran over to her table.

"Hey, where's the fire?" she responded.

"You will never in a hundred million years guess what just happened to me in study hall!"

"What, did Mr. Buford swallow his whistle?"

"No, that would be pretty funny, but I'm trying to be serious, so stop making jokes." I didn't even know where to begin. I wanted to say everything at the same time, afraid I might leave something out. "Guess who just talked to me?" she knew. I knew she knew.

"Liam Larson?"

"Yes!"

"Oh my God! Tell me everything. What did he want?"

"I can't believe it, Kendra. He never comes to study hall. You know, the coach always gets them out of class so they can watch films and go over plays. Well, today I'm just sitting there, and he comes up behind me and sits down!"

"Go on."

"Well... you're right."

"I'm right? About what? Jenny, get on with it. I can't stand this rambling." She had scooted her chair in as close to the table as possible, hanging on to my every word.

"You're right about him liking me!"

"What?" She gasped, closing her open mouth with her hand. "Ahhhh... I told you so! I told you so! I told you so! Oh my, God Jenny, keep talking!"

"Well, he pretty much told me that he's liked me for a while, and he's just been too nervous to approach me. Can you believe that? Liam Larson too nervous to approach a girl? Anyway, he saw Friday night as his opportunity."

"What about Shanna, I thought they were still an item?"

"Me too, but apparently not. I guess it's been over for a while."

"What about your confrontation with her on Saturday?"

"I know, that came up too, but he made it perfectly clear that it was over between them."

"Oh my God, I told you, Jenny. I told you that there was something to this!"

"I know. I'm sorry I didn't believe you. Honestly Kendra, I think I need to pinch myself to make sure I'm not dreaming."

"Hey, wait a minute." Kendra's tone immediately changed. "I thought you didn't want anything to do with him?"

I sighed. "I know. I know, and I don't know what's going to happen. It definitely has to go slow, that's for sure. But you had to hear him, see the expression on his face, to hear his voice, he was being so open and honest with me. I think I'm in shock. But I will admit, he is cute."

"Cute?" Kendra said. "That's the understatement of the year. Wow, this is good, Jenny, even for you."

We were laughing, enjoying the moment, when I noticed Shanna a few tables down sitting with Kelli and some of the other cheerleaders. She was pissed, and I knew it was because of me. She had been crying, and her eyes were blood-red and swollen. She glanced my way and turned away abruptly when she saw me look at her. I looked away too. I had enough on my plate without adding her to it. Before we realized it, the bell had rang and lunch was over.

Kendra and I left for our fifth period Spanish class. The class flew by, and before I knew it, it was time for sixth period English. As we entered the classroom, I searched the room for Liam, but he wasn't there yet. Kendra and I took our seats. In a way, I was glad he wasn't there. I was still trying to process the last couple of hours and he would definitely be a distraction for me. The final bell rang, a warning to all students still in the hallway to get to their designated class. A few more kids trickled into Mrs. White's English class but not Liam. The disappointment still surprised me. *Oh well, this was probably better anyway.*

Mrs. White asked if anyone had their *To Kill A Mockingbird* papers done. Kendra and I happily pulled ours out. *Cha-Ching for the bonus points.* The fifty-minute class seemed like two hours. I didn't think it would ever end. I didn't pay much attention in class. My thoughts were preoccupied with what had just happened to me. Liam Larson liked me, Jenny King. I was smiling to myself when Kendra looked over at me. I gave her an embarrassing giddy grin without realizing it. She knew exactly what I was thinking. Finally, after the longest fifty minutes in history, class was dismissed.

I darted quickly from my seat and headed for the last class of the day, band. I grabbed my batons, and Kendra and I ran to the field for marching practice. By the time practice began, the rain had finally ended, but the field was still extremely wet making marching particularly difficult, not to mention messy. Every time I took a high step I would sling mud on the back of my jeans. Besides this, I forgot to wear my boots, so my tennis shoes were completely encased with muddy goo. Linda had decided that we should practice our routine at the top of the bleachers where it was concreted. I was more than happy to oblige. Mr. Hawthorne blew his whistle to give us our break, and Kendra caught up with me on my way to the band room.

"Can you believe that awful routine we have to do with the drums?"

"It doesn't look that bad. I thought it looked pretty good."

"You don't have to do it. Marty and Mike are loving it though. So..." Kendra said, "when are you going to hear from Liam again?"

"He's supposed to call me tonight after he gets home from football practice."

"What time?" Kendra said, wasting no time beating around the bush.

"Umm, I think seven."

"I want you to call me as soon as you get off the phone with him, understand?" I laughed at her enthusiasm. "You promise?" She said.

"Yes, I promise, as soon as I get off the phone I'll call you."

"Great!"

"Oh, by the way, Kendra, you're the only one I've told so far, do you mind not saying anything yet?"

"Yeah, but why? I'd be telling the whole world if Liam Larson liked me."

"I know, I'm just not ready to be bombarded with questions. I'm still digesting everything myself, you know?"

"Okay, that's cool. My lips are sealed until you give the word."

"Thanks, dawg!" With that, Mr. Hawthorne blew his whistle warning us that we had only a few minutes left of our break.

"I gotta go get my other baton, Kendra."

"Okay, see ya later!"

We giggled and went our separate ways. I ran to the band room to get my baton. I was also dying of thirst and wanted to grab some money so I could get a water before Mr. Hawthorne blew his final whistle. The band room was situated at the end of the high school, right on top of the cliff. By the time I made it to the room I was exhausted and out of breath. I ran into the room. My money was in my jacket, and my jacket was under a pile of about fifty others. I threw the other jackets in a chaotic manner, frantically looking for mine. The clock slowly ticking down from fifteen minutes. I had to hurry if I was to get a water from the machine. Finally, after going through the whole pile, I found mine. Grabbing the money from its pocket I dashed out the door bee-lining my way to the vending machine. I was rushing, which is never a good thing. I tried to put my change in way too fast, and it fell to the ground, most of it rolling down the sidewalk.

"ARRGGGH, why is this happening to me?" I yelled.

I started chasing my quarters in hopes of not losing any of them. I bent down trying to pick them all up at the same time, when a hand reached down next to mine.

"Hello," Liam said softly.

"Hello," I said, trying to look composed while trying to retrieve my change.

"Looks like I'm always helping you recover your money."

"Oh, yeah, I guess you are," I said, laughing nervously.

He handed me my change, cupping it in my hand and pressing his hand against mine. We slowly raised up together, almost bumping our heads as our eyes met each other. He was dressed in his practice gear for football.

"Are you going to be able to practice today?"

"Not really. I can walk through some of the drills, but I can't do anything until I get clearance from Dr. Garrett, and that's not until tomorrow."

"Oh, I see." Mr. Hawthorne blew his whistle; he was very regimented.

"I gotta go, Liam. If I'm late, Linda will have my head. I already got the cold shoulder from her for being late on Friday after the halftime show."

He looked puzzled. "Are you known for being late?"

"Not really, but I better not make a habit out of it."

"I understand. Can I still call you tonight?"

"Yeah, I'm looking forward to it."

"Me too."

His grin was almost as beautiful as his eyes. We began our walk down the hill, all eyes from both the football team and the band were glued on the two of us. I tried to ignore it but found it utterly impossible to do so. The sheer notion that Liam was even standing next to me, much less walking beside me still seemed unreal to me. I tried to soak it in as best as I could while at the same time ignoring the gasps and whispers from the onlookers.

He leaned into me at the bottom of the hill. "Have a good practice."

"I will, you too."

I quickly turned to walk over to where the rest of the majorettes were when I felt a tug at my baton. Liam had grabbed the other end of it. I turned to see what the hold-up was. He just smiled and gave me that same wink. I couldn't help but smile back.

"See ya later, Jenny."

I pulled my baton away slowly and prepared myself for the interrogation I knew was coming.

"So," Linda said, "what's up with you and Liam Larson?"

I felt myself becoming immediately defensive. *Why should I have to tell her anything? It's none of her damn business. I won't even give her the satisfaction of an answer.* But then again, I thought that would be stupid. *She was being nice enough. I'd be interested too if the shoe was on the other foot. I am going to have to start answering questions about him sooner or later, especially if this ended up being something between us.* I was just hoping it would be later instead of sooner.

I braced myself and replied. "Oh, I don't know. We just started talking, and he walked down with me. We were going in the same direction." I was watching their reaction, hoping this would be a sufficient enough answer for them. I should have known better.

"Just walking down the hill together, huh?" Allison said. I knew Allison wouldn't resist the moment. She was notorious for being into everybody's business. My eyes went straight to hers.

"Yeah, what's wrong with that?"

"Nothing, I guess, except he was holding onto your baton with you." I had forgotten that gesture.

"Well, it's nothing, really guys."

I could feel my heart racing. *Why couldn't Mr. Hawthorne or somebody interrupt us so we could move on from this subject?*

But instead I received devious smiles from all the girls as if they knew I wasn't telling the whole story. I started twirling my batons, trying to ignore their looks and remind them that we were here to practice.

"Guys, can we just get on with this." I was pleading.

"Okay," Linda said reluctantly.

But I knew that this wasn't over. In fact, it was only the beginning. Mr. Hawthorne kept us for an extra half hour, it was way after five before any of us were able to leave. I kept thinking that I had told Liam I would be home by now. The only good thing was that he was still practicing too, so he knew that I was still here. I couldn't believe I even cared about that. Plus, I had til seven, plenty of time. I quickly gathered my things, not saying goodbye to anyone. After my first interrogation with the squad, the last thing I wanted was an interrogation from my friends. Avoidance was imperative. Fortunately for me, the rest of the girls were still getting instructions from their squad leaders. I took the cue and started my walk home. I took the shortcut through the baseball field and cut five minutes from my time and hopefully would avoid the girls when they drove by. I looked back, Kendra and Missy were waving. I waved back but didn't wait for them. I was homeward bound.

I went through the mangled baseball fence that looked as if kids had taken steel clippers to cut an opening in the fence. It made my exit faster than usual. I was more than half way home when the traffic from practice started passing me. I noticed Missy's car turning in the opposite direction. I was off the hook for a while. Then the trucks started passing, which meant one thing, football practice was also over. At least eight trucks passed me when I noticed the hum of a familiar motor. I turned to see whose it was. The black Ford pick-up truck approached me slowly. I stopped as his truck pulled to the curb next to me.

"Do you want a ride?"

He looked cute as he leaned into the steering wheel wearing an old, blue and white flannel and jeans. His wet hair hung down and looked longer than I remembered. It easily graced the top of his shoulders. As I leaned into the door, I could smell a fresh scent. I couldn't tell if it was his air freshener or his deodorant.

"This is becoming a habit."

"I hope so," he said.

"Thanks, but I'm practically home already."

"Come on, get in. Please, I promise I won't bite."

His devilish grin made me think otherwise. I looked around, not really caring if anyone saw me but at the same time hoping nobody did. I placed my books and batons on the messy floor. I hadn't noticed the mess before. I was glad. By the super clean exterior of his truck, I was afraid he might be a neat freak. But there was the usual mess found in most teenager's cars: CDs on the floor, his football equipment, an empty can of pop and some school books.

"How was practice?"

"Great," I said, "And yours?"

"Good. I couldn't do much, but I didn't care. I was able to watch you."

I felt my face beginning to blush.

"I'm really not that good and not much to look at."

"Oh, I would have to disagree. I've always enjoyed watching you."

He had scooted himself closer to me. I couldn't help but think that the last girl to sit here was Shanna Smith. I tried to keep some distance between us, but he made it very difficult. I looked down at his legs. His soft cast was missing.

"You're not wearing your cast?" I was nervous and was trying to make idle conversation so he wouldn't notice my anxiousness.

"I took it off. My leg is feeling better. It just hurts a little, besides it's a nuisance when I have to drive." His right arm was resting on the back of my seat. "Is everything okay, Jenny?"

"Yeah, why do you ask?"

"I don't know, you seem nervous or something."

"No, not nervous." My voice quivered.

"Jen, did I upset you this morning?"

"No, not at all."

"I hope not. I've been thinking about you all day."

A smile crept its way onto my face. "You have?"

"Yeah." He leaned in further to me.

"Liam, I don't want to go too fast. This has been a head rush for me all day, I'm still trying to absorb everything."

"That's fine. As I told you, no pressure." Obviously it didn't matter what I just said because he scooted closer. I had nowhere to go. My back was against the door. "Jen?"

"Yeah?"

"Did I tell you how much I like you?"

"Uh-huh," I whispered, my heart pounding.

Then without any warning he moved over to me before I could react. His face was practically on top of mine. His lips grazed mine as he spoke but still without kissing me. "I do, I think I've fallen for you big time." I could feel my lips quivering and was positive he could feel them too. I was so nervous, and he seemed to be so under control. "Have you considered your feelings for me?"

I couldn't say anything. I had thought about my feelings for him, but the jury was still out. I didn't answer him. Had I, my lips would have moved, and indicated that I wanted him to kiss me, but then again maybe I did want him to kiss me. The two of us just breathed. Our breaths encircling each other. Our eyes met. He whispered my name as his right arm pulled me into him. As if we could get any closer, his left arm grabbed the back of my neck and he gently and cautiously pressed his lips to mine. He was so tender, but I could feel the urgency in his kiss, he didn't hold back. I didn't move, letting him kiss me. I could tell he wanted me to respond, but I was shaking. Then as if I had no control over my body, my arm reached for his waist. I was holding onto him, pulling him even closer to me, giving in, obliging to his will. He groaned softly. I first thought of his injured leg, but then he pressed himself closer, tighter to me. I knew then it was a moan of desire. His lips were soft, and his mouth was sweet. His wet hair fell on my face.

With hesitation our lips parted, and we were still holding each other, not moving, both of us breathing but barely breathing at the same time. He was staring at me through his hair. I pulled it to the side so I could see his face. His eyes were so blue. I felt dizzy and was glad to be sitting or I would have easily lost my balance. It was our first kiss.

"I've been wanting to do that for a long time, Jenny," he whispered.

I kept breathing, wondering how long he meant. I felt weak. I couldn't believe how numb I felt when I was around him or how I allowed myself to be overcome by him. "You have?" My voice was barely audible. He pulled himself to me again, his lips touching mine.

"Uh-huh," he said. "You still didn't answer my question."

I had completely forgotten the question. Smiling, as I said, "I think I just did."

He kissed me again, giving me no time to breathe. I felt like I was going to suffocate, but I didn't care. The way he made me feel was too important to ignore. After a few minutes, we finally came up for air.

"I really should be getting home now."

"Okay. I'll take you home," he said reluctantly, "but I'm not letting you go, Jenny." His response was serious. There was something deeper going on, but I didn't know how deep. "Let's go," he said.

I looked at his clock on the dashboard. It was 5:42 and Mom and Dad were going to be worried.

"Don't worry. I'll have you home in no time."

He put the truck into drive, and away we went. It took less than a minute for him to get me home. The ride was silent, but no words were needed. He pulled into my driveway and leaned over.

"Seven still?"

"Yeah, Seven." I started to get out, but he stopped me. His lips were on mine again.

"I thought we were going to take this slow?"

"We are. Believe me, my first thought was not to let you get out of my truck."

"Oh," I said as he squeezed my hand.

"Until seven?"

"Yeah, seven."

I slipped out of the cab of his truck and watched him back out and drive away. I was still numb from head to toe as I tried to manipulate my way up the steps without falling down. I walked inside the house not realizing how I had gotten there. I was losing it. My brain was a fog. I threw my stuff on the bench. The house smelled of Mom's apple cake.

"Hi, Mom, I'm home!"

"Hi, honey. I was wondering when you were coming home. The phone's been ringing off the hook for you."

"Who's been calling?"

"Well, Kendra called twice, Missy, Shauna, Frannie, Brenda, everybody and they all want you to call them back."

I breathed heavily. "Maybe later, Mom. I'm starving!"

"How was practice?"

"Good. We're learning our new routines for the festival this weekend."

"Oh, great, I can't wait to see them."

I sat down at the table. "Where's Dad?"

"Dad had to go to Charleston on business. He won't be home until late tonight, so go ahead and eat." She handed me a plate, and I scarfed the food down in record time.

"You must have been starving," Mom said.

She had no idea. After dinner, I helped Mom with the dishes. Since it was just the two of us, clean-up was a breeze. The kitchen clock read 6:44. I had plenty of time to take a quick shower before my phone call.

"Do you need anything else, Mom?" Hoping her answer would be no.

"I think we're good. You go ahead and go. If it's alright, I'm going to go visit Ann. She hasn't been feeling well, and I want to take her some apple cake."

Perfect, I thought. I would have the house to myself when Liam called. Mom kissed me goodbye, and I headed up the stairs.

"Jen, love you."

"Love you too, Mom, see ya later!"

I raced up the remaining steps and rushed like a mad woman to get my shower. It felt good to clean up. I put on a pair of my favorite yoga pants and a cami and jumped on my bed. The clock read 7:04. Hmm... He hadn't called yet. I kept my cell with me in the bathroom so I could hear it ring. *Well, it's only been five minutes. I'm sure he'll be calling any second.* Rrrrrrinnng, *finally!* I thought. I jumped to answer it. I almost picked it up, and then hesitated. I didn't want to seem too eager. I let it ring a couple more times before answering.

"Hello?"

"Jenny, why haven't you called me back!" Kendra was almost screaming at me as she spoke.

"Kendra, I can't talk now. Liam is supposed to call me any minute. I thought you were him. I gotta hang up!"

"Okay, but you call me as soon as you're off the phone with him, understand? I want details!"

I laughed. "Okay, okay, now let me go."

I lay back on the bed, laughing at how funny Kendra had sounded. I glanced over, the clock now read 7:11 p.m., still no call. Trying to keep busy, I picked up my English paper and pretended to work on it. By seven-thirty, I stopped and got up. Feeling uneasy, I tried to rationalize why I hadn't heard from him yet. *Maybe something came up? Maybe he forgot my phone number. Damn it, I should have given it to him again. I knew he wouldn't be able to remember it.* Then reality started to sink in, maybe he wasn't calling. *I knew I shouldn't have gotten my hopes up. Slow down, don't rush into things*, I kept saying to myself. *This is only going to lead to heartache.* And it had.

By nine-thirty, I had finished off a pint of cherry-nut ice cream and was sulking and hating myself for letting him get to me this way. I felt stupid for allowing him to kiss me and for me to kiss him back. *What was I thinking? I let my emotions take control of me.* I had known it was a mistake. I went upstairs. The clock read 10:11pm. I never went to bed this early, but I couldn't think of a better place to be. At least I could go to sleep and not think about him. As I drifted off, I thought I could hear my cell ringing, I glanced at my clock, and it was 10:29. Kendra must be calling me back. I never called her; *she'll want answers, and I don't have any to give her.* The ringing continued. I was groggy, too groggy to answer the phone and in no mood to talk. *I'll talk to her tomorrow.* I closed my eyes as the ringing slowly faded away.

Chapter Six
The Festival

     I awoke the next morning, feeling tired and sluggish. I was still reeling from the fact that I allowed Liam to play me for a fool. The sun was casting an ominous shadow in my room, and I rolled back and forth in bed contemplating whether or not I should get up. I didn't feel like doing anything but laying under my covers and escaping from what lay ahead. I had questions to answer. My friends were still waiting to hear about the great Liam Larson. Little did they know that he was a conniving liar who played with your heart before ripping it to pieces.

     Furthermore, I was sure he was with Shanna last night. She would be reveling in all her glory, knowing she was back in the good graces of her precious little Liam. It was enough to make me want to vomit. I stared at my cell. Still no ringing, just like last night. *He didn't call.* I just couldn't believe it. But did it matter anyway? At least now I knew what kind of person Liam was. I could move on before he did any more damage. This was short and quick. I would explain to my friends that it just wasn't going to work out between Liam and me and that would be that. I'd be convincing. They wouldn't have any other choice but to believe me, and I would avoid being hurt and embarrassed any further. I would put on a good show in front of Liam too. He would be none the wiser, and by the end of the day, everyone would have forgotten that Liam had even given me the time of day. *It would work; it had to. Besides, we weren't really even dating, no, he only just professed that he was crazy about me and couldn't stand to be away from me. That's all. The jerk!*

    I could hear commotion downstairs. Mom and Dad were already getting their day going. I looked over at my clock, 6:50am My first class was in less than a half hour. I was going to be late. All this sulking and deliberating over Liam was going to cost me a detention. He had already messed with my heart. I wasn't about to let him mess with my near-perfect attendance record. I sprinted from my bed, looking into the mirror as I groaned in disbelief. The lack of sleep had wreaked havoc on my appearance. There were dark circles under my already blood-shot eyes. *Uggh!* I was a complete mess. I groaned in despair, knowing I needed a miracle or at least a lot of make-up to repair the damage. With no time for pity, I ran into the bathroom, grabbing my jeans and my all-important makeup bag, and went to work. I made it to school in record time, thanks partially to Dad allowing me to take the car. The hallway was practically empty. Most of the kids were already in their designated class. I ran to my locker. Luckily, none of my friends or Liam were in sight. I wanted to avoid him at all cost. I threw my batons and jacket in, and slammed the door. To my utter horror, I ran right into none other than the one and only person I was trying to avoid.

    "My God, Liam, do you have to sneak up like that and scare the living hell out of me?"

I tried to keep my cool while regaining control of my already out of control heart rate. Mad or not, Liam could instantly make my heart pound and my stomach turn with one single look. I had to learn to control this behavior before it did me in. Before he could speak, I turned to walk away. I was instantly pulled back by his firm grip on my forearm.

"Wait, Jenny, I'm sorry about last night."

"Sorry? About what?"

"Jenny, don't. Please, I know you know what I'm talking about. I was supposed to call you last night."

"Oh that, I had completely forgotten you were supposed to call." I was such a liar and a bad one at that. I turned to walk away again, only to be stopped by Liam's ever-so firm grip on my arm.

"Jenny, listen."

"Liam, there's no need to explain. It's not like I have tabs on you or anything. It's perfectly okay, and honestly, I didn't think you would call. Besides, it's better this way. Yesterday was moving a little too fast for me, and this way we can just make a clean break of things before anything even gets started."

"Jen, you don't, can't mean that."

I turned to walk away again trying to avoid eye contact with his baby blues as the bell for 1st period began ringing.

"Liam, I have to go. Class is going to begin any second." I knew it was common for him to miss class but not for me; besides, I desperately needed to get away from him. I felt used and I didn't want to hear his explanation.

"Jenny, you have to let me explain."

"Listen, there's nothing to explain. I told you it was okay. You don't need to do this."

He tightened his grip on my arm. "Jenny, don't walk off like this, not until I can tell you my reason for not calling you. I'm sorry."

"Can you please let go of me?" I tried, to no avail, to pull my arm away, but his grip held firm.

"No, I'm not. Not until I can talk to you without you trying to get away from me." He was as stubborn as he was cute. The final bell rang.

"Liam, I don't know about you but I've got class right now. You have to let me go." He reluctantly loosened his grip and allowed me to walk away, but before I could open the door to Geometry, Liam grabbed my arm again.

"I can't let you leave until we talk, Jenny. You'll just have to miss class."

"I can't believe you. Do you always get your way like this?"

"When it comes to you, I'm going to have to say yes. I've waited way too long to have you in my life to lose you now."

I was shocked by his last statement. *Did he really mean that, or was he still playing the debonair man about campus?* It was too early to tell, and against my better judgment I followed him outside to find out. But before he could even get two words out, Mr. Reynolds, the assistant principal, told us both to get to class.

"Jenny, please wait for me after school. I promise I will explain everything to you then. I'm not going to be in school after lunch. I have to get my leg x-rayed one last time, but I'll come back and meet you by the band room, deal?"

My rational voice told me to say no and to do it right away, but my heart told me to say yes. At least I could hear him out, even if it was against my better judgment.

"Deal."

He smiled from ear to ear. "Great, I'll see you then."

Before I could move, he effortlessly kissed my cheek and gave me his wink. I felt torn the rest of the day. I wanted to be upset with Liam, but he made such a convincing argument this morning that I felt compelled to believe him. By the time band rolled around I had convinced myself that he was telling the truth and that I had jumped to a stupid conclusion. I dealt with the barrage of questions from my wonderful girlfriends and answered them as best as I could. As far as I knew, for now at least, Liam Larson and I were just friends. That's all they needed to know, at least until I talked to him after school. And as for Kendra, who could read me like a book. She knew I would let her in on all of this in good time.

I was relieved when band was finally over. By five-thirty, most everyone had left the premises, and there was still no sign of Liam. I sat on the back steps to the rear entrance of the band room, re-reading the same sentence in my book over and over again as I waited patiently to see Liam's black truck pull into the parking lot. By six, even the custodians had left. Liam was nowhere in sight, and by the looks of it, he wasn't going to show. I had been duped again by the one and only Mr. Larson. I grabbed my things and made the walk home, concluding that even if he did show I wouldn't pay him the time of day. I was done being made a fool of by him.

It was finally Friday, and the official start of the Black Walnut Festival, as well as a day off for the schools. Normally, I was over the top about the festival, but not today. Liam had taken care of that by again letting me down. I was bound and determined not to dwell on his rude behavior and just concentrate on the weekend ahead and the majorette competition. I had too much at stake. This was my final year for competing, and I needed to focus and give it my all, without distractions. It was turning out to be a gorgeous day. The rain had finally ceased, and the sun was giving way to a beautiful, crisp, sunny autumn day. The town was pulsating with excitement. The side streets had been closed to allow for vendors from across the state to set up booths to showcase their must-have items. The National Guard Armory was stationed to hold the candy and baked good items that the locals had made: everything from fudge, bread, cakes, pies and ice cream. Mom always entered one of her apple cakes, adding black walnuts to go with the theme. Two years ago she took first place.

Main Street had been partitioned in certain areas in order for chairs and stadium seats to be set up along the parade route. Close to five thousand spectators were at last year's parade, and the festival committee had predicted at least that many this year, if not more. There were dozens of craft kiosks as well. You could find everything from hand-knitted sweaters, to hand-knitted cup holders. And then there was the carnival. People from miles around would come into town just for this. People that I've never seen before in my life would show, making the town of Spencer question how many people actually lived in the area. Kendra and I used to wonder where they were the other three hundred and sixty-two days of the year.

The carnival had grown over the years, starting simply as a Ferris wheel and a few kiddie rides, into one of the largest attractions to come to these parts. Almost thirty rides emerged overnight in the town parking lot. Everything from a gigantic slide to a tilt-a-whirl to a monstrous haunted house. It was amazing and always a lot of fun. The festival had definitely gotten underway. It was quite an event and something everyone in the town took pride in. The town looked great in all of its festival regalia. The streets were lined with gold and brown banners, and autumn flags hung from the light posts. The baskets that were once filled with summer impatiens and petunias were now filled with hardy mums in their glorious colors of autumn.

My older sister, Ashley, who lived in Ohio, came home often and never missed the festival. I couldn't wait. We usually spent at least one night together during her weekend visit, and this year should be no exception. Luckily for us we got along brilliantly as sisters and didn't share the usual sister animosity that most siblings do. The mood in town was exhilarating and exactly what I needed to keep my mind off of him. It was almost noon before I realized it, and I hadn't even been downtown yet. Mom and Dad were on the festival committee this year and had already left for the day before I had even woke up. Thankfully I would be spending it with Kendra who was already running late to pick me up. Ashley would arrive tonight, so between the two of them I wouldn't have a chance to think about Liam. Just as I was ready to call Kendra, she knocked on my door.

"I thought you'd never get here."

"I would have been here an hour ago, but the traffic is horrible. I had to park on the side of the road and walk here. Looks like our best bet is to walk anyway, there's no parking downtown either."

The two of us grabbed our jackets and followed the sounds and smells of the festival. The short walk it took to arrive downtown showed us exactly how busy the day was going to be. It was bumper to bumper traffic as far as the eyes could see, and the streets were packed with patrons. We struggled our way through the kiosk lined streets for most of the day until we both had grown tired of the sightseeing.

"Are you feeling okay, Jenny?"

"Yeah, why do you ask?"

"Well, you've been quiet for most of the day, and I don't know. I haven't heard you talk of Liam once. Is something going on?"

Actually nothing was, I thought to myself.

"I don't know, Kendra, it's weird. I can't figure him out and I guess I've come to the conclusion that he's more of a conniver than I thought."

"What? Liam? What do you mean?" Kendra was totally dumbfounded by my statement.

"It's just that he tells me one thing and then he doesn't follow through. He said he would call me Wednesday night, and he didn't, and then he said he wanted to explain after school yesterday why he didn't call, and he never showed up. It's one lie after the other."

"Jenny, come on, I don't think you've given the boy a fair enough chance."

"A fair enough chance? Kendra, I've given him two chances, and he hasn't come through once. How many does the boy need?"

"I just mean that I'm sure he has a good enough explanation to why he didn't call you. You just need to give him the chance to explain, that's all."

"That's just it. I tried to give him the chance, but he didn't show up after school. I waited for over an hour, and he never showed. I wasn't going to stay there all night."

"Jen, I completely see where you are coming from. All I'm saying is you might be making a mountain out of a molehill. Why don't you just wait and see what happens. I can't believe Liam would go to all the trouble he has with you to blow it so easily."

Maybe she was right, but I really didn't want to find out. Being duped by him twice in a row was two times too many for me. It was getting late in the afternoon, and if we wanted to take in any of the rides before the game tonight we had to do it now. The town was even more jam-packed than before. The loudspeakers were blaring with some country song about lost love and hardship, and every kiosk vendor was trying to lure us to their tables. But the only thing enticing Kendra and I were the sights and sounds coming from the parking lot, the carnival. We made our way through the crowd and finally found our way to the rides. It was awesome. Just the sight alone was breathtaking, not to mention the smell of cotton candy and taffy. It was as busy here as the streets were, and it looked like half the school had shown up as well. We saw Frannie and Steve going into the haunted house, Brenda and Drew at one of the shooting galleries, and Missy and Eric on the Tilt-a-Whirl.

"Wow, everybody is here," Kendra said.

"Yeah, everybody seems to have a date."

"Stop it, Jenny. You're gonna make yourself crazy at this rate. Just let it go. Besides, I thought you were mad at him?"

"I am mad at him, but it wouldn't hurt to see him."

"I can't figure you out."

I had to agree, I was in a complete state of flux over Liam Larson, and there didn't seem to be any cure for it.

"Come on," Kendra said grabbing my arm.

"What are you doing?"

"We're going to go ride the Ferris wheel. You need to get your mind off of Liam and have some fun."

"And you think riding the Ferris wheel is going to do that?"

"It's a start."

Kendra made me stand in line for the ride while she went to buy our tickets. She was right, it would take my mind off of him. The ride was coming to an end, and our turn was fast approaching with Kendra nowhere near the front of the ticket line. My only option was to allow the people behind me to go ahead and wait for Kendra when from out of nowhere I was pushed from behind and pulled onto the ride. Liam was sitting by my side. The operator closed and locked our door, and we started our ascent. I watched Kendra as she smiled and stared at me in disbelief. He looked great. His gorgeous eyes were as blue as an afternoon sky, and he had his hair pulled back in its signature ponytail. I began to speak, but he quickly put his finger against my lips.

"No talking until I have my say." He was in total control. I tried to speak when his forefinger again planted itself on my lips. "I told you i was going to talk. You can just sit next to me and listen." I didn't say a word, and when he was sure I wasn't going to try to speak, he began. "First of all, I'm sorry I didn't meet you after band yesterday. My Grandpa had a flat tire. I had to help him repair it. He was in Ripley, and I had no way to contact you. I didn't have my cell with me and Grandpa, well he doesn't own one. We were in the middle of nowhere. By the time we got back in town, it was after midnight. Secondly, if you would check your cell, you will see that I tried calling you last night when I got in. You should have at least six or seven messages from me." I did have a bunch of missed calls, but I never checked to see who they were from. "Finally, about Wednesday night, I did call you."

"No you didn't." Liam's finger went back to my lips.

"Shhh, I said I was doing the talking. Like I was saying, I did call you, but it was much later than I told you I would, but you never answered. The phone just rang and rang. After I left you on

Wednesday, Parker came over to my house to hang out for a while. He was helping me bring the horses in when one of them ran away. I couldn't leave her out there. She has a bad leg and needed to be in the barn. We looked everywhere for that damn horse. It took us half the night to find her. Once we got her settled in the barn, I immediately called you. But, like I said, you never answered. So there, in a nutshell, Jenny King, I've told you why I didn't call and why I didn't show up after school yesterday. You can make your judgment on me now if you want, but I will tell you, you're not getting off of this Ferris wheel until you forgive me. I gave the operator twenty dollars' worth of tickets and told him I had more if needed."

"So that was you calling so late on Wednesday?" I finally said.

"Yes."

"I thought you were Kendra. When you didn't call at seven, I had given up. When the phone rang, I just didn't answer it." The Ferris wheel was going around and around, but I was so caught up in what he was saying that I didn't even realize we were moving. I looked down at one point to see that Kendra had found Shauna, and they were now in line for the tilt-a-whirl. "Liam, I didn't give you a chance. I'm sorry. After the way I acted at school, and then I didn't see you the rest of the day, so I thought... well it doesn't really matter what I thought." I didn't continue, not wanting to say or even think that he might not want anything to do with me anymore. I hadn't made up my mind about him yet, but I knew I didn't want him out of my life. I looked down as he took his arm and put it around me. I felt completely at ease, all my inhibitions about him were gone. I think the Ferris wheel was still moving, but I still couldn't tell.

"I told you I'm crazy about you. You're not getting rid of me that easy, and I told you I'm not letting you go. It just about killed me last night when you didn't answer your phone. I couldn't even sleep, all I could think about was you and that I needed to straighten things out with you. I was on my way to your house today when I saw you and Kendra here at the carnival. I couldn't get to you fast enough."

Before I had a chance to say anything, his lips were on mine. I wanted to pull back from him, but this felt so right. I wanted Liam to kiss me, and I wanted to kiss him back. I clutched his ponytail, undoing it so his hair would fall on my face.

"I could get used to this," he said.

"Me too."

Out of nowhere, we heard the operator say, "Hey you two, this isn't a make-out ride." Liam handed the guy a bunch more tickets and told him we weren't done yet, the operator mumbled something under his breath while he locked us back in. When the ride finally ended, the operator unlocked our hatch allowing us to leave. Liam helped me down, and closed his hand over mine, our fingers tightly intertwined. I looked back at our seat. It was number eleven. *Funny, the same number as Liam's football jersey, must be fate,* I thought as a smile crept over my face. Walking away, I noticed Liam's limp was gone.

"Hey, you're not limping!"

"You noticed. I didn't get the chance to tell you how my doctor's appointment went."

"Is everything good?"

"As good as gold. Dr. Garrett cleared me so I can play in tonight's game."

"There's no chance you could re-injure it?"

"Well, I guess, but I'll be careful. Why, are you worried?"

"No, of course not," I said, trying to act blasé about the whole matter. But I knew better, and so did Liam. "Maybe a little."

This time last week, I didn't care at all. Strange how things can change in a matter of days.

"You know, Liam, when you didn't show yesterday I was ready to call this whole thing off."

"You were?"

"Yeah, I thought you were just being a jerk by leading me on. When I didn't see you, it really hurt, more than I wanted it to."

He stopped and abruptly turned me to face him. "I know it looked bad, that's why it was so important for me to talk to you. You're becoming very important to me. I knew that when I saw you last night."

"What? But you didn't see me last night, what do you mean?"

"Well, in a way I did. You just didn't see me." I was totally confused, and by the expression on my face, he knew it too.

"After we returned from Ripley, I took a little drive into town to your house."

"My house?"

"I pulled in your driveway and sat there for a while."

"Why, didn't you let me know?"

"I wanted to, especially after yesterday morning, but I didn't think your parents would be too thrilled to see me at eleven o'clock at night, asking if I could see you."

"I guess you're right, but you still could have tried."

"That's okay, I saw you turn off your light. I didn't want to bother you. Anyway, I was fine. I was near you, and that's all that mattered to me. It was good enough just to be that close to you."

I felt my insides melting like butter.

"Liam, I don't know what to say, except I am so sorry about yesterday."

"That's okay, you have a long time to make it up to me." He leaned in, kissing my cheek.

We spent the rest of the day together as we enjoyed the festival. I looked for Kendra, but she was nowhere to be found. It was almost 4 o'clock by the time Liam walked me back to my house.

"Do you want to come in?"

"I can't. I have to be at the field house by five, and my football stuff is still at the house."

"That's okay. I need to get ready for tonight too."

"Jenny, can I take you home after the game?"

My heart was in my throat. "Yeah, I would like that."

"Great, I'll see you at the game."

He leaned into me, gently kissing me on the lips and holding both of my hands in his. I looked up at him. I barely came to his chest.

"Liam, I think you're winning me over."

"I hope so."

And with that, he turned around and ran down my steps, taking them two at a time. You couldn't even tell that just a few days ago his leg was in a cast. I laughed as I watched him, waiting until he was clear out of sight before I went inside. I found Mom and Dad in the living room.

"Did you have a nice time downtown?"

"Yeah, I did."

I wanted to tell them about Liam, but this was not the time. I had to be at the school by five-thirty, and if I brought up that I spent the afternoon with a boy I would have the interrogation of a lifetime. Instead, I ran upstairs where I found my neatly pressed uniform waiting for me on my bed. I put it on and ran downstairs to grab my boots.

"See ya guys at the game!" I shouted to them, as I ran out the door.

"Jenny, wait."

"What, Mom?"

"Dad and I have been asked to be one of the judges for the art show tonight. We won't be at your game. I'm sorry."

"That's okay, see ya later."

I began my descent down the front steps when I realized that they wouldn't know Liam was bringing me home. In a quick turn, I headed back up to the house.

"Jen? Did you forget something?" Mom asked.

"No, but I forgot to tell you that Liam will be bringing me home tonight."

"Liam?" Dad asked sternly.

"Yes, Dad, he's the boy who's brought me home from practice a couple of times."

"Oh right, he has the black truck. I told you about him, Henry."

"Are you two going out after the game?" Dad asked.

"I'm not for sure, Dad. Maybe to Lougini's."

"Well, just remember your curfew now is twelve-thirty. Don't be late."

"I won't."

The stadium was filled to capacity. The Spencer Yellow Jackets were facing the Parkersburg Big Red, another fierce rivalry for both teams. Parkersburg had beaten us the past three years in a row, and the Yellow Jackets were determined to end the streak tonight. I took my place with the majorettes and could see Liam on the field warming up with the other football players. He was in the front line along with Parker and Tony, all three of them were captains for tonight's game.

By the time the game started, the rain had returned, making the field a slippery mud pit. Both teams were covered in it, making it difficult to even tell who was who. The entire bleachers were covered with blue and gold raincoats and umbrellas. The rain poured down in sheets making it a miserable evening to watch the game. What had started out as a nice evening had turned into a cold night of torrential rain. At halftime, Mr. Hawthorne allowed the band to wear their raincoats for the performance. That was nice for them, but not for the majorettes. It was hard enough to twirl a baton when it wasn't raining, but adding rain coats to the mix made it next to impossible to perform. Furthermore, Linda had vetoed the coats. By the end of our show, we looked like ninety-five rain-soaked mudrats on the field. Everyone was covered in thick wet mud. Marty Skinner even managed to lose one of his shoes during the performance, which we hoped wouldn't cause a problem during the second half of the game. We were a calamity of errors, and all of us were all too eager to get the show over with and get off the field.

As the teams made their way back into the stadium, the heavens broke through and cleared the skies. An ominous foreshadowing of what hopefully was to come for the Yellow Jackets, and without fail, the second half turned out to be much better, not only weather-wise but point-wise for our beloved team. Within the first eight minutes of the 3rd quarter, the Yellow Jackets scored two touchdowns, increasing their lead to over twenty-eight points. Victory looked imminent. Liam was having one of his best games ever, scoring all but one of the five touchdowns so far.

When the game ended the Yellow Jackets had won, Liam had scored another touchdown as well as Parker Hanson. The game turned out to be history making for us, going down as the highest scoring win for the team in over thirty years. Leading the Yellow Jackets in that victory was none other than the Liam Larson. His leg injury from the previous week had been forgotten, allowing him to run for over one hundred fifty yards, making six out of the seven touchdowns, and retrieving three fumbles. He had been on fire that night, and the crowd was in a state of euphoria for him. I felt the same excitement and rush of emotion as everyone else, not only for the win but also for Liam. I was falling for him and felt like throwing caution to the wind. There was still that little voice in my head that kept nagging me, but I didn't really care. For now, all was right with the world and all was right with Liam. I still didn't have all the answers I needed, but I did know that he seemed to be genuine about his feelings for me, and for now, that was enough. Mr. Hawthorne blew his whistle to get everybody's attention.

"Great show, guys, even with the rain. See you at the park tomorrow morning at ten sharp for the parade."

The crowd in the stands were still in a state of pandemonium, no one seemed to care that it was cold and wet. No one left the stadium. They were throwing tons of blue and gold confetti in the air, and in the midst of all this was Liam. Their all-American boy being hailed as the hero of the night. I watched him from the stands. He and Parker were body bumping each other and high-fiving everyone in reach. They were celebrating a great win, and it was nice to see him in his element, enjoying the moment with his team, especially after last week's loss. I headed to the band room to gather my belongings. I knew I wouldn't see Liam for a while. He would be on the field for some time still, being congratulated by every Tom, Dick, and Harry who could get close to him. Back in the band room everyone was trying to dry off and clean up. I had never in my life seen so much mud in one place. I felt sorry for the school custodian who would eventually have to clean up the mess that we were leaving behind.

"So, what's the plan for tonight?" Kendra asked while gathering her things.

"Liam's taking me home. Sorry, I forgot to tell you."

"That's okay, I kinda figured that much anyway. So what's going on between you two? Are you two an item now?"

"An item? That's a good one. I don't know."

"What do you mean you don't know?"

"I don't know. I don't know what's going on yet."

"Really?" Kendra asked surprisingly. "Well, I think you two are. Frannie heard Liam talking to one of the guys earlier before the game, and they were all joking that Liam was off-limits now. I can only guess that's because of you."

"Wow, I don't know. I guess I'm going to have to wait and see." I took a deep breath, reminding myself to take things slow and just breathe. It was so easy to lose my senses when it came to Liam. The last thing I wanted to do was to get my hopes up. Right now, I was just going to enjoy it day by day. No pressure, right? That's what Liam said.

"What are your plans for tonight, Kendra?"

"Shauna invited me to go to Lougini's with her, and then we're going to go to the carnival."

"Sorry, I can't go with you, but tomorrow, okay?"

"Definitely. I'm looking forward to it, and your sister, she's coming right? She's such a crack-up!"

"Yeah, she'll be there."

"I gotta run. I want to stop off at home and change. I'm caked in this mud! Have fun with Liam, tonight."

"Thanks, I will."

I looked down at myself and saw that I too was covered in mud, and I had no way to clean up before I saw Liam. There was nothing I could do. Liam's going to have to see me this way whether I want him to or not, I thought. I looked at the door and saw Kendra waving franticly my way, motioning to me that Liam was outside. That was quick, I thought to myself. I thought he would still be in the midst of his celebration with the rest of the team. I walked outside to find him sitting on the steps waiting for me. Although, I would have to wait my turn to see him. Half of the band, along with Mr. and Mrs. Hawthorne, were congratulating him on a job well done. I watched him from a distance. He looked like he was fresh from the shower. His hair still wet and in wavy curls. Not a speck of mud on him. He was wearing a gray and white flannel shirt that was only half-way buttoned up, showing a very tight and toned upper chest. I wanted desperately to get near him, but instead I held back, waiting my turn.

"Hello," I finally said after minutes of waiting. He jumped to his feet at the sound of my voice. He instantly grabbed me around the waist, ignoring the others who were congratulating him.

"Hey there."

I smiled at him. "Nice game tonight."

"Thanks. Ready to go?"

"Yeah, but are you allowed to leave? I thought you would still be on the field or talking to the coach or something."

"Nah, I had enough. I'm not really big on all that stuff. I told the coach I needed to leave, so I snuck out. Besides, Parker is the one who won the game for us, I just caught the ball." A humbling remark, I thought. "I had more important things to do tonight."

"Oh yeah, like what?" I asked innocently.

"Seeing you."

"Oh," I said.

He grabbed my stuff and took my hand in his. We walked down to his truck that was parked next to the curb. As he opened my door, I looked at myself. I was a dirty mess.

"Umm, Liam, do you have a towel or something? I really don't think I should get in your truck like this." As pieces of dried mud literally dropped from my body.

He gave me a once over looking at me from head to toe showcasing a devious grin. "You look great. I like the mud."

"You're incorrigible."

He didn't say a word, only grinned that same devious grin. He grabbed a blanket from the back of his cab and laid it on the seat for me.

"For you, my lady." He motioned his arm to the empty seat.

"Thank you." I smiled and playfully curtsied to him.

He ran around to his side of the truck and jumped in.

"So, are you hungry?" He asked, squeezing my left hand.

"No, not really, but if you are we can get something to eat."

"No, I'm not, but I know you always go to Lougini's, so if you want to go we can."

"Thanks, but really, I'm not at all hungry."

"Then do you mind if we go for a ride?"

"That would be nice."

"Great, I was hoping you would say that."

Liam squeezed my hand tighter and pulled me closer to him. I loved how it felt, but in the back of my mind, I was still questioning his intentions. It had only been a couple of days since we started seeing each other, and I had to be sure. We drove for a while before ending up on the outskirts of Spencer. He pulled off the main road and took a dirt road up a hill called Brush Creek Road. Once we reached the top, we were met by a beautiful midnight blue, star-filled sky. The dark and ominous clouds that lingered earlier were now nothing more than a distant memory. Liam found a pull-off area and parked his truck there, right where there was a flat, grassy area. The road was narrow and the pull-off looked like an area used for avoiding oncoming traffic.

"Here," he said, as he put the truck in park. "What do you think?"

"It's so pretty here."

He was looking at me. "Yeah, I might even say beautiful."

"I meant the view."

"So, did I."

He looked absolutely gorgeous, and I looked absolutely filthy with the mud.

"I am so sorry. I'm turning your truck into a complete pig sty." I turned the mirror in my direction to look at my face. My rain-soaked hair had dried into a stringy, tangly mess. "I look awful."

"On the contrary, you look nice; like I said, beautiful."

I stared at him in disbelief. How could he think I look anything but disgusting? I continued to mess with my hair, trying to get the bits of mud out of it, and comb it with my fingers the best as I could, when he pulled me to him.

"Stop," he whispered in my ear. "I don't care about the mud."

"Liam..."

He interrupted me. "I want to kiss you. Please stop talking."

He carefully moved towards me, holding me gently, taking his left hand to grab my neck while his right arm found the center of my back, making my body come towards his. His movements were so swift and smooth, that my mind barely had time to register what he was doing. He held me, kissing me softly, gently biting my lower lip. His breathing was soft but labored. I arched my head backward, making it easier for his lips to find my neck. He was being so tender, and I felt myself melting in his grasp. He moved himself closer to me. Our bodies were touching. The weight of him forced me to lay down in the seat. His lips never leaving mine, I took my hands and pulled him to me. My welcomed invitation made him kiss me harder.

"Liam," I finally said, "I need to breathe."

"I'll breathe for both of us," he said, never once stopping his lip-lock on me. I ran my hands through his hair. It was still damp, and even with his hair disheveled he looked great.

"Liam?"

"Yeah?" He stopped his sensual search of my face with his lips to look at me. I couldn't believe he wanted me. I was at a loss for words.

"Why? Why me?" I asked. "There are a hundred girls who would kill to be with you, to be in my shoes right here, right now. Why do you want me? We barely know each other."

He sat up, bringing me with him. He leaned back in his seat, both of us straightening our clothes. His face tightened, making the lines of his chiseled features more defined. He looked at me with such intensity that I backed away from him slightly.

"Do you know the first time I saw you?"

"No," I said, not sure when he actually meant.

"And I mean really saw you. I've always known who you were, but the first time I really looked at you and realized who you were was this past August. I had just gotten to school for football practice and was walking up the hill with Parker and Tony. We were headed to the field house, and as we came up the hill, there you were. You were laying on the grass above the cliff, with some other girls, twirling your baton and laughing about something; I don't know what, but it sounded beautiful coming from you. You took my breath away. I almost fell over when I saw you. It was the first time I had actually seen you. I even remember what you were wearing, a striped shirt and a pair of shorts. Isn't that insane?! I remember every detail of you... about you. God, you were... are so beautiful. The sun was shining down on you, and your hair was laid out on the grass. Your face, I can still see you. I have that memory etched in my brain forever."

I listened to him, feeling somewhat embarrassed about how he was describing me.

"I dropped my football gear and almost fell over it. Parker and Tony had to grab me. They had wondered what had come over me, but I was barely able to keep my balance. It was then that I really knew I had to find out more about you. I just knew I had to get to know you, and I knew from that moment on that somehow, someday I would. I asked everybody about you, trying to find out anything and everything I could on you. Every day I would wait in my truck to see you, watch you walking to school, or driving your car, trying to bring myself to say hi to you. I'm surprised you never noticed because I followed you everywhere. I practically stalked you just trying to get my nerve up to approach you. That's what I meant when I told you Parker is very happy about what's happened. I was driving him crazy. And football practice was just as bad. Just knowing that you were down at the other end of the field was driving me insane. Sometimes Coach Green would call my name two or three times before I even heard him. I would be in some sort of trance just watching you at the other end. I'm surprised I could even remember the plays during the games. I found myself looking for you in the stands, hoping to see you somewhere."

I couldn't believe what I was hearing, knowing that for months he was doing this, and I didn't know anything about it.

"Liam, why did you wait so long to talk to me? I mean, I see you talking to people all the time. Face it, you're definitely not hurting for friends... or wanna-be girlfriends."

"It's different with you. When I'm hanging with my friends, I'm just being me, a goofball." An adjective I wouldn't have used to describe him. "I'm one of the guys, you know. I've grown up with them. We've done everything together from playing football, hanging out at each other's house, even having our first beer together. But with you, Jenny, I can't describe it, when I see you I get nervous. My hands become sweaty. I get this funny feeling in my stomach. I know it sounds corny, but it's true. There's no other way to explain it." His hands were squeezing mine tightly, and he inched himself closer to me. "Jenny, I'm dead serious when I tell you I'm crazy about you. I've never lied about my feelings for you. You've become my refuge." His blue eyes met mine. They were soft and glistening in the light of the moon with flecks of black encircling them. "With you I can be me, not the football player, not the all-American, just me. You don't seem to care about how many touchdowns or sacks or yards I've ran, and I like that. I think even some of my friends hang around me because of who they think I am, but it's not who I am. This is who I am, right now, here, with you, in this truck, tonight, this is me. I'm just a country boy who is crazy about a red-hair girl. You're the first person who's ever made me feel like that, Jenny."

"Even Shanna?" I had to ask.

"Even Shanna."

I watched him, and I could tell this was different. I knew from tonight on things would be different between us. I still wasn't sure what was going to happen, but I knew he was going to be a part of my life. *How could I not believe him?* My heart pounded in my chest. I had gotten the answer I was desperately searching for.

The clock read 12:11am when we finally surfaced for air. The bond that we had formed had been sealed with a night of enduring and passionate necking. He was still the gentleman, never going too far but letting me know his feelings for me were real.

"Liam, I've got to be home in twenty minutes." It would not matter to Mom and Dad how great a guy or football player Liam was or even how he won the game for Spencer tonight. If I was more than one minute late, I would be in trouble, and no hero of any game would be able to save me from the wrath of breaking curfew.

"Okay," he groaned reluctantly, "I'll have you home in time, but we're not leaving yet."

"Liam, we have to." I remembered how long it took us to get here, there was no way we were going to make it back in twenty minutes. "You don't understand my parents, especially my mom. She'll be livid even if I'm the tiniest bit late. We have to go."

His head was on my lap, and I pulled him off of me to help him back in his seat so he could tell that I was serious about leaving. The windows of his truck were fogged over, obviously caused by our heavy make-out session. I rubbed them the best I could with my hand.

"Okay, babe. Let's go."

Liam leaned over once more to me and kissed me tenderly on the lips. He gave me an easy, laid-back, contented smile. I brushed his hair out of his eyes.

"We're never going to make it home if you don't stop kissing me."

"I know," he said as if his hopes were not to leave at all. Then he pulled himself back and put the truck in reverse, pulling the truck around, and gunning it down the hill over the muddy road as if there was nothing to it. I was nervous. The clock read 12:17. We were never going to make it. I was already trying to think of an excuse, but Liam must have felt my anxiety. He pulled me to him, driving with his left hand, keeping his right arm around my waist.

"I'm going to get you home on time, I promise."

I smiled at him, too nervous to speak. Then, as if time stood still, Liam was in town. We were passing the high school, the carnival, and the closed kiosks for the festival. He pulled into my driveway with a minute to spare. I couldn't believe it.

"Wow, you did it! But how?"

I didn't have time to question his brilliant driving skills. I was just thankful to be in my driveway, knowing that I had narrowly avoided a confrontation with Mom.

He just smiled and kissed me on the forehead. "I told you I would have you home on time."

"Thanks."

"Good night. And, good luck tomorrow."

"Thanks." I waved bye to him as I left his truck.

He gave me a wink and pulled out of my driveway. I stood there watching as he drove away and listening to the hum of his truck's engine as it slowly faded into the distance. The sound gave me goose bumps, just knowing that it was Liam's, and when I heard it, I would know he would be near. It was just then, from out of nowhere that I was abruptly knocked from behind by a huge white German Shepherd. It was Shasta, Ashley's dog. Ashley was home.

Chapter Seven
It's Official

"Hey sis, where've you been? I've been waiting for you for hours?"

"Ashley! I'm so glad you're here."

Shasta continued to jump on me with her eager enthusiasm, desperately trying to knock me down so she could cover me with her wet kisses.

"Down girl, I'm glad to see you too." I looked up at Ashley in astonishment, still amazed she was here. "When did you get in?"

"A couple of hours ago. I thought you would be here, but Mom and Dad told me about the game, and that you were with some guy tonight?" I smiled sheepishly at her, looking down the street where I had last seen Liam's truck.

"Yeah, I was. That was just him."

"So, sis, give me the scoop. I haven't seen you this happy since Dad took you and Kendra to your first rock concert."

"His name is Liam Larson, and he's a really good friend and maybe more."

"Maybe more? What's that supposed to mean? Are you guys dating?"

"It's complicated. I think so, but he hasn't officially asked me. But I do know he likes me, and there seems to be no one else in the picture. The past couple of days, it's just been us."

"Okay, sounds like you're dating."

"No, I'm not sure. But, I'm definitely having fun."

Ashley shrugged her shoulders, meaning she was satisfied, and I was off the hook, for now at least. I wasn't ready to dive into the past couple of weeks with her. Although, I did want to ask her about something else that had been bugging me, but now was not the time. It was late, and tomorrow was officially here. I had to get some sleep if I was going to be any good for the competition that was only hours away.

The alarm rang in my ear. Ashley and Shasta were still fast asleep, not even budging. I aimlessly tried to turn the deafening noise down only to push the volume up. Finally finding the off button, I slowly rose out of bed. The sky was dark and cloudy out my bedroom window. It looked like it was going to be another rain-soaked performance. I could hear my parents downstairs talking. The smell of coffee and dad's famous scrambled eggs with ham were wafting up the stairs. I got out of bed, grabbed my stuff, and headed for a much-needed shower.

"Hey, Jen, good luck today," Ashley said as she covered her head with her pillow.

"Thanks, sis. Looks like it's going to rain though."

Ashley leaned over to look out the window. "Yeah, I wouldn't bother much with your hair and make-up, looks like the rain will take care of that today."

I gave her a half-hearted grin and walked to the bathroom. By the time I had made it downstairs Mom, Dad, and Ashley were eating breakfast. A plate with my name on it was waiting for me too.

"Mom, I'm not really hungry, besides I have to be at the park in ten minutes, so I'm just going to go."

"You have to eat something, Jen, you won't get another chance until this afternoon."

I grabbed a banana and downed a glass of orange juice. "There, I've eaten."

Mom looked at me with defeat, knowing she wasn't going to win this one. "Okay, but take some money with you in case you have a chance to eat later."

I grabbed my batons and boots and waited for Ashley to drive me to the park. When we arrived, there were at least thirty other bands already lining up and preparing for the start of the parade. I took my place with the majorettes. Linda was droning the routine over and over again, constantly saying it out loud, "heads up, 1,2, 3, step once, step twice." And then she would start all over again. Mrs. Hawthorne was busying herself by handing out throw-away rain ponchos that she had purchased at the local dollar store. Since we were being judged on our twirling ability, we opted again not to wear them. I looked at the sky. It was still dark and threatening, and in the distance you could hear the sound of thunder rumbling. I knew it was only a matter of time before we were pummeled with more rain. I looked for Kendra, but she seemed to be nowhere in sight. The flag corps marched in the back of the band, and we were in the front. I would have to hook up with her after the parade.

Mr. Hawthorne blew his whistle. "Lineup, five minutes, guys!"

Everyone got into formation. Linda stood in front of us with the rest of us in line right behind her. I was on her right side, a very important position in the line-up. It was my duty to make sure that we stayed in a straight line and didn't move too close to Linda, or fall too far behind.

"Two minutes guys, two minutes!"

Mr. Hawthorne went down the side of the band, checking everyone's line position. Mrs. Hawthorne was now feverishly pinning our numbers on our uniform. These numbers were used to judge us during the competition. They would become every girl's identity during the festival today.

"There you go, Jenny," Mrs. Hawthorne said.

I looked down, and my mouth dropped open as I stared at the number that Mrs. Hawthorne had just pinned on me. It was number eleven. It was too surreal. Mr. Hawthorne blew his final whistle and motioned for Kirk Phillips, the drum major, to move forward. The parade had started and so had the rain. There were literally hundreds of spectators lining the sides of the parade route, some two and three rows deep. It was next to impossible to make out anybody along the route. Everyone was either covered in rain gear or hiding under an umbrella. I never saw my parents or Liam, but I did see my sister. She was front and center with her camera in hand, taking every picture she could as I marched my way down the road. She was like the postal service: not rain, sleet, or hail could stop her from getting her job done. By the time the parade ended the band had less than a half an hour before its performance at the competition. The mighty Blue and Gold always performed first, a tradition that had started with the beginning of the festival. Finally finding Kendra, we ran into the school bathroom to try and fix what we could of our rain-drenched hair and mascara-soaked eyes.

"Okay, we've only got a couple of minutes, tell me, what did you and Liam do last night?"

"Nothing, he took me for a drive, and we ended up parking at the top of Brush Creek Road and just talked."

"Just talked? You can do better than that."

I looked at her, and she knew me too well. "Okay, well we did make out... a little... well... a lot."

"I figured that much from the Ferris wheel. I want to know the dirt. What happened?"

We didn't have enough time for me to go into explicit details.

"Look, things seem to be moving a little faster than I thought. He likes me, really likes me, and I think I like him too." Mr. Hawthorne's whistle was blowing. We both knew there was no time to continue. "Listen, I'll tell you tonight when we go out with my sister, okay?"

"Fine."

Kendra and I rushed with our hair and make-up and darted out the bathroom door. The band and majorette competition went on for hours. Over thirty bands and twenty-five majorette corps were competing for titles. At the end of the day the Blue and Gold walked away with four trophies: one going for the drum solo performance by Marty and Mike Skinner; one for best marching band; and two for the majorettes. Linda ended up with a runner-up to Miss Majorette, and I was awarded an honorable mention.

All in all, a job well done for being a very messy day. Because of the weather the competition had been delayed three times due to the thunder and lightning. By the time the last trophy was awarded it was past nine o'clock. As the fans left the stadium, I looked everywhere to see if Liam was in sight, but I couldn't find him anywhere. I felt a little disappointed. He hadn't said one way or the other if he would be here, but I thought in my heart that he would. No matter, we hadn't made plans to see each other. I definitely wasn't going to turn into one of those girls who had to know where their guy was all the time. Besides, rain or no rain, Ashley, Kendra, and I were still going to have a great time together at the carnival.

"Hey, Kendra, do you mind if we don't talk about Liam tonight? I just want to have a good time with you and Ashley, and I don't want to go into all the details regarding what's going on between us right now. Ashley doesn't even know a tenth of what's happened, and I'd rather not have to explain it tonight."

"Sure, no problem."

"Thanks, anyway she already saw Liam bring me home last night. I know she's just waiting to corner me so she can bombard me with questions."

"I completely understand Jenny. Are you ready? We should go if we ever want to make it to the carnival."

"Sure, let's go."

I grabbed my batons and gear, and we headed downtown to meet up with Ashley. People were jam-packed in the streets and cars were bumper to bumper on the roads. The music that was being piped through the speakers was filling the air. Kendra and I found Ashley along with Mom and Dad at the entrance to the carnival.

"Hi girls," Mom said as she hugged us both. "You did a great job, both of you and congratulations Jen on the honorable mention. We're so proud of you."

"Thanks, Mom."

She grabbed my number eleven that was still pinned to my skirt. "I'm going to take this home along with your other stuff."

"Okay, we'll be home later."

"Great job, sweetheart." Dad gave me a bear hug, almost lifting me off my feet. "You should've won. You were the best one out there." And not to make Kendra feel left out he added, "you did an awesome job too, Kendra, you both should be so proud of yourselves."

"Thank you, Mr. King," Kendra said

"Okay girls, see you at home. Ashley, no later than twelve-thirty for them."

"We better get a move on if we're going to ride anything, it's already ten o'clock," Ashley said as she looked at her watch.

The line for tickets was wound like a snake between the rides. We took our place at the back of it and waited. It was actually nice not to be moving. The whole day had been about getting from one place to the next, and I enjoyed the temporary moment of being stationery. I was a people watcher, and we were all having fun looking at what everyone was wearing and who people were with.

"Have you seen Liam today?" Kendra asked.

"No, I thought maybe I saw him during the parade route, but I couldn't tell."

I found myself looking for him around every corner. Any time I saw a boy with dirty-blonde hair that was shoulder length my heart would jump into my throat. But to my dismay, he wasn't there. I had gotten used to seeing him, and I didn't like not seen him all day. The line finally moved, and Ashley was next. She handed the ticket lady her money, and she handed Ashley a sleeve of tickets.

"Okay, what do you want to ride?"

We all knew that was a rhetorical question. It was a tradition for the three of us to always ride the Scrambler first. This was a ride that went in a fast and furious crazy star pattern, back and forth, forcing the person sitting on the outside to be squeezed to death by the other people sitting next to them. Ashley was always the outside person, with me in the middle and Kendra on my side. We found the ride and took our place in line again.

"This is going to be so much fun," Ashley said. "You guys didn't eat anything did you?"

"No! You think we're stupid?"

The last thing we wanted to do was to ruin the night by throwing up on the very first ride we rode. It was our turn, and we handed the boy our tickets. Kendra went first, then Ashley, and I followed closely behind. We were led to an empty car. The seats were damp and muddy from the weather, but it didn't matter to us. This made the experience even more fun. We sat down, taking our seats in the proper order. The boy clicked our door shut and jiggled it to make sure it remained locked.

"Okay, this is it. Prepare to fly, girls!" Kendra said as all three of us clenched our handles so tight that our knuckles turned bone white.

The ride started with Poison's "Talk Dirty To Me." It began slow but gained momentum with each turn. The three of us couldn't help but scream as the ride accelerated in speed. We were whipped around at an unbelievable pace. Faster and faster the ride went, our screams drowned out by the sheer sound of the ride. Kendra was pushing against me, easily allowing enough room for a fourth person to sit down. I was pushed against Ashley, and Ashley was pushed into the side of the car. We could hardly breathe but found enough strength to scream and laugh as hard as we could. Our hair was being whipped into our faces, the breeze from the ride felt good, and the slight rain that was still falling felt invigorating as it hit our skin. It was fantastic, and then, as quickly as it had started, the ride began to slow down until it came to a complete stop, leaving all three of us breathless. The g-force that had pushed us into each other had let up, and we were finally able to compose ourselves and position ourselves back into our seat without squeezing the life out of each other.

"That was awesome, let's do it again!" Ashley said as we exited the ride.

My equilibrium was off. Although I wasn't sick, the ground was moving. "No, sis, I need to sit down for a minute. I'm still spinning, and I know I'm not still on the ride."

"Kendra, you and me?" Ashley asked.

"Okay. Jen, we'll be back."

"Fine, I'll just keep the ground from moving while you're gone."

I found a bench near the ride and took a seat, still feeling nauseated but laughing at how much fun we had just had. I leaned my head back and closed my eyes. My stomach was feeling more nauseous by the second, and it didn't help to smell the aroma of sausage and onion sandwiches in the air. I kept my eyes closed with my hands over them. "Just breathe, Jen, just breathe," I kept telling myself. I felt a slight breeze pass by me and then the feeling that someone had sat down next to me. I didn't have the strength to look at them so I graciously moved over to allow them ample room to sit. To my surprise, every time I scooted so did they. I was already at the edge of the bench. Any more moving and I would be on the ground, which in my mind was still moving. I felt like I was being watched. *How rude. Couldn't this person give me the dignity of getting sick without an audience?*

Then, he spoke. "Hey, babe. Having fun?" I knew that voice. My hands fell to my side as my eyes focused on Liam. "Hi there beautiful," he said, looking amazing as usual. His hair was down, and one side was pulled behind his ear. He had a white t-shirt on with a pair of body hugging jeans with the right knee worn out.

"I didn't think I was going to see you today."

"I know. I'm sorry I couldn't make it to the parade. Grandpa and I had a lot of work that needed to get done on the farm. We just finished about an hour ago. How did you do today?"

I looked down. "Okay, I guess. I didn't win Miss Majorette if that's what you're asking, but I did get an honorable mention."

"That's still really good, but you should've won."

"Yeah, you and Dad seem to think alike, but it's okay. I'm not upset. It was fun, even in the rain. And guess what my judging number was today?"

"What?"

"Eleven! Can you believe it, same as yours."

"Must be kismet," Liam said with a wink.

I smiled. "Yeah, definitely." Thinking that we definitely could be each other's destiny.

He leaned in to kiss me. It felt good to see him. He had made me completely forget that I was sick to my stomach. I couldn't believe how much I had missed him. Just as our lips were to touch, we were interrupted by an "Ahem," from Ashley and Kendra.

"Hey sis, Hi, Kendra."

Kendra spoke first. "Hey there, Hi Liam."

"Hi, Kendra," Liam said in return.

Ashley was staring at Liam, waiting for her introduction.

"Ashley, this is Liam; Liam this is my sister."

Liam stood up. His six foot plus frame towered over my sister.

"Hi, nice to meet you."

"Hi, Liam, nice to meet you too. So you okay, Jen?" Ashley asked with concern.

"Yeah, much better. Only the sky is moving now." I was trying to be funny, when in reality I was telling the truth.

"Why, what's wrong?" Liam asked.

"Nothing, I just got a little dizzy from riding the Scrambler, that's all."

Kendra was now sitting with her head between her legs next to me. "Are you okay?" I asked.

"No, I think I'm going to be sick. I think once was enough for that ride." She was holding her hand over her mouth, and her stomach was heaving up and down.

"She's going to throw up!" Ashley exclaimed.

"Come on, let's go get you something to drink," I said

"Nah, it's not going to stay down. I need to get out of here." We found a port-o-potty, but it was too gross to use.

"Hey, we're real close to my house. Let's take you there, and you can lie down," I said.

"Sounds like a good idea," Ashley chimed in.

I looked at Liam. "Sorry, I gotta go."

"I understand. Can I see you tomorrow?" He grabbed my hands.

"Yes, definitely. Call me okay?"

He leaned in to kiss me. This time not allowing for any interruptions or distractions. His mouth was sweet, and the kiss lingered. I was glad he was holding my hands because between the dizziness from the ride and the way he made me feel, I was in no shape to stand on my own two feet.

"Tomorrow," he whispered.

He slowly let go of my hands, and gave me his wink. Parker Duncan was waiting by the Ferris wheel.

"Nice to meet you," he said to Ashley as he and Parker walked away.

"He's cute, sis. I can see why you didn't wait at home for me last night."

"Yeah, he's okay."

"Okay? He's definitely more than okay," Ashley exclaimed.

I felt myself staring at Liam, his butt still in plain sight.

"Can we go? I'm really not feeling well," Kendra said pitifully.

"Sorry, let's go."

Kendra ended up puking three times when she got to our house. Mom made her drink some ginger ale and laid a wet washcloth on her forehead. Her color was slowly returning to normal by the time her mom came to pick her up.

"Sorry guys. I turned into such a party pooper."

"Don't worry about it. We still had fun, and you're not a party pooper. Remember, I got sick first."

"Well, at least you didn't throw up."

I laughed. "Yeah, but you did enough for all three of us."

"Ha ha. Very funny. See you guys later. Bye, Mrs. King; thanks for your help."

"Anytime, Kendra. You get some sleep."

"Wow, what a day," I said after Kendra closed the door behind her.

"You said it, sis," Ashley said as she sat next to me in the living room.

"You girls stay up as long as you want. We're going to bed. Good night."

"Good night," I said, walking into the kitchen.

"You hungry?" Ashley asked as she followed me.

I actually was. We found some fried chicken and homemade potato salad in the fridge. Ashley and I watched the town slowly close down from our bedroom window. The music had faded away, and the lights from the carnival had been dimmed. It was reminiscent of a ghost town, with nothing but the debris left behind from the hundreds of spectators hours earlier. Ashley and I enjoyed each other's company, laughing and talking about the day's events and how Kendra had ended our night. We became quiet, and I knew what was coming.

"So, you gonna tell me about Liam or not?" I smiled, still playing with the food on my plate.

"Ashley, I can't explain it. He literally just entered my life a week ago. I mean I didn't even really know who he was until this week, and now it's amazing. I definitely think I have fallen for him. And he definitely seems to have fallen for me. In fact, he's the one who approached me first, and apparently he's had a thing for me for a while."

"You didn't know?" Ashley asked.

"No, I mean most people associate Liam with football. He's an awesome player, and honestly Ashley, he's always been linked with Shanna Smith. But this week he just started talking to me. I didn't think much about it but, to be frank, I thought he was being a jerk. He became relentless, and he was always coming up to me. Then one day in study hall he found me and…"

"And what?"

"He told me he how he felt about me. He said he was crazy about me and had been for a while. I didn't know what to think. I was in shock, I think I still am. I thought him and Shanna were still an item. If you ask her, they are, but he told me they've been through for a long time. I still don't know what to think, but he's so convincing when he's around me, and he treats me like I'm the only girl alive. We've spent some time together and I think he's telling me the truth."

"And how do you feel about him?"

"Well, in the beginning, I thought he was playing me, but sis, when I'm with him he's so sincere. He's definitely winning me over. I do like him. And God, is he cute!" We both started laughing.

"Jen, he seems nice enough, just be sure, okay?"

"Don't worry, I will. But you know it's weird…"

"What, what's weird?" She asked.

"I don't know. I think I'm thinking too much about it, but it just seems that ever since Liam has been in my life I have seen the number eleven."

"The number eleven? What are you talking about?"

"Well, for one thing, that's Liam's football number, and then it's other stuff too. Like when I look at the clock, it's 12:11 or 8:11; and when I'm with him, I'll see the number eleven; or I'll go to buy something, and my change will be eleven cents. And today, my number for the majorette competition was eleven. I know it sounds silly, and there's probably nothing to it, but it's just weird how it's popping up so much, and I never noticed it before."

"I wouldn't put too much thought into it. You're probably just more aware of it because that number is associated with Liam, and now you're just noticing it more than you used to."

"You're probably right." I leaned back on my bed with my eyes focused on my clock, "but look, Ashley!" I motioned to the clock on my nightstand.

"Oh My God!" The clock read 2:11am

"See, I told you."

"Pure coincidence, sis. Let's just go to bed."

Easy for her to say, I thought, and then I drifted off into a much needed deep sleep. Sunday morning, I awoke to the sound of Shasta scratching at my door. I looked over, but Ashley was already gone. I got up and opened the door for Shasta. She was a gentle giant. Her looks were intimidating, but her soul was as sweet as can be. She was a protector and just wanted to love you. She especially loved my sister and hardly ever left her side. I'm sure that's why Shasta was so insistent on getting out of my bedroom. Ashley was already downstairs. I could hear people talking. The smell of coffee was in the air. Mom and Ashley were laughing as they worked in the kitchen. I could also hear Dad talking, but he wasn't in the same conversation as Mom and Ashley's. I didn't recognize the fourth voice, but I figured it must be one of Dad's employees or one of the tenants. It was not uncommon for someone to be at our doorstep looking for my dad. I figured I had better get my shower. *Who knew who was downstairs.* I took my time, and the hot water felt good on my body, especially after yesterday's cold, damp day. Instead of drying my hair, I towel-dried it and put some conditioner in it. It needed a rest from the constant blow drying I had been giving it lately. I pulled on my favorite blue cami and yoga pants and sprinted downstairs. Mom and Ashley were at the kitchen bar drinking coffee and nibbling on some cinnamon buns.

"Mmm... those smell and look great," I said as I entered the kitchen.

"Good morning, sleepy head, did you finally decide to wake up?" I hugged Mom and glanced at the oven clock, it was after one o'clock in the afternoon.

"Oh my God, I can't believe I slept in so late. Why didn't you guys wake me up?"

"You were sleeping so soundly, hon, I didn't have the heart to disturb you. You've had a couple of busy days. Your body needed the rest. Plus, I tried to wake you, and so did Ashley, but you wouldn't budge."

"Yeah, Shasta, even climbed on you at one point, and all you did was pull the covers over your head."

I groaned and scratching my head as I eyed the cinnamon buns.

"Would you like one?" Ashley asked with a smirk.

"What's that look for?" I asked, as I grabbed a bun and sat down.

"Oh nothing, just thought you might want one of these cinnamon buns."

I looked at her wondering what she was getting at. "You're acting very weird. I think the Scrambler messed with your head last night."

I could hear Dad talking to his friend, and it sounded like they were outside on the porch swing. The swing quietly squeaking as it moved back and forth.

"Mom, these are great. Did you make them?" I asked devouring the bun.

"No, Jen."

"Well, if you didn't make them, where did they come from? I don't remember seeing them here yesterday?"

"He brought them."

Mom and Ashley were both looking at the front door. I turned around to face the direction of their stares. Dad was walking in, and right behind him was Liam. I quickly turned around in my chair. Mom and Ashley both were quietly smirking at me.

"Why didn't you tell me Liam was here?"

I was furious. I looked a mess, and now I was trapped with no place to hide. I quickly ran my fingers through my hair, trying desperately to make myself look presentable. I was giving my sister the evil eye. I thought for sure, she, out of everybody, would have come upstairs to let me know Liam was here. Instead, she just smiled at me.

"Hi, honey, you finally woke up," Dad said.

"Hi, Dad." I leaned in and gave him a kiss on the cheek.

"Look who's here." Dad motioned, as Liam came into view.

"Hi, Jenny."

"Hi, Liam."

I didn't know if I should get up and acknowledge him the way I wanted to, or if I should just stay in my chair. I opted for the latter.

"What are you doing here?"

"Why? Aren't you glad to see me?"

"Yes, of course, I am. I'm just surprised to see you in my house, that's all. I thought you were going to call me first."

"I did; three times. You've been asleep. So, I finally decided just to come over and see you. So here I am, cinnamon buns in hand."

I still had part of a bun in my hand. I dropped it immediately.

"Liam, these are delicious," Mom interjected.

"Thanks, Mrs. King. It's a family recipe that my Grandpa has mastered."

I looked at him, motioning with my eyes to move outside so I could talk to him alone. He smiled at me and politely excused himself.

"If you don't mind, Mom, we're going outside for a while."

"Sure, honey, but grab your jacket. It's cooled down considerably."

I grabbed a sweatshirt from the hall tree and pulled it over my head as we headed to the porch. I turned to give my sister a scowl, letting her know I would deal with her later. She just gave me that same sweet smirk and went about her business. Once outside and out of view of my parents, Liam grabbed me around my waist. Before I could speak, he kissed me with such intensity that I felt my body arching backward.

"I've been wanting to do that since you had to leave me last night."

"Liam, you've got to be careful. I'm sure Mom and Dad are watching."

"You don't think they approve of me?"

"No, it's not that. I don't think they would approve of your intentions right now."

He smiled that thousand-watt smile that I loved so much. His eyes were a deep, contented blue today. We sat down on the swing, being careful not to make it squeak too loudly.

"I still can't believe you're here."

"I couldn't wait any longer. I missed you."

I smiled at him. "I missed you too. What were you talking to my dad about?"

"Oh nothing, just you, and how crazy I am about you, and how when I'm with you I just want to attack you. Just your normal conversation you have with your girlfriend's dad."

I leaned back to look him in the eye, ignoring the statement about attacking me, and startled at the last part.

"What?"

"You called me your girlfriend?"

He pulled me close to him. "Well, aren't you? I mean that's how I feel about you, and that's how I think of you. Is that okay? I mean, you do want this don't you? I know I do."

His lips were close to mine. His breath was hot against the cold air. I didn't say a word. He pulled away from me.

"Jenny, do you feel differently?"

I could tell he was worried when I didn't give him an immediate answer, but I did want it; I just couldn't speak. I was so overcome by hearing those words that I was still absorbing them. I lowered my head.

"Jenny, what's wrong? Did I say something to upset you?"

I looked up at him, tears feeling my eyes. Trying to hold back what I knew was inevitable, I just shook my head no.

Finally, I said, "I'm just happy."

"You had me worried," he laughed.

"I'm sorry. It's just that I didn't know what to think. I thought we had something, but I didn't know for sure."

"Jenny, I told you I'm crazy about you. I mean that. I've always meant that. Everything that's happened between us this past week was real. Nothing has changed for me."

I turned my body to face his, wrapping my legs around his waist. I kissed him softly while he held me in his grasp. We must have gotten lost in the moment. The next thing I felt was a pair of eyes on us. It was Ashley.

"Hey, you guys sorry to interrupt, but, Jenny, I've got to go home soon."

"What? You just got here. I thought you were staying until tomorrow?"

"I wish I could, but my boss called. I have a sales meeting at eight tomorrow morning, and I'm not the least bit ready for it."

I frowned. She only made it home a few times a year, and I wasn't ready for her to go back. I was also torn. I looked at Liam. I wanted to be with him too, but I wanted to spend time with my sister as well. Thankfully, Liam understood, and it was his idea to leave.

"Hey, I'll talk to you later, and I'll definitely see you tomorrow at school. Spend the rest of the day with your sister." He kissed me on the forehead.

"Thanks, Liam."

He got in his truck and sped off. The rest of the day Ashley and I just hung out. We took a long drive in the country and talked about everything from Liam to Ashley's life in Ohio. The day flew by, and by that evening Ashley had gone back to her home. I went upstairs and watched the midnight sky from my window, another starry-filled night. The weekend had turned out to be perfect, and today had been the icing on the cake. I couldn't wait for tomorrow.

Chapter Eight
Homecoming

Monday morning came with a vengeance. I awoke to a horrible, pounding headache, and my eyelids felt like they weighed a ton. Every muscle in my body ached with agony.

"Mom!" I weakly yelled.

"Jenny, what's wrong?"

"I don't feel so good."

"Oh, Jenny, you don't look so good." She pressed her hand to my forehead.

"You feel hot. You're staying home today."

"Mom, I can't. I'll be fine. Let me get a shower and something to eat, and I'm sure I'll feel better."

I tried to get out of bed, but as soon as I moved, my whole body ached, forcing me to lay down again. Besides the aches, I was shivering. Mom placed two extra blankets on my bed, and I still couldn't get warm.

"You just stay in bed. I'm going to call the doctor."

I didn't fight it. I knew I was sick. There was no way I was going to make it into school today. I was sure Liam would be waiting for me in the parking lot. He would soon find out that I wasn't going to be there. I lay in bed, listless, half awake and half dead. I felt miserable. I was almost in a comatose state when Mom walked back into my room.

"Well, sounds like you have the flu. Dr. Garrett said to stay in bed and drink lots of fluids. It's got to run its course which could take a few days."

"A few days? Mom, I can't miss that much school."

"You're going to miss a lot more if you don't do as I say. You're run down, and your body has finally given in. School will still be there and so will Liam."

She was good. She knew exactly what I had meant. I gave in and spent most of the day asleep. It was almost 6 o'clock when I awoke to the house phone ringing. I could hear Mom at the bottom of the steps talking to Liam. I tried to get up, but every time I did, I felt nauseous and yelling would be useless. My throat was also on fire. The loudest I could speak was barely above a whisper. I would have to wait for Mom to come to me. Minutes later she walked up the steps carrying a tray.

"Here, I made you some soup." I just looked at it. The smell made me want to vomit.

"No," I whispered. "My throat hurts, and my stomach is still upset. I don't want anything." I pushed the tray away and rolled over. "Who was on the phone?" Already knowing the answer.

"Liam. He's called all afternoon. He's worried sick about you."

"What did you tell him?"

"Just that you had the flu and you wouldn't be in school tomorrow either."

"Mom, you don't know that. I'm kind of feeling better already," I lied pitifully.

"Jenny, you're sick. Don't worry; he understands. Now listen, I told him I would be in touch, and if you're feeling up to it later I'll let you talk to him. I promise. Kendra and Shauna called too. Kendra said she would talk to you later and if you needed her to get your homework to let her know before school tomorrow."

"Okay, thanks."

I slumped in bed. I couldn't believe my luck. Just yesterday everything was great, more than great; things were perfect. Today, I'm stuck in bed with the flu. I looked out my window. The town was slowly returning to normal. All the gold and brown banners that had decorated the buildings were down. The street crews were busy sweeping all the debris and trash left behind from the spectators. It was a gloomy sight, perfect for how I felt. I decided to fall back to sleep. *A little nap might help me feel better, and I would be in better spirits when Liam finally calls.*

I could feel the warmth of the sun on my face as I opened my eyes. It looked like a beautiful day. My clock read eleven o'clock, but that couldn't be right. It was just six o'clock not too long ago, and if it was eleven o'clock it should be dark out, not light.

I sat up in bed and took a drink of water. The pain in my throat was almost gone.

"Good morning, how are you feeling today?" Mom said as she entered my room.

"Good morning? What you do you mean good morning? What day is it?"

"It's Tuesday, hon."

"Tuesday! You mean I slept through the night?"

"Honey, you've been sick."

"What about Liam? I was supposed to talk to him last night. Did he call?"

"Yes, four times. That boy doesn't give up does he? He's been so worried. At one point, he insisted on stopping by, and I had to convince him not to."

"What did you tell him?"

"I just told him that you were sleeping."

"What did he say?"

"Honey, relax, he understood. He said he would call you this afternoon after football practice." I calmed down but still wished I hadn't slept through the night missing his call. In the background, the doorbell rang.

"I'll be right back."

"Mona?" Dad yelled.

"Coming Henry, hold on."

A few minutes later, Mom was back in my room holding a bouquet of pink and yellow roses.

"Jenny, these just came for you."

"Wow, they're gorgeous. Who are they from?"

"Who do you think?"

She placed the flowers on my bed as I opened the card. "I'm sure you look just as beautiful as ever, even with a fever. Please get better soon, I miss you more than I can say. Love, Liam." I smiled, holding the card near my chest.

"Here, let me put these in a vase. Did he have something nice to say, honey?"

"Um-hmm." I laid back in bed, hugging the card close to me. Before leaving, Mom put her hand on my forehead.

"Ahh, nice, fever's gone."

"Can I go to school tomorrow?"

"We'll see. Let's get through tonight first."

Liam called precisely at 5:33pm, I saw the digits on the clock.

"Hello," I said hoarsely.

"Hey, babe, how are you?"

"I'm doing much better. Thanks so much for the flowers. I love them. They're so beautiful."

"You're welcome, but they can't be half as beautiful as you are."

"You are such a smooth talker."

"No, just honest."

"Are you going to be able to come to school tomorrow?"

"I think so. Mom said she would make up her mind in the morning. As long as I don't have a fever, I think I can."

"I hope so. It's been a hell of a week without you here. I need to talk to you about something anyway."

"What is it, Liam?"

"Oh, nothing that can't wait until tomorrow."

"Should I be worried?"

"No, not at all. I shouldn't have even said anything. Just get better, and I'll see you at school."

"Okay."

"Jenny?"

"Yeah, Liam?"

"Sweet dreams tonight."

"Thanks, you too."

By Wednesday morning, I felt as good as new. My fever was completely gone, and I was able to hold down dinner from Tuesday night and breakfast from that morning. Mom okayed me to return to school, so Dad decided he should drive me. He pulled up to the back entrance next to the band room.

"Have a good day, honey, and call us if you start feeling sick."

"Okay, Dad, I will."

I grabbed my books and headed up the hill. I looked for Liam's truck in the school parking lot. I didn't see it. No matter, he might not even be here yet. Before I could round the corner, I saw her, my arch nemesis, Shanna Smith. I tried to avoid her, but it was too late. She was headed straight in my direction.

"Hello there, Jenny."

"Hello, Shanna."

"Well, looks like you've got the prize goose."

"What do you mean, Shanna?"

"Liam, silly girl."

"Look, Shanna, I'm not going to get into this with you again. This is none of your business."

"I guess not, but don't get too attached to him. He does this from time to time when he needs a break. I've learned to accept it. He always comes back to me."

"Does what, Shanna?"

"You, Jenny, spending time with you. Don't get your hopes up that this is serious between you two. It's how Liam plays. You'll learn. It's just sad that you fell for his trap. You're such a sweet girl. It's a shame you're gonna get your heart broken."

"Shanna, you're such a pathetic loser and liar. Why don't you just go crawl under the rock where you came from! I'm done with you. Don't ever come near me again!"

I was furious. The first thing I had to see after being gone all week was her. Not exactly the way I wanted to start my first day back to school. I stormed off leaving Shanna standing in her spot.

"Hey, wait up." I turned around to find Kendra running towards me. "Welcome back, girl."

"Hey, Kendra, thanks. How are you feeling? The last time I saw you, you were a little green under the gills too."

"I'm fine. I'm sure it was just the ride. You're looking good."

"Thanks, I'm feeling much better. Although, if you would have asked me that a minute ago, I might have answered differently."

"What do you mean?"

"I just ran into Shanna."

"Really? What happened?"

"You wouldn't believe the nerve that girl has. She's still trying to tell me that Liam and her are an item and that I'm just setting myself up for heartbreak."

"You're kidding?"

"I wish I was."

"Did you tell Liam?"

"No. It just happened, and I haven't seen him yet."

"Well, I gotta go. I just wanted to say welcome back. I need to study for a Spanish quiz. Don't worry, since you've been absent, I'm sure you won't have to take it today. I'll try to tell you what's on it if I can."

"Thanks, see ya."

"Oh, by the way, Jenny, what's going on with homecoming? Are you and Liam going together?"

"Oh my God, Kendra, homecoming completely slipped my mind. I don't know, we haven't even discussed it."

"Well, don't worry about me, I've got a date."

"You do… who… when… how?"

She was laughing. "Stop, Jenny, actually it's one of Liam's friends, Tony Williams."

"What? I don't believe it. That's great, but when? I didn't even know you guys knew each other?"

"It all happened this week while you were out. I can't go into details, but Liam had something to do with it. I gotta go. I'll tell you all about it later."

I was speechless and very happy for her.

By the time fourth period arrived, I had become very anxious. I still hadn't seen Liam yet, not even in the hallways. I was hoping he would be in study hall instead of skipping it like he usually did. Mr. Buford was in rare form that morning, blowing his whistle a full minute before study hall was to begin. I found my usual seat and still there was no sign of Liam. *Oh well, I guess I'll see him when I see him.* I pulled *Moby Dick* out of my book bag. I hadn't read any of it since last week when Liam confessed his feelings to me. I only had a week left before this report was due, so maybe it was a good thing I had no distractions. Just as I had gotten comfortably situated in my seat, I felt his hand around my neck.

"Hey, babe, welcome back." He was holding a single red rose in his hand. "For you, beautiful."

"Ah, Liam thank you. You shouldn't have. You already got me flowers."

"Yeah, but those were for when you were sick. This is because I missed you and you're back." I leaned over and gave him a quick kiss.

"You want to get out of here?"

"Sure, in about fifty minutes when class is over." Liam was staring, and I could tell he meant right now. "You mean now? You can't be serious? We can't leave. Mr. Buford will see us."

"Don't worry, I've already worked it out. Parker is going to distract him so we can slip through the door, he'll never know we're gone."

"No way, Liam, we'll get caught."

"Trust me, Jenny."

I looked around. Most of the kids were too absorbed in their own little world to notice what Liam and I were doing. I saw Parker at the other end of the auditorium, and I could tell he was waiting for Liam's signal.

"Are you sure about this?"

"Trust me, babe."

I put away *Moby Dick* and waited for Liam's cue. "This is crazy."

"Yeah, but it'll be worth it, I promise."

I saw Liam lean back in his seat and make a hand signal to Parker and at that very instant Parker got up and started coughing horribly, as if he was choking. Mr. Buford jumped into action, running to Parker's side to assist him. Parker motioned with his hand to go on. All eyes were on Parker, perfect for us to make our escape. Liam grabbed my hand and in an instant we had gone through the exit door. We were laughing hysterically.

"I can't believe you, Liam. You're insane!"

He pulled me to him, "Yeah, for you. Now come on." He took my hand in his, and we ran down the hill to his truck that was parked by the curb. He pulled me to his side of the truck, opened the door and helped me up, never once letting me out of his reach. I scooted over to make room for him only to have Liam scoot me back to his side.

"What are we doing? We can't leave, I just got back."

"Don't worry, all you're missing is study hall and lunch. We'll both be back for Mrs. White's wonderful English class." He started his truck. "Oh, I forgot to do something."

"What?"

"This." He closed in on me, took me in his arms and kissed me, holding me with a vice grip. "I missed you."

"You certainly have a nice way of showing it."

"Just wait Jen. It's only the beginning." He put his truck into drive and pulled away.

"So, where are you taking me that couldn't wait until school was out?"

"You'll see. Just enjoy the drive."

His right hand was tightly secured around my left leg, and I couldn't move if I wanted to. We drove out of town for about ten minutes when Liam pulled off onto a dirt road. It reminded me of the muddy road at Brush Creek Road, but this road was much narrower with trees and brush obscuring part of its drive.

"Where are we, Liam?"

"Just wait. You'll see. We're almost there."

The road snaked around for a couple of miles, it seemed he was taking me to the middle of nowhere. At one point, Liam had to drive through a creek bed that was swollen from the weekend's rain. His big truck handled it fine. Then in the near distance, I could see a clearing. Liam drove through it, and there before me stood a beautiful, turn of the century, two-story home with a wraparound porch. You could tell the house was in need of some repair. The white paint was visibly worn and chipped. The steps leading up to the porch were crooked, and it looked like the first one might even be broken, but the house itself was beautiful and full of character.

"Here we are," Liam said as he stopped the truck.

"This is beautiful, Liam. Is this your home?"

"Yeah, well, mine and my grandpa's."

"I love it."

Liam opened his door and grabbed my hand instantly. Instead of allowing me to get out on my own, he gently pulled me out of the truck on his side, tenderly picking me up to place me on the ground.

"What do you think?"

"I think it's great."

The house stood on top of a clearing with two big oak trees bordering it. On the far right side of the house on top of a hill stood a huge, old barn. It too looked like it was about the same age as the house and in need of repair. There was an old tractor parked next to the barn and behind the barn you could see a clearing where three horses were grazing in a field. He took me inside.

"Grandpa, it's Liam, are you home?"

"Is he expecting us?"

"In a way. I told him I was bringing someone very special to the house today. I just didn't tell him when." Liam gave me his famous wink.

"Where is he?"

"He could be anywhere. It's almost eleven-thirty. He's probably out in the field somewhere with Blue, our dog. Here, sit down. I'll be right back."

Liam led me to an oversized stuffed couch that had a yellow and blue rose pattern on it in what looked like to be the living room. The room was spacious with high walls and a cathedral ceiling. Besides the couch, the only other furniture in the room was a coffee table and two Victorian chairs with the same rose pattern on their seats. The windows were ceiling to floor with white shears covering them. On the mantle above the fireplace were three pictures. One was of Liam in his football uniform standing next to his grandpa. Another was a picture of a couple on their wedding day, and the third was a beautiful picture of a young woman with long, dirty blonde hair and striking blue eyes. This must be his mother, I thought to myself. Her eyes were exactly like Liam's. The home looked cozy, but I could tell it had lacked a female touch for quite a while. I walked over to look at the picture of whom I thought was Liam's mom. She was very beautiful, with striking features. I wondered what had happened to her, when Liam walked in.

"Are you ready?"

"Ready? Ready for what?" I asked. He was smiling, a mischievous smile; he was definitely up to something.

"Here," he held out his hand for me to place mine in his. "Follow me, but you have to keep your eyes closed."

I covered my eyes with my left hand while Liam held my right. "Liam, what are you doing? Ouch!" I had stubbed my toe on the corner of something.

"Are you okay? Sorry 'bout that," he said giggling.

"Yeah, I'm fine."

He walked slowly. I could tell we were going into another room, and then he took me with both his hands and gently seated me in a chair. "Okay, no peeking, and keep your eyes closed."

"Okay, but the suspense is killing me, hurry up." I could tell he had sat down next to me. His hand was on my knee.

"Okay, babe, open your eyes."

I opened them to see that we were sitting down at a beautiful mahogany table in the dining room. I gasped. "Liam, what have you done?" The table was covered with an antique white lace tablecloth and covering it were literally hundreds of red rose petals. In the center of the table was a huge teddy bear holding a single red rose in its paws. There was cheese and fruit on the table too with a bottle of sparkling grape juice being chilled in a cooler.

"Do you like it?"

"Like it? I love it. You did this for me?"

Liam clutched my hands in his, "Yeah, Jen, just for you."

I looked at him. My eyes were filling with tears. "I don't know what to say, Liam."

"Don't say anything, Jen."

I wrapped my arms around his neck pulling his ponytail out, so his hair could fall on my face. I kissed him emphatically, "Thank you." I repeated in between kisses. "Why? Why would you do this?"

"I missed you this week. I hated it that you didn't feel well and I couldn't be there to see you. This was my way of showing you how much I care and how much you mean to me."

My feelings for Liam were deeper than they had ever been. If there was ever a doubt about how I felt for him before, this moment had washed them away. I knew I was just as crazy for him as he was for me. Nothing mattered anymore but Liam. I knew that more than ever at that exact moment.

"Liam, you've made me so happy."

"That's all I've ever wanted."

I got up out of my chair and sat on his lap, facing him with my legs wrapping around the back of the chair.

"I'm crazy about you, Liam, definitely crazy."

"Jen…"

But I didn't let him finish. I took his lips to mine, kissing him with all the same emotion that he had for me. He leaned me against the lace covered table, moving the trays of food and the teddy bear out of the way. He was on top of me, pushing his weight against my body. His lips were securely on mine, and his hands found their way around me.

"Jenny, I..." but before another word was spoken we both heard the front door open.

"Liam?" A rough voice yelled out. "Liam are you home?"

"It's my grandpa."

We both stood up quickly, composing ourselves as best we could. I quickly straighten the tablecloth and repositioned the food and teddy bear back on the table.

"Grandpa, we're in here," Liam answered back.

I heard his grandpa's footsteps drawing nearer and nearer. They were heavy and slow. His one step made a louder thud than the other one as it hit the floor, possibly from a limp. He rounded the corner. He was tall like Liam, with the same brilliant blue eyes. His face was permanently tanned with a chiseled look to it. There was a scar that ran from the corner of his left eye down to his left ear with another scar following the same pattern on the left side of his neck. He wore an old cowboy hat that looked to be the same age as he was. He was a handsome man, and I could see where Liam got some of his features.

"Hi, Grandpa."

"Hello, Liam, I thought you were home." His grandpa looked right at me.

"Umm, Grandpa, this is Jenny, the girl I was telling you about."

He took his cowboy hat off and nodded politely. "Hello, Jenny, nice to finally meet you. Liam has told me a lot of nice things about you."

I looked at Liam with my eyes wide open. "It's nice to finally get to meet you too, sir. Your house is beautiful."

"Well, I can't take any of the credit for it, but thank you. And forget about the sir. You can call me Grandpa."

"Thanks, I will."

He was peering over our shoulders, looking at the table covered in rose petals. "Looks like I interrupted something."

"No, Grandpa, not at all. Please stay."

"No. Thanks anyway. I just came in to get a drink of water. Old Blue and I need to get back to work. Jenny, I hope you come back real soon. Maybe next time I'll be able to visit longer."

"Thanks. I'd love that."

"Liam, don't forget I'm going to need your help tonight getting the horses in from the field."

"Sure, Grandpa, right after practice."

"You guys have school today?"

"Yeah, we just came here for lunch."

"Well, alright then. See you later. Nice to meet you again, Jenny. Come back."

Liam's Grandpa tipped his hat to me and walked out of the room. I began to breathe.

"Oh my God, I thought I was going to throw-up. I've never been so nervous in all my life."

"Don't worry, he's harmless. Anyway, he knows all about you."

"It seems he knows more about me than I know about him."

"I told you that you're all I talk about."

"I thought you meant Parker and your friends, not your grandpa."

"Come here." Liam pulled me close to him, and we stared at each other with undivided attention. "You know, I need to ask you something."

"That's right, you did say that."

"I know this is really short notice, but you don't have a date for the homecoming dance do you?" I just smiled, remembering I was off the hook since Kendra now had a date.

"No, I don't have a date, but I do know of a guy who might be interested in taking me."

"Who is it?" Liam asked abruptly, not realizing I was referring to him.

"You, silly."

"Oh. So you'll go with me?"

I leaned up on my tippy toes to bite his lip. "Uh-huh, maybe with some persuasion."

"No problem." He leaned down and picked me up in his arms. I wrapped my legs around his waist. "So, is this a yes?" He asked.

"Definitely, yes."

The rest of our time at the house we spent in each other's arms. We talked a little about the weekend, but for the most part we just stayed in each other's embrace. We both knew that our feelings for each other were growing stronger. In the short time that I had really known Liam, I had never felt so strongly about another person. It was scaring me that it was moving so fast, but I didn't care. The only thing I did care about was him. We were somehow connected to each other, and it was beyond anything that Liam and I could control. We both knew it. I could have stayed at Liam's house the rest of the day. I felt right at home right from the start, but before we knew it, it was time to leave. We got in his truck, my new teddy bear in my arms, and headed back to school. The drive back was quiet. George Strait was playing in the background, one of Liam's favorite singers. I leaned my head on his shoulder, and he kept his right hand on my thigh.

"Jenny, I want you to know that you're the first girl who's ever met my grandpa."

I sat up. "Really? I don't believe that. What about Shanna, surely she's met him?"

"No. Not even once."

"But you guys were together for over two years. How can that be?"

"Well, two years technically. We broke up about a dozen times within those two years. Our relationship was not what most people thought it was. She was a convenience at times and for the most part it was her pursuing me, and not the other way around."

"But we've been together for only a short time. Why did you want me to meet your grandpa so soon?"

"Because before you, my grandpa was the only important person in my life. Now I have you. Why wouldn't I want the two people I care about the most to meet?"

I smiled at him and leaned my head back on his shoulder while placing both of my hands in his free hand.

"Thanks, Liam."

He gently kissed the top of my head and drove on.

The rest of the week flew by. Kendra and I both were on the homecoming committee, and any spare time we had was spent decorating the halls and cafeteria for the dance. Friday night's game against Ripley turned out to be another win for the mighty Yellow Jackets. Liam scored two touchdowns, and his friend Tony Williams ended up running for eighty-seven yards, his best game ever. Needless to say, Kendra was happy. Apparently since the weekend, Kendra had become smitten with Tony, and Tony with her. And it all started that same night at Lougini's when I fell on Liam. Kendra caught Tony's eye, and after much persuasion on Tony's part, Liam introduced him to her which resulted in Tony asking her to homecoming.

It was Saturday morning. The dance was to start at 7p.m., so I had less than ten hours to make myself look decent for Liam. My dress was freshly dry-cleaned and hanging on my closet door. Kendra was coming over in a little bit, so we could help each other with our hair and do our nails together. My stomach had been in knots since Liam dropped me off the previous night from the game. He said he would be here at 6 o'clock sharp to pick me up. I didn't think I was going to make it. I was messing with my hair in my mirror when my phone rang.

"Hello," I said sweetly.

"Hey, beautiful, ready for tonight?"

"I'm ready to see you, but I don't think I'm going to be ready for the dance. I wish I had a few more days to prepare for it."

"You'll look beautiful. How can you mess with perfection?"

"You're way too kind and way too smooth for your own good."

"I call it like I see it, babe, and like I've always told you, I only tell you the truth."

"I can't talk long, Kendra's on her way over. We're going to help each other with our hair and make-up. She's pretty excited about going with Tony."

"So is Tony. That is all he talked about last night. I haven't seen him this nervous in a long time. So, see you tonight, then?"

"Yes, I can't wait."

"Me neither, babe. Oh, by the way, you should be getting a delivery soon, so watch for it."

"What did you do?" I asked.

"Nothing, just something for my girl. See you tonight."

He hung up the phone. I was smiling from ear to ear. Liam was spoiling me with not only his attention but with his gifts as well. The flowers he had sent me when I was sick earlier this week were still in bloom, and the teddy bear that he gave me from the other day was still holding a rose. What could he be sending me now? Not two minutes later did I find out.

"Jenny?" Mom yelled from downstairs. "You better come down. There's something here for you."

"Coming, Mom."

I bolted down the stairs taking two at a time. At the bottom of the steps, Mom was waiting for me holding another beautiful bouquet of red roses.

"I think these are from Liam."

"They're beautiful, Mom. I can't believe him," I whispered out loud.

"I think he likes you, hon."

"I think so too."

I ran upstairs, taking the roses with me. I jumped on the bed and opened the card. "Until tonight, something to remind you of me, love, Liam." I stared at the bouquet. I couldn't believe him. I grabbed the phone to call him, but before I could, I laid it back down. The bouquet looked different, beautiful, but something about it was wrong. I concentrated on them, trying to figure out what it was when I noticed that there only seemed to be eleven roses instead of the usual twelve.

"1, 2, 3, 4, 5, 6, 7, 8, 9, 10, 11... hmm eleven?" Not a dozen. I counted them again making sure I didn't miss one. Okay, maybe the florist forgot one. I picked the phone up again, dialling Liam's number quickly.

"Hello," he said.

"Liam, the roses are beautiful. You've got to stop this though. You're spoiling me."

"Do you like them?"

"I love them, just like the others you've gotten me. But hey, I think you got short-changed."

"What do you mean?"

"Well, there's only eleven. I think the florist forgot one."

"No, they didn't. I've got the last rose. I'm giving it to you myself." I couldn't speak. "Jenny, are you there?"

"Yes, I'm here. It's just when I think I have you figured out you do something like this. I don't deserve it."

"Nonsense, Jenny, I'd give you the world if I could. These flowers are just a small token of how I feel about you."

"But, Liam, this is way too much too soon, we've only been together a short time."

"Jenny, it's only been a week for you, but it's been months for me."

"I don't know what to say."

"You don't need to say anything. I'm just glad you like them. I'll see you tonight."

"Okay, bye."

"Bye, babe."

I took the flowers downstairs and put them in a vase. At this rate, I was going to have to invest in more vases. Kendra showed up at precisely three o'clock, her dress, make-up kit, and shoes in hand.

"Can you believe we both have dates for tonight?" she asked.

"I know. It's pretty unbelievable considering this time last week we were going together. I guess we looked pretty pathetic. What time is Tony picking you up?"

"Not until six-thirty. What about you and Liam?"

"He said he would be here at six."

"These flowers are gorgeous, Jenny. I can't believe how many he's gotten you this week."

"I know. It's crazy. No boy has ever paid this much attention to me or showered me with as much as Liam. He's definitely spoiling me."

"Not a bad way to be spoiled, if you ask me," Kendra said enviously.

By five-thirty, Kendra and I both looked ready for the dance. Kendra had on a pale pink, floor-length halter dress with a rhinestone jewel in the middle of it. Her hair was swept up in a loose bun with tendrils of spiraled hair falling on both sides of her head. The cream colored dress that I had bought a couple of weeks ago had to be taken in on the sides. I had obviously lost some weight since Liam had entered the picture, and it didn't help that I had gotten sick this past week either. Mom secured the sides with neatly hidden safety pins adding an antique brooch that belonged to my grandmother to help conceal it.

"There, that should do it." Mom stepped back. There were tears in her eyes. "You look so pretty, Jenny, and so do you Kendra. I can't believe how grown-up both of you are."

"Thanks, Mom."

"Thanks, Mrs. King."

"Now don't go anywhere you two. Dad and I want to take some pictures."

"Ugh," we both groaned in unison.

Mom and Dad came back with their camera in hand. After what seemed like a hundred pictures in a hundred different poses, Mom finally stopped the photo session.

"Now, all we have to do is wait for Liam to take some with him."

"Mom, you can't be serious? You've already taken enough for the year."

Kendra glanced down at her watch. "I gotta go. Mom wants to take some pictures too. It's already six o'clock."

"Six o'clock? Liam is supposed to be here any second." And as soon as I mouthed the words, I saw his shiny, black truck pull into my driveway. "He's here!" I ran upstairs to check myself out. I didn't want to see him walk up the driveway. "Bye, Kendra, see ya tonight."

"See ya, Jenny. Oh Jenny, he looks sooo hot!"

"Stop it, Kendra!"

I ran into the bathroom, giving myself a once over, checking my hair, making sure there was no lipstick on my teeth, and then with a spritz of cologne in all the right places I waited for Mom to call me.

I heard the doorbell ring, "Hello Liam, come on in. You look so nice."

"Hello, Mr. and Mrs. King. Here these are for you Mrs. King."

"Liam, more flowers? You shouldn't have. They're so pretty."

"It was nothing, really. I hope you like them."

"Jenny, Liam's here."

I slowly walked down the steps, stopping at the landing. I couldn't see Liam's face yet, but I could tell where he was. He was standing in the foyer right next to our grandfather clock; Mom and Dad were to the left of him. I continued my descent down, picking up my dress to keep me from falling down the stairs and making a complete ass of myself. At the bottom landing, Liam walked over to me. He was carrying the single red rose.

"Hi, Jenny. You look gorgeous." He handed me the rose, kissing me on my cheek.

"Thanks, Liam. You don't look so bad yourself."

He was dressed head to toe in a black suit. He wore a cream colored shirt that was buttoned halfway up, revealing the definition of his well-chiseled chest. Around his neck was a silver cross that hung right below his neckline. His hair was pulled back in its tight ponytail, secured with a black holder. Kendra was right; he looked hot.

"Oh, these are for you too."

He pulled his arm from around his back to reveal more flowers. This time a wrist corsage to match my dress. There were four cream-colored sweetheart roses accented with baby's breath and crystals, followed by strands of light blue ribbon cascading down from the corsage.

"Liam, it's so pretty. Thank you." I had a million butterflies dancing in my stomach and I could feel the room spinning. I thought at any moment I was going to pass out, the only good thing was I knew Liam would catch me and I couldn't think of a better place to fall than in his arms. He helped place the corsage on my wrist, giving my hand a squeeze in the process. His hands felt sweaty. Liam Larson was also nervous.

"I have something for you too," said Mom, handing me a box that was sitting on the chair next to our piano. I opened the box to reveal two cream colored sweetheart roses, a boutonniere for Liam. I took the pin out of the box and almost stabbed myself in the process. I placed the boutonniere on his lapel and nervously pinned it on him.

"I hope I don't stick you. I'm not very good at this." I couldn't believe how bad my hands were shaking.

"Don't worry. You could never hurt me." I looked at him and smiled. He motioned with his mouth, "Let's get out of here." I nodded in agreement.

"Well, I guess we're ready." I looked over at Mom and Dad, who were both beaming, looking like the proud parents that they were.

"Oh no, you guys don't, not until I can get some pictures of you two. You're not getting away from me that fast."

"Mom, really, we're going to be late."

"A couple of pictures will not make you late. Now here, smile." A flash went off in our eyes, blinding us both. "Just a couple more."

I was becoming agitated. "Mom really that's enough."

"It's okay, Jenny, I don't mind," Liam said, appeasing my mom.

"See, Liam doesn't mind."

I growled at him under my breath. He laughed at my gesture. Finally after twenty more minutes of Mom's relentless photography session, we were allowed to leave.

"Have fun guys, see you at one. No later!"

We walked hand in hand down the steps. Liam, taking his time so I wouldn't trip on my dress, was always the gentlemen.

"Did I hear your mom say you have until one?"

"You heard right."

"But the dance is over at ten."

"Um-hm," I said with a sly smile.

"Oh, you're good, and I thought I was the sneaky one in this relationship."

"Not tonight you're not, I thought it would be nice to have some time together away from the dance."

"I like your thinking, babe."

"I thought you would."

We arrived at the dance to find the parking lot completely full.

"Wow, I can't believe all the cars here," I said as I helped him find a spot. "There's one over at the end." I motioned as a car pulled out of a spot after a parent dropped off some kids.

"Great eyes, Jen."

"Thanks, yours are pretty nice too."

Liam backed into the parking spot with such ease that it made him look like he drove that way on a regular basis.

"There. Ready to do some dancing, babe?"

He pulled me to him. "Yeah, are you?"

"No, not yet. First this."

He put his lips on mine, kissing me long and hard. His tongue encircled mine in my mouth. He held me tighter as he continued, taking his hands to explore my exposed back.

"I hope I don't stick you. I'm not very good at this." I couldn't believe how bad my hands were shaking.

"Don't worry. You could never hurt me." I looked at him and smiled. He motioned with his mouth, "Let's get out of here." I nodded in agreement.

"Well, I guess we're ready." I looked over at Mom and Dad, who were both beaming, looking like the proud parents that they were.

"Oh no, you guys don't, not until I can get some pictures of you two. You're not getting away from me that fast."

"Mom, really, we're going to be late."

"A couple of pictures will not make you late. Now here, smile." A flash went off in our eyes, blinding us both. "Just a couple more."

I was becoming agitated. "Mom really that's enough."

"It's okay, Jenny, I don't mind," Liam said, appeasing my mom.

"See, Liam doesn't mind."

I growled at him under my breath. He laughed at my gesture. Finally after twenty more minutes of Mom's relentless photography session, we were allowed to leave.

"Have fun guys, see you at one. No later!"

We walked hand in hand down the steps. Liam, taking his time so I wouldn't trip on my dress, was always the gentlemen.

"Did I hear your mom say you have until one?"

"You heard right."

"But the dance is over at ten."

"Um-hm," I said with a sly smile.

"Oh, you're good, and I thought I was the sneaky one in this relationship."

"Not tonight you're not, I thought it would be nice to have some time together away from the dance."

"I like your thinking, babe."

"I thought you would."

We arrived at the dance to find the parking lot completely full.

"Wow, I can't believe all the cars here," I said as I helped him find a spot. "There's one over at the end." I motioned as a car pulled out of a spot after a parent dropped off some kids.

"Great eyes, Jen."

"Thanks, yours are pretty nice too."

Liam backed into the parking spot with such ease that it made him look like he drove that way on a regular basis.

"There. Ready to do some dancing, babe?"

He pulled me to him. "Yeah, are you?"

"No, not yet. First this."

He put his lips on mine, kissing me long and hard. His tongue encircled mine in my mouth. He held me tighter as he continued, taking his hands to explore my exposed back.

"Liam, wait, the dance." His breathing was erratic, his hands still fondling the back of my body, inching their way down. "Liam, the dance."

"Oh, right, the dance..." Liam just stared at me as if he needed to tell me something, "Jen... I" and before another word could be spoken, Parker Duncan was honking his horn.

"Oh my God, that scared me," Liam said as he gave Parker a hand gesture that I knew was only meant for Parker to see.

"Come on, let's go."

He opened his door and got out, never once letting go of my hand. I scooted over to climb out, and Liam picked me up and gently placed me on the ground.

"You know you don't have to do that."

"Yes I do, and I want to." He was staring at me again with that same eagerness from a few moments earlier. "Jen..." I thought he was going to say something else to me, but instead, he just said: "You look absolutely beautiful tonight."

He took his hand and glided it across my cheek so gentle that I could barely notice the roughness of his skin. We took our time walking to the school, neither of us interested in the dance anymore. It was in full swing by the time we made it through the cafeteria doors. Everybody was there and dancing to the music. The room looked amazing. There were blue and silver streamers cascading down from the ceiling with silver stars and iridescent moons dropping in between them, very appropriate for the theme, Moonlight Serenade. I looked around for anybody I knew. It didn't look like Kendra and Tony were there yet. I did see Shauna and Paul along with Missy and Eric on the dance floor.

"Do you want to go find a seat?" Liam asked.

"Yeah, but first I would like to hang my wrap up."

"Sure, let me take it for you."

I handed Liam my wrap and he took it outside in the hallway to be checked. I waited for him at the entrance of the cafeteria and watched the kids dancing to Big and Rich, Save a Horse, Ride A Cowboy. The room was dark, but the silver stars and streamers that hung from the ceiling lit up the whole room. I was impressed with the job we did; the room looked magical. I turned to see Tony and Kendra walk into the room.

"Hey, dawg."

"Hey there," I replied. "I'm so glad you're finally here Kendra."

"Me too. We got held up because Mom was taking so many pictures."

"I feel your pain."

"So, where's Liam?" Tony asked.

"He took my wrap and checked it for me. I didn't want to lug it around." Tony looked at Kendra, wondering if he should do the same courtesy.

"Do you want me to take yours Kendra?"

"Sure, thanks, Tony."

We were giggling as Tony walked away. "He's not much for talking, is he, Kendra?"

"Well, not yet, this is really the first time we've been together. It's been a little awkward, if you know what I mean?"

"Don't worry. You guys stick with us. Between the three of us, we should be able to loosen Tony up."

A few minutes later, Tony and Liam were back.

"So, girls, do you want to find a seat?"

"Sure."

We found a table in the far back corner of the cafeteria, near one of the exit doors. Even though the rumor mill had been running rampant about Liam and I being a couple, I was still amazed at the number of gawks and stares we received when we entered the room. Most of them were well intended, but there were a few that weren't, especially the stares that came from Shanna Smith's table. Shanna was with Chris Crowder, a bad seed all the way around. Chris didn't play sports or play in the band. He found his hobbies elsewhere, and they usually included getting into trouble with the law. On more than one occasion, Chris had been suspended from school for trying to sell marijuana on school property. Kelli and Parker were both sitting with them, and as we passed by, Shanna didn't look up until Liam was in sight.

"Hi, Liam," she said in a very seductive tone.

Shanna was barely wearing a strapless yellow and black dress. Her hair was pulled to one side in a ringlet ponytail, and she had the brightest red lipstick on I had ever seen. She definitely was trying to get noticed. Liam looked the other way, only squeezing my hand in an effort for me to move faster as we passed her table. I felt bad for Liam. Parker Duncan was one of his best friends, but Parker dated Kelli Hanson, and she was Shanna Smith's best friend. It was a tangled web, one that I didn't want to get caught up in but felt that I was already. We finally sat down at our table, only to have Liam and Tony pull us to the dance floor. *Big and Rich, Save A Horse, Ride A Cowboy* was still playing, and these two country boys weren't about to let us sit this one out. For the next hour or so,

Liam never left my side. We danced every dance possible, taking full advantage of the slow dances to be as close as possible. The night was going perfect, and it didn't seem like anything could go wrong. We were having a fantastic time together. Kendra and Tony also seemed to be hitting it off, and by the time homecoming court was announced, they had made plans for a second date. Even Shanna was leaving us alone which seemed to be a feat in itself since her eyes seemed to be glued to our table. One of the best parts of the evening was hearing them announce Frannie as the homecoming queen. Kendra and I both squealed in delight because it was an honor well deserved for our good friend.

"Let's go congratulate her, Jenny."

"Of course, let me tell Liam, and I'll meet up with you at Frannie's table."

Liam was supposed to be getting my wrap, but I saw he was talking to Parker and Kelli. I honestly didn't want to interrupt them for no other reason than I just didn't get along with Kelli. But if Liam and I were going to be together, running into her was going to be part of the packaged deal. Confrontations were going to be inevitable. I knew I had to just bite the bullet and get it over with. Kelli didn't seem to want to make the first move anyway.

I walked up behind Liam, "Hi guys," as I looked straight at Parker and Kelli.

"Hello, babe," Liam sweetly said as he took my hand in his.

"Hi Parker, hello, Kelli."

"Hi, Jenny."

"Hi," Kelli said coldly.

"Your dress is gorgeous, Kelli. That color looks great on you." I was trying.

She seemed in shock that I would pay her a compliment. "Umm, thanks, you look nice too."

Trying to break the ice with your arch nemesis' best friend is never easy, but at least I was trying. The trivial back and forth banter between us seemed to be over, neither one of us knowing what to say next, so I diverted my attention to Liam.

"I'm going over to Frannie's table for a while. I want to congratulate her on her win."

"Okay, tell her congrats from me too."

"I will. Well, I guess I'll see you guys later. Bye Parker; Bye Kelli." I smiled and walked off feeling pretty proud for taking the first step with Kelli. At least I knew we could be civil with one another if the need arose.

Frannie's table was nothing but a roar of squeals and laughter. It was great to hang out with my friends and just talk and laugh. It had only been a couple of weeks since I had hung with them, but I didn't realize how much I had missed. Within fifteen minutes, I had been completely updated on all the latest gossip and scoops, including what was being said about Liam and me. After clearing up that Liam and I weren't engaged and after making plans to have a girls' night in the near future I left the table to find Liam. He didn't seem to be anywhere in sight, although it was quite difficult to see with the dimmed lights and the multitude of kids dancing haphazardly throughout the room.

Our table was empty. Kendra and Tony were at the snack table and most of Liam's friends were either on the dance floor or at their table. So by a matter of deduction, I had come to the conclusion that he was retrieving my wrap in the hallway. I wasn't the slightest bit cold now, so there was no need for it. I walked into the hallway only to discover the hallway had turned into a make-out alley. Obviously the teachers were too caught up in the dance to realize the real action was going on out here. I ignored the groping and heavy breathing as best as I could as I made my way to the coat check, only to find that there was more of the same going on there as well. I literally ran into a couple as I walked into the room.

"I am so sorry, I was just," but before I said another word, my heart stopped. Standing in front of me was none other than Shanna and Liam, her arms around his neck and her lips on his. I stared in disbelief and utter shock, unable to move or speak.

"Oh, Hi, Jenny," Shanna said as she wiped her mouth with her hand. "Oops!" she said with a sarcastic giggle. I just stared, not believing what I was seeing. I felt like I had just had the wind knocked out of me. Liam quickly shoved Shanna away from him, but before he could get to me I turned and ran off.

"Jenny, come back here!" he screamed as I ran down the hallway, pushing my way through the barrage of couples who were doing exactly what Shanna and Liam were doing moments ago. I couldn't get to the exit door fast enough. My eyes filled with tears, and I could hardly see. Running into people, I made my way to the door. I didn't care. I just needed to get out of there and as far away from the school and Liam as my feet could take me.

"Jenny, wait up!" Liam screamed again. I ignored his futile pleas as I pushed my way through the exit door. The cold air hit my body like a ton of bricks taking my breath away and for a moment my tears. Liam would be upon me in seconds I was sure. He was fast and I would be no match for him if he were to open the door right now. I quickly ran down the hill making my way to the parking lot breaking my shoe and ripping my dress in the process.

"Great, just my luck," I added pity to my list of bereavements for the night. The tears were streaming down my face like running water now; there was no stopping them, not that I wanted to stop them anyway. I felt awful, and my only consolation was that maybe I could cry my feelings out and rid myself of Liam forever. I looked around; there was no sign of him. I sat there amidst the debris and gravel that made up the parking lot crying uncontrollably. My breath becoming shallow and labored from the excessive amount of emotions I was enduring. I knew I couldn't stay there. Liam would soon come this way looking for me. I needed to make my exit and make it soon. I scoped the area adamantly. He was nowhere to be seen. I gradually stood up and snuck around the parked vehicles making my presence inconspicuous as I hobbled my way towards home on a broken shoe.

Maybe Liam got the message and decided to return to the dance to be with Shanna. Maybe that was the plan to begin with. Maybe they had plotted this devious scheme weeks ago to embarrass and hurt me just for the fun it. But why? It was something Shanna would do and enjoy. She was known for her cruel and wicked tricks, but it didn't seem like Liam. It didn't seem like him at all. *Why in the world would he want to embarrass me like this? To put me through this? I thought he was different.*

But I had thought so many other past relationships were different too and look where they had gotten me, nowhere. It didn't matter anymore anyway. He had made his choice, *like there was one to make.* His choice must have always been Shanna. *She had been right.* He had just gotten bored with her, and now he was ready to go back to her. I was just a diversion for him for a while. A fling.

I had hardly made any headway on my journey home. My feet were killing me, and it didn't help that I was walking in the gravel to keep myself hidden as much as possible from the traffic. I didn't want to see or talk to anyone, and at this point I just wanted to crawl home and die. But before I could do that, I needed to trash my shoes. I sat down near an overgrown bush and slid my shoes off. I heard the sound of Liam's truck coming around the corner, driving slowly as he searched for me. I sat very still, hoping the bush concealed my identity. He drove past me, and I breathed a sigh of relief. Then the truck came to a screeching halt. He jumped out of his cab and ran in my direction.

"Jenny, here you are!"

"Get away from me, you bastard!" I jumped to my feet, throwing my shoes in his direction.

"Dammit, Jenny, stop. You almost hit me!"

"That was my intention!"

"Stop, you have to listen to me. It's not what you think."

"I know what I saw, Liam. Leave me alone!" I turned to walk in the opposite direction of him when he pulled my arm forcing me to stop and face him. "Don't, Liam. I don't want to do this." I was crying so hard that the words were coming out in berated breaths.

"My God, Jenny. Please, it's not what you think. Please don't shut me out like this. If you would have just waited instead of leaving like you did."

"Waited? For what? To watch you and Shanna in another lip-lock? No thank you, I saw enough to last me a lifetime." I tried to pull my arm free from his grip to no avail. "Liam please let go of me." My plea fell on deaf ears. Instead, he held onto me tighter pulling me closer to him.

"I'm not letting you go until I explain."

"Explain? There's nothing to explain. I know what I saw; you and Shanna were kissing!"

"No! Jenny, Shanna kissed me. I didn't kiss her. You have to believe me. I went to get your wrap, and she followed me out there. She started coming on to me. She's drunk and acting crazy. I told her to back off, but she wouldn't listen. When you came around the corner, that's when she flung herself onto me. Babe, I swear to you, I'm telling you the truth. It's not what you think. I told her to stay the hell away from me, but she wouldn't listen. Please, listen to me!" His voice was desperate, and his eyes filled with tears. I didn't want to listen. I jerked myself around, losing my balance, and falling to the ground, pulling him down with me. "This isn't my fault, just give me a chance to explain. You owe me that much at least."

"Owe you? I don't owe you a damn thing! Why did you even bother with me? You could have just left me alone and saved us both all this drama and pain! Why did you even bother with me in the first place? I was doing just fine before you entered my life!"

"But I wasn't, Jenny. You're the best thing in my life." He was on his knees. His neatly black pants were now covered with dirt and grass stains. He brought his face close to mine. I looked the other way. I was too confused and hurt to face him. "Leave you alone? Are you kidding? I've been happier these past couple of weeks than I've ever been." His words cut straight to my heart.

"Liam, I don't know. I don't like feeling like this. Shanna's always going to try to put a wedge between us. I don't know if I can do this."

"Don't say that. I'm so sorry. I promise she'll never interfere with us again." I turned away from him again. I had heard his apologies before.

"Jenny." His voice trembled as he spoke. He looked as awful as I felt. His face was etched with pain, and his blue eyes were muddled with tears.

"How can I believe you?"

"Because I'm telling you the truth. I told you I would never lie to you, and I'm not going to start now. I promise, she threw herself at me. I don't want her; I only want you. She'll never have my heart. It belongs to you, babe, for always."

He cupped his shaky hands around mine, pleading with me to believe him. I could tell he was scared. Scared of what just happened, and what could happen.

"Liam…"

He stopped me and forced me to look into his eyes. "Jenny, don't you see how much you mean to me? Do you honestly think I would go to all this trouble if I didn't…" He paused for a split second.

"If you didn't what, Liam?"

"Jenny, if I didn't love you." He was still on bended knees, lowering his head as he said those three prophetic words.

"You what?"

"I said I love you, Jenny. I… I love you."

"What?"

"I think I've loved you from the first time I set eyes on you."

Before I could react, he pressed his lips against mine, wrapped his strong arms around me and pulled me tightly to his body. I forced myself from him. Was he still playing with me, with my emotions, with my heart?

"Liam, you can't do this to me. You can't say that if you don't mean it." I was crying harder than ever.

"But I do mean it. I've never meant anything more in my life. I'm not expecting you to say it back. I mean, I hope one day you will, but that's not why I'm telling you. I'm telling you because I can't keep it to myself anymore. I need you to know how I truly feel about you. I do; I love you." He whispered again as he pressed his lips on mine, kissing me even more passionately than he did before. I wanted to believe him more than anything, but I couldn't relent to him so easily.

"Liam, that hurt me to see you two like that. It's more than I can take."

"I swear to you on my life, if you just give me one more chance you'll never hurt again. I don't want Shanna. I want you. What more do I have to do or say to make you believe me?"

"I don't know. I just know I never want to feel this way again. It hurts too much."

He took his hand and wiped the mascara stained tears from my cheek. "Baby, you never will, I promise." This time he softly kissed me, slowly, waiting for my reaction. I hesitated, still feeling the pain, but he felt so good against me. I wanted him to kiss me. I wanted him. I pushed back, reciprocating his kiss.

"I love you, Jenny."

"I know, Liam. I know." We both gave in, buckling into each other's arms as we lay on the ground.

"I thought I was going to lose you." His voice still trembled as he pulled me tightly to him and held me.

"You don't know how I felt when I saw you and Shanna. I wanted to die." He pulled himself from the ground, bringing me with him.

"Come on. We're getting out of here." He picked me up in his arms and carried me to his truck. "You mean more to me than life itself. Shanna means nothing, never has and never will. " He helped me into the truck as he climbed in next to me. I told you, I'm never letting you go. I meant that." He put his truck into drive and sped off away from the school.

"Where are we going?"

"Some place we can be alone. I don't want to be at the dance anymore, and I don't want to share you with your friends. I want to be alone with you."

I looked in his mirror and assessed the damage that my crying fit had done to my face. It was almost beyond repair. My eyes were bloodshot and swollen, and my face had mascara-stained streaks running down my cheeks. Liam wouldn't let go of my left hand, and to be perfectly honest, I didn't want him to. We drove for nearly fifteen minutes when he made a familiar turn off the road. I recognized it immediately. It was the road that led to his house. It was only eight-thirty. We had over four hours to be together I thought.

"Is your grandpa here?"

"No. He's delivering horses to an auction in Ohio. He won't be home until tomorrow night. It's just you and me."

I was still rattled, but felt more at ease as we approached his house. I loved it there. There was an unforeseen feeling that made me feel always welcome and at home. The house looked eerily vacant tonight as he parked the truck, as though no one had lived there for years. There was a cool breeze in the air, and I shivered as Liam helped me out of the truck.

"Are you cold?"

"Just a little," I remembered my forgotten wrap back at school and the circumstances that led me from not getting it.

"Here," Liam took off his jacket, and wrapped it around my shoulders, "better?"

"Yeah, thanks." He looked good in his cream colored shirt and black pants. His body was in perfect condition, and his clothes accented his frame nicely.

"Let's go inside." Liam grabbed my hand as I followed him up the steps. I noticed as I pulled my dress up how badly I had ripped it and that my bare feet were covered in dirt.

Liam instantly noticed me looking at myself. He gave me a smile and lifted me into his arms in one gallant sweep. I wrapped my arms around his neck. His hair was still pulled back into its tight ponytail. I carefully pulled it out and watched his hair fall, framing his beautifully masculine face. He walked into the living room and sat me down on the blue and yellow floral covered sofa, never once taking his eyes off mine.

"Liam, I…" I started, but he didn't let me finish. His body was positioned over me.

"Jenny I'm so sorry about tonight. I never thought Shanna would stoop so low. I'm sorry you had to see that. I meant what I said earlier. I am in love with you."

I didn't say anything, not knowing what to say. Instead, I pulled him to me and kissed him emphatically. He willingly obliged, taking me in his arms as he leaned me back onto the sofa. I unbuttoned his shirt, pulling it off of him. His sun-kissed skin was gorgeous, and my mind was having a field day with all the thoughts that were running through it about him. I sat up, forcing myself on his lap, wrapping my legs around him as best as I could. We were wrapped in each other's embrace, giving in to each other's desire, not holding back, not hindering to what we both wanted. Every part of my body was on fire as though the very tips of my nerves were exposed, and I knew the only thing that could save me from my fiery realm was Liam's touch. He read my mind, touching my body, making his way down my legs, lifting my dress as he made his way back up my thigh. His touch, sending shivers down my spine.

"Jenny."

"It's okay, Liam."

He carefully kissed my neck, making his way down my body, removing the straps of my dress as he caressed me. He picked me up in his arms.

"Where are we going?" I whispered.

"Upstairs. I don't want to make love to you on a couch."

I squeezed my legs tighter around his waist. "Liam?"

"Yeah, Jen."

I had a million thoughts running through my head. I knew what was about to happen. I wanted it. I wanted it more than anything, and I wasn't scared. I longed for him. My body ached for his skin on mine, for us to become one. Never had anything felt more right than this, but I couldn't find the words to express those feelings. But it didn't matter; Liam knew. He could see it in my eyes and in the way I kissed him. He knew exactly how I felt.

"It's okay, babe." He touched his lips to mine, slightly biting my lower lip. The steps that led upstairs seemed endless. Liam never took his eyes from mine as he carried me down the hallway to his room. He kicked the door open. The room was large and decorated with trophies and awards from his football accomplishments. The number eleven stared at me from every direction, but what I noticed more than anything was the huge four poster oak bed covered in a black comforter that took up most of his room. He placed me gently on it, leaning over me as we

"Here," Liam took off his jacket, and wrapped it around my shoulders, "better?"

"Yeah, thanks." He looked good in his cream colored shirt and black pants. His body was in perfect condition, and his clothes accented his frame nicely.

"Let's go inside." Liam grabbed my hand as I followed him up the steps. I noticed as I pulled my dress up how badly I had ripped it and that my bare feet were covered in dirt.

Liam instantly noticed me looking at myself. He gave me a smile and lifted me into his arms in one gallant sweep. I wrapped my arms around his neck. His hair was still pulled back into its tight ponytail. I carefully pulled it out and watched his hair fall, framing his beautifully masculine face. He walked into the living room and sat me down on the blue and yellow floral covered sofa, never once taking his eyes off mine.

"Liam, I..." I started, but he didn't let me finish. His body was positioned over me.

"Jenny I'm so sorry about tonight. I never thought Shanna would stoop so low. I'm sorry you had to see that. I meant what I said earlier. I am in love with you."

I didn't say anything, not knowing what to say. Instead, I pulled him to me and kissed him emphatically. He willingly obliged, taking me in his arms as he leaned me back onto the sofa. I unbuttoned his shirt, pulling it off of him. His sun-kissed skin was gorgeous, and my mind was having a field day with all the thoughts that were running through it about him. I sat up, forcing myself on his lap, wrapping my legs around him as best as I could. We were wrapped in each other's embrace, giving in to each other's desire, not holding back, not hindering to what we both wanted. Every part of my body was on fire as though the very tips of my nerves were exposed, and I knew the only thing that could save me from my fiery realm was Liam's touch. He read my mind, touching my body, making his way down my legs, lifting my dress as he made his way back up my thigh. His touch, sending shivers down my spine.

"Jenny."

"It's okay, Liam."

He carefully kissed my neck, making his way down my body, removing the straps of my dress as he caressed me. He picked me up in his arms.

"Where are we going?" I whispered.

"Upstairs. I don't want to make love to you on a couch."

I squeezed my legs tighter around his waist. "Liam?"

"Yeah, Jen."

I had a million thoughts running through my head. I knew what was about to happen. I wanted it. I wanted it more than anything, and I wasn't scared. I longed for him. My body ached for his skin on mine, for us to become one. Never had anything felt more right than this, but I couldn't find the words to express those feelings. But it didn't matter; Liam knew. He could see it in my eyes and in the way I kissed him. He knew exactly how I felt.

"It's okay, babe." He touched his lips to mine, slightly biting my lower lip. The steps that led upstairs seemed endless. Liam never took his eyes from mine as he carried me down the hallway to his room. He kicked the door open. The room was large and decorated with trophies and awards from his football accomplishments. The number eleven stared at me from every direction, but what I noticed more than anything was the huge four poster oak bed covered in a black comforter that took up most of his room. He placed me gently on it, leaning over me as we listened to each other's labored breaths. He brushed the hair out of my eyes.

"We don't have to do this," he said. "I can wait. I don't need to do this to show you how I feel about you. I do want this, but only if you do."

"It's okay. I want this too."

"I really do love you, Jenny and I'm not expecting you to say it just because I did. I just needed you to know how I felt."

"I know, Liam."

My feelings were strong for him, very strong. I wanted to say the same to him, but I wasn't ready, not yet. I had fallen into that trap with other guys only to have my heart broken and left feeling like a fool for confessing what I thought was real. This time I wasn't going to make that same mistake. If I did love him, then I was going to make sure. It was enough to know how he felt for me for now. He pressed his body harder against me this time, our bodies perfectly aligned to each other's shapes as he held me tenderly in his clutch. There were no inhibitions between us. We were both willing participants to each other's wants and desires. Our bodies were shaking, and our breathing was labored as we undressed each other. Nothing in the world had ever seemed more right than this. The heat that had ignited between us was producing a desire that seemed to take over both of us.

"I want this moment to last," he said. "This is more than an act for me. This is me loving you."

"Liam," I whispered in his ear, "please come here."

He leaned down towards me, taking me into his arms.

Chapter Nine
Mom and Dad

    The next couple of months found Liam and me inseparable. If we weren't together, we were on the phone with one another. School was going good, and the football team was becoming nearly unstoppable. They had made it all the way to state before being defeated by the Ravenswood Red Devils in overtime. It was an incredible game that was led by none other than Liam and his buddy Parker Hanson. Liam scored four touchdowns and ran for an incredible three hundred eleven yards, but in the end, the Ravenswood Red Devils took control of the game by scoring a field goal from fifty-six yards out to win the title. Still, both teams were congratulated for playing such an awesome game and for making it all the way to State and commended on jobs well done for their entire seasons.

    At the high school football banquet, Liam was awarded the highest honor given by the school. His football jersey, #11, had been retired by the coaching staff. He had reached school records over the four years he had played football for the Spencer Yellow Jackets, running for 7,411 yards, having 542 tackles and completing 111 touchdowns. When Coach Green called Liam to the podium he received a standing ovation that brought all of us to tears. Not bad for a small town country boy.

By Christmas, his grandpa and my family had become more than acquaintances but actual friends, sharing stories about their lives in Spencer as well as stories about Liam and me. We were comfortable with each other and with each other's family. Liam's parents hadn't been in the picture for a long time. His grandpa had raised him since he was six years old. He liked being around my family and enjoyed the whole family unit. He had missed that growing up with just his grandpa.

Kendra and Tony were still dating, although they were more off than on. We did some double dating with them once in a while, as well as with Parker and Kelli. Kelli realized I wasn't the mean bitch Shanna had made me out to be. She had warmed up to me instantly, realizing that we had much more in common than dating football players. Kendra, on the other hand, was fickle. Whenever she thought someone was getting too serious with her, she would start to lose interest. Tony had fallen for Kendra head over heels, and in the process almost scared her away.

For Liam and I though, homecoming had been another turning point in our relationship. We knew the feelings we had for each other were stronger than we ever thought possible, even early on. We didn't take each other for granted and didn't let things step in the way of how we felt about one another. We kept things open and honest with each other and always expressed how we felt no matter the circumstances. Shanna's name was never brought up again, and for her part, she kept her distance from both of us.

Right before Christmas week, Liam took me out to Brush Creek Road. The road wasn't muddy anymore, now it had been replaced with a thin layer of snow, but the view was just as I remembered it, breathtaking. The sky was as clear as a crystal ball showcasing the luminous stars that twinkled and danced against the horizon. I felt content in Liam's arms. We were in tune with each other and could sit quietly in each other's presence without the awkwardness of silence.

"What are you thinking about, babe?"

"Oh, nothing in particular." My head rested against his chest as the beat of his heartbeat was slowly putting me to sleep. "I was just thinking about the first time you brought me here."

"You remember?"

"How can I forget? I was covered in mud from head to toe from that awful performance I had to do in the rain, and you still thought I looked beautiful."

"Well, I've never lied about that."

I kissed him on the tip of his nose. He took his hand and lifted my chin up to his face.

"You missed," he said as he brought his lips to mine.

I sat up, looking seriously in his face.

"What, Jen?"

I had been wanting to talk to him about his family for a long time but never felt comfortable enough to do it until now.

"Liam, can I ask you a question?" He always seemed guarded about them and bringing the subject up was making me nervous.

"Of course."

"Are you sure?"

"Definitely, you know you can ask me anything, ask away."

"I was just wondering, why you never mention your family, your mom and dad? He looked away. Sighing heavily, he gripped the steering wheel tightly.

"Did I say something wrong?"

"No. It's just that I don't talk about them."

"I'm sorry, I didn't mean to bring something up that would be uncomfortable for you to talk about. It's just that I care about you and wanted to know more about you. If you don't want to talk about them then just say the word, and I'll never mention them again."

He leaned into me. "I want to tell you. You more than anyone should know. I'm sorry I've never said anything to you."

He took a deep breath before proceeding. "You know the picture on the mantle in the living room?"

"Yeah, there's one of you and one with your grandpa and you in your football uniform."

"Yeah, but not those two. I'm talking about the one with the young woman in it."

"I remember. She's quite beautiful. Is that your mom?"

"Yes, it is."

"I thought so. You have her eyes."

"I only have a few pictures of her. She died when I was six. I don't remember much about her, only that she loved to cook and sing."

"I'm sorry. I would have never asked if I'd known I was going to dredge up something so sad. You don't have to go on if you don't want to. If it's going to be too painful, I'd rather not know."

"No, I want you to know. I don't have many memories of her, but I do remember that she died," he paused before continuing. Then he looked me straight in the eye, "because of my dad, Jenny."

"What?" I asked wondering if I had heard him right. "Liam, I'm so sorry."

He breathed in deeply and looked earnestly at me. I stroked the hair around his face, placing it behind his ear.

"No, Jenny, it's okay. Like I said, I don't remember much. It's just that, you know, I miss her. I can't really say that about my dad, but I do miss my mom." He turned his face away from me, and I was positive that he wiped a tear from his cheek. "It was a Friday night. Dad was working late. It was just me and Mom at home. She had just made dinner and was beginning to make her cinnamon buns."

"You mean the ones your grandpa made for us?"

"Yeah, those are the ones. Actually they're my grandma's recipe. Anyway, it was getting late, and Dad still wasn't home. He was known to go have a beer after work on Friday nights, but he never stayed out long. It had to have been close to eleven, and he still wasn't home. Mom was worried. She called Grandpa, but he didn't answer. So she called our neighbor Russ Browning who lived up the road from us. Russ was a loner. He had lost his wife to cancer a few years earlier and pretty much stayed to himself. He knew my dad worked long hours and always told my mom if she ever needed anything to just let him know. I heard later on that he actually had a thing for Mom, but, to be honest, I don't think Mom ever knew, and if she did, she would have never cheated on my dad. She really loved him.

"But, that night she was worried, more than usual. Something seemed different. Dad never stayed out that late unless he called. He was always home at a decent hour, so Mom knew something had to be up. Mom, out of desperation, called Russ, and he came over right away. I remember Mom was crying. She tried to keep it from me, so I wouldn't worry, but I could hear her when she went out of the room. I knew something was wrong. She wasn't one to get so emotional.

"By the time Russ came over, I was sent to my room. She was becoming hysterical, thinking the worst had happened to Dad, and seeing her like that was frightening me. Russ was trying to calm her down when Dad walked in the door. Dad had been drinking and drinking a lot. He wasn't a heavy drinker normally, but Mom and Dad were going through some rough times.

"They had been having a lot of financial problems, and we both noticed that Dad seemed to take to the bottle a lot more often. It bothered Mom, but she never did or said anything about it to him. She only hoped he knew what he was doing and knew when he had enough. He was barely coherent that night, stumbling into the door, knocking things over. To be honest, I don't know how he drove home in his condition. The first thing Dad saw was Russ's arms around Mom. Russ was trying to console her, but that's not what Dad thought. He went ballistic, screaming and swearing at the top of his lungs. Mom tried to calm him down, trying to explain why Russ was there, but Dad wouldn't listen. He was a very jealous man. He knew how beautiful Mom was, and he was always questioning why she was with him. He also knew that Russ was a little too friendly with her.

"Dad was on a rampage, knocking things down, breaking mirrors, throwing anything he could get his hands on through the plate glass front door. She tried everything in her power to stop him, but he had gone crazy, he was enraged like some kind of wild animal and acting like a deranged lunatic. His personality changed with a blink of an eye. Russ tried to help too, but it was like adding fuel to the fire. It only made things worse. I was upstairs in my room listening to everything: the screaming, the arguing, the glass breaking. It was horrible, Jenny. I just kept rocking myself back and forth, closing my eyes, and trying to wish that this was all a bad dream and when I opened them everything would be back to normal again.

"It was a bad dream, only I wasn't sleeping. I was wide awake, and it was getting worse by the minute. The arguing and screaming got louder. I kept singing this song over and over again in my head that Mom would sing to me at bedtime, doing anything to drown out the horrible sounds coming from downstairs. Then I noticed that everything grew quiet for a moment, it was too quiet and just when I thought it was over, I heard my dad running up the stairs. He was charging them, making it sound like a herd of horses trampling them. I remember running under my bed. I was so afraid. I could tell Mom and Russ were behind him. Mom pleaded with Dad to listen to her. She tried to explain that the only reason Russ was there was because she was worried about him. Dad didn't see that. All he could see was that another man was in his house with his wife. I heard him go into their bedroom. Mom was screaming at him to calm down, and then her voice changed. The pleas and desperation turned into pleas of fright and panic. I could tell by her voice that she was afraid. I heard her scream out the word, 'no'. There was sheer panic in her voice.

"She kept repeating it, 'no, no, no, no!' saying my dad's name over and over again. 'Please Allen, no!' and then out of nowhere there were two loud shots. The sound reminded me of firecrackers you hear on Fourth of July. I held my breath, waiting patiently to hear Mom's voice again, but there was nothing. The house was silent. There was no sound or movement from anyone, just this uneasy, eerie feeling that had come over me. I knew something bad had happened. I kept waiting to hear my mom's voice. I wanted to yell out to her, but I was too afraid Dad would turn his anger on me.

"I finally decided to open my door, something now I wish I had never done. When I did, I found Mom in Dad's arms, lying on the floor in a pool of her blood. He was pleading with her, whispering her name over and over again. 'No Jessica, I'm sorry. Please Jessica, get up!' He kept saying it over and over again. Her eyes were still open, but there was nothing in them. I knew right then she was dead, and beside her was Russ, he was just lying there too, both of them motionless. I yelled out to her.

"Dad looked at me. He had this terrified, wild look in his eyes. A crazy look. I yelled at him. 'What did you do to my mom?!' He just stared at me, saying nothing. He was crying hysterically. He whispered to me that he was sorry and ran down the stairs, leaving Mom there as her blood blanketed her on the floor. I stood there staring at her lifeless body, her eyes still open, as if at any moment they would blink and I would see life return to them. I kept staring at her praying for her to wake up, holding myself as a rocked back and forth when I heard another shot come from outside. I ran down the stairs to find that Dad had shot himself in the head in our front yard. It was July 11th."

I didn't speak right away, just absorbing what Liam had divulged to me. "I don't know what to say except that I'm so, so sorry. I never dreamed in a million years it was that bad. I can't imagine what you've had to go through." I took him in my arms, holding him close to me, trying to protect and shelter him from the pain.

"It's okay. I'm glad I told you, besides it was a long time ago. I'm doing fine now, especially with you in my life. It felt good to talk about it. I haven't ever told anyone except Parker and now you. Grandpa and Parker are the only ones who know the truth about what happened that night."

"What do you mean the truth?"

"Most people think Mom and Dad died in a car accident. That's how I want it. It's too painful and personal to tell what really happened to them."

"I won't say a word. I promise." I brought him closer again, hugging him with all my might. "I promise Liam. Is that how you ended up with your grandpa?"

"Yeah. Grandpa showed up soon after my dad shot himself. He found me lying over Mom's body. I was just crying, pleading with her to wake up. After the whole incident, Grandpa closed up the house, selling it to the first buyer that came along. That's when I moved in with my grandparents."

"Your Grandma was still alive?"

"Yeah, but not for long. My mom was their daughter. Grandma was never the same. It just about killed them both. Grandma always had health problems, and after Mom died, she got worse, not caring if she lived or died. I don't think she had the will to live if I'm being honest She passed away five months after Mom. So, it's been just me and Grandpa for the past eleven years."

"Liam, I don't know what to say."

"You don't have to say anything. Just having you here with me is all I need."

"I'll always be here for you, Liam, always. I just don't know how you got through that."

"I don't think I would have if it hadn't had been for Grandpa. He's been my strength, my rock. Believe me, there were plenty of times I think he wondered if I would ever be the same. I was so young when it happened. I guess that could be a good thing, but no kid should see their Mom in the condition I did, or their dad. I spent a lot of nights crying myself to sleep. Grandpa would just let me, holding me, and letting me get it out of my system. As I got older, things became a little easier, but I kept to myself a lot. Grandpa was definitely worried about me. The only thing I liked to do was play football, and I wasn't even doing that. Eventually, he made me play pee-wee football here in town. I didn't want to. I didn't want to be around anybody, but he forced me to, it was the best thing he ever did for me. Football became my therapy, my release. When I was playing, I forgot all about my troubles. It didn't hurt that tackling people and knocking them down helped release some of my aggression too. When I wasn't practicing on the field, I was practicing here with Grandpa. He was, and is to this day, my biggest supporter. He believed in me when I didn't believe in myself, pushed me to be the best I could. I wouldn't be where I am today if it wasn't for that old man. I love him."

"Liam, that's beautiful. I think what you and your grandpa have is priceless. It's epic. I'm envious of it. I can definitely tell how much he means to you."

"Yeah, he's something special. I don't know what I would do without him. I'm glad I told you."

"Me too, babe."

After a long period of silence, Liam sat up and looked me straight in the eyes.

"Enough sadness, Okay?"

"Okay," I said with an encouraging smile.

"Tell me something about you?"

"What do you want to know?"

"Well, what's your favorite color?"

"That would have to be blue. And yours?"

"No fair. I'm asking the questions."

"No way. I only asked you one. If you're going to find out some of my favorites, then I want to know some of yours as well."

"Fair enough, black."

"Black?"

"Yeah, that's my favorite color."

"But it's so dark and mysterious."

"Yeah, like me," he said with a crooked grin.

"Okay, good enough then."

"My turn again. Silver or gold?"

"Definitely silver. I've never been a gold chick."

"And you?"

"Silver also," he said as he grabbed the silver cross hanging around his neck.

"Your favorite food?"

"Lougini's pizza with everything on it except anchovies."

"And yours?"

"Fried chicken."

"Really? I took you for a steak man."

"Steak's okay, but give me a fried drumstick any day, especially Grandpa's."

Liam continued. "Favorite holiday?"

"Christmas."

"Really?" he said.

"Yeah. I love the whole idea of it: decorating the house, the smell of things baking in the oven, and of course Christmas trees. I love Christmas trees. What about you?"

"I don't know if I have a favorite holiday. Does football season count as a holiday?"

"No, it doesn't, but I guess in your case I'll give it to you."

"What about after high school? Any plans. Jenny?"

"I guess college, but I haven't decided where though."

"Do you know what you want to do?"

"I've always thought I would go into business, so I could come back and help my dad with his store. What about you? I'm sure you're going off somewhere to play college ball aren't you?"

"No," he said matter of factly.

"No, to college ball or no to college altogether?"

"No, to college. I'm not really school material. After high school, I've always planned to stick around here and help Grandpa with the farm. He's got a pretty good business with raising and selling horses, and I've always wanted to help him. I like tinkering with cars too, so who knows, maybe I'll do something with that. But if you're going away to school then I might have to reconsider. I don't think I could stand it if you were too far away from me."

"Me too, Liam."

"I'm not worried. We're meant to be together. Something as trivial as college can't separate us. Now, let's move on with the questions. I'm not done interrogating you.

Who's your favorite group?"

"That's a hard one. I don't know if I can narrow it down to just one."

"Okay, give me your top three."

"I don't even think I can narrow it down to three," I said laughing. "I'll give you my top six: Guns N Roses, Def Leppard, Bon Jovi, Shinedown, Avenged Sevenfold, Three Days Grace, and 311."

"That's seven," Liam said laughing.

"Oh yeah, I guess so. I like so many. It's hard to narrow them down."

"Wow, I'm dating a hard rock chick."

"Through and through. What about you?"

"Well, I like rock, but if I'm going to say a favorite it would be George Strait."

"George Strait? He's country!"

"Yes he is. I'm all country, baby."

"I like country boys."

"I hope you like just one country boy."

"Oh, and who would that be?"

Liam closed in on me, pinning me to the seat. My heart still skipped a beat whenever he was this close to me. "Me, babe."

"Yeah, you'd be the one," I said as I melted into his arms.

Chapter Ten
Racing Rumors

      Our conversation at Brush Creek Road had been a revelation for us. We were closer than ever and felt totally at ease with each other on everything. Of course, the physical attraction between us was amazing. We had this insatiable desire for one another, but even with that we knew that our relationship was so much more than the physical attraction between us. What we had ran deep and in time we would find out just how deep. We were connected, and in that connection it allowed us to be in synch with our bodies and our minds as well.

      Liam, of course, continued to spoil me, showering me with flowers. In fact, the very next day after playing twenty questions he sent me a dozen roses. This time they were a pale lavender, the closest color to blue I had ever seen on a rose. The card simply read "If I had known your favorite color was blue I would have adorned your house with these a long time ago. Love you always, Liam." He was a hopeless romantic, and I couldn't have been happier. We had an innate understanding of each other's feelings. I don't know if it's possible to find your soul mate so early in life, but in the short time Liam and I had been together it had made me consider that we had. Even though I hadn't professed my love for him, it was there, inside of me and growing stronger every day.

Since football and marching band season was over, Liam and I had more time to spend together. When he wasn't with me I knew exactly where I could find him, with his buddies: Tony and Parker and their trucks. His second favorite thing besides me was his black Ford F-150. Liam and his friends could literally spend hours working and playing with their over-sized four-wheeled toys. It was a true obsession that I was only now learning more about since football season was over. It didn't matter if the trucks already looked like showcase models, they could always find something that needed to be replaced, repaired or rebuffed. It made the ordinary man's car look downright dowdy next to theirs. And when they weren't working on them they were driving them and not just around town. These trucks were designed for speed, and that's exactly what Liam and most of the male population between the ages of sixteen and twenty-one did in Spencer: they raced.

Beginning in December, every Saturday night there was a drag race going on somewhere on one of the back roads. These were highly secretive and well-guarded races. Usually, a couple of days before the race, word would spread to where and what time the race would take place. It was nearly always done late at night, and the venue changed weekly. This was to keep the police at bay and to make the races more interesting. Money was a huge factor for the boys to race as well. The winner took half of the purse on whatever bets were made, but more importantly, it was the draw, the attraction that made it worthwhile, not to mention the competitive tension between the boys.

These races drew participants from surrounding counties. The same boys who played against each other in football competed against each other off the field and on the road. If we had beaten them in football, this was their chance to get even and believe me, there were a lot of boys still holding onto some past hostility. I had never been witness to these races, but I had heard about them. Not until Liam entered my life did I realize that there was truth behind the rumors. The police would try to patrol the streets and the back roads hoping to catch these races in the act, but they never were fortunate enough to come across them. The boys were always one step ahead of them, using a walkie-talkie system to track and keep an eye out for police or potential traffic. The last thing anyone wanted or needed was to have a car drive up on them during the middle of a race. Not only would that spoil the race, but more importantly, it could easily cause a serious accident.

The races were meant to determine who was the fastest, sometimes reaching speeds of eighty miles per hour within seconds. Having an outside car come from out of nowhere could cause devastating consequences. Liam knew I didn't agree with his racing, but it was a part of him and something he did long before he knew me. He could hardly contain himself on the days that there was a race, and even though it bothered me that he raced, I never said anything to him. Instead, I would put on a brave smile and lend him my support. But accidents do happen, and that's what worried me the most. There was no way that these boys could race at such high rates of speed every weekend without disaster finally occurring. A few years back a couple of boys did get hurt and pretty badly when one of their trucks careened into the other causing both of them to spin out of control. The local paper said that the one boy had fallen asleep at the wheel, but everyone knew better. This was part of the secret, the pact. If the boys wanted to continue to race, all involved guarded the races and their outcomes with their lives. For all the danger involved, it was some of the best damn fun this town had to offer them.

Chapter Eleven
The Accident

    On the last day of school before Christmas break, everyone was anxious to leave Spencer High for a while. It had been a long semester, and it seemed everybody's brains had turned to mush over the past couple of weeks cramming for their exams. Exams had been brutal, and Mrs. Harris' Social Studies exam had been the worst of them all. Her four-page paper had one hundred questions covering everything from the war of 1812 to John F. Kennedy's assassination. It was almost too much for the mind to absorb. Kendra and I had spent most of our time studying together since we had all but two of our classes together. I helped Liam in English, helping him to ace his *Moby Dick* paper that Mrs. White had so graciously given him more time to write. Thank goodness Mrs. White's exams were always take home, or I think Liam would have never passed. I had often wondered how he had gotten by before me. But then again, he is Liam Larson, I'm sure he had plenty of wannabe girlfriends who were always too happy and eager to help him out in all dilemmas such as these though. I didn't see much of the other girls, all of them caught up in their own lives. Frannie and Steve were still an item and so was Missy and Eric Manns.

Shauna was single and loving it, enjoying the freedom to date whomever she pleased, whenever she pleased. Brenda had decided that having a boyfriend took too much of her time, so after homecoming she and Drew both agreed that they were better off as friends. With Christmas break finally upon us, I was hoping that all of us could finally get together like we had discussed at the homecoming dance. The digital clock, when the final school bell rang, read exactly 2:36pm; releasing all of its prisoners for their two-week break. Liam was waiting for me as usual by the band door. He had become a permanent fixture there after school since October.

"Hey there, beautiful," he said as he grabbed me and smothered me with a wet and delicious kiss.

"Mmmm, not a bad way to start the break," I said as I held onto him.

"The only way to start the break if you want my opinion." Liam seemed to be in a particularly good mood, smiling from ear to ear.

"What's up with you?"

"Oh nothing, just in the Christmas spirit and happy to see my girl, that's all."

"You seem like you're up to something. Anything you want to tell me?"

"No. Nothing I can think of. Are you hungry? Do you want to grab a bite to eat?"

It was Friday, and there were only four days until Christmas. I had promised Mom that I would come straight home from school to help her bake, but I knew she wouldn't mind if I showed up a little late, plus Friday meant pizza at Lougini's.

"Sure, what did you have in mind?"

"We could go to Lougini's, or to my house."

"Your house? You have something to eat there?"

"I might."

"Okay, your house it is."

"Great, I was hoping that would be your answer."

I had a feeling that his house was the only answer that he was willing to accept. He grabbed my hand in his and took my books in his other as he led me down to his truck. We arrived at his house just in time to see Grandpa Mack leaving.

"Hi, you two."

"Hi, Grandpa, where are you off too?"

"I've got to run over to the next county. I'm out of feed for the horses, and the feed store in town is out of what I need. I won't be gone long. You guys make yourself at home." He gave Liam a wink as he drove off, a wink that I had seen Liam give me a hundred times.

"What was that?" I asked curiously to Liam.

"What?"

"That wink your grandpa gave you, it looked very suspicious."

"You are reading way too much into stuff. It was nothing. He was just saying goodbye."

"Goodbye? Okay, if you say so, but I think you two are up to something."

"You're crazy, girl."

Liam squeezed my hand as he pulled the truck to the front of the house. I was in awe at the sight before me. The porch railing was covered in pine roping with red and silver bows, and the front door had a huge Christmas wreath with tiny lights encircling it.

"This is beautiful, did you do all this?"

"Yes, well, Grandpa and me. You know, Jen, this is for you. It's the first time since my grandma has been gone that Grandpa has wanted to decorate the house. He really cares for you. He knows how much you love Christmas. He wanted the house to look extra special, just for you."

"I don't know what to say, but wow, thank you. I love it! I can't wait to thank Grandpa, I just can't believe you guys would do all of this just for me." I couldn't help but smile.

I squeezed Liam's hand as he opened the front door for me and guided me into the living room. The mantle was adorned with the same pine roping, but instead of red and silver trim, there were blue and silver bows. On top of the mantle were four silver candles, two on each side. But the sight that took my breath away was in the far right corner of the room. Standing before me was a huge Christmas tree adorned with silver and blue ornaments. Twinkling white lights were entwined throughout the tree, and on top stood a silver angel holding two candles in her hands. Silver icicles hung from each branch creating a shimmering effect.

"Liam, your tree, it's gorgeous."

"It's your tree, Jenny. It's part of my Christmas to you."

I stared at him in disbelief. I couldn't believe anyone could care for someone as much as Liam cared for me. "Are you kidding?"

"Do you like the decorations on it? You said your favorite color was blue and that you loved silver."

"Oh my God, Liam. It's perfect, just perfect. And, the angel, she completes it. It's the prettiest tree I've ever seen."

"The angel represents you, you're my angel. You entered my life and saved me from being alone." It was a corny statement, but I believed him.

"I don't deserve you. This is the nicest thing anyone has ever done for me."

"It's only part of what I want to give you. I'd give you the world if I could." He wrapped me in his warm and strong embrace. I felt so secure and safe when I was with him, and more importantly, I never had felt more loved.

"You're going to put my gift for you to shame," I said.

"You've already given me my gift: you."

"You're too smooth with your words."

"No, just honest, Jen, if I never received another gift in my life, my world would be complete because I have you." We both became silent, knowing the moment was turning serious. Liam stared at me with so much love in his eyes. I wanted to tell him how I was feeling when he told me to sit down on the sofa.

"I'll be right back. Close your eyes and no peeking."

"What are you up to?" He slowly backed away, facing me the entire time as he walked out of the living room. "What are you doing, Liam?" I asked impatiently.

"Just wait babe. Don't peek. I'm watching you." I giggled at his playful manner.

A few minutes went by, and I kept my hands over my eyes, not swaying to the temptation to peek through the slits of my fingers. I heard Liam come back into the room. He was making a lot of noise. The sound of clinking glasses and liquid being poured was apparent. Finally, after minutes of me being in complete suspense, Liam allowed me to remove my hands from my eyes. He was sitting next to me. He had covered the coffee table with a red and white checkered table cloth, a single lavender rose was perched in a crystal vase. There were two crystal goblets filled with what looked like sparkling grape juice in them, and on a platter was a huge Lougini's pizza with everything on it.

"Are you hungry?"

"Oh my, God, I can't believe you! This is so sweet. You are by far, hands down, the most thoughtful boyfriend in the world."

"I aim for perfection, babe," he said in a sweet but still narcissistic manner.

"This looks great. When did you do this? I saw you at school today. I know you didn't leave the school, and I know you didn't have time to go to Lougini's?"

"You can thank Grandpa. I asked him to help me set this up."

"Aha, the wink, I knew you two were up to something."

"You're too good babe, very observant."

"I don't miss a trick."

"Well, are you hungry or not?"

"I'm starving."

Liam handed me a glass of the sparkling grape juice, and we proceeded to eat the entire pizza. After an hour of pure gluttony, I knew it was time for me to go home, even though in my heart I could have stayed there forever. It was close to six o'clock, and Mom would be needing my help.

"This was the perfect afternoon, but I really need to get home, I'm sure Mom is waiting for me."

"Okay," Liam reluctantly replied. "Come on, let me get you home before I change my mind and decide to kidnap you and keep you here for myself."

I chuckled at the thought. "Sounds like a plan, but I think my parents would come after me. Am I going to see you this weekend?"

"I don't know. I'll call you. I have to help Grandpa bring back some horses he bought from another farmer. It's going to take most of the day tomorrow, and I'm not sure where we're picking them up at."

"Okay, I understand, no problem."

We walked out of the room, turning off the lights except for those on the Christmas tree. The reflection that they gave off, lit up the entire corner of the room, creating the effect of a starry night on the walls and ceiling. It was mesmerizing, bringing a true calm over me.

"Liam, you don't have to give me another thing for Christmas. Everything I need or want is in this room." Liam said nothing, only holding me close to him in his ever so protective embrace.

We eventually walked out of the room hand in hand. The drive to my house was quiet. Liam had Brooks and Dunn playing on the radio. Life was good. By the time Liam pulled in my driveway, it was past six-thirty, and I could see Mom working diligently through the kitchen window. I kissed Liam goodbye and walked into the house to find Mom had transformed the kitchen into a full-fledged bakery. There were pies, candies and cakes stacked everywhere.

"Hi, hon, did you and Liam have a nice time?" Mom was covered from head to toe in white flour.

"Yeah, Mom, it was nice."

"I bet you're glad school is done for a couple of weeks," Dad said as he came into the kitchen.

"Definitely."

"Well, hon, I'm almost done with the filling for the pumpkin pies. Why don't you help me with them, and then we'll start on the apple cakes. I'll need you to start peeling those apples over there."

I looked at the kitchen sink. There had to be all the apples left in Spencer in our kitchen. There were at least eight bags full of Granny Smiths, McIntosh and Golden Delicious. "Mom, how many cakes are you making? There's enough here to feed an army!"

"Well, I'm really not for sure. I'm going to give some to the church, and I wanted to make some extra for friends and family."

I reluctantly rolled my sleeves up and grabbed a paring knife in the utensil drawer, wishing I had taken Liam up on his offer to kidnap me. Mom and I worked through most of the night, and by morning I woke up in bed with my hands stiff and sore. I stretched in bed, pulling my blankets close to my face. I looked out my window to find a fresh blanket of snow on the ground. The thought of staying in bed all day had crossed my mind. My warm blanket and comforter seemed much more inviting than the idea of rising out of bed. I thought about Liam and his grandpa and how cold it would be for them to herd the horses and bring them back on such a snowy day. I made a mental note to be sure and thank Grandpa Mack when Liam called me later today. I closed my eyes, imagining my beautiful Christmas tree at Liam's house with its blue and silver ornaments hanging from it, wishing I was there with Liam instead of here in my room by myself. I could see Liam and I sitting on the floor next to the tree, a warm fire in the fireplace, and Liam's arms wrapped around me, no one else in the world but us. I fell back to sleep with those beautiful thoughts going through my head.

"Jenny, wake up. Honey wake up!"

"Huh, what is it Mom?" I looked at my clock. It was past eleven in the morning. "Mom, what is it?" I asked groggily as I rubbed my eyes.

"Jenny, it's Liam. There's been an accident."

"Mom, what?!! What do you mean an accident? What's wrong?"

"I don't know, but you better get up. Parker Duncan is downstairs waiting to see you."

Parker? I thought to myself, why would he be here? Something must be seriously wrong if Parker is here at my house. I bolted out of bed, grabbed my robe, and ran down the stairs as fast as I could. I found Parker sitting in our living room waiting for me, his face subdued and timid.

"Parker, what's going on, what's wrong? What's happened to Liam?" I asked frantically.

"Jenny, I'm sorry, but Liam and his grandpa were in an accident this morning."

"What? They were going to go pick up the horses today. What happened?"

"I'm not sure. Grandpa Mack was driving and somehow lost control of the truck. The roads were really slippery, and they think he may've passed out behind the wheel. The truck swerved out of control and down an embankment."

"Oh my God, are they okay? I have to see them!"

"Calm down, Jenny," Mom said, trying to be the voice of reason.

"No, Mom, I can't. You don't understand!" I felt my world crumbling around me, my knees buckling beneath me. Yesterday had been so perfect. How could this be happening today?

"Parker, where did they take them?" Mom asked.

"They're at the hospital."

"How did you know what happened?"

"Liam called me last night asking me to go with them. He said they could use an extra hand with the horses. I said I could, but I decided to drive separately. I was following them when it happened. I saw the whole thing."

I began heading for the door, ready to leave at that very instant.

"Jenny, where are you going? You're not even dressed," Mom said looking at me in my pajamas.

"Parker, can you wait? I'll only be a second."

I ran upstairs, throwing on whatever I could put my hands on first, not caring if it matched. I frantically pulled my hair back into a disshelved ponytail and ran back downstairs.

"Okay, let's go. I'm ready." I was on the verge of crying. My body shook uncontrollably. Mom and Dad both tried to reassure me as they met me at the bottom of the steps.

"Listen, hon, you've got to pull yourself together. You're not going to be any good to Liam if he sees you like this."

Parker was nodding in agreement. "Yeah, Jen, anyway that's why I'm here. Liam asked me to come get you. He wants to see you."

"Mom, Dad, do you mind if Parker takes me to the hospital instead of you guys?"

"Sure, honey, but we want you to call us as soon as you know anything, okay?"

"I will," I said as I grabbed my purse and walked out the door with Parker. Parker's lime-green pick-up truck was parked at an angle in our driveway as though he had hastily pulled into it. He opened the door for me. The step up into his cab wasn't half as high as Liam's. "Is he okay, Parker? You have to tell me the truth."

"Jenny, I don't know. They took Liam and Grandpa Mack away before I had a chance to find out anything. I only saw Liam for a minute, and he asked me to get you. I wish I had more to tell you, but I don't know anymore. The doctor hadn't even seen them when I left for your house."

The drive to the hospital was the longest in my life. All I could think about was Liam and his grandpa at the bottom of some embankment. My worst thoughts repeating through my mind.

"Parker, you would tell me? I mean, you're not keeping something from me just to protect me, are you?" I was scared to hear his answer.

"Yes, Jenny. I promise. I'm telling you all I know. I will tell you Liam's banged up pretty bad, but he was awake the whole time, never losing consciousness. He actually got out on his own and pulled Grandpa from the truck."

"Oh my God, I don't know what I'll do if something happens to either one of them."

"Don't worry, they're in good hands right now. Everything's going to be fine. Jenny?"

"Yes?"

"I don't know if it's my place to say anything to you or not, and you can stop me if you think I'm speaking out of line, but I think you should know that the whole time all he talked about was you. He didn't want you to worry. He was so concerned about how you were going to take the news. He loves and cares for you more than anything. I know it's true. I've known Liam since we were in second grade. There's never been anybody in his life that he has cared for more than you. I know he loves you. I can promise you, it's coming from his heart. I've known him too long, and I've seen him when he's with you and when he's not with you. I know that this is the real thing for him. I'm sure you know this already, but I thought you should hear it from someone else besides him. You really are his world. You're the best thing that's ever happened to him."

"Thank you, Parker. That means so much to me."

"You're welcome."

I already knew. I think I knew from day one. I was just determined to make it hard for Liam to prove it. The way Liam made a point to see me, to talk to me, and then how he opened up to me on that fateful day in study hall. It made sense. His feelings for me were strong even then. I was just too stupid and naïve to realize it. We finally made it to the hospital. My heart was pounding in my chest as I grabbed Parker's arm.

"Parker, I don't think I can go in. I'm scared."

"It's alright. Liam needs to see you." Parker gave me a reassuring squeeze on my arm. "Now come on. I'm right beside you."

I never liked the idea of hospitals, not that anyone does. I think it was the stark white walls and the smell of disinfectant that bothered me. Everything was too clean, and it didn't help to see nurses and doctors walking around with their clipboards, analyzing their patients with grim looks on their faces. We walked in to find empty cots and wheelchairs in one corner while nurses and doctors were walking from room to room. I looked around to see if Liam or his grandpa were visible. I didn't see them anywhere. The only sight I saw was a little boy being treated for what looked like a broken arm, and an elderly lady who was sitting in a wheelchair with an IV hooked up to her arm. The little boy was crying out in pain and asking for his mommy. The sound of his voice unsettled me. Parker and I looked around to see if there was a nurse or doctor who could help us.

"Excuse me," Parker said as we found a nurse sitting at the nurse's station. "We're looking for Mack and Liam Larson. They were brought here earlier this morning by ambulance after being in a car accident."

The nurse looked down at her board, musing over the writing in front of her. "Oh, here it is. They're both still being treated here in the emergency room. If you take a seat, someone will be right with you."

"Are they okay?" I asked, trying to seem calm.

"Miss, I'm sorry. I don't know their condition, but if you take a seat someone will be right over who can help you."

That wasn't the answer I wanted to hear. I looked down the hallway, and I knew that Liam and his grandpa were behind one of those closed doors. I had to find them myself.

"Where are you going, Jenny?" Parker asked, as I made my way down the hallway.

"I can't wait Parker. I need to see Liam now."

He grabbed my arm. "Jenny, wait, you're not going to do anybody any good if you get us kicked out of here. Now let's just take a seat. The nurse said she was going to get someone to come talk to us."

He motioned to a seat. I didn't want to sit down, but I reluctantly did. That lasted for a few minutes. I was too nervous to sit. I got back up and paced back and forth. My eyes zoned in on the closed doors down the hallway. The palms of my hands were cold and sweaty, and I had a knot in my stomach the size of Texas. I hated not knowing what was going on. I watched as a doctor walked in one of the closed doors. *Was that Liam's room?* I thought to myself. *Another person, maybe another doctor or intern, I couldn't tell, ran into the room holding a syringe in their hand. What was going on? Why wasn't someone coming to talk to us yet?*

"Parker, I can't stand not knowing. I have to find out what's going on."

"Hold on. Let me go see if I can get some more information." He walked back to the nurse's station, only to return with a solemn look on his face. "We have to wait, Jenny. They're short on help today, so she's doing the best that she can."

I lowered my head into my hands. I was nauseated and dizzy. Tears were finally streaming down my face. I couldn't hold them back any longer. Parker took me in his arms held me and let me cry as hard as I needed to.

"Jenny, Jenny King? Is that you?"

I looked up to see Dr. Garrett staring down at me. " Dr. Garrett, you don't know how happy I am to see you. Liam and his grandpa are here. They were in a car accident."

"Yes, Jenny, I know. I'm the one treating both of them."

"Are they okay? What's wrong with them?"

"Liam has suffered a pretty severe concussion. He has some contusions on his body, and he required some stitches on his right shoulder. He's going to be fine, but he's going to be sore for a few days. I want to keep him overnight for observation, but I think he'll be ready to go home tomorrow."

"What about his grandpa?"

"I'm afraid Mr. Larson suffered a mild heart attack. We think that's what caused the accident. We want to keep him a little longer to run some tests."

"Oh my, God," I said as I covered my mouth. "Is he going to be okay?" I felt as if the floor was going to swallow me alive. My knees were failing me.

Dr. Garrett put his comforting hand on my shoulder. "I think so. He's going to have to take it easy for a while, and like I said, we want to keep him here for a while for precautionary reasons."

"Can we see them?"

"Sure, but not too long. They've been through a lot, and we want to get them to their rooms, so they can get some rest. You must mean a lot to Liam," Dr. Garrett said as he walked us down the hallway.

"Excuse me?"

"The whole time I was treating him, all he talked about was you and how he didn't want you to worry about him. He wanted to make sure you would be alright."

"If I would be alright? Liam is the one hurt."

"Yes, I know, but he didn't want you to be upset over what had happened. He's been very agitated with us for not bringing you to him sooner."

"See, I told you, Jenny," Parker said.

I just looked at him, smiling weakly. I was still too upset to feel anything but worry.

"There's one more thing you should know."

"What's that?"

"Liam saved his grandpa's life. If he hadn't pulled him out of the truck, his grandpa probably would have drowned."

"What do you mean? I thought the truck just went over an embankment." I looked straight at Parker.

"It did," Parker said, "but the truck landed upside down in a swollen creek bed."

I grabbed my stomach, trying to hold onto something to keep from falling down.

"Are you okay, Jenny?" Dr. Garrett asked.

"Yes. Just give me a second."

I took a deep breath and motioned to Dr. Garrett and Parker that I was ready. We walked down the hallway. Dr. Garrett opened the door to reveal a bright room filled with monitors and IV's and a single bed with a nurse standing next to it. She was giving Liam a shot in his forearm. I walked slowly to his bed, approaching his side hesitantly as I mentally prepared myself to see what the accident had done to him. I heard the constant beeping of the heart monitor behind his bed. His right arm was hooked to an IV. The nurse gave me a reassuring smile and a gesture to come closer.

"Looks like the girl you were telling me about is finally here."

Liam opened his eyes and met mine instantly. "Hi there, gorgeous. I thought you'd never get here." His voice was groggy and weak.

"Liam, I'm so sorry I didn't get here sooner. How are you feeling?"

"Much better, now that you are here." I tried to fight back the tears, but it was useless. They were cascading down my face like a waterfall.

"Hey, don't cry, babe. I'm going to be just fine, just a few bumps and bruises, that's all." His voice seemed so drained and exhausted.

"You're impossible." I buried my head into his good shoulder as he softly let out a groan. "I'm sorry, did I hurt you?"

"No babe. You're fine. It feels nice having you next to me. I've missed you."

"It's only been a day, Liam."

"Yeah, but a very bad day, babe." He took my hand and brought it up to his lips and kissed it.

"Hey, Parker," Liam said as he looked over to see his friend at the foot of the bed.

"I told you I would bring her to you."

"Thanks, bud, I owe you one."

"Don't mention it. You doing okay?"

"I'm okay. My head is killing me though. I have the worst headache."

"The doctor said you suffered a concussion."

"Well, that explains it then," he said as he covered his head with both hands.

"Do you know anything about your grandpa?" I asked.

"Not much. I've been trying to find out, but they won't tell me anything. They just keep telling me not to worry." The look on my face must have said it all. "You know something, don't you?"

"Grandpa suffered a heart attack. That's why he passed out when he was driving."

"Is he okay?"

I looked at the nurse.

"Don't you worry. It was a mild heart attack. I'll have the doctor come in and talk to you. He can fill you in on all the details concerning your grandpa."

"I'm sorry, babe. Dr. Garrett told me outside before I saw you. I thought you might already know," I said.

Liam was always the strong one around his friends. The only time he ever showed his emotions was around me. But here in front of Parker, Liam couldn't hold back any longer. He was upset, and it didn't matter who saw him.

"Baby, I'm sorry. Dr. Garrett said it was a mild heart attack, and he should be okay. They want to keep him for observation for a couple of days, but they think he's going to be fine."

Liam looked at me in disbelief. "What do you mean a mild heart attack? For Christ's sake, Jenny, don't you think that's enough?"

I pulled myself away from Liam. "I'm sorry. I didn't mean it like that. Honestly, I was just trying…"

Before I could finish, Parker came over to my side. "Hey, Jenny, let's go. Liam, I'm going to take Jen outside and see if we can talk to Dr. Garrett. You get some rest. We'll be back in a little bit." I turned from Liam's side to walk away when he spoke.

"Jenny, please come back. I'm sorry, I didn't mean to snap at you like that."

In the couple of months that I had known Liam, I had never seen him act like that. I tried to shrug it off, tried to not take it personally, rationalized that it was because of the trauma he had been through and that he wasn't thinking clearly. But deep inside, it really bothered me.

I walked back to his side. "Liam, it's okay. Parker's right. You need some rest, and I want to go talk to Dr. Garrett."

He stopped me, bringing my face to meet his. "Here," he said as he softly kissed me on my lips. "That's all the medicine I need, babe. Forgive me?"

I smiled at him. "There's nothing to forgive. We'll be right outside, okay?"

"Just don't go too far."

I walked outside trying to hold back the tears that needed to come out again.

"Are you okay, Jen?" Parker asked.

"Yeah, thanks."

"You know he didn't mean to act like that towards you. I know Liam. He's just upset about his grandpa."

"I know that. I'm going to go call my parents. Can you see if you can find out anything more on Liam's grandpa."

"Sure. I'll meet you back here."

I went to the volunteer station. One of Mom's friends, Flossie West, was working at the desk.

"Hi Mrs. West."

"Hello, Jenny. What brings you to the hospital?"

"My boyfriend and his grandpa were in a car accident this morning."

"Oh dear. I'm so sorry to hear that. Are they going to be alright?"

"Yeah, I think so. Dr. Garrett is taking care of them."

"Well, if Dr. Garrett is taking care of them, they're in the best of hands. Don't you worry, honey."

"Thanks, Mrs. West. That's good to know. I was wondering if you knew where I could make a phone call. I forgot my cell, and my parents are waiting to hear from me."

"Oh, sure. You can use the phone over there. Just dial nine to get an outside line." She directed me to a phone located across from her desk.

"Thanks, Mrs. West."

"Sure thing, honey. I'll keep your boyfriend and his grandpa in my prayers. Tell your mom hi for me too."

"Will do and thank you again."

I called Mom's cell, and the phone rang and rang. "Come on pick up." Right when I was ready to hang up, Mom answered the phone.

"Hello."

"Hi, Mom, it's me."

"Jenny, we've been waiting here on pins and needles. How are Liam and his grandpa?"

"They're doing alright, I guess. Liam has a concussion. They want to keep him overnight, but they think he'll be released tomorrow."

"Oh, honey, I'm sorry, but that's much better news than we were expecting to hear."

"Yeah, I guess."

"How is his grandpa?"

"He suffered a heart attack. That's why he blacked out at the wheel."

"Oh dear. Is he okay?"

"I think so. I haven't seen him yet. Mom?"

"Yes, Jenny?"

"Liam saved his grandpa's life. Apparently the truck flipped over an embankment and into a creek bed. Liam pulled his grandpa out. Dr. Garrett said if he hadn't had done that, Grandpa most likely would have drowned."

"How's Liam handling that?"

"I don't know. I guess okay. He still seems pretty shook up though. He hasn't got to see his grandpa yet, and it's really getting to him."

"Well, of course it would. How are you doing?"

"I'm fine."

"Do you want us to come to the hospital?"

"No, really, I'm fine, and besides, they're going to take them to their rooms soon. I know Dr. Garrett wants them to get some rest, so I don't think they're going to be able to have visitors for a while. I'm going to stay here if that's okay. I'll call you later."

"Okay, Jenny. I love you."

"I love you guys too."

"Tell Liam we're thinking about them."

"I will. Bye."

"Bye, hon."

I hung up and let loose the tears again that I held back from Mom. I felt like I was going into total meltdown.

"Are you okay?" Parker came up from behind me.

"Yeah, sorry, just me being a total basket case, that's all."

He gave me a half-hearted laugh. "I think you're allowed to be upset."

"Did you see Dr. Garrett?"

"Yeah, they just took both of them upstairs to their rooms."

"What did he say?"

"Liam's going to be able to go home tomorrow, and his grandpa can go home in two or three days. So far, his tests have come back fine. It was just as Dr. Garrett thought: a mild heart attack. They think they might have to put in a stint, but they didn't seem to find any more reason for concern."

"That is so good to hear." I gave him a big-hearted hug. "Where are they?"

"Liam is in room 218, and his grandpa is in intensive care in room 211, down the hall from Liam."

Room 211 and 218, "Eleven," I thought to myself. How strange, eleven again.

"Jenny, what's wrong? Jenny? Earth to Jenny."

"What?"

"You were spacing out on me. Are you alright?"

"Oh, sorry. I was just thinking about something. It's nothing though. Come on, let's go see Liam."

We took the elevator to the second floor. Room 211 was down the hall to the right, and room 218 was in the other direction.

"Don't you think we should see about Liam's grandpa in case he asks us?"

"Absolutely. Good thinking," Parker said as we walked over to the nurse's station.

"May I help you?" the nurse asked, sounding as if she had been bothered one time too many today.

"Yes, we were hoping to inquire about how Mack Larson was doing. I believe he's in intensive care." The nurse sighed heavily as she looked down at her chart.

"Oh yes. He was just put in his room. It looks like he's resting comfortably. Are you relatives of Mr. Larson?"

"Well, not technically. I'm dating his grandson who is also here. They were in a car accident this morning. It's just the two of them. There's no other family members. I guess I would be the next closest relative."

"Only family members are permitted to see Mr. Larson."

"I'm Parker Duncan. I'm a close friend of the family. I'm sure if you spoke with Dr. Garrett he would let us see him."

The nurse looked at us with trepidation. "Wait here. I'll be right back." She walked to the other side of her station as she paged Dr. Garrett.

"Don't worry. Dr. Garrett will let us see him."

"I hope so." I looked at the clock; it was 1:11 in the afternoon. That damn number again. I was beginning to get freaked out about it and knew this wasn't the time for it. I was obviously tired and allowing my head to mess with me.

"Hello, Jenny, Parker."

"Hi, Dr. Garrett."

"What can I do for both of you? Have you had a chance to see Liam's grandpa?"

"No, the nurse said only family members could, so we were hoping you could tell her that it would be okay for us to see him."

"Sure, I'll speak to the nurse right now, but listen, he's really tired, I want him to get some rest. Only stay for a few minutes."

Parker and I walked down the hallway, counting the room numbers as we passed them; 209; 210; then finally 211. We quietly opened the door, being careful to not to disturb Grandpa Mack in case he was sleeping. His bed was on the far wall next to the window. From my view, I could clearly see Liam in his face. They both had the same rugged exterior and jaw line, and now more than ever, I could see the family resemblance between the two of them. Grandpa Mack had the same sparkling blue eyes as Liam too. His face was older of course, but there was no denying the Larson lineage. I walked to his side.

"Hello, Jenny; Hello Parker. How nice of you both to come see me." He gave a beautiful but weak smile. The same smile as Liam's.

"Grandpa, I'm so sorry this happened. How do you feel?" I grabbed his left hand and firmly held it in mine.

"Oh, I'm fine. They said I'll be as fit as a fiddle in a few days."

"Grandpa, you know you suffered a heart attack don't you?"

"I know, dear. I also know if it wasn't for Liam I wouldn't be here right now. I heard he saved my life. Parker you were there; is that right?"

"Yes sir, Liam pulled you out of the truck."

"I should never have been behind the wheel. I shudder to think of what might have happened."

"But, Grandpa, everything is going to be fine now," I said.

"No, you don't understand Jenny. I mean I shudder to think what might have happened to Liam. I could have killed him. I'd never forgive myself if something were to happen to that boy." Grandpa's voice quivered as he spoke.

"Grandpa, you can't think like that. Just be thankful that you're both going to be okay. That's what's important, not the what if's and maybe's."

"I don't know how Liam found you, but I'm sure glad he did. You're a precious thing, honey, not only to my grandson but to me too. I can't begin to tell you the change you've made in my boy. He loves you so much, and so do I."

"Oh, Grandpa, thank you." The tears were back. At this rate, I should be tearless by day's end.

"And, Parker, I owe you a huge thank you too. I heard you were right there, helping us after the accident. You were the one who got the ambulance to us so quickly. Thank you, son."

"Don't mention it sir. I'm just glad I was there."

"Jenny, have you seen Liam?"

"Yes, Grandpa, but only for a minute. He was still pretty out of it when I was with him, but he's okay. He suffered a mild concussion and needed some stitches."

"A concussion?"

"Yeah, but it's not bad. Dr. Garrett said he would probably be able to go home tomorrow. They just wanted to keep him overnight for observation. It's standard procedure, nothing to worry about."

"Will I be able to go home too?"

I hesitated. "No Dr. Garrett thinks you should stay here for a while, just a few more days."

"But, Liam will be by himself at the house. He'll have no one to watch out for him."

"He can stay at my house until you get home. It'll be great. He's there half the time anyway, and my parents would be more than happy to have him," Parker said.

"Are you sure, son?"

"Definitely, consider it a done deal."

"Thanks, Parker. That's very generous of you. Tell your parents thank you for me too. I'll rest a lot better knowing he's not at home by himself." Grandpa looked like he had been through hell and back.

"Well, we're going to let you get some rest. If you need anything, just ring for the nurse. I'm going to stay here at the hospital for a while. If you need me just let the nurse know, and she'll come find me. Okay?"

"Okay, dear. Thank you. Are you going to go see Liam now?"

"Yes, but just for a minute. I'm sure he is resting too."

"Tell him not to worry about me. Tell him I'm fine."

I looked down at this man. In my mind, he possessed the strength of ten men but lying here in bed, he looked weak and fragile. He was still trying to put on a good face though, even after suffering a heart attack, his primary concern was for his grandson. Grandpa Mack was an admirable man. I kissed his forehead lightly and gave his left hand another squeeze.

"I will, Grandpa. Get some rest." Parker and I walked out of the room as I breathed a sigh of relief.

"Jenny, if you're okay. I'm going to go home. I'll be back. I just want to get ready for Liam. You know, tell my parents and everything."

"Sure, Parker, I understand. Hey, thanks for being here. I know it meant a lot to Liam and to me. I can see why Liam considers you his best friend."

"You're welcome, and if you don't mind me saying, I can see why Liam is head over heels for you. He's been crazy about you for a long time. You guys are good for one another. It's as if you two were meant to be together, you know, like soul mates or something."

I gave Parker a hug. "Thanks."

"Will you need a ride later? I can come back to get you and take you home."

"No, my parents can come for me. Anyway, I'm not sure how long I'm going to be here."

"Alright then, tell Liam I'll talk to him later."

"Okay, bye."

"Bye."

I stood in the hallway as the elevator doors closed behind Parker. I turned towards room 218. I walked into Liam's room to find him fast asleep. All the lights were off and the curtains were drawn shut leaving the room in darkness. Thankfully, the bed next to him was empty. No noise or interruptions from another patient. I pulled a chair next to his bed as quietly as I could. I sat back and allowed my legs to rest on the end of Liam's bed. It had been a long day for everyone concerned. I looked at Liam. He was resting peacefully. Even after a car accident he was still as gorgeous as ever. I placed my hand on his, closed my eyes, and fell asleep next to him. The next thing I remember was Liam's hand rubbing mine. I opened my eyes to find him staring at me.

"You're awake. I'm sorry. I didn't mean to fall asleep on you."

"Don't be. I enjoy watching you sleep. Did you know your nose twitches when you're asleep?"

"What?" I grabbed my nose. Feeling slightly embarrassed as Liam softly laughed at me.

"It's actually quite cute. You're very entertaining to watch."

I rolled my eyes. "Liam, really, you should have been sleeping too, not watching me and my nose twitch."

"Come here," he said softly as he patted the side of his hospital bed.

"What?"

"I've been waiting for you to wake up."

I leaned down to him, and he grabbed my neck and pulled me closer to him as he gave me a long and much-needed kiss.

"I'm sorry for how I acted earlier. I was just so upset over what happened. I think I was more scared than I have been in a long time. I thought I might lose him, Jenny."

"Liam, it's okay. You don't need to apologize to me. I completely understand. I would feel the same way."

"You and Grandpa are the most important people in my life. I shouldn't have snapped at you the way I did."

I leaned in to kiss him again, but Liam stopped me. "What's wrong?" I asked

"Nothing." He leaned over to look at the vacant bed. "Are we alone?"

"Yes," I said. "Why?" Liam scooted over in his bed. "What are you doing?"

"Lay with me, Jenny. I want you next to me."

I stared at him in astonishment. "I think you got hit harder on the head than they thought. I can't do that. The nurse's station is right outside. We'll get caught, and I'll get in trouble."

"They'll never know. Please." He again patted his hand next to the spot he had cleared for me.

"Liam, you're crazy."

"Yeah, crazy for you."

I looked at the door, my head told me no, but my heart disagreed. I cautiously climbed in his bed, careful not to hurt him.

He had been pretty banged up from the accident, and his hospital gown clearly allowed me to see the multitude of bumps and bruises that the crash had inflicted on him.

"Liam look at your bruises. What if I hurt you?"

"Babe, there's no way you could hurt me. Besides, they've been giving me medicine for the pain," he said with a wink. "I can't feel a thing," he added giving me his devilish grin.

He moved closer to me. "There. Much better."

"If we get caught, I swear they're going to throw me out."

"Then I go too."

I pulled his face to me, making sure he didn't have to move much. I kissed him, playfully biting his lower lip.

"You know, I think this is the first time I ever made out in a hospital bed."

"My first time too. I guess you could say we're virgins at this."

"Very funny." Without thinking I slapped him on the chest.

"Ouch," he said, as he rolled over on his back.

"Oh, sorry. I wasn't thinking. Did that really hurt?"

"It's fine. It's just the stitches. There in a weird spot, and every time I lay on my back I can feel them. You know they had to give me eleven. I didn't think the cut was that deep."

I instantly sat up in bed. "Did you say eleven stitches?"

"Yeah, why?"

"Oh, no reason, I thought Dr. Garrett said you only needed a couple, that's all."

"No, the nurse said there was eleven."

I leaned my head back down on his good shoulder. My mind repeated the number eleven over and over again.

"Jenny, did you see Grandpa?"

"Yes, I did. He's doing fine. Dr. Garrett doesn't think there is any permanent damage to his heart. They still want to keep him for a couple of days, but they said he's going to be fine."

"Are you sure? You're not just saying that to make me feel better?"

I looked at him squarely in his crystal blue eyes. "He's going to be fine, Dr. Garrett told me so himself. I would never hide or keep anything from you, especially when it concerns Grandpa Mack. He just needs rest like you do. He did want me to tell you not to worry about him. He's more concerned about you than he is of himself."

"That's Grandpa for you."

"Oh, also, I think Dr. Garrett is going to release you tomorrow from the hospital and you're going to stay with Parker."

"What? Why?"

"Well, your grandpa would feel better if you weren't alone. Since he's going to be in here for a few more days, Parker offered, and your grandpa took him up on it."

"I'll be fine."

"I have to agree with your grandpa. You can't take care of yourself right now. Anyway, Parker wants to help, and it will only be for a couple of days, just until your grandpa comes home. You'll both be home by Christmas, I'm sure." Liam didn't say anything. "Please, Liam, do it for me. It's either that, or you can stay here till your grandpa is released and eat hospital food."

"Okay, I'll go, but I don't think it's necessary."

"Thanks, babe," I said as I hugged him, forgetting about his injuries.

"Ouch!" He screamed.

"Sorry, I keep forgetting."

"It's okay. I like the pain, especially if you're inducing it."

"Liam, you're crazy."

"Like I said, baby, crazy for you. Now come here. I need to feel some more pain," He said with another wink.

I stayed with Liam for the next hour. After he finally fell asleep, I quietly snuck out of his bed. I knew Mom and Dad were probably waiting to hear how Liam and his grandpa were, so I thought another phone call was in order. Besides, I was starving. I hadn't had anything to eat all day. I walked quietly out of Liam's room, tiptoeing to make as little noise as possible. I took the elevator downstairs to the floor where I had first used the courtesy phone and called home. There was no answer from Mom's cell, and the land line just rang. I finally realized that they must not be home and hung up.

I made my way to the hospital cafeteria. The cafeteria left much to be desired: turkey and rice soup with a roll and salad or tuna fish salad on a croissant. I opted for the tuna. I found a seat in the far corner of the cafeteria. I wanted to be as far away from people as possible. Aside from a couple of nurses, I was the only person in the room. For not eating anything today, I was having a hard time finding my appetite. I couldn't stop thinking about the accident and the irony of how eleven seemed to be playing a role in it. *What was it with this number and me lately? Am I deliberately trying to see it or were other circumstances bringing it to my attention?* I thought back at the similarities that seemed to plague me. There was the obvious, Liam's jersey number; my cell number; the Ferris wheel cart; my majorette number. And then the clock always ended in eleven, and of course Liam's parents death date. *This is too weird and creepy, what does this mean? Is it supposed to mean anything?*

I looked down at my sandwich. In the process of scrutinizing my thoughts, I had picked away at it until there was only a plate full of crumbs and half-eaten bites. I took my plate and threw the uneaten sandwich away and walked out of the cafeteria. Obviously it was easy to associate certain things in your life when you have seen them before, but this was just a little too coincidental. *Should I even tell Liam? Would he even care? Of course he would, right? Or would he think this was all just a bunch of nonsense and that I was letting my imagination run wild?* Nevertheless, now was definitely not the time to bother him with it. Until I had more concrete evidence, I wasn't going to worry about it either, if that was even possible. In the hallway, I saw a much needed and welcome site coming in my direction.

"Mom, Dad, when did you get here?"

"Hi, honey, just now."

I hugged them tightly, the way I had when I was a little girl and was afraid of the dark. I needed them right now more than ever. The whole day had been too nerve racking and unsettling for me to handle alone, especially after Parker had left.

"Thanks, I'm really glad you're here."

"How are Liam and his grandpa?" Dad asked earnestly.

"They're doing better. Liam is hopefully going to be released tomorrow, and they're going to keep Grandpa Mack for a couple more days. Dr. Garrett said he didn't see any permanent damage to his heart, but they just want to run a few more tests for precautionary reasons."

"Oh, I'm so glad to hear that. What a relief. Can we see them?" Mom asked.

"I think so. Dr. Garrett gave Parker and me permission to see them so I wouldn't see why you guys couldn't also. I'm sure it will be okay. I know they would both be happy to see you."

We took the elevator up to the second floor and went to the nurse's station. "Hi, I'm Liam Larson's girlfriend. Dr. Garrett gave me permission to visit with his grandpa. Would it be okay if my parents saw him too?" It was a new nurse, and she seemed much more relaxed and willing to interact with people.

"Yes, it says here that you and your family are allowed. Go right in, but please be quiet, and I must ask that you only stay for a few minutes."

"Sure, no problem."

We walked down to room 211 to find Grandpa Mack sitting in an upright position.

"Well, hello there. What a nice surprise," Grandpa Mack said cheerfully as he extended his hand. My mom and dad walked briskly to his side. My mom planted a soft kiss on the side of his cheek.

"How are you, Mack?"

"Oh, I'm fine, just fine. I really think I should be able to go home, but they won't let me."

"Grandpa, you have to take it easy. I think you deserve to have some down time, and this is the best place to receive it," I said.

He smiled at me. "You've got a great girl there, Mona and Henry. I don't know what Liam or I would do without her. She's been a blessing to us both."

"Thank you, Mack, she feels the same way about you and Liam." I felt embarrassed as I stood there listening to them talk about me as if I wasn't in the room.

"If it's okay with you guys, I'm going to let you visit with each other. I'm just going down to see how Liam is doing."

"Okay dear, we'll come get you when we're ready to leave, what room is Liam in? We want to see him too."

"218, down the hall from here."

"Bye, Grandpa. I'll talk to you later."

I made it to Liam's room only to find him too sitting upright in bed. "Hey, what are you doing? Shouldn't you be lying down? How's your head feeling?"

"Hey, beautiful. I was wondering when you were coming back."

I leaned down and kissed him and found myself being held by him.

"I missed you. Where did you go?"

"I thought you needed some sleep, so I went to the cafeteria to grab a bite to eat."

"Hey, did you hear? Dr. Garrett said I could be released tomorrow."

"That's great. I thought you would. Have you talked to Parker?"

"Yeah, he just called. He's going to be here tomorrow morning with his parents. I guess you were right. I'm going to their house."

"You knew that."

"Yeah, but I can take care of myself, and besides, I know this great girl who could be my nurse."

"Oh really? And who would she be?"

"I think you know her. She's quite beautiful. She's about your height, with this gorgeous head of red hair, and sparkling hazel eyes, and ..."

"Okay, okay, I get the picture," I said as I interrupted his description of me. "Liam, stop joking around. You know the best place for you is at Parker's house. Especially with your grandpa still here, and besides, you're still recovering yourself. You need to lay low for a while and just let your body heal."

"Yeah, babe, I know, but that's where you come into the picture. you know with your bedside manners."

"You're impossible."

"I know; that's what they keep telling me."

"But seriously, how are you feeling?"

"Not bad, my headache's a little better." Just then, Liam was interrupted by his door opening.

"Liam, hon, how are you?"

"Hi, Mr. and Mrs. King. I'm doing fine."

"Oh, honey, we were so worried about you and your grandpa. You're both very lucky; you know that don't you?"

"Yes, I do."

"Are you sure you're okay? Do you need anything?"

"No, Mrs. King. Really, I'm doing just fine. Besides, I get to go home tomorrow."

"That's wonderful news, but you're not going to your house by yourself, are you?"

"No, Mom, he's going to stay at Parker Duncan's for a couple of days."

"Oh, good. Well, you know if you need anything you can always call us too."

"Thanks, I'll keep that in mind." Liam looked right at me as he gave me a slight wink.

"Mom and Dad are going to take me home. I'll call you in the morning okay?"

"Okay, babe."

"Mom, Dad, I'll be ready to go in a minute." Hoping they would get the message that I would like to say goodbye to Liam without them watching.

"Oh, right, well, we're so glad you're okay. You be sure and call us if we can help in any way. That goes for your grandpa too."

"Alright, thanks for stopping in."

Mom gave Liam a hug, and Dad patted him on his sore shoulder. Liam held his breath and tried not to show the immediate pain my dad had inflicted upon him.

"I'll be right there," I said, as Mom and Dad exited the room.

"Are you okay?"

"I'm fine. He has a hearty pat though."

"At least your sense of humor didn't get hurt."

Liam's eyes were dark and blood-shot. He was succumbing to the effects of the accident. His movements were stiff, and the bruises were more evident than ever.

"I'm going to go. It's been a long day, and if you're going to be released tomorrow, you need to get a good night's sleep. Call me tomorrow, okay?"

"I will, but you don't have to go. I really would like you to stay and keep me company."

"Me too, but I don't think you would get much rest if I did."

"Jenny, I love you."

I smiled sweetly at him. I wanted to say the same to him, but my head wouldn't allow it, not yet, at least. It didn't matter though. I think Liam knew how I felt. I leaned over and gave him a long and tender kiss.

"Sweet dreams."

"Definitely," he said.

I left his room reluctantly. I didn't want to leave either.

The next morning, I awoke to the phone ringing.

"Hello?"

"Hey, beautiful, wake up!"

"Liam? What time is it?" I asked, my brain still on sleep mode.

"It's after eleven in the morning, sleepyhead. You've slept the whole morning away."

"Oh no! It can't be? I'm sorry, I must have been more tired than I thought. Let me get dressed and come see you before you leave the hospital."

"You can't."

"Why not?"

"I'm not in the hospital. I'm at Parker's."

"What? Already? You've already been released? I'm sorry. I was wanting to be there."

"It's okay, babe. You needed the sleep."

"Yeah, I guess," I said as I rubbed my eyes, earnestly trying to wake up. "How do you feel? What did the doctor say? Do you still have a headache?"

"What is this twenty questions?"

"No, I just want to know."

"I'm fine. The doctor gave me a clean bill of health. I just have to take it easy for a couple of days."

"Are you sure? You're not keeping anything from me are you?"

"Like I could if I wanted to."

"What about Grandpa?"

"Dr. Garrett said he's doing fine. All the tests came back good. He might be home as early as tomorrow. They even took him out of the intensive care unit and put him in a regular room."

"That is so good to hear. So that means you might only have to stay at Parker's tonight?"

"Yeah, although they've extended me an open invitation to stay as long as I'd like, but I want to go home. One night is good enough, and besides, Grandpa will need my help when he gets home. And it's almost Christmas."

Christmas! It had totally slipped my mind. With everything that had happened over the past couple of days, Christmas was the last thing on my mind. There was so much I wanted to do to make it extra-special for Liam and me. It was going to be our first Christmas together, and I wanted it to be memorable.

"Oh my, God! Christmas is two days away!"

"Yeah, I can hardly wait, babe. Are you ready?"

I had bought Liam's gifts weeks ago, but the thought of the actual holiday took me off guard.

"Yes, I am, believe it or not."

"Well good, because I am," Liam said confidently.

"What's that supposed to mean?"

"Oh, nothing. You'll just have to wait and see, now won't you?"

For being such a popular guy and always in the mix of things, Liam had a very private and reclusive side to him. This was the side of Liam I loved more than ever. He was himself, his guard was down, and I saw him for who he truly was: a down home country boy who loved to laugh, listen to country music, and make other people feel important and happy. Liam seemed to receive his greatest joy from watching the reactions of others when he had done something nice for them; whether it was filling his grandpa's truck with gas, helping the coaches with the freshman team, or decorating a Christmas tree for his girlfriend with her favorite colors. He made people feel special, and I understood why people wanted to be near him. It wasn't about Liam; it was how Liam made those who were near him feel. I knew that whatever he had planned for Christmas, he had put his heart and soul into it. I couldn't wait, and that's why I had to make sure that I made him feel just as special as he always made me feel. I had to make this Christmas the best.

"You know it's not nice to tease your girlfriend only two days before Christmas."

"It isn't?"

"No, it isn't, you may find all you get from me is a lump of coal."

"A lump of coal you say? Well, babe, if it comes from you it'll be the best damn lump of coal I have ever received."

"You're impossible."

"I know; that's what I keep hearing. Hey, I gotta go. I'll call you later."

"That's fine, I need to go anyway. Mom and I are going to Charleston to do some shopping. I'll talk to you later."

I got dressed and found Mom downstairs ready to go. Things were good again. Liam was out of the hospital, his grandpa was going home tomorrow, and our first Christmas was only two days away.

Chapter Twelve
Merry Christmas

Mom and I got home from Charleston late on Sunday evening. The stores were complete mayhem with everyone and their brother trying to find that one perfect gift that would complete their lists. In other cases, they were just starting. I had finished my shopping for Liam over a week ago. It was my family that I had nothing for yet. I was normally on top of things like this, but Liam hadn't been in the picture before. But all got taken care of when Mom and I made our last trip to the mall. I carried my bags upstairs to my room, plopping them and myself on my bed. It was late, and I was tired. The whole weekend wreaked havoc on my physical and mental state, causing me to finally cave in from exhaustion. My eyes were almost closed when Dad entered my room.

"Hi, Dad," I said sleepily.

"Hey honey. Sorry to disturb you."

"That's okay. I was just closing my eyes for a minute."

"Looks like you and Mom cleaned house."

I chuckled at his attempt at humor as I made room on my bed for him to sit down. "We gave it our best shot."

"I just wanted to let you know Liam called. He said his grandpa was being released tomorrow, and that he and his friend Parker were going to pick him up. They should be home by tomorrow afternoon for Christmas Eve."

"That's great!" I was so elated that I jumped into my dad's arms and gave him a huge hug.

"What's this for, honey?"

"Oh, I don't know. I'm just so happy. Everything seems like it's finally working out. You know, Liam is fine, his grandpa is going to be okay, and it's almost Christmas. I'm just extra happy and warm all over. You know that fuzzy feeling you get when everything seems right."

"You know, Jen, I need to tell you something. I've never told you this, but I think you should know that your mom and I think a lot of Liam. He's a very nice young man. We weren't too sure in the beginning. You know it's hard to read with these teenage boys. But Liam has proved to be a nice, polite young man, and we're very happy for the two of you."

"Oh, Dad, you don't know what that means to me, especially coming from you. Thanks."

"You're welcome. I just thought you should know our thoughts about him. Well, honey, I'll leave you alone. Mom needs my help downstairs. Are you hungry?"

"No, I'm fine. I think I'm just going to go to sleep."

"Alright, see you in the morning. Love you."

"Love you too, Dad."

I went into the bathroom and started washing my face when I heard the house phone ring.

"Jenny, it's for you."

"Okay, coming. I'll be right there, who is it?"

"It's Liam."

I scrambled to find a towel to dry my dripping face. Mom met me halfway up the stairs, the phone in her hand. I grabbed it from her, water still dripping from my chin.

"Hello."

"Hey, beautiful, how was your shopping trip?"

"It was nice. Mom and I had a lot of fun."

"Did your dad tell you my good news?"

"About your grandpa? Yeah, he just did. You know you guys are really lucky, don't you?"

"Yeah, people keep telling me that."

"So, when are you picking your grandpa up from the hospital?"

"Sometime in the morning. I'd like to have him home by noon."

"Great, I've got something for the both of you when you get home."

"What is it?"

"Oh, nothing. You'll just have to wait and see, now won't you?"

"You're sounding very sneaky, a lot like me."

"I've learned from the master."

"So, does that mean you're going to be at my house when we get there?"

"If you want."

"I want, I definitely want."

We laughed. It had only been a day since I had seen him, but I missed him more than anything. I was finding it harder and harder to be away from him.

"Well, I better go. It's late. I just needed to hear your voice."

"I can't wait to see you, Liam."

"Yeah, me too, and it's Christmas Eve. You're still planning on spending it with me, aren't you?" He asked.

"Of course, there's no other place I'd be than with you."

"That's, exactly how I feel too, Jen." He said with much love in his voice. "See you tomorrow."

I woke on Christmas Eve morning to find my parents already preparing the Christmas Day dinner. The house was bustling with activity. Not only were we preparing for Christmas, Dad's employees were making regular stops at the house to pick up their Christmas bonus checks. Dad was known to be a generous man, but at Christmas time he really showed how much he appreciated his employees and all the hard work they did for him. He always wanted to make sure they knew it. One year, one of Dad's employees, Roger Curtis, had his house catch on fire while he and his family were away. When Dad found out about it not only did he give them a substantial bonus to keep them on their feet, he also allowed them to stay in one of our apartments rent free until their house was ready for them to move back. This kind of generosity made my parents well liked in the community. They were always ready to lend a helping hand, no matter the circumstance. I could hear the commotion downstairs. It was only eight-thirty, but it might as well have been four o'clock in the afternoon by the sound of the chatter going on.

    I quickly showered. I had a lot to do today, and if I wanted to get things ready for Liam and his grandpa, I needed to get moving. I spent the next couple of hours wrapping Liam's gifts and then preparing food for their homecoming. Mom and I had decided that Liam and his grandpa would be hungry when they got home, and being that both of them hadn't been in their house for a while, groceries were in order. I went to the store and grabbed whatever I could from off the shelves. Coffee, pop (Coca-Cola to be exact, Liam's favorite), sandwich stuff, and some other necessities that I thought they might need. I bagged everything up and then headed back to my house. Mom had prepared Liam's favorite, fried chicken with all the extras.

    I was anxious to get out of the house. It felt like grand central station during rush hour: people were coming in and out on a non-stop basis and the phone wouldn't stop ringing. I stayed out of the way and concentrated on what I needed to get accomplished. I was running out of time. The clock read 10:11am (of course). Liam had said that he wanted to be home by noon. That gave me less than two hours to get to his house, put away the groceries, do some light cleaning, and put their presents under the tree.

    I loaded Dad's delivery van and headed to Liam's. I couldn't wait to see their expressions when they walked through their door.

They both had made me feel so much a part of their family that I couldn't wait to repay them with the same kindness. I made the drive to Liam's house in record time and began unloading the van. I had to hurry if I was going accomplish all that I had planned. I loved their cozy and inviting home, being decorated for Christmas; it made it twice as inviting.

I looked at the Christmas tree Liam had given me. It was still as beautiful as when I first saw it. I went over and plugged in the lights. *Beautiful"* I thought to myself. The sun shone through the windows making the crystal decorations on the tree sparkle against the wall. I found myself mesmerized by its enchantment and realized nothing was getting accomplished. I tore through the house like a tornado: putting away groceries, setting the table, and warming the food in the oven. I called for Blue, I had no idea the last time he had eaten or had water. I filled his bowls and placed them on the back porch hoping he would come running soon. I had about twenty minutes left if Liam was right about when they were getting his grandpa. I rushed around the house, giving it another once over.

When I heard the truck coming up the drive, I went to the porch. Parker was the first person I saw. He was helping Liam's grandpa out of the truck. I looked around for Liam but didn't see him anywhere. Then I noticed a ponytail rising from behind the truck. Liam saw me as soon as he stood up. I couldn't wait. I ran to him and threw myself into his arms.

"Oh my God, Liam, I missed you." I gave him a huge kiss, not even caring that Parker and Grandpa Mack were only a few feet away.

"Baby!" He shouted as he bear-hugged me back.

It was as if we had been separated for weeks instead of just a couple of days. We embraced each other tightly, neither of us letting up on our grip.

"Ahem, excuse me, if you two lovebirds don't mind, we should probably get Grandpa in the house." Liam and I were still locked into each other's gaze as Parker cleared his throat again.

"Right, of course, Parker. Sorry, Grandpa."

"Don't be. I'd forget I was here too if I had a reception like that."

"Hi, Grandpa, how are you feeling?" I went over and took his hand.

"Much better, now that I'm home. What are you doing here?"

"I just came over to make sure your house was in order and to bring you and Liam dinner."

"Jen, you didn't need to do that," Grandpa said.

"Yes, I did, besides it's Christmas Eve. Where else would I be? Now come on, let's get you inside."

I held onto Grandpa's hand as he gingerly walked into the house. Good ole Blue must have heard the truck pull up as he bounded towards Liam and Grandpa from out of nowhere, welcoming them the way only a hound dog could. Liam and Parker followed behind us carrying the numerous paraphernalia that had inundated their short hospital stay.

"Jenny, the house looks great. You shouldn't have gone to the trouble."

"Honestly, Grandpa, it was no trouble at all. You and Liam are probably the cleanest guys in the whole town. You put me to shame."

I helped Grandpa Mack into the living room and to the sofa next to the fireplace. Liam and Parker went upstairs.

"We'll be right back Grandpa. We're just taking all this stuff up to your room."

I sat on the couch next to Grandpa. "Can I get you anything? Are you thirsty or hungry?"

"Thanks, Jenny, not right now, but something sure smells good. What is it?"

"It's dinner, whenever you want it."

"Thank you. I think I'm going to rest for a bit first. I guess I'm more tired than I thought."

"Take a nap. I'm going to go finish what I was doing in the kitchen." I kissed him on the forehead as he closed his eyes.

"Jenny?"

"Yes, Grandpa?"

"Thank you."

I smiled down at his face. It looked softer than usual. The rugged and worn exterior was replaced now with a more fragile look of a thankful and humble man. I gave him a reassuring squeeze on his arm as I pulled a blanket over his legs.

"Get some rest, Grandpa."

I walked into the kitchen. Almost everything was ready for dinner. I heard Liam and Parker running down the stairs.

"Shhhhh," I said as I stopped them. "Grandpa is resting."

"Oh, sorry. We didn't mean to be so loud," Liam said as they came down the last few steps.

"Well, be quiet. He's tired and needs the rest."

"Okay, Mom," Liam said playfully.

The room became awkwardly quiet. Parker stared at both of us.

"Liam, if you don't need me for anything else, I better go. I still have to get home and get a shower. I'm going over to Kelli's tonight for Christmas Eve."

"Thanks, bro', I'm good."

I gave Parker a hug. "Thanks again for this weekend."

"Don't mention it, Jen. You guys have a great Christmas."

"You too, Parker," Liam and I said in unison.

They walked out together, and I could tell Liam felt indebted to him for everything he did over the weekend. Parker was probably more like a brother to Liam than his friend, and I think the weekend solidified it. I continued working in the kitchen. The fried chicken Mom had made smelled delicious, and there was enough to feed an army.

"What's this, babe?" Liam asked as he entered the kitchen.

"I told you I had something for you and your grandpa when you got home. This is it: dinner from my parents."

"Really? They didn't have to do this."

"I know, but they wanted to, and besides you had nothing here to eat. You were going to have to have cereal for Christmas

Eve. I wasn't about to let that happen. And I stocked your pantry, so you don't have to worry about running to the store."

Liam cornered me against the kitchen counter. "You know, you better be careful Jen. You might just make me fall for you if you keep this up."

"Oh really? I wouldn't want you to fall for me now, would I?" Liam's body was pressed against mine. I could feel my heart beating through my chest. I grabbed him and pulled him closer to me, if that was even possible. "I missed this."

"Me too, babe."

He kissed me softly. Our bodies strained to touch each other's, ached to be closer than they already were. I pressed my lips hard against his as he leaned into me, balancing me against the counter. He lifted me onto the counter as I wrapped my legs around his waist.

"Jenny?"

"Yeah, Liam?"

He was tender and subtle with his touch. His hands easily found their way under my shirt.

"I love you."

"I know you do." I went to kiss him, but he leaned away from me. "What, Liam?"

"I'm serious. I need you to listen to me. I'm…" his eyes shifted to the kitchen floor.

"Liam, what?"

He looked back at me with a serious expression. "Jenny, I'm more in love with you than you'll ever know. I know I can't live without you."

"I'm not going anywhere. I'm right here."

He looked at me earnestly. "I'd die without you. Do you know that? I didn't realize how much I needed you in my life until this accident. Please don't ever leave me."

"What are you talking about? Where is this coming from?"

"I don't know. I had a lot of time to think in the hospital, and it was mostly about you and me. I just care about you so much. Nobody has ever meant this much to me. You've filled a void in my life that I didn't even know was there. I know this sounds stupid, and you might think I'm just being nutty because of my injury, but nothing has ever felt more right than how I feel about you. Honest." His gaze went right through me.

"Jenny, ..."

I put my lips back on his, where they belonged and ached for. Liam picked me up off the counter as I wrapped my arms around his neck.

"Where are we going?" I asked him already knowing the answer.

"Upstairs, shhh. I don't want to wake Grandpa."

I put my head against his neck and softly giggled as he carried me. His hair fell around my face. "Your grandpa is going to wonder where we are."

"Don't worry. He knows I wanted to spend some time alone with you."

"But what about your head? Doesn't it hurt?"

"No, it's not my head that hurts."

He carried me down the hallway to his room; he had become an expert in holding me while opening his door. He placed me on his bed carefully as he laid next to me. The room was dark with shadows dancing on the wall from the sun's rays that trickled in, yet still it was easy to see the homage to his career in football. The number eleven was sporadically placed throughout his room. Pictures and newspaper clippings of Liam playing football covered every inch of space on his walls.

"Merry Christmas, Jenny."

"Merry Christmas, Liam."

We were facing each other. Our legs entwined in each other's while our hands never left each other's grasp. There were no words needed at this moment; both of us were content to be with each other, to be next to each other. He gingerly touched my arms, making his way to the side of my face. His touch was sensual and soft, the way a feather would feel gliding against my skin. It sent a sensation down my body that I couldn't ignore. The emotions that I felt for him left me breathless. I moved in on him, allowing no space between our bodies. I grabbed his shirt and pulled it carefully over his head. He didn't flinch or say a word. He just responded to my primal needs and helped me in my quest to undress him. I pushed him onto his back, being careful of his stitches. I positioned myself on top of him.

"Jenny," he whispered my name in the most beautiful and melodic tone.

"Shhh, "I leaned down and nibbled his ear as I ran my fingers through his wavy hair. He smiled as he brought himself to me. His eyes were still on mine, and our thoughts were the same. Our bodies became one.

Time stood still when we were together, but it was getting late in the day. The sun was going down and the shadows it produced in his room were now being replaced by the moon's magic.

"Hey, don't you think we should go and check on Grandpa? I'm sure he's awake, and I don't think he would be too thrilled to learn that I've been in your room for most of the afternoon."

Liam was cradling me from behind. His fingers were caressing my bare shoulder. "I guess, but I'm sure he's still asleep. But you're right. We should get up. It is Christmas Eve." He was smiling his infamous crooked smile as he sat up. "Time for presents." He shot up out of bed and pulled on his jeans. "You stay here. I'll be right back."

Before I could answer, he was out the door and down the steps. I lay back on his bed and brought the covers to my face. They smelled like him, and the more I breathed them in the more I realized I could easily become drunk off of his scent. I quickly put my clothes on as I took my time scoping out Liam's room. It was a small room with only enough space for his bed, dresser, and a small desk by his window. It was somewhat messy but nothing out of the ordinary. If anything, most of the mess was a result of us knocking things over in the heat of the moment. I knew he had a lot of football memorabilia, but not until I started really looking at his room and analyzing it did I realize just how much he had.

Liam literally had dozens of pictures of himself playing football strewn on his walls. There were candid shots of him scoring touchdowns, running down the field, giving high fives with his teammates and countless others of him posing for local media. It was insane the amount of attention he had received over the years due to his playing ability. I was in awe staring at it and felt somewhat bad that I didn't pay more attention to him throughout the years. He obviously was a very good football player.

The number eleven was displayed everywhere. He even had one of his football jerseys encased in a beautiful black frame. I felt as if the number was antagonizing me, staring at me from all directions, trying to let me know it was real and so were my feelings regarding it. I wanted to tell Liam about this, but I still couldn't. The timing had to be perfect, and tonight of all nights wasn't the night. Just then, Liam walked back into the room. He had his left hand behind his back and a lavender rose in his right.

"For you, beautiful." I took the rose, inhaling its sweet scent. "Merry Christmas." I looked down. His left hand came from behind his back. In his hand was a tiny blue box with a silver bow on top. I took the box and sat down staring at it intensely. My heart was beating a mile a minute. "Well, aren't you going to open it?" He said as I continued to blankly stare at it.

"Yes, of course, but I don't have your present with me. It's downstairs. I need to go get yours. It's not fair that I should open mine without you having something from me to open."

"Stop it. I don't care about a present. I've got you, and that's all I've ever wanted. Here now, stop procrastinating and open it."

He sat down next to me. I carefully took the bow off the box as I took a deep breath. Carefully I unwrapped the silver paper to find a black velvet box.

"Liam, what is this?"

I froze as I stared at the ominous and intriguing dark box that was giving me so much trepidation in my hands. Liam placed his hands on top of mine, instantly calming my nerves.

"Open it, please," he said smiling.

I slowly pulled back the lid, unveiling a beautiful silver necklace with three charms hanging from it. The first charm was a small silver heart, the second charm was Liam's number, #11; and the third charm was a silver cross. It was the most beautiful necklace I had ever seen. My mouth literally dropped to the floor leaving me unable to speak and hardly able to breathe.

"Well, do you like it?"

"Liam, I love it. It's beautiful, I don't know what to say, you shouldn't have done this."

"Yes I should have."

I stared at the charms. On the back of the heart I noticed writing, the tiny words read, "you n me, 4ever."

"I can't believe you did this. It's perfect."

"That's how I feel, you and me forever."

"I love it, babe, thank you, and your number?"

"I wanted that to be close to your heart. Do you recognize the cross?"

I studied the cross as I moved it between my fingers. "Liam it's beautiful, but I don't recognize it."

"It's my cross, the one I wear around my neck." I looked at his neck. His silver chain was there, but the cross that dangled from it was missing.

"But this was yours. I can't take that."

"I want you to have it. It belonged to my mom, and now it belongs to you."

"I don't know what to say."

"I told you I loved you. I hope you realize it now. You now have my heart, my soul, and my love forever."

I clutched the necklace in my hands and held it close to my own heart.

"Liam, I'll cherish this forever. Here, help me put it on." I turned my back to him, allowing him to put the necklace around my neck. I could feel myself shaking and only stopped when Liam touched my skin. The necklace fell into place, stopping right below my collarbone, all three charms falling into place.

"Merry Christmas, Jenny."

"Merry Christmas, babe. Now it's your turn. I have something for you."

"I told you all I needed was you."

"Even still, I do have a present for you."

I walked downstairs being careful not to wake Grandpa Mack just in case he was still asleep. I tiptoed into the living room. The soft murmurs of his breathing answered my question that he was still sleeping soundly. Ole' Blue laid by his side. The blanket that I had laid on Grandpa's legs was on the floor, and I carefully picked it up and covered him again. He rustled softly as he took the blanket and pulled it up to his waist, snoring softly in the process. The tree's lights were casting a beautiful glow in the living room. I immediately grabbed Liam's present and tiptoed my way back upstairs to his room, being careful not to stumble. Liam was lying down on his bed, his arms behind his head, but he instantly sat upon my arrival.

"Here, for you, Merry Christmas."

He took the present from my hands and kissed me. "Thanks, babe. What is it?"

"You're going to have to open it."

Liam was much more aggressive in his unwrapping than I was. Where I was careful, Liam was savage. He tore through the ribbon and box in one sweep of his hands, manhandling the package as if his life depended on it. All the tedious time I had taken to wrap the package so it would look just perfect was ruined in seconds flat. Inside he found a leather bracelet, on the ends of it were two silver and turquoise nuggets.

"Do you like it?" I was nervous. Liam didn't wear much jewelry except for the silver cross that was now mine, and I wasn't for sure if he would wear this. But this was a very rugged bracelet. It looked like Liam to a 'T'.

"I love it Jen, thank you."

"The one silver nugget has your number on it, and the other has our initials."

"You're kidding?" he said as he played with the stones between his fingers. "It's great, Jen. I'll wear it all the time. So what about the turquoise? Does that mean anything?"

"Well, partially. It's my favorite stone, and the color reminds me of your eyes."

"It's perfect, just like you. Come here." He pulled me to him. "It's the best present I've ever been given and even more special because it's from you."

"I'm glad you like it. I have one more gift for you."

"What? No, Jen, this was more than enough."

"I know, but I saw this and thought of you. Come with me. I couldn't carry it up the stairs."

I pulled on his arm, dragging him with me to the living room. Grandpa Mack was still snoring. The covers were now positioned up to his neck. Only his head peeked out, and it was nestled deeply in the crevices of the sofa pillow and the blanket. We carefully walked over to the tree.

"Here, sit down and close your eyes," I whispered. I watched as Liam put his hands over his eyes. "No peeking." I started giggling as he playfully peeked through his fingers. "There," I said, "you can open it now."

Before him was a box with a complete set of tools inside it.

"Jenny? Really? I can't believe you did this. This is awesome. These are for me?"

"Yeah, they're not quite as romantic as the first gift, but I know how much you like to work on your truck and how you're always borrowing tools from your friends; so I thought you deserved to have your own set."

He sat flabbergasted, running his hands over the shiny silver gadgets. "I can't believe you Jenny. These are great. I can't wait to use them. You're the best babe." We leaned in to kiss again when we heard a noise from the couch.

"There you two are." Grandpa Mack had awakened from his slumber.

"Oh, sorry, Grandpa. We didn't mean to disturb you."

"Don't be. I'm glad you did. I would have slept right through Christmas. It is still Christmas Eve, isn't it?" He asked, somewhat worried.

"Yeah, you haven't missed it. Merry Christmas, Grandpa," I said.

"Thank you, dear, Merry Christmas to you too. Oh, I see Liam gave you your present. It looks perfect around your neck."

"I absolutely love it. How are you feeling? Do you need anything? Are you hungry?"

"I am, and I could eat a horse."

"Well, I don't have a horse, but I do have some fried chicken. Will that do?"

"It'll do just fine."

"But wait, I have something for you." I went to the tree and grabbed the present that was still under it. Liam stared at me with intense curiosity. "Here, Merry Christmas." Liam and his grandpa both continued to look dumbstruck.

"Jenny, you shouldn't have. I wasn't expecting anything. I don't have anything for you, dear."

"Grandpa, just having you out of the hospital is my present."

Liam sat down next to his grandpa, still bewildered that I pulled one over on him. Grandpa's hands were still a little unsteady and shaky as he tried to open the present. Liam, being the person he is, helped him as Grandpa's hands began to shake even more.

"Jenny, I can't believe your thoughtfulness. This is so nice of you."

Inside the silver box, Grandpa found a black leather photo album. As he opened it, he and Liam found pictures of Grandpa with Grandma, Liam with his mom, and numerous ones of Liam's football career.

"Jenny, when did you do all of this, and how?"

"I have my ways. Some of these are pictures my mom has taken, the other ones, well I guess you could say I stole them from your house. They're not all there, just some of them. I figured you could fill in the rest of the book on your own."

"I love it, Jenny, thank you."

"Yeah, I can't believe you did this. This is really nice, and I can't believe you did this behind my back," Liam said still bewildered.

"Well, I can keep a few secrets."

The rest of the evening, the three of us enjoyed our time together, browsing through the album as I listened intently as Liam and his grandpa reminisced on the pictures that held so many wonderful memories for them.

Chapter Thirteen
Lies and Deceptions

      Aside from Ashley being away on a skiing holiday, Christmas had turned out to be a wonderful day for both of our families. After a memorable Christmas dinner that featured my dad's famous turkey and stuffing, everyone ended up around our piano as Mom entertained us with her favorite renditions of show tunes. Liam even surprised us by playing his guitar, a gift from his grandpa. Needless to say, we were all impressed by his new talent, most of all me. He never failed to surprise me. He was just as gifted off the football field as he was on it. Liam and Grandpa were feeling better day by day, and by the end of the week, they were back to their usual routines.

      Liam had been given the okay by Dr. Garrett to resume his driving, something he had been doing anyway. Grandpa had been given a clean bill of health and permission to resume most of his normal duties. By the end of the first week of Christmas break, we had spent every evening together.

Break was halfway over, and I still hadn't seen any of my girlfriends. We both agreed that on Saturday we would take a day off from each other and spend with our friends. Kendra had been dying to see me. Apparently she and Tony were more of an item than I knew. He surprised her on Christmas Eve with a dozen long stem red roses and a note saying she was the only one for him. She, of course, had decided she was over the moon about him too and couldn't wait to tell me all the explicit details. I was thrilled for her. It would be fun to have someone to talk to about guy stuff, and who better than my best friend.

Liam called me first thing on Saturday morning, a ritual he had begun after we officially became a couple. He wanted his voice to be the first thing I heard when I woke up. For a guy, he had the sweetest disposition and some wonderful attributes that are uncharacteristic for a so-called jock. It was going to be an unusually warm day for the end of December, and Liam had made plans with Tony and Parker to work on their trucks. He had been busting at the seams to try out the new tools I had given him, and he had the perfect excuse to use them. After our phone conversation, I grabbed a cinnamon bun from the kitchen table and drove to Kendra's house. We were both looking forward to hanging out with each other. It had been a month since we had some girl time that didn't involve school work, and we knew we were way overdue for it. I arrived at her house to find her in her room, picking up piles of clothes off her floor. Kendra was notorious for not being the cleanest person around.

"Hey, nice mountain of clothes you've got going on here. Is this a science project or are you just turning green on me?" I said as I kicked my way through the avalanche of clothes and paraphernalia.

"Ha, Ha. They're clean; they just haven't made it to my closet. Mom said I had to put them away if I wanted to hang out with you today."

"Here, let me help then." I grabbed a bunch of clothes, and without knowing where they belonged, started stuffing them in different drawers. We worked for an hour before we could finally see Kendra's yellow carpet.

"There, all done. Thanks for the help."

"Don't mention it," I replied as I plopped on her bed. "Where are your parents? I haven't seen them since I arrived."

"They left for the day. Dad gave Mom this God-awful orange sweater for Christmas. She's taking it back to exchange it for something much more expensive. She thought Dad should at least pay for buying her such an ugly gift, and I do mean that literally. I've never seen her so upset over a gift."

"Ugly, huh?"

"You wouldn't believe how ugly. I couldn't believe my dad even thought that she would even remotely like it. It looked like someone threw up all over it."

"Ooooh, not good."

"Yeah, so to make up for it, Dad's going to let her pick out whatever she wants, and then he's taking her to dinner and a movie. They'll be gone for the entire day."

"Great, that leaves the whole day for us. My parents are driving to Ohio for the day to see Ashley, so I'm free as well."

Kendra sat down next to me and rearranged the roses Tony gave her that were on the nightstand next to her bed.

"Those are gorgeous. That was really sweet of Tony. Were you totally surprised when you received them?"

"Yes, you know, Jen, things were just going so-so with us. We were having lots of fun when we were together, but I couldn't read him to save my soul. I could never tell if he liked me or not. One day I thought he did, and then the next he would totally ignore me. It was so frustrating. That's one reason I wasn't so sure about us. I could never figure him out."

"So, how did this all come about with the roses?"

"Last Friday, before the break, I was leaving the building when I saw Tony standing next to my car. He said that he couldn't see me on Saturday. We had planned to go to the movies. I was devastated Jenny. I really had decided that I liked him, and I didn't understand the last minute change of plans. So anyway, I just said okay and brushed it off. I didn't hear from him the entire weekend. I was so miserable. I just moped around the house the whole time. Mom and Dad thought I was coming down with the flu. I did not dare tell them the real reason. You know they already think no guy is good enough for me. If they were to know how I felt about Tony and how he had practically just dumped me, they would have been so mad at him. I would have never had a chance with him.

"Anyway, I thought for sure that that was it and it was over. I was crushed, but I was accepting it. Then on Christmas Eve the doorbell rang, it was the delivery guy with these flowers. I couldn't believe it, Jenny, I called him right away to thank him, and he said he was so sorry for the way he had acted. He was nervous about getting too close to me, and he realized over the weekend that he really liked me too. I started crying. He ended up coming over, and we spent Christmas Eve together."

"What about your parents? How were they?"

"Oh, you know, they still don't think he's the right guy for me, but it did help that Tony brought Mom a gift."

"He did? What did he bring her?"

"Here, let me help then." I grabbed a bunch of clothes, and without knowing where they belonged, started stuffing them in different drawers. We worked for an hour before we could finally see Kendra's yellow carpet.

"There, all done. Thanks for the help."

"Don't mention it," I replied as I plopped on her bed. "Where are your parents? I haven't seen them since I arrived."

"They left for the day. Dad gave Mom this God-awful orange sweater for Christmas. She's taking it back to exchange it for something much more expensive. She thought Dad should at least pay for buying her such an ugly gift, and I do mean that literally. I've never seen her so upset over a gift."

"Ugly, huh?"

"You wouldn't believe how ugly. I couldn't believe my dad even thought that she would even remotely like it. It looked like someone threw up all over it."

"Oooooh, not good."

"Yeah, so to make up for it, Dad's going to let her pick out whatever she wants, and then he's taking her to dinner and a movie. They'll be gone for the entire day."

"Great, that leaves the whole day for us. My parents are driving to Ohio for the day to see Ashley, so I'm free as well."

Kendra sat down next to me and rearranged the roses Tony gave her that were on the nightstand next to her bed.

"Those are gorgeous. That was really sweet of Tony. Were you totally surprised when you received them?"

"Yes, you know, Jen, things were just going so-so with us. We were having lots of fun when we were together, but I couldn't read him to save my soul. I could never tell if he liked me or not. One day I thought he did, and then the next he would totally ignore me. It was so frustrating. That's one reason I wasn't so sure about us. I could never figure him out."

"So, how did this all come about with the roses?"

"Last Friday, before the break, I was leaving the building when I saw Tony standing next to my car. He said that he couldn't see me on Saturday. We had planned to go to the movies. I was devastated Jenny. I really had decided that I liked him, and I didn't understand the last minute change of plans. So anyway, I just said okay and brushed it off. I didn't hear from him the entire weekend. I was so miserable. I just moped around the house the whole time. Mom and Dad thought I was coming down with the flu. I did not dare tell them the real reason. You know they already think no guy is good enough for me. If they were to know how I felt about Tony and how he had practically just dumped me, they would have been so mad at him. I would have never had a chance with him.

"Anyway, I thought for sure that that was it and it was over. I was crushed, but I was accepting it. Then on Christmas Eve the doorbell rang, it was the delivery guy with these flowers. I couldn't believe it, Jenny, I called him right away to thank him, and he said he was so sorry for the way he had acted. He was nervous about getting too close to me, and he realized over the weekend that he really liked me too. I started crying. He ended up coming over, and we spent Christmas Eve together."

"What about your parents? How were they?"

"Oh, you know, they still don't think he's the right guy for me, but it did help that Tony brought Mom a gift."

"He did? What did he bring her?"

"Some fancy hand lotions and soaps."

"Oh my God, that's perfect. She loves that stuff. He was definitely working it, that's for sure."

"Is that the necklace Liam gave you?"

I grabbed the charms in my hand. "Yeah, isn't it beautiful?"

"Wow, Jenny, I can't believe how things have changed in the past couple of months with the two of you. When I think back to when all this started, I never would have dreamed in a million years that you guys would end up together. You hated him. Now look at you guys. I never see the two of you apart from each other."

I giggled. "I know. I can't believe it myself sometimes, but, you know, he's totally not the guy I thought he was. There's a real sweet person behind that tough guy exterior, and that's the Liam that I fell for. He's so much more that the jock on campus, he totally won me over."

"I'm happy for you, Jenny. I miss our time together, but I understand. You glow when you talk about him, and, of course, we all know that he's over head over heels for you. I really get why you want to be with him now because that's how I'm feeling about Tony. I can't stand to be away from him."

"You know the best part is now the four of us can double date."

"I know. It'll be awesome. So, Jen, are you going to the drag races tonight?"

"What drag races? I don't know anything about them."

"You don't?" Kendra asked, stumped in amazement.

"No, should I?"

"Well, I just thought since Liam was racing in them you would have known about it." I looked at her in complete disbelief. She realized she may have said something she shouldn't have. "Jenny, I'm sorry. I thought for sure Liam would have told you about it. I know it's been planned for a couple of days now."

"Liam didn't tell me anything about it, Kendra. That doesn't make any sense. How did you know?"

"Tony told me last night. That's why he and Parker are at Liam's house as we speak. They're working on their trucks, priming them for the race."

I sat motionless. I knew I shouldn't be upset. It wasn't like he had to report to me or ask me for my permission, but why wouldn't he at least tell me he was racing? I was hurt and felt jilted, as though I had caught him cheating on me. It was the same feelings I felt the night of homecoming.

"Jenny, I'm sure he meant to tell you. It was probably just an oversight on his part."

"Yeah, I guess, so what time are the races?"

"They're tonight at eleven. I know there are some guys coming from other counties to race in it too. Tony said Johnny Bryant from Walton would be there along with some guys from Ripley."

"Do you know where they're racing?"

"Yes, Ripley Road near Tuckers Run."

"Are you kidding? That's the most dangerous road of them all!"

"I know it is, Jenny, but Tony said they had plenty of lookouts. Besides, Liam isn't even racing till close to the end. By the time it's his turn, they'll either be done with it, or they'll have it mapped out so that Liam will know exactly what to do. Don't worry. He's not racing until after Tony races. Race eleven."

"What did you say, Kendra?" I heard the number ringing in my ears.

"I said Liam is racing after Tony. He's either next to last or is the last race."

"No, what number did you say?"

"I said he's in race eleven."

I shot up off Kendra's bed with that stupid number ringing in my ears.

"Jenny, what's wrong, are you okay?"

"Yes... no, I don't know, Kendra. I... It's nothing, but I need to talk to Liam. Where's your cell? My battery's dead."

Kendra handed me her phone. I was so upset that I had to call Liam's number three times before I got it right. The phone rang and rang. I knew Liam was probably outside and couldn't hear the ring.

"Damn it!" I said as I heard his recording. I tried to remain calm on the phone, but my tone would tell him otherwise. Liam would know that I wasn't myself. I left my message giving him Kendra's number to return my call.

"What's up? You're acting really strange," Kendra said.

I stood there holding her cell in my hands, wondering if I should tell Kendra about my feelings with this daunting number. Why not? I had nothing else to lose, I decided.

"You're going to think I'm crazy, but it's just that when you said he was racing tonight, and that his race was number eleven, well, it kind of sent me over the edge."

"What are you talking about? It's just a number."

"No, it's not actually. Well, it is, but it's just that..."

"Jenny, what is it? You're mumbling."

"Okay, I'll just come out and tell you." Both of us sat back down on her bed with pillows on our laps. "It's this number eleven, Kendra."

"Okaaay?" She was more confused than ever and trying to decide if I was going insane or not.

"Okay, listen. I don't know how to explain it except that ever since Liam and I have been together I see this number. I mean I see it everywhere."

"What do you mean?"

"Well, first off the obvious: it's Liam's football jersey number. Not a big deal, I know, but after Liam and I started dating I started seeing the number everywhere else. Like the night of the carnival when Liam found me. You left with Shauna, and we rode the Ferris wheel, and we were in cart number eleven."

"So, that doesn't mean anything."

"I know, but that was a very important night in our relationship. It was one more step in bringing us together, and that's not all. Every time I look at the clock it seems to have the number eleven in it. It will read 2:11, 1:11, 6:11, or it would add up to eleven like 1:28 or 10:37. Liam would call me, and the time would be on the eleven." Kendra was listening intently to me, but her look was odd as though she was just trying to appease me rather than really believing me.

"Look, I just mean that it seems this number is playing a part in our lives, and when I look back on it, it's always been here. Like my address and my phone number, both have the number eleven in it, and Liam's address has eleven in it too. That first night at the football game when I dropped my baton, that was on the eleventh. Liam and Grandpa Mack's accident last week, did you know it happened on Route Eleven? The police report says that Parker called in the accident at seven-eleven that morning!" I pulled my hair back in frustration watching Kendra's reaction to all this.

"Jenny, look, I don't know if it means anything or not. It just seems that this number is merely a coincidence. Of course you started seeing it more than you did before; you probably also notice black Ford pick-up trucks more than you did before you started dating Liam. Honestly, I don't think there's anything to it."

"Maybe you're right, but I can't ignore it. When you said Liam's in race eleven tonight, well, it's just one more time that the number has come up." Kendra looked at me. She was trying to be understanding, but I knew she found this hard to fathom. "Look, I guess I'm super-sensitive about it and that Liam didn't tell me about the race. You know those races are dangerous. Plus the cops are always on the look-out for them. It just doesn't seem like a good omen."

"How can you say that? You should look at it as the glass half-full instead of half-empty," Kendra said, trying to remain positive for me.

"What?"

"I mean, you're looking at this number in all the wrong ways. The only bad thing that involved the eleven is Liam's accident, and that actually turned out to be just fine. Liam is better and so is his grandpa. You yourself said the accident could have been a lot worse. What about the positive things that are related to this number like Liam and you getting together. Even the night of the football game, that was the start of all this. It looks like there's more good to the number than bad."

"I guess you're right, but I still don't feel good about tonight's race. Ever since you told me about it, I've had this strange feeling in my stomach, and I don't think it's going to go away until I talk to Liam about it."

"Have you talked to Liam about the number?"

"No, you and Ashley are the only ones. I want to, but it just never seems to be the right time. Plus I'm not sure how he would react. I keep thinking he would say I am being silly or something. But I plan on telling him. I have to. I'm constantly thinking about it, and I find myself looking for the number now. It's like a toothache that won't go away. It's constantly gnawing at me."

Just then, Kendra's cell began to ring. "I'll get it," Kendra said as she took the phone from my hand. "Hello? Hi, Liam, yeah, she's right here. Hold on." She handed me the phone. I looked over at the clock it was eleven minutes after four. I motioned to Kendra, and her mouth dropped when she saw the time.

"Hi, Liam."

"What's up, babe? You seemed upset on your message?"

I started to tell him why when I caught myself. I decided it wasn't worth interrogating him about why he didn't tell me about the races tonight. If Liam didn't want to tell me about them, then I was not going to bring it up, and the eleven would have to wait as well. There was no need to bring it up either when I couldn't talk to him face to face about it. Besides, I didn't want to upset or bother him. If he was determined to race tonight, then he needed a clear head and not be bothered with trivial stuff like daunting digits.

"Umm, it's nothing. To be honest, I can't remember why I called. Kendra and I have been having such a good time catching up with each other. It's totally slipped my mind."

It was a lame attempt at a lie, but it was the best I could come up with so quickly. Kendra was staring at me as if I was crazy. Her arms flapped at her sides in a gesture that showed that she was wondering what I had just done.

"Are you sure, babe?"

"Positive. I guess I just wanted to hear your voice. Are you guys having fun?"

"Yeah. I love my tools, Jen, thanks."

"I'm glad, and you're very welcome."

"What are you and Kendra going to do later?"

"I'm not sure. We're just playing it by ear. Right now, we're just hanging out in her room listening to music." At least that much was true. "What about you?"

He hesitated. "I'm not sure either. We're probably just going to stay here and get a pizza or something."

My heart sank. How could he deliberately keep this from me?

"Great, sounds like you have a plan."

Liam was silent a few seconds before answering. "Yeah, I guess. Jenny?"

"Yeah, Liam?" Here it was. I was moments from hearing the truth.

"Love you." Although I loved hearing him say that to me, it wasn't what I was hoping to hear. My heart sank further, located now somewhere in the depths of my knotted stomach. "I'll call you later, okay?"

"Sure. If I'm not here, I'll be home."

"See ya, babe."

"See ya."

I handed Kendra her cell and fell back on her bed covering my face with a pillow. "He didn't tell me, Kendra. I gave him the chance, and he still didn't tell me about the races tonight."

"Jenny, there must be a reason why he's not telling you. I can't believe he would keep something like that from you if there wasn't a good reason. It just doesn't sound like him."

"Yeah, I guess, but I still don't like it. If he can so easily keep this from me, who's to say he won't or hasn't kept other things from me too."

"Why didn't you bring it up yourself? You had the perfect opportunity?"

"I know, but I just couldn't. I thought it should be his place to tell me, not the other way around." Kendra didn't respond.

The rest of the day dragged by, and we spent it in her room listening to music. After feeling jilted and slighted from Liam's phone call earlier, the last thing I wanted to do was anything fun. I felt like sulking and drowning in my own misery, and nothing Kendra did or said brought me out of it. By dinnertime, Kendra and I had listened to over six hours of music. We were both starving and had decided a Lougini's pizza was in order. Lougini's was packed as usual upon our arrival.

"We should have come earlier," Kendra said as we scoped out the restaurant. "There doesn't look like there's a table. Why don't we just order a pizza to go? We can watch a movie at home and just chill at my house? I really don't want to hang out here anyway. It's way too crowded and I don't even see anybody we know."

I agreed. We placed our order, and after only fifteen minutes or so we were on the road again and back at Kendra's.

"I'm going to get some plates. Why don't you take the pizza into the family room and find a movie?" Kendra said.

Kendra's family room was tiny, barely bigger than her bedroom. There was an over-stuffed sofa that had been there for as long as I could remember and a coffee table that Kendra said dated back to her great, great grandmother. The room was filled with her mother's antique glassware and vases, and the scent of lavender enveloped the air. I was in the process of picking a movie on TV when Kendra's cell rang.

"Jenny, it's Liam."

"Hey," I said with no emotion in my tone

"Hey, babe."

"Hey," I repeated again.

Liam's voice was quiet and reserved. "What's going on?"

"Kendra and I were getting ready to watch a movie and eat some pizza. What's up with you?"

"Oh, nothing, Parker and I were just sitting here having a beer."

"A beer? Does your grandpa know you're drinking?"

"Jenny, don't worry. I've only had one, and no, he doesn't know."

"Where's Tony? Isn't he still with you guys?"

"He just left. I guess he's picking Kendra up in a little bit. Why?"

"No reason. Just wondering. Kendra and I are still hanging out, so I thought Tony would still be with you guys."

"No. He left a little a while ago. He wanted to get a shower before he picked her up."

Oh, so much for pizza and movie. Thanks for telling me you were also going, Kendra, I thought to myself while I became hurt and more pissed off than I already was. I was quiet; and the more I thought about it, the angrier I became. I could hear Liam talking on the other end, but for the life of me, I didn't hear one word he said.

"Jen, are you there? Jenny?"

"Yeah, sorry. I must have zoned out for a second."

"Finally. I thought you had hung up on me. You were so quiet. Is anything wrong?"

Yes, there is. Why didn't you tell me about the damn races tonight? Why do I have to hear it from Kendra and not you? Are you trying to keep something from me? And to top it off, I'm being blown off by my best friend as well, I blurted out in my head.

"No, I guess I'm just tired. That's all," I said.

and had decided a Lougini's pizza was in order. Lougini's was packed as usual upon our arrival.

"We should have come earlier," Kendra said as we scoped out the restaurant. "There doesn't look like there's a table. Why don't we just order a pizza to go? We can watch a movie at home and just chill at my house? I really don't want to hang out here anyway. It's way too crowded and I don't even see anybody we know."

I agreed. We placed our order, and after only fifteen minutes or so we were on the road again and back at Kendra's.

"I'm going to get some plates. Why don't you take the pizza into the family room and find a movie?" Kendra said.

Kendra's family room was tiny, barely bigger than her bedroom. There was an over-stuffed sofa that had been there for as long as I could remember and a coffee table that Kendra said dated back to her great, great grandmother. The room was filled with her mother's antique glassware and vases, and the scent of lavender enveloped the air. I was in the process of picking a movie on TV when Kendra's cell rang.

"Jenny, it's Liam."

"Hey," I said with no emotion in my tone

"Hey, babe."

"Hey," I repeated again.

Liam's voice was quiet and reserved. "What's going on?"

"Kendra and I were getting ready to watch a movie and eat some pizza. What's up with you?"

"Oh, nothing, Parker and I were just sitting here having a beer."

"A beer? Does your grandpa know you're drinking?"

"Jenny, don't worry. I've only had one, and no, he doesn't know."

"Where's Tony? Isn't he still with you guys?"

"He just left. I guess he's picking Kendra up in a little bit. Why?"

"No reason. Just wondering. Kendra and I are still hanging out, so I thought Tony would still be with you guys."

"No. He left a little a while ago. He wanted to get a shower before he picked her up."

Oh, so much for pizza and movie. Thanks for telling me you were also going, Kendra, I thought to myself while I became hurt and more pissed off than I already was. I was quiet; and the more I thought about it, the angrier I became. I could hear Liam talking on the other end, but for the life of me, I didn't hear one word he said.

"Jen, are you there? Jenny?"

"Yeah, sorry. I must have zoned out for a second."

"Finally. I thought you had hung up on me. You were so quiet. Is anything wrong?"

Yes, there is. Why didn't you tell me about the damn races tonight? Why do I have to hear it from Kendra and not you? Are you trying to keep something from me? And to top it off, I'm being blown off by my best friend as well, I blurted out in my head.

"No, I guess I'm just tired. That's all," I said.

"Are you sure? Cause I'm getting the feeling something's wrong."

I sighed heavily. This back and forth nonsense was exhausting me. If he didn't have the decency to be open and honest with me, then I wasn't going to tell him. If he wanted me to know, he would have told me by now, and I was tired of this cat and mouse game. It just wasn't worth it anymore.

"No, Liam, really. It's just been a long day. Kendra and I have been busy all afternoon. I'm just tired. I think I'm going to go home and go to bed anyway. If Tony's on his way over, she's going to have to get ready."

"Want me to call you later?"

How can you if you're racing down Ripley Road at a hundred miles per hour? I thought to myself.

I bit my lip to hold back my growing frustration and anger. "No, it's not necessary. Have a good time with Parker. Bye."

There was hesitation on Liam's end. He knew that I was not acting like myself. He had never heard me act so coy and evasive. Maybe deep down, he knew that I knew about the races that night. It wouldn't take a genius to figure it out. He's the one who kept it from me. Why else would I be upset? He would have to realize that Kendra wouldn't keep something like that from me. He's the one who messed up. All he had to do was be up front and honest with me, something he couldn't seem to do. I never ended our conversations with such a casual goodbye either. He undoubtedly realized something was wrong.

"Bye, Jenny... love you."

The silence was deafening, and Liam was waiting for a response, any response, but nothing was coming out of my mouth.

I was angry, and I couldn't give in. Instead, I ended our conversation by saying, "I know."

"You definitely seem like something is wrong. Are you sure you don't want to talk about it?"

I looked at Kendra. She was messing with her hair, trying to decide if she wanted to wear it down or back in a ponytail. This was not the time or the place to bring it up. "No, positive, I'm fine. I'll talk to you tomorrow."

"Okay," he said as we both hung up.

I tried to contain my composure as I began to cry, fighting the tears back with a vengeance by biting my lower lip until it became numb. I did not dare let Kendra see me in this state of mind. Everyone thought Liam and I were the perfect couple with no problems. Everything was always so great. I wasn't about to start off a string of rumors over this, especially if it turned out to be nothing at all. There still could be a rational explanation for all of this. I had to wait and let him tell me in his own time, or at least by tomorrow.

"Hey, Kendra, I think the movie and pizza are going to have to wait. Liam told me Tony already left his place to pick you up."

"He has? I'm not ready though. He said he wasn't coming until later. Just like a man to not give you enough time to get ready," she said frantically as she aggressively brushed her hair. She stopped immediately when she noticed me. "Hey, are you okay, Jen?"

"Yeah, I'm fine. He still didn't mention anything about the races though, Kendra. He acted as though he and Parker were going to hang out at his house all night. I just don't understand it."

Kendra put her arm around me as she tried to reassure me. I didn't want it from her. I just wanted to go home. I left feeling betrayed and let down. I went home glad to find that Mom and Dad were still gone. Tonight I needed to have the house to myself. I grabbed a water from the fridge and headed off to bed. It was half past ten when I heard the doorbell ring. I quickly grabbed my robe and walked to the stairs to see who it was. I carefully leaned over the banister, trying desperately to look without being noticed. If it was one of Dad's employees or tenants, I was more than willing to let them ring our doorbell until their fingers fell off. But to my surprise it wasn't for Dad, it was for me. Standing at my door ringing the hell out of my doorbell was Liam. A wave of emotions came over me: happiness that he was at my doorstep, anger because I was still mad at him and sadness because I didn't know why he lied to me. I casually walked down the steps and opened the door.

"What are you doing here? You're supposed to be at the r..." I stopped myself, realizing I was about to let the cat out of the bag.

"I had to see you. I didn't feel right after we hung up earlier."

I let him in, looking around to make sure there were no nosy neighbors watching. He picked me up and squeezed me tightly, and engaged in sucking the literal breath out of me. "I missed you, babe."

I lead him away from the window and into the living room where our curtains were drawn.

"What are you doing here? I thought you were with Parker tonight?"

"I was. I mean I am. I'm supposed to pick him and a couple other guys up in a little bit."

To go to the races, I presumed.

We sat down with Liam almost sitting on top of me he was so close.

"Jenny, is anything wrong?"

"Why? Is that why you're here?"

"Yes, plus I wanted to see you of course, but you seemed so distant on the phone tonight, and I don't know why. Did I do something?"

I looked away from him, knowing full well if I looked him in the face I wouldn't be able to hide my feelings anymore.

"What is it?" he asked.

I finally brought myself to face him in the eyes, those gorgeous crystal blue eyes that melted me every time. Liam looked nice tonight. His hair was pulled back in its ponytail, and a small strand was falling next to his right cheek.

"Are you going to tell me what's wrong or not?"

"Liam, do you feel that we have a good relationship?"

He placed his arms around the inside of my robe, holding onto my waist. "Of course, babe. I think we have a fantastic relationship," he said as he moved in closer to my face. I pushed him away.

"I don't mean like that. I mean do you think we have an honest and open relationship. Do you feel we can tell each other anything?"

He moved back a little to read my face. "Yes, Why?"

"I mean that we should always be able to talk to each other and not keep things from each other, right? Be honest with no secrets, don't you agree?"

"Yeah, I've never kept anything from you, Jenny."

I looked at him in sheer astonishment. Did he actually say that to me without even hesitating once? I shot up off the sofa. I felt my face turn a hundred shades of crimson red. I was so furious with him that I wanted to spit at him.

"What's going on?" he asked.

I took a deep breath and tried to compose myself as I turned towards him. "I can't believe you! I can't believe the gall and audacity you have to sit here in my house and outright lie to me as though there was nothing to this!"

"What are you talking about? I don't understand where this is coming from. Calm down and come here, please. Sit back down and let me in on why you're so mad at me." He grabbed my arm, and I yanked it from his grasp and walked away from him.

"What am I supposedly lying to you about?"

At this point, I was fuming. I could feel the steam rising from my face, and I could tell he was becoming agitated with me for beating around the bush. "The god damn races, Liam! The damn races that you are going to tonight." Liam's mouth dropped to the floor. "You didn't think I knew about them did you? Well, I do. You know it would be one thing to find out about them from you. But no, I had to find out about them from my best friend who is also going to the races with her boyfriend that she has only been dating a few days. Obviously they have a much stronger trust in their relationship than we do!"

I was screaming at this point, and I didn't feel the need to hold back. All the anger and frustration that had been pent up inside of me since Kendra's was finally coming out of me, and I wasn't going to try and stop it. Liam sat there looking dumb-struck. "You know, I really don't care if you go or not. It might not be something I totally agree with, but you know I wouldn't keep you from doing something you enjoy. What hurts the most is you couldn't be honest with me. You lied to me all day about these races. I gave you every chance to tell me, and you didn't."

Liam slowly rose from his sitting position and approached me. His hand reached for mine again. "Babe, I'm sorry. I knew you weren't a fan of them, and I knew you thought they were dangerous, so I thought the best thing was not to tell you at all."

I pulled my hand back. "So you'd rather lie to me than tell me the truth?" He knew I was right.

"I guess I didn't think it through, Jenny. I figured if you didn't know then no harm was done."

"No harm was done? What do you call this? Do you think I live under a rock or something? That I never talk to my friends? Come on, Liam, you blew it this time. Of course, I was going to find out if not today, sometime. People do talk to me you know. You're not the only one with friends!"

"Jenny, I'm sorry. I'm..."

I didn't let him finish. Sorry wasn't going to cut it.

"Just go Liam. You're going to be late if you need to pick up your friends. Anyway, it's almost eleven. If Kendra was right, you'll be racing soon."

Liam looked more hurt than I'd ever seen him before, and I didn't care. He wasn't going to be able to get out of this that easy. How could I trust him after this? Maybe it was a minor detail, on the grand scale of things. It's not like I caught him cheating on me or anything, but if I let this go, then it'll be that much easier for him to lie to me again next time.

"Jenny, please, you've got this all wrong. Look I won't even go if that's what you want. I don't want to leave you like this."

"Liam, I want you to go."

"You know, I was just trying to protect you. I didn't want you to worry about me. I hope you know that's why I didn't say anything to you. It wasn't anything else. It wasn't because I didn't want you there, or that I was sneaking around or anything like that. I just didn't want to upset you, especially since last week's accident. But I guess it doesn't matter. You're upset anyway."

I didn't look at him. I could feel the tears flowing down my face.

"Yeah, whatever Liam."

I ran to my room and slammed the door, leaving him standing in the living room alone. I waited at my door to hear Liam's next move. After several minutes had passed, I heard my front door slam shut and the screeching of Liam's truck pulling out of my driveway. I fell on my bed and drowned myself in tears.

Chapter Fourteen
The Apology

    I must have fallen asleep because the next thing I remembered was my cell ringing. Instantly, I thought of Liam and the drag races. Even though I was still feeling the same tormented rage, there was nothing worse than being awakened by the phone at an ungodly hour of the night. I picked it up immediately.

    "Hello?" I said nervously.

    "Jenny, it's Mom. Are you still up, or did I wake you?"

I breathed a huge sigh of relief. "Hey, Mom. No, I was asleep. What time is it?"

"It's after midnight, dear. I was just calling to let you know that Dad and I are not going to be home tonight. Ashley wants us to spend the night. We'll be home sometime tomorrow. Will you be okay?"

"Sure, Mom."

"If you need anything just call. Love you hon, goodnight."

"Love you guys too, 'night."

"Oh, Jen, you did lock the doors before you went to bed didn't you?"

"Yeah, I think so, but I'll go check again. See you guys tomorrow."

"Alright, dear, bye."

I lay back in bed and stared at the ceiling. I felt horrible. I was sick to my stomach yet relieved that the phone call wasn't about Liam being in another accident, but I was also reminded about how we had left things. It was never my intention to get so hot-headed with him, and I let my emotions get the best of me. It was our first major fight, and I felt like crawling under the proverbial rock that I had told Liam I didn't occupy. I sighed heavily. I was too emotional and upset to go back to sleep. I laid there thinking about how tonight's events unfolded and wondering if Liam was feeling as bad as I was, *probably not*.

It was almost half past midnight. *The races were probably over, or were they?* I didn't have the slightest clue how long they lasted. I guess it all depended on how many raced and how they played out. I wondered how Liam did, if he won and if he was okay. He was right on one point though. I didn't like them. It was a dangerous game that the guys played, and I wasn't a fan.

Too many people had gotten hurt, and I wasn't trying to be uptight, but after the accident last week, I had reason for concern where Liam was involved. Nevertheless, I would have loved to have been there to support him and cheer him on. The thought crossed my mind to get dressed and see what all the fuss was about. I could call Kendra and ask her, but then it might sound like I was checking up on him, so I resisted my urge. *On the other hand, Liam still might call me.*

I looked at my phone, staring at it, hoping I could somehow mentally make it start ringing. Nothing happened. There was only silence. I could feel my anger subsiding. Guilt and feeling sorry for myself replaced it. There was no need to lay here in my own self-pity though. Liam wasn't going to call. *Anyway, it was late, and besides, I was the one who gave the impression that I didn't want to talk to him anymore. I was the one that walked away from him, leaving him standing alone in my living room. I didn't blame him one bit. I wouldn't call me either. I never gave him a chance.* He wasn't going to make the next move. The ball was in my court, but my stubbornness wasn't allowing me to make the call either.

Instead of picking up the phone, I went downstairs to eat my way through a pint of mint chocolate chip ice cream. After a good twenty minutes of self-pity consumption of the dairy concoction, I could tell it wasn't helping me. I still felt as bad as ever, and to make things worse, I felt like a pig for eating almost the entire container. Gaining five pounds over a stupid argument wasn't going to solve anything. The only solution would be to talk to Liam, but it was too late to do that.

I headed back upstairs when I remembered Mom's last words to check the doors. I walked around the house checking all of them. They were all locked except the front door. I turned the knob, and it opened. I remembered that Liam was the last to leave, and I guessed he hadn't locked the door behind him. I turned the key and heard the click. Locked. I turned around to head back to bed when a shadow of a truck in my driveway caught my eye. I strained my eyes to look out the window. The black truck with silver edging was a dead giveaway. I walked outside into the frigid air to see why Liam was here. I wasn't wearing my robe, and the cold air embraced my body as I made my way towards his truck. His truck sat so high off the ground that it made it next to impossible for me to look inside. I had to step up on the truck's step to actually see anything. There sat Liam, asleep behind the wheel. I opened the passenger side door and slipped in, instantly waking him.

"Jenny," he said sleepily.

"Liam, what are you doing here? It's almost one o'clock in the morning?"

"I came back after the races. I wanted to talk to you. You were so upset. I didn't think you would want to see me though. So I just sat here in my truck. I guess I must have fallen asleep."

"Did you... race?" I asked, hoping his answer would be no.

"Yeah, Jen, I did. I know it's probably not what you want to hear, but I did. You know, I almost didn't. After you walked out on me, I left your house with every intention of just going home. But I found myself driving out to Ripley Road, and you know, I decided to go ahead with it. I'm sorry. I won't ever lie to you again, and if you're interested, I would love to take you next time I race."

I sat there on his cold seat looking down at the new floor mats that my parents had given him for Christmas. I was confused. I was so happy to see him, but at the same time, I still couldn't get past the lying, and even after everything that happened between us tonight, he still decided to race. I didn't know how to comprehend that.

"Liam, I don't know. I'll have to think about it."

I kept my face down, not daring to look at him. I was still unnerved, and I knew the littlest gesture could cause me to begin crying again. Instead, I rocked myself back and forth to try and stay warm. Through the corner of my eye, I could see Liam make his way towards me. I moved closer to the door to send a message that things still weren't settled between us.

"Jenny, please don't. It was stupid for me not to consider your feelings. Honestly, I never would have done this if I thought this was going to happen."

He was next to me now, and I had nowhere to go. I was pinned against the passenger door as he lifted my chin to meet his eyes.

"Jenny, I love you. I hate this, this tension between us. Please, I'm telling you I'm sorry. Why else would I sit out here in my truck, in the freezing cold, in your driveway, in the middle of the night if I didn't mean it?"

I softly chuckled. I didn't know any other boy that would do what Liam was doing. I just didn't know if I could trust him. Those two words should go hand in hand, and tonight they weren't. It did seem trivial, but my heart had been broken before by guys I thought I could trust. I didn't want to go down that road again.

"Liam, I still don't understand why you couldn't just tell me about the races. If they're no big deal, then why keep me in the dark? Maybe you're thinking I'm agonizing too much over this, but if you can intentionally keep this from me, how do I know you won't keep other things from me also? I need to know I can trust you. I've never lied to you. Why did you think it was alright to lie to me?"

"I don't have an answer for you. I was thinking that I was protecting you by not letting you know. I know these races can be dangerous, and I guess I thought it would be better if you didn't know about them. That way you wouldn't worry. But instead of protecting you, I made a mess out of everything."

"Well, you're right about that. They are dangerous. I thought you would have enough common sense to not intentionally try to kill yourself."

His brow furrowed down. "Jenny, you know you're the most important person in the world to me. I would never do anything stupid, but I've done these races a hundred times. They're not half as dangerous as you're making them out to be. The stories you hear are usually just that: stories. The guys who have gotten hurt were because they were doing something really stupid while they were racing, like drinking or being high. I don't do that. Me and the boys just enjoy doing it for the thrill of it. It's like an adrenaline rush, that's all. That's where we get our high, not from doing stupid shit like drinking or taking drugs before we race."

"But you were drinking. When I talked to you on the phone earlier, you said you and Parker were having a beer."

"We were, but that was hours before the races, and I only had the one, honest."

I looked at him skeptically. "Were you planning on telling me if I hadn't had brought it up first?" He didn't answer. He didn't have to. His silence was all the answer I needed. "That's what I thought." I felt a tear slowly descending down my cheek, and I quickly tried to wipe it away, but Liam did it for me.

"Jenny, please don't cry. I don't know what else to say. All I can do is tell you that I won't keep things from you again, and hopefully that will be enough for you."

He put his arms around me, and his embrace sent a warming sensation throughout my body. I was colder than I thought.

"You're like an icicle." He took off his letterman's jacket and placed it around me. It smelled like him, and even better, it felt good around my frigid body.

"Thanks, but this doesn't mean I'm forgiving you."

"Maybe not, but consider this a peace offering. You know you can't stay mad at me forever."

He leaned in to kiss me and hesitated. He waited to make sure I wanted it. I didn't move, but I couldn't resist him either.

"I'm so sorry. I never meant to hurt you like this."

"I know." I looked at his clock. The time read 1:11 in the morning; that damn number again.

"Am I forgiven?" Liam's lips were touching mine as he spoke.

"I'm thinking about it."

"Why don't we go in your house, and I can try to convince you some more?"

The thought of having Liam all to myself for the entire night with no parents in the house was almost too tempting to pass up, but I knew it wasn't the right thing to do. For one thing, I had no idea when my parents would be returning tomorrow. Even though they were in Ohio, they have been known to get up in the middle of the night and drive home. I wouldn't put it past them to do it again. I could just see the look in their eyes when they opened my bedroom door to find Liam lying next to me. Talk about losing trust. Any and all that I had with them would be vanquished forever.

Furthermore, our one elderly tenant across the street, Mildred Jones, was known for her innate snooping abilities. She had been my dad's secretary for over thirty-five years. She was the eyes and ears of the business when he couldn't be around, more or less a business confidante to him. She always had my dad's back. About five years ago, her husband, Arnold, passed away of a sudden heart attack. She was devastated. They had no children, and Arnold was her life. Mom and Dad took it upon themselves to take care of her, handling all the funeral arrangements and helping her close up their house. Mildred felt deeply indebted to them. I think that's why she felt so compelled to keep an eagle eye on our place and the business when they weren't around. It was a lovely gesture on her part but very annoying when it interfered with my own personal life.

It was much easier to face the disappointment in Liam's face than to deal with the flack I would receive when Mom and Dad found out from Mildred that I had Liam over unsupervised for the entire night. In a word or two, all hell would break loose. I looked at Liam as he waited patiently for my impending yes to invite him in. My heart ached over what I was about to say. It would be one of the first times I had refused him, something I'm sure he wasn't ready to hear.

"I don't think we should. I want you to, really, but I don't think tonight. I'm really tired, and I'm sure you're grandpa is worried about you. Besides, even though my parents are gone, it doesn't mean they won't know. There are eyes everywhere. Trust me," I said, a phrase that seemed flippant after tonight's argument. "My luck, we'll get caught before we walk in the front door. Do you understand?"

"Yeah, I do, but that doesn't mean I don't want to," Liam said as he snuggled closer to me.

His attempt to change my mind was admirable but futile. His body felt warm, and I was slowly begun to thaw out. "You're sure you don't want me to come up if anything, just to keep you warm? I'm sure nobody will see us. It's too late. Everybody's asleep."

He was hard to turn down, but I had to think with my head and not my heart. "No, not tonight. I just don't think it's a good idea."

"I'm being rejected, aren't I?"

"Come on. That's not fair."

"I know. I'm sorry. I understand, really. I guess I just didn't want this to end. Making up is so much better than fighting, don't you agree?"

I smiled at him. "Thanks for understanding. Call me tomorrow?"

"You know I will, babe."

I gave him a quick but meaningful kiss and hugged him tightly. He got out of his truck and walked around to open my door, always the gentleman, even at one in the morning.

"I'll talk to you tomorrow."

"Here's your jacket."

"You keep it."

I was glad. I didn't want to give it up anyway. He walked backward without taking his eyes off of me. He threw me a kiss and placed his hand over his heart. I was halfway on the doorstep when I heard his voice.

"By the way, you never did ask me how I did in the races tonight." He was beaming with pride.

"I'm guessing by the smile on your face that you must have done pretty good?"

"You know it, babe. I won both heats in record time."

"I wouldn't have thought otherwise."

"Thought you would like that. I had the best time the last race, 11.9 seconds, a personal best for me."

He blew me another kiss and hopped down the steps two at a time. I stood frozen in my spot. I murmured his time, 11.9 seconds. Even when you add the numbers together, they equal eleven. This was becoming incredibly strange. Liam was already down the road before I realized I was still standing in the doorway, allowing the frigid air to enter the house. I quickly turned to go inside, stopping only to check out Mildred's window. *No curtain movement, thank, God!*

I went inside and ran up the stairs, all the while repeating the number in my head. This had turned into more than just an interest. It was becoming an obsession, an obsession that I couldn't ignore anymore. It was slowly and intuitively taking control of every thought I had. I paced in my room while I tried to figure out what this meant. *This has to mean something, but what?* I looked at my laptop. The drive to stay up and Google the number was very appealing. *If I wasn't already half asleep on my feet, I would.* My body was beckoning me to lie down before I fell down. I passed my mirror and stopped in wide-eyed bewilderment at what I saw. I couldn't believe what was staring back at me. The number eleven I never noticed it before. I froze as I became enthralled with the digit. Liam always wore this jacket. The number was huge, taking up most of the jacket's sleeve in bright gold thread. I ran my hand over the soft fringe that made up the daunting digit. It was as if a higher being was calling to me, forcing me to stare at it. It was mesmerizing to look at it with such clarity, as though it was trying to speak to me, to let me know I wasn't crazy. It was real, and it was making itself known to me. I scoffed at the thought.

I pulled myself away from the mirror and forced myself to stop staring at the image. I was tired. It had been an emotionally long and draining day. I didn't even remember my head hitting the pillow as I fell fast asleep, protected by number eleven's embrace. A few hours later, I heard the sound of Mom and Dad opening the front door.

"Hello, Jenny we're home." Mom yelled from the foot of the steps.

I reluctantly opened my eyes. I looked at the clock. It was only six-thirty in the morning. My body needed more than the five hours of sleep it had just received. I rolled over, throwing my covers over my head as I heard Mom's footsteps coming up the stairs.

"Jenny, are you up?" Mom whispered as she entered my room.

"Hey, Mom, not really. I didn't get to bed till late. What time did you leave Ashley's? It had to have been in the middle of the night?"

"Oh, shortly after I called you. You know you're dad. He can't sleep unless he's in his own bed. Your sis only had a pull away bed, and it wasn't very comfortable. But anyway, go back to sleep, honey. I didn't really mean to wake you. I just wanted to check in on you."

She leaned in and gave me a nurturing kiss on my forehead. "Hey, what's this?" She was looking at Liam's letterman's jacket that I was still wearing.

"Oh, this? Liam gave it to me last night. He stopped by to say hello before he went out. I was cold, so he let me wear it. I guess I forgot to take it off when I went to bed."

She looked at me doubtfully. "You mean you wore it all night? What time did he stop over?"

"I don't know. It was pretty early. Like I said, I was cold. I just wore it around the house while I watched TV."

I tried to sound convincing, but it was hard, especially when I was still half asleep.

"Well, okay, dear. Go back to sleep. We'll talk later."

"Glad you're home, Mom."

She closed the door behind her, and I laid there in bed clutching Liam's jacket. I was wide awake now, and there was no point in trying to sleep. Even if my body was yelling for me to try again, it was pointless. The more I tried, the more awake I became. I felt that nagging sensation like a toothache coming on again about the number eleven. I took Liam's jacket off, opting to wear my robe instead, just in case my parents felt the need to berate me some more over it. I sat down at my laptop, staring at the blank screen.

"Where to begin?"

I started with the obvious. I Googled the number eleven. Hundreds of entries popped up: everything from histories of numerology, the Wikipedia's definition of the number, famous people who were born on the 11th, and so on. I scrolled down the list choosing my selection carefully, opting for the obvious and hopefully the easiest to understand. The entry entitled just "11", popped up, it didn't provide me with much useful information. Stating merely the obvious that it came after the number ten and before the number twelve. *Great information if I was teaching a kindergarten class the chronological order of the numbers one through twelve.* I continued on. *This one got me nowhere.*

Then I came across a definition, the meaning of the number eleven. I clicked on it. *Well, at least this was a little more informative than the first one I tried.* The entry stated that the number eleven was referred as a master number, dating back to the beginning of time. There were many biblical references to the number as well as positive and negative connotations. *Interesting, I thought, but what does it mean to me?* None of this information seemed to reflect any reason why it was popping up so much in my life. I continued. *Let's see what the positive and negative references have to say.* "Nervous energy... could mean subconscious attachment," *hmm, I pondered, this could be something.* "Heightened awareness," *well that is definitely true. I am much more aware of the number.* I continued to stare blankly at the screen. All of this was very interesting, but I needed more information and something with more substance that could lead to why it was making itself known to me.

I was completely absorbed when I heard Mom call up to me. "Jenny, it's for you. Are you still asleep?"

"No, I'll be right there."

I quickly saved my information to my favorites and turned off my computer. I tied my belt around my robe and rushed downstairs.

"It's Liam."

"Thanks, Mom... hello?"

"Hey, babe, whatcha doin?"

"Hey there. Nothin. I actually just got up a couple of minutes ago. You caught me just in time. I was about to get in the shower."

"Ooh, perfect timing."

"Honestly, is that all you ever think about?"

"Where you're concerned, I would have to say yes."

"So, why are you calling me so early?"

"You know I want to be the first voice you hear."

"I'm sorry to disappoint you, but you're second today. Mom was the first."

"Yeah, she answered your landline. You weren't answering your cell. I thought they were still visiting your sister in Ohio?"

"Dad couldn't sleep there. Ashley's mattress was uncomfortable or lumpy or something, so they drove through the night."

"Wow, I guess it's a good thing I didn't come in last night."

"You're telling me. That would not have been fun to explain. So what are you doing?"

"Nothing really, just sittin' around with Blue. Grandpa went into to town to have breakfast with someone."

"Anyone I know?"

"I don't know. I don't even know who he is. Grandpa had already left when I got up this morning. Just left a note saying he was having breakfast with an old friend."

"Oh, okay."

"Jenny?"

"Yeah?"

"Are you still mad at me?"

I was. I knew I was. I was letting his little white lie get to me more than it should. Even if he tried to make up with me, there was still a piece of me that didn't want to let it go.

"No. Not really. I don't know, maybe a little. I guess I'm still questioning why you did it."

"I said I was sorry."

"I know you did, but it just bothers me that you did it. If you care about me as much as you say, then I don't think we need to have secrets."

"You're right. We don't. My bad. Like I said, it won't happen again. How can I make it up to you?"

"You don't have to make it up to me. It's just me now. I have to let it go."

"Can I see you later?"

"Yes, I'd like that."

"Great, I'll pick you up in a half-hour."

"A half-hour? I thought you meant later in the day. That hardly gives me anytime to get ready. I just got out of bed. I'm a mess!"

"You can't look any worse than after we've been together, and you've always looked great then. You could have green slime oozing out of every part of your body, and I would be turned on by you."

"You're absolutely crazy!"

"Yeah, I know. I'll see you in thirty."

He hung up the phone before I had a chance to lobby for more time. I quickly grabbed my clothes and darted to the bathroom. Liam was never late, and I didn't expect him to start today. I was in and out of the shower in record time, allowing no time to wash my hair. I spritzed it with my favorite body splash and pulled it back in a neat and tidy ponytail. With only minutes to spare, I brushed my teeth and applied my favorite pink lip gloss. I darted down the stairs, taking two at a time to await his timely arrival.

"Where are you off to so early in the morning?" Mom said as she met me at the foot of the stairs.

"Liam's picking me up any minute. We're going to take a drive."

"So early? Where are you guys going?"

"I'm not sure. Probably just around town. He didn't really say."

"Well, I'm off to bed. I can hardly keep my eyes open, and Dad's already asleep. Be good, and be careful."

"Always am, Mom."

The doorbell echoed in the background. "That's him. Gotta go." I gave her a quick peck on the cheek and headed for the door.

"Hey, babe, ready?" I yanked on his arm and headed towards his truck.

"Whoa, what's the rush?"

"I just wanted to get out of there before Mom started asking more questions."

"Why? What's the matter?"

"Nothing, I don't think. It's just that Mom was a little suspicious of me having your jacket on last night."

"So," he interrupted. "What's wrong with you wearing my jacket?"

"Nothing, except that... well..." I was almost too embarrassed to tell him. "I slept in it."

"Oh, you did, did you?" He asked with a triumphant smile on his face. "Did you have sweet dreams?"

"Wouldn't you like to know?" I asked as he grabbed me around my waist.

"Yeah, actually I would. Do you ever dream about me?"

I thought about that. I couldn't remember dreaming of Liam. I'm sure I had at least once. Don't all girls dream of their knight in shining armor? I lied. "Yeah, all the time."

"Really? 'Cause I dream of you a lot!"

"You do?"

"Yes, even before we started dating. Like I've always told you, I can't stop thinking about you, even when I'm asleep." He pulled me close to him and kissed me softly on my lips.

"Umm, you taste good."

"Colgate," he replied with a snicker. He held me in his clutches. "Are you ready to go?"

"Yes, let's hit it, Mr. Colgate."

"Anything you say my dear. Your wish is my command."

He grabbed my hand and pulled me to his side of the truck, opened the door, and helped me inside. Following right behind, he situated himself behind his steering wheel. I scooted over to allow him more room.

"Oh no, you don't. Get back here girl. I missed you way too much to have you sit over there. You're not leaving my side all day."

"All day?" I said.

"Yep, you're mine till tonight, if that's okay?"

"That's very okay."

I nuzzled myself closer to him as he pulled me back to his side, forgetting all the anguish I had been keeping pent up from last night. His authoritative demeanor was a huge turn on.

"Where to, babe?"

"I don't care. Wherever you want."

He paused and bit his lower lip as he thought of a destination. He pulled out of my driveway and drove down the street.

"Where are we going? Did you decide?"

"Yes I did, and you'll know soon enough."

He squeezed my left leg with his right hand before settling it between my thighs, a gesture that he began from the first night we were together. The roads were nearly empty, probably because it was still early in the morning. Liam drove for about fifteen minutes when I recognized instantly the destination we were headed to: Brush Creek Road.

"I thought it would be nice to come here, especially today. You can see for miles."

He pulled his truck to our spot and positioned it so we could see the entire town of Spencer and beyond. The sun was hovering above the horizon, and beautiful hues of pink, blue, orange, and crimson painted the sky.

"It's still just as breathtaking, Liam."

I could feel his magnetic blue eyes wearing down on me. "Yes, you are Jenny. Come here." He pulled me to him.

"I didn't get a wink of sleep last night. All I could think about was how I hurt you. I never want you to feel that way again over me."

I was still hypnotized by his eyes. "Liam, stop beating yourself up over this. I'm over it." This time I meant it.

"Are you really?"

"Yes. I was holding a grudge for all the wrong reasons, when Kendra told me about the races, my heart sank. All I could think about was that it hadn't come from you. I was positive it was an oversight that you just hadn't had the chance to tell me. When I spoke with you that day and you never brought it up, I lost it. My imagination started going wild. I did actually think that maybe the races were a reason to meet a girl… maybe Shanna."

"Shanna?!" Liam shouted as he pulled away from me. "You honestly believe that I would go behind your back to meet up with her?"

"Well… I,"

"Jenny, first of all, Shanna and I are over, finished, kaput, done with, understand?" Liam placed his hands on my shoulders and held them firmly in his grasp.

"Yes," I said solemnly, not daring to look away from him.

"Secondly, I would never in a million years cheat on you. Why would I mess up the best thing that has ever happened to me? Remember when I told you that you were my refuge. I meant that. I can be myself with you. No one can hold a candle to you, especially Shanna. I would be lost without you."

The look in my eyes must have clued him in on how tightly he was holding on to me. He automatically loosened his grip only to run his hands down my arms until they found my hands. I looked at him intently. I'd never seen him speak with such tenacity. I began to feel ashamed for even thinking that he would try to lie to me.

"Liam..." Once more, he stopped me from speaking. This time he spoke softly though, and his voice and eyes were calm and subdued.

"Jenny, I want to marry you."

"What? What did you just say?" I could feel my heart beating a thousand beats a minute.

"I know this is unexpected, and believe me, I don't think I meant to say it so soon, but I've never meant anything more in my entire life. I've felt this way for some time now, and I can't imagine you not being in my life. It's probably presumptuous and premature of me to bring it up so early in our relationship, but I know it's you. I love you, and this isn't going away for me. My feelings are only growing stronger for you."

He stopped talking and waited patiently for my response. I had often thought that someday he would ask me, but I never thought it would be so soon. I wanted to say something, anything, but nothing would come out of my mouth. Everything felt in slow motion. It was surreal. I never had an out of body experience, but I was positive that this was how one felt. I became absorbed in what Liam was saying to me, but at the same time, I was paralyzed. My emotions controlled my physical ability to speak, or even move.

"I love you. I've loved you from the minute I saw you sitting on the hill that first day, and I know it's too soon to actually get married, but one day I want to. I want to spend the rest of my life with you."

"Liam, I…" Again, Liam's voice interrupted me.

"Jenny, I've wanted to tell you this from the beginning, but I knew it would be too soon. I didn't want to scare you away. I can't keep it in anymore. I love you, babe, and I want you forever."

He was beaming. The elation that exuded from him could only be compared to the times I saw him playing football and he had run for the winning touchdown. I waited, thinking that as soon as I tried to speak that he would interrupt me again. But this time he was silent. Only his eyes were talking to me now. Those beautiful crystal blue eyes confessed the same feelings that he had announced seconds ago.

"Liam, I'm sorry I ever doubted you."

I could feel my entire body beginning to tremble. He moved closer to me. His arms wrapped themselves around me. I wasn't cold in the slightest; I had his jacket on, but I couldn't keep from shaking.

"Jenny, you'll never lose me. It's me who should be worried about that."

I looked at him in utter confusion. "You're afraid of losing me, why?"

"You're beautiful. Don't you see it? I know everyone else does. You don't notice how guys turn and stare when you walk into a room?"

"You're crazy, Liam. No guys take the time to look at me."

"You could have any guy in Spencer. Hell, the entire county. I see them, and I hear them. When you walk into a room, guys are always checking you out. Sometimes it's all I can do to keep my hands to myself and not punch them out. I feel like the luckiest guy in the world because I'm with you. Why do you think it took me so long to get my nerve up to talk to you in the beginning? I was scared to death you wouldn't have anything to do with me."

I continued to stare at him in disbelief. "Are you kidding me?" I couldn't believe the irony here. The Liam Larson, the cutest guy in the tri-county area, was telling me that he was the fortunate one, that he felt lucky to be by my side. It was mind-boggling. Everywhere he went, he was a magnet, attracting guys and girls to his side. Everyone wanted to be next to him, and he didn't see it. Instead, he put me on the pedestal. "Liam, it's you who could have any girl you want. You're the all-American football player, the leader of the pack, the guy everyone looks up to, and every girl wants to be with. How in the world can you say you're the lucky one? No one acts like that around me."

"But that's where you're wrong, Jenny. You just don't see it. Listen, I know what you're saying. I know people clamor to be around me, but that's just because I played football. If you actually paid attention to who sticks by me through thick and thin, it's my friends, my true friends: Parker and Tony. If I didn't perform well on the field, I can guarantee you I wouldn't have the same posse following me. That's why you're different. You didn't care about how many touchdowns I scored, or even who I was. I can be myself with you and let my guard down. That's why you became my refuge. That's why I love you and one day I will marry you. That's a promise."

He pulled me to him. The clock in his truck read 10:11, and in that instant I knew that the meaning of this number had to play a part in our relationship. For what it was worth, I was betting on it being a good thing. I had to stop worrying about the negative and concentrate on the positive. My sister and Kendra were right; the glass was half full. Almost everything connected with this number was somehow right, like a tie or bond that brought Liam and me together. I didn't understand it yet, but I would, and in time, Liam would too.

Chapter Fifteen
The Revelation

Liam and I spent the rest of the morning at Brush Creek Road.

"What are you thinking about?" He asked me.

"How happy I am, and how my life has changed since you entered it. You know, if you were to have asked me if I would be sitting here next to you a few months ago, I would have said no."

"Why do you say that?"

"Because we ran in different circles. We never saw each other. Besides you playing football, I didn't know anything about you, and I wouldn't have imagined you knew of me."

"Trust me, I knew a lot about you."

I kissed him gingerly on his lips and moved my hands to the back of his head. I pulled his ponytail out and twisted my fingers through his hair. He turned his body to meet mine. We had become experts in entangling ourselves in the limited space his truck allowed. He pushed me gently down until I was prone on the seat. My hands were still wrapped around his hair. He brought his lips to mine while his hands explored my body. He wasn't saying a word, and he didn't have to. I could read his body movements instinctively. I wrapped my left leg around his waist and forced him closer.

"Jenny, I want to take you back to my place." He arched my body to his and kissed my face and neck. "I don't think I can wait though."

I didn't want him to stop either. We had done a lot in his truck but never that. I wasn't sure if it was possible, but I was more than willing to find out. I grabbed his shirt and pulled it over his head. He immediately helped me out of his jacket, taking my shirt with it. Before I knew it, we were moving together, loving each other with no conviction.

Liam's head rested on my chest and my left leg was still wrapped around his lower torso, and my arms were around his neck. I looked at his clock. 12:11 on the dot. Not again, I thought. He lifted his head to look at me. He kissed me as he met my gaze.

"I guess we didn't make it back to my house."

I started laughing. "No, but we can still go if you want. I definitely could continue where we left off."

"I like the way you think, girl!"

I couldn't ignore him, but I also couldn't keep from thinking about how I kept seeing eleven all morning. Two monumental moments happened when the time read eleven. First, when he confessed his desire to marry me, and second, our most recent rendezvous. That had to mean something. My concentrated expression caught Liam's attention.

"Babe, you okay? You look like you're off in your own little world."

"Yeah, I'm fine, perfectly fine."

I maneuvered myself up, allowing both of us to sit up. A couple cars passed by and we decided we better get dressed. Most of our clothes were on the truck's floor. Only a couple articles of clothing clung to us, and they were strategically placed. We laughed at the thought of someone seeing us. We really didn't care; we really were loving one another. It was us showing our heart and soul to each other in the rawest of forms. Another car passed and this time slowing down. The man driving rolled his window down.

"You guys okay? Having car trouble?" The elderly man asked.

Liam opened the back cab window. "No. Thanks though. Just enjoying the view," he said and pointed to the horizon.

"Oh, you kids have a great spot to enjoy the scenery." He drove away.

Liam was completely dressed, but I was still trying to pull my jeans on, and my top was nowhere to be found.

"Yeah, the view isn't so bad in here either old man," Liam said, as he handed me my shirt.

"Liam!"

"What? I'm just telling the truth," he snickered and planted another kiss on my never deprived lips.

"What do you want to do now?" He asked as I put on his jacket.

"I'm starving. Let's go get something to eat."

"You're always starving after we do that."

"I can't help it. I guess I work up an appetite."

"Hmm..." he said with a smile.

"Why don't we go back to my house? I've got leftover pizza from last night."

I was starving, and pizza sounded good, especially since Kendra and I never got to eat the one we ordered the previous night. "You guys really got pizza last night?"

"Yeah, I told you we were. You didn't believe me?"

"Well, at the time I guess I didn't."

"Silly girl. When are you going to realize I don't keep things from you, well most things," he said as he remembered the races.

He put his truck into drive and pulled me to my usual spot next to him.

"I guess now," I said

"Good. Don't ever think otherwise."

He squeezed my waist and drove to his house. The house looked empty. Grandpa Mack's old Chevy truck was nowhere in sight, and Blue didn't come running to greet us as we drove up.

"Is your grandpa still out?"

"Yeah, looks like it. He didn't really say when he was coming home."

He parked his truck next to the house, opened his door, and grabbed my hand as we stepped out. We went into the kitchen, Liam opened the fridge, and a Lougini's pizza box was presented to me.

"Just like you like it: everything but anchovies. You get a couple of plates, and I'll heat up the pizza."

I went to the cupboard and grabbed two porcelain plates, cautious not to break Liam's grandma's favorite china. They had been in Liam's family for over a hundred years, passed down until they had ended in Grandma Larson's possession. They were beautiful: off-white with a beautiful blue rose pattern and green leaves filigreed throughout the plates. I'd never seen Liam or his grandpa use any other. He once told me that his grandparents believed in using things instead of simply admiring them. "What's the use of having it if you're not going to use it," his grandparents had always told him. It put the Corelle dinnerware we used at home to shame.

I placed slices of pizza on our plates. Lougini's pizza didn't belong on Grandma Larson's china. It was like wearing your old favorite tennis shoes with your wedding gown. They just didn't go together, but then again, the pizza did look pretty good on them. *Maybe tennis shoes and wedding gowns would also work.* We grabbed a couple of drinks and made our way into the living room.

My Christmas tree was still there and as beautiful as ever. The crystal and blue ornaments that hung from the tree still took my breath away. It was in my opinion, besides the necklace Liam gave me, the sweetest gesture he'd ever done for me. We sat in silence for a few minutes while we consumed the pizza. Both of us were hungrier than we thought. Blue must have smelled the food because he sauntered in from the back door wagging his tail and plopping himself next to Liam where he watched and waited patiently for us to drop some pepperoni. I handed Blue a couple of pieces to satisfy his hunger. He licked my fingers appreciatively and resigned himself to the fact that he had gotten all he would get. He was asleep within minutes.

"Hey, you okay?"

"Huh?" I must have had that same spaced out look on my face from earlier. "Yeah, I guess I was just thinking."

"About what?" he asked curiously.

I knew there was never going to be a better time than now to bring up my concerns about the number eleven, but I still didn't know if I should or not. The morning had been perfect, and I didn't want to spoil it with my stupid preoccupation. But that was always my excuse. I never wanted to bring it up because I thought it would spoil the mood. Procrastinating was becoming my forte.

"Liam." I paused, wondering how to begin.

"Yes?" He put his plate on the end table and laid down on the sofa, propping his head on my lap.

"We can talk to each other about anything, right?"

"Of course, I thought we've already had this conversation?"

"We have, but this isn't about last night. This is something else, something that's been on my mind for a while."

"Oh, okay. Shoot. I'm all ears." He snuggled himself closer in my lap and began playing with the buttons on my shirt.

"You won't laugh or anything will you?"

"Laugh? No Jen, just tell me already."

I took a deep breath, positive that as soon as he heard how ridiculous this sounded he would burst out laughing and would have to apologize for saying he wouldn't.

"It's just that—and please don't call me crazy—but it just seems that over the past couple of months since we've been together, I keep seeing this number."

"Number?"

"Everywhere I look, I keep seeing the number eleven."

"The number eleven? You mean my football jersey number?"

"Yes, but not just that. When I look at the clock, it will read 3:11 or 10:11. You'll call, and the minute will be on the eleven. I thought it was just a coincidence at first, but it's happening all the time. Then I started thinking back on things you've told me and things I remember, and I realized that it was playing a part in other areas too."

"Like what?" He was still messing with the buttons on my shirt, trying to strategically place his face in my stomach.

"Are you listening?"

He had successfully unbuttoned two of my bottom buttons and was now licking my stomach, "Yeah, you just taste good. I was still hungry for dessert."

"You're hopeless! I'm trying to be serious!"

"Jenny, I'm listening. I'm listening, please go on. Where else have you seen the number?"

"Everywhere Liam. I thought back on when you told me the first time you saw me. Remember when you were going to football practice, and I was sitting on the grass during majorette practice? That was on the 11th, August 11th, and the night at Lougini's was on the 11th."

He sat up and faced me. "So what? Some important events in our life just happened to have fallen on that date."

His smile was always reassuring to me. He gave me a wink, trying to express to me that this preoccupation meant nothing.

"But don't you see? It's as if there's some outside force playing a part in our relationship. There have been too many instances for it to be just a coincidence. Plus, that's your number; everyone associates you with that number. All people have to say is 'number eleven', and we all know they're talking about you. And it's just not those things. Remember the night at the Black Walnut Festival when you met up with me. I was with Kendra?"

"Yeah, I was looking for you and found you at the carnival."

"Right, and you and I rode the Ferris wheel together. The cart number, it was eleven."

Liam looked at me with his blue eyes. "Come on Jen, that's nothing."

"Maybe not, if that was the only time I noticed it."

"But everything you've mentioned have been good things, maybe it's just a good omen."

"Possibly. I was thinking that too until last week when you and your grandpa were in the accident. The accident happened on Route 11, and when Parker called in, the accident report said the time was 7:11 in the morning. You said you received eleven stitches in your shoulder, and your hospital room number had the number eleven in it." I felt I was rambling. "Liam, how can all these be coincidences?"

"What are you trying to say? Do you think that some supernatural force is behind this?"

"I don't know. It's just that I've been keeping this inside, and I've wanted to tell you, but I didn't know how you would react. I don't know what it means, but I can't ignore it anymore. I see it on such a regular basis that if I don't see it I wonder why." I had worked myself up to the point where I started shaking. Liam noticed and pulled me to him, wrapping his arms around me.

"Babe, you're shaking like a leaf. It's okay." I nestled into him and inhaled the scent of his body. "You're really upset about this, aren't you, Jen?"

"Yes I am. You know last night when you thought I overreacted about the race; well I was upset about you deceiving me. But Kendra told me you were supposed to race in heat eleven. When she said that, I just about lost it. It was that damn number again. That's why I called you yesterday afternoon. I thought maybe it was a sign of something bad. I wanted to warn you. All I could think about was the accident last week. I was scared to death that you might be in another one, all because you were racing that night and in that race. But when you called me back I couldn't tell you. I didn't know how, and I didn't want to bring it up over the phone, especially with Kendra there."

"Did you tell her about how you were feeling?"

"Yeah, I did. I had to. I couldn't bring myself to tell you yet, and I had to get it off my chest before I exploded."

"What does she think?"

"She thinks I'm overreacting. I also told my sister and of course she basically said the same thing. Maybe I am, but it all seems to be related to me and you."

"But that's a good thing." He sat up and held my hands. "Listen, I don't think you're crazy, and I don't think you're overreacting, but I do think that there's nothing behind this. Maybe you're just noticing it because it was my football jersey, and you're seeing it more often. Hell, in my room alone you're going to see that number at least fifty times. It's all over my walls."

"I guess so, but please, can you promise me that you'll just be more aware of it and be careful. Humor me with it, please?"

"Anything for you, Jenny." He kissed the top of my hands and brought his lips to mine.

"Better?" He asked.

"Yeah, thanks for listening. And Liam?"

"Yeah?"

"Thanks for not laughing at me." I placed myself back into him, and he leaned back on the sofa as we snuggled closely.

"Jen?"

"Yeah?"

"Look what time it is?" I glanced over at the grandfather clock in the far corner of the living room. 2:11 in the afternoon.

"See! What did I tell you?"

"Yeah, spooky isn't it?"

"Exactly my point."

"You know you could have told me this in the very beginning. You didn't have to keep this bottled up. I would have listened."

"You tell me that now, but we had just started dating when this all started. I didn't really know you all that well. I was still trying to figure you out for myself. I couldn't bring this up until I was sure about us."

"You mean you had doubts about us?"

"Of course. It's only natural. You do have a reputation that precedes you, you know. I had to make sure you weren't the egotistical jock that everyone made you out to be. You know the love 'em and leave 'em type, wham bam thank you ma'am."

"I can't believe you even considered that to be true of me!" He seemed truly surprised by my remark.

"I don't believe it now. I do know you a little better. I didn't have anything to base it on then. The rumors held more substance at the time, but don't worry, I'll defend your honor now. You've proven your character to me."

"Well, thank you for your vote of confidence."

"Anytime babe, anytime."

He started tickling me when the front door swung open.

"Hey kids."

Liam immediately stopped upon hearing Grandpa's voice. "Hey Grandpa, what's up?"

"Nothing much, Liam. Just went into town and had breakfast with an old friend."

"Anyone I know?"

"I don't think so. His name is Ott Banner. He still has some family in this area and was just passing through town. How are you, Jen?"

"Great Grandpa, now that Liam is done tickling me to death."

"You gotta watch out for that boy. He's got an ornery streak in him."

"I'm finding that out. Thanks for the advice."

"Well kids, I'll be outside. Looks like we're expecting some more snow tonight, and I want to fill the hay troughs for the horses. I'll see ya later."

"Grandpa, leave that for me. I'll do it later."

"Don't worry about it Liam. Let me do it. You've been treating me like an invalid ever since we got home from the hospital. I'm more than capable to put some hay in some troughs without supervision." He walked out of the room in a huff.

"What was that all about?"

"Oh nothing, he's just been on edge ever since the accident. He's not the type to be waited on hand and foot, and he's having a hard time letting me take over some of the chores that he's always done."

I stared at Liam with admiring eyes. All of a sudden I was looking at him in a whole new light, a whole new perspective, a clarity. He carried himself with such confidence for being only seventeen years old. He had the maturity of a man much older. Maybe it was because Liam and his grandpa had never had anyone else in their lives for so long that they had to depend on each other. I could see the love and respect Liam held for Grandpa Mack. It ran deeper than what they portrayed, an unspoken bond. But for whatever reason, it made me love Liam even more. *Love*, I thought to myself. *I love him.* A huge smile came across my face. It was an epiphany. I knew right then that I was totally head over heels in love with Liam Larson. I couldn't help but start laughing at my revelation. Liam looked at me with a puzzled expression.

"What's come over you?"

I threw my arms around his neck, squeezing him with all my might.

"Hey, what brought all this on?"

I didn't answer him. Instead, I pressed my lips so hard against his that we fell backward onto the couch. When I finally did look at him, I swear I could see his soul through those magnificent blue eyes.

"I love you, Liam."

He stared intently at me. "What? What did you just say, Jen?"

"I said I love you. I love you, Liam, with all my heart."

"You do? You're sure? You're not just saying that for my sake? Not just because I told you how I felt? Because I don't think I could…"

I put my finger over his lips to shut him up. "Yes, I love you more than anything."

The same smile I was wearing came across Liam's face too.

"Whoo-hooo!" he exclaimed.

He got up off the sofa, picked me up in the process, and swung me around and around in the middle of the living room. He was moving so fast that I became dizzy. The fireplace, the Christmas tree, and the grandfather clock were nothing but a blur. I buried my head into his shoulder so I wouldn't get sick from the spinning, and finally after six or seven turns, Liam gently placed me down only to kiss me long and hard.

"Jenny, you've just made me the happiest guy in the whole wide world. Are you sure you feel this way?"

"Yes. I think I have for a while, but not until right now did it hit me. You're the most caring and loving guy I know, and you love me. I can't believe I didn't realize it before now."

He picked me back up in his arms. His sore shoulder from the accident was just an afterthought. "Please babe, I don't think my stomach can handle any more spinning." Liam laughed as he held me tightly in his grasp.

"What's all the ruckus about?"

Grandpa Mack blurted out as he came back into the room. Liam slowly put me down and grabbing my hand.

"Sorry about that Grandpa. We were just... um horsin' around."

I couldn't tell if Liam was going to tell his grandpa the real reason for the commotion or not. He looked at me as if he was waiting for me to give him the go ahead. I smiled and squeezed his hand.

"She loves me!"

Grandpa Mack stood there staring at us with the same beautiful crystal blue eyes of Liam's. "Well, I could have told you that."

Grandpa Mack wasn't much for words, but when he did speak he was direct and to the point. No thrills or emotion, but you always knew how he felt. He gave me a wink, a gesture I had come to know and love.

"Alright, I'm gonna go outside and do some work now. I'll talk to you two lovebirds later," He said as he walked out of the room.

Liam turned my body to his. "I'm never going to let you go girl."

"I know, Liam."

The rest of the day, we helped around the farm, even though Grandpa insisted we didn't. We both knew he could use our help. The accident had been a week ago, and Grandpa did not want to relinquish to the fact that he still wasn't fully recovered. He didn't make much fuss over the help, just a few grunts, and moans when he realized he needed it. Although I've never worked on a farm, I did my best to help out where needed. With a little guidance from Liam, I had learned to operate a full-size tractor with ease, a big accomplishment for a girl who had never set foot on a farm until a couple of months ago.

By nightfall, the snow had begun falling in huge fluffy flakes, and within an hour, there was enough on the ground to make snowballs. I seized the opportunity. Grandpa had called it a night and had already gone to bed. Liam was putting away some hay bales and closing up the barn. I waited outside by the tractor that I had conquered when I grabbed some snow and shaped it into a perfect snowball, all the while not taking my eyes off Liam. Any suspicion from Liam would mean total defeat for my planned sneak attack. I had to be careful. He didn't have a clue as he walked towards me as if he didn't have a care in the world. I gave him a friendly smile with my hands held strategically behind my back. When he opened his mouth to speak, he didn't have a chance. Before he could say one word, I attacked. I threw my precisely made snowball directly towards his face with the grace and ease of a football player.

Bam! Direct hit. The look on Liam's face was priceless. Snow dripped from the top of his head and cascaded down his rugged chiseled chin. I started laughing uncontrollably. He stopped dead in his tracks. I froze, holding onto the tractor for support. *What is he going to do?* His expression changed swiftly, and I couldn't make out his next move. I had to be ready for anything. A devilish smile crept onto his face. I could tell his diabolical mind was working a mile a minute. He was planning his move. This time I didn't have a chance. I started easing my way backward. For every step I took, Liam took one too, mimicking mine exactly. I couldn't read his face.

"Liam, now come on, stop right there. It was just a snowball, one teensy, bitsy snowball." He wasn't listening, only moving closer to me and smiling. I had suddenly turned into the prey, and the predator was positioning himself to strike. I slowly backed away, trying to circle around the back of the tractor. I needed to barricade myself from him. He was quick, and I had to think fast. I quickly scoped the area. There was nowhere to run or hide. He was cornering me. He didn't care. As soon as I moved, Liam pounced and missed me by inches. I screamed.

"Don't you dare! It was just a snowball." He walked slowly around the tractor, not allowing me to be out of his sight. The barn was directly behind me. *If I can make it there, I might have a chance to gather more ammo. It's worth a shot.* I positioned myself, not daring to take my eyes off Liam. On the count of three, I was going to make a run for it.

One, two, three...THUD! I fell backward, tripping on the tractor's wheel. I immediately looked up to see where Liam was. The snow was falling in buckets and made me feel disoriented. It was too dark to see anything except the snow. Liam was nowhere in sight. He had become a ghost in the night. I quickly took advantage of my position to make another snowball, this one much larger than my first. I slowly rose up, keeping myself in a crouched position at all times behind the tractor. I looked everywhere.

"Liam, where are you?" Nothing, just dead silence. I gathered more snow. I had to be prepared. It looked like this was going to be a sneak attack from him. Then, from behind, *BAM* again! Direct hit to the back of my head. I fell to the ground, and Liam raced to my side, falling on top of me laughing hysterically.

"Gotcha!" He roared in triumph as he pulled me into his arms. His look quickly became serious. His laughing stopped as he whispered to me. "Gotcha forever, Jenny." He gazed through to my soul. "I love you."

"I love you too, babe."

Chapter Sixteen
Johnny Bryant

It was January and time to go back to school. The hubbub and excitement that the Christmas break had brought was nothing more than a memory. I was relieved though. I needed some normalcy in my life. I had professed my love to Liam, and that made up for all the misconceptions that we had gone through over the course of the break. Liam had once said that it was love at first sight for him. But I, on the other hand, needed more convincing and a little coaxing. He was The Liam Larson, the most popular boy at Spencer High. He could have any girl he wanted just by saying the word, and I had to be sure I wasn't going to end up as another notch on his belt. Most girls would have given their front teeth to be where I was. So I had to be sure, and finally, I was.

Liam didn't care for anyone but me. I was his refuge, as he put it. He could be himself with me, and he truly adored me. I knew it. I belonged with him, and he belonged with me, and nothing in the world was going to change that.

Of course, there was my little obsession with the number eleven. I had beaten myself up over it, and for the longest time, it had kept me from telling Liam. I was so worried about his reaction to my obsession over the number that I almost let it come between us. *Stupidity should be my middle name.* Liam didn't belittle or chastise me. Instead, he listened with open ears and made me feel better. The eleven was still there. It didn't go away, but I knew it would be okay. For whatever reason, this number was in our lives. *I know we can get through this; I have his love and support.*

I still saw the number more than ever. Of course, I saw it in the usual places, like the time of day and the fact that it was Liam's number. His bedroom was a shrine to the oddity. But now it was popping up in other places too. I would be driving down the road, and the next exit would be eleven miles away, or I would be number eleven in line at the store. It was still driving me crazy, but instead of dealing with this on my own, I could now openly talk to Liam about it. He tried to stave it off, never berating me, only listening with open ears. Even still, I felt as though I was seeing this number for a reason; as if everything I had seen so far was nothing more than foreshadowing of something else that was going to happen in our lives. I still had this unsettling suspicion that I was being prepared for something more monumental. I just hadn't pinpointed it yet. In my mind, it hadn't happened, everything that had happened up until this point were only signs. *There has to be more to this than mere coincidences, but a missing piece to the puzzle is still needed.* The only thing I didn't tell Liam about the number was that it scared me. It was stupid, I know, but I couldn't help it. And until I knew why, I was going to make sure that Liam and I were cautious in everything we did.

With the New Year came new beginnings. For one, a new class schedule for the second half of the school year. This was it: five months until graduation, countdown to freedom. *Where had the time gone?* Luckily for Liam and me, Liam was able to drop and add classes to his schedule in order to make ours match. It didn't hurt to be Liam Larson at Spencer High. Even though football season was over, he was still their boy with the golden touch who could do no wrong. All he had to do was wink and even the teachers fell under his spell, male teachers included. I do believe all the female staff had a crush on him, and all the male staff wanted to be Liam's best friend. It was crazy and something I was still getting used to.

    I never got much notice in school. I did my thing, and that was it. I blended with the crowd, an anonymity that I relished. Now things were different. I was Liam Larson's girlfriend. If I wasn't getting stares of admiration from the people who were happy for me, I was getting stares and glares from those who weren't happy for me. Either way, I was receiving more attention than I deserved or wanted. I never understood how Liam could stand it. *Thank God he doesn't take it seriously.* He always said that the accolades and attention meant nothing to him. All that was important to him was that he played good football and that his Grandpa Mack was proud of him; and more recently, that I cared.

    I didn't have to worry about asking Mom and Dad for the car anymore. Liam was at my doorstep bright and early every morning at seven sharp in his big black Ford truck to take me to school. He was even my alarm clock, calling me at five-thirty so he would be the first voice I heard. If there had ever been any doubt in my parents' minds about him, they had diminished. Liam had won them over too, not that it took much for Liam to win anyone over. He had a way about him that made him likable and approachable.

    Even with the New Year and new classes, school had become less than desirable. I was so over it. I felt as if I was going through the motions instead of actually being a part of the class. Maybe Liam had something to do with it. He definitely was more fun to think about than the history of France. I had to force myself to concentrate, an activity that was new to me. The first week of classes was monotonous. There were no tests or papers due and no homework. This was the week when the teachers explained what the semester would entail and what they expected from us. Ugggh, boring to the tenth degree. The best thing about the class was Liam. He always sat next to me and would constantly write or text me messages expressing his undying love for me and other things that were too inappropriate for class. We were having a blast. We were young, happy, and totally in love.

With the New Year also came new faces. One of them was Johnny Bryant, Liam's arch nemesis in football, or so I thought. He had transferred over to Spencer High from Walton. His parents grew up in the Spencer area and had decided to move back after the holidays and before Johnny graduated. Even though I didn't know him, I felt for him. How horrible to spend your entire life in one school, growing up with the same friends, and then have your life disrupted, all because your parents wanted to move back to their old stomping grounds. Luckily for Johnny, he acclimated easily. He knew most of the boys from our school from playing sports. He had been accepted into the group with open arms, and to my surprise, Liam was one of the first to welcome him.

"I'm really surprised that you and Johnny Bryant are on friendly terms."

"Why does that surprise you, babe?" He asked as he scribbled figure eights on the back of my hand during study hall.

"Because he's from Walton, our arch rival. He's the enemy."

"Just because he played on a rival team doesn't mean we can't be friends. Actually Johnny and I have known each other since pee-wee football."

"Oh really?"

"Yeah, I guess I didn't mention him because he was at a different school. We hang out, and we've been going to the same parties and haunts for years, even raced against each other." He hesitated.

"The drag races?"

"Those would be the one."

The races were still a sore subject between us. He immediately took his eyes off of mine and concentrated on the figure eights he was still drawing so meticulously on the back of my hand.

"Would you mind telling me what you're doing?" I asked, as I failed miserably to pull my hand from his tight grip.

"Not at all. I'm getting you back for the sneaky snowball attack."

"Oh, I see, payback?"

"Yeah, you know what they say about payback?" He leaned down and kissed my tattooed hand.

"Yeah, I do."

The bell rang, and as usual, we waited for our cue from Mr. Buford to leave. Only one more class and the weekend would begin. Mr. Buford gave his signal, and Liam took my books in his hand as we headed to Advanced English.

"So babe, Lougini's tonight?"

"Sure, sounds great."

"I'll pick you up after 6. I've got to help Grandpa with the horses first."

"Not a problem, I need to help Mom and Dad in the store anyway. That'll give me a chance to get that out of the way."

We walked into Mrs. White's Advanced English class. The class was full and only a few seats were available. Liam and I found some vacant seats in the back. There was a boy seating to the left of me, and Liam gave him the look, and in two seconds he changed seats.

"Why did you do that?"

"I wanted to be on this side, and I don't think he minded."

The boy was cowering down in his seat, looking at Liam in fear.

"You don't think he minded? You probably scarred him for life. He'll end up failing this class because of you. He'll be too preoccupied worrying about you to know what the class is about."

"Don't be so dramatic, babe. I just let him know that he was in my seat."

"Your seat?"

"Yeah, if it's next to you then it's my seat, plain and simple. Most of the kids know that. He just didn't get the memo."

"The memo? You sent out a memo on seating arrangements?"

"Well, not exactly, but most kids figure it out that where you are I'm right next to you. Everybody knows that."

He leaned over, grabbed my hand, and kissed it tenderly. The figure eights now looked like a Rorschach design on my hand. He let up his grasp, keeping my pinky in his clutch.

Mrs. White called the class to order as the final bell rang. "Good afternoon, cl…"

But she wasn't allowed to finish. Her classroom door swung open with such force that it hit the side wall, causing an echoing effect as it hit. All eyes were diverted towards it.

"Sorry, I'm late. I got lost."

She gave the intruder an unpleasant glance. "Please take a seat."

It was the one and only Johnny Bryant. He was much taller than I realized, easily matching Liam's height with dark brown hair and eyes. He never made eye contact with the class, only scanning the room fervently for an empty seat. He found one, on my right side and smiled harmlessly at me.

"Hi."

"Hi," I responded back.

Liam leaned over to put himself in view, "Johnny, hi!"

"Liam! Hey, finally a familiar face."

"How are things?"

"Good, except for getting lost."

They reached over and gave each other a knuckle bust.

"Johnny, this is Jenny, my girlfriend."

"Nice, to meet you, Jenny. So you're the famous Jenny King. It's finally nice to meet the girl who stole Liam's heart."

"Thank you. I think," I said, puzzled by his comment.

"Believe me, it's a good thing. I haven't seen Liam so happy in a long time. I can see why he's so crazy about you, you're beautiful."

I couldn't help but smile at his innocent compliment.

"Thanks again."

"I told you were the one, babe." He squeezed my pinky a little tighter.

Mrs. White directed her eyes to us. "If you three are done with your conversation, I would like to continue with class."

"Sure thing Mrs. White, go right ahead," Liam said with all the authority of a teacher.

After class, Johnny caught up with us in the hallway.

"Liam?" Johnny said. "What are you doing tonight? Me and some of the guys are going over to Jake Pittman's place. You wanna come?"

He looked at me. "Can't, I'm going to be with Jenny tonight, But thanks anyway. Call me and maybe we can hook up this weekend."

Johnny gave me a peculiar grin. "No problem, if I had a girl like Jenny, I wouldn't go either. I'll talk to you later."

Liam and I walked to the parking lot and headed for his truck. Johnny seemed nice, but I couldn't get over how forward he was in front of Liam.

"What's up, babe?"

"Nothin' really, I just thought it was odd that Johnny complimented me so much in front of you. Didn't you think that was a little forward considering I'm your girlfriend?"

"I guess. If it would have been someone else, but Johnny's cool. I think he was just being nice. And you are quite beautiful. He was just stating the obvious." Liam's lips touched mine. "I'm sure Johnny just realizes how lucky I am, Jen. I know I feel lucky."

I swung my arm around Liam's neck and played with his ponytail. "You know, I think I'm kinda lucky too."

"You do, do you?" Liam had that devilish look on his face. His hands found their way inside the top of my jeans, and they barely rubbed the sides of my stomach, sending a shiver up my back.

"Uh-huh…" but before I could finish, Liam pushed me against his truck door, pressing his body against mine. Our books fell to the ground. His breath was against my neck.

"You wanna go back to my place?"

"Uh-huh," I repeated.

I pulled his ponytail down, always an indicator that I wanted him. Liam lifted me into the truck, and we sped away to his house.

It was late when we heard Grandpa Mack's truck. We had been so caught up in our afternoon delight that we had totally forgotten about anything else.

"Shit." Liam jumped out of bed and grabbed his jeans. "I was supposed to get started in the barn before Grandpa got home."

I pulled the sheets up to my chest, frantically searching for any article of clothing I owned. He found my shirt and threw it my way, kissing my forehead at the same time.

"Sorry, babe, but I better go meet him downstairs. Go ahead and get dressed. I'll keep him outside until you come down."

He started to leave when he glanced back at me. In a heartbeat, he jumped back in the bed, throwing me backward against the headboard. He forced his body against mine and gave me one more kiss.

"I love you."

"I love you too," I said, softly giggling.

He raised his finger to his lips, motioning me to be quiet.

"I'll meet you downstairs," he whispered.

I tried reluctantly to keep him there with me but knew I knew had better let him go. He winked and went downstairs. I quickly pulled myself together, making sure the buttons were all in the correct place and combing my hair with my hands.

"Well, this is as good as it's going to get."

I quickly made my way downstairs. I could see Liam and his grandpa still outside. I went to the kitchen and grabbed a glass of water. Maybe if I had something in my hand, it wouldn't look so obvious that we were messing around upstairs. I took a seat in the living room and pretended to read a magazine. Perfect timing, Liam and Grandpa Mack walked in seconds later.

"Jenny, hon, nice to see you." I got up and gave Grandpa Mack a hug. "What's that for?"

"I'm just glad to see you. How are you feeling?"

"Good, good, hon, I'm plugging along. It's going to take a lot more than a measly old heart attack to get this old man down." Liam nodded for me to go into the kitchen.

"Well Grandpa, I'm glad you're feeling better. I'm going to take my glass to the kitchen and then I'm going to have to go."

"So soon, why don't you stay for a while?"

I looked at Liam, who was already standing by the kitchen door, shaking his head.

"Umm, no, I can't tonight, but I'll definitely be back. I promise."

I walked into the kitchen. "What's going on?"

"He's not feeling well, Jen. I think I better stay home tonight and help him out. He wants to go put the hay in the barn by himself. It's too much for him. Do you mind if we don't go out?" Liam reached for my hands.

"No, not at all, definitely you should stay." I leaned up on my tiptoes and kissed him.

"You're really the best, Jen. Do you know that?"

"Yeah, I know."

"Oh... we're not modest are we?"

I laughed. "No, not in the slightest."

"Let me get my keys, and I'll take you home."

Liam parked in front of my parents' store and walked me inside. Johnny Bryant was talking to my dad.

"Hi, Jen; Hi, Liam."

"Hi, Dad."

"Hi, Mr. King; Hey Johnny, what are you doing here?"

"Getting a job."

"A job? Here at Jenny's dad's store?"

"Yeah, I need to make some dough, and my parents told me to try here. I didn't know this was Jenny's dad?"

"Yeah, this is him." The four of us stood there in awkward silence.

"So," I said, "your parents know my parents?"

"Yeah, I guess so." I looked at Dad for more answers.

"Johnny's dad used to work for me, years ago. He called me up the other day asking if I had anything for their son. Do you guys know one another?" Johnny gave me the same smile from earlier today.

"Umm, actually I just met him today at school through Liam. They've known each other apparently for a while."

"Oh, good then." Johnny finished signing some papers and handed them back to my dad.

"You can start next week, Johnny. Welcome aboard." He shook my dad's hand.

"Thank you, Mr. King. I look forward to it." He was looking straight at me.

"So Liam, you still want to get together this weekend?"

"Give me a call. Johnny I'd like to, but I don't know what's going on."

"Well, maybe I'll see you two tonight."

"No, plans have changed. I've got to help my grandpa on the farm."

"That's too bad. See ya guys later. Thanks again Mr. King." Johnny walked right by me, brushing his body against my arm. "See ya," he said under his breath as he walked away, giving me a very uncomfortable feeling.

"You okay, Jen?"

"Yeah, I'm just going to miss you tonight, that's all."

"I'll miss you too. I'll call you later."

Dad was still in earshot range. Liam leaned down and kissed my cheek, whispering in my ear, "love you."

"Me too," I whispered back.

"Bye, Mr. King."

"Bye, Liam. See you soon."

I watched as Liam drove off. I turned around and walked with Dad as he price checked different items in the store. I couldn't get Johnny Bryant off my head. Something about him made me feel very uneasy, and I couldn't put my finger on it. He seemed too confident about himself, especially in front of Liam. *Johnny couldn't be the type of guy to try and horn in on one of his friend's girls, or could he?* I tried to shrug it off.

By eight-thirty, I had helped dad do the entire inventory for the front part of the store. "Thanks, hon."

"You're welcome."

We didn't spend a lot of time with each other, so I was happy that we were able to put in a couple of hours together. I went home and grabbed a quick shower. I put on my favorite sweats and grabbed a book on numerology that I had gotten from the school library when my cell started vibrating. I looked at the face of it, 11 missed messages, all from Liam except for one I didn't recognize.

"Hello?"

"Where've you been?"

"I was helping Dad in the store. I just got home. Did you finish helping your grandpa?"

"Almost, but I'm done for the night. It's getting too dark to do any more work. Why don't I pick you up, and we'll go to Lougini's?"

"That sounds great. I'll be ready in eleven minutes."

"Funny," Liam said. "I'll be right over."

I stared at my un-open book. "This will have to wait until later."

Lougini's was packed. Luckily Tony and Kendra were already there and sitting at a booth by themselves. When they saw Liam and me, they motioned for us to join them.

"Thanks for letting us sit with you guys." Liam and Tony gave each other the familiar knuckle knock.

"So, what's going on dawg? When did you guys get here?"

"We've been here for a while but just got a table a couple of minutes before you guys walked in."

I looked around. There wasn't an empty seat to be found. "Lucky for you guys, and us."

"Jen, I was just going to pick some music out. Wanna come?"

"Sure. I'll be right back," I told Liam.

"Don't go far, babe."

"Never."

Kendra and I walked over to the jukebox, a modernized rendition of an older jukebox that played CD's instead of vinyl records.

"So, how are you and Tony?"

"Great, really great. You and Liam seem to be doing very well, if that smile of yours is any indication."

I couldn't help but smile when it came to Liam. "Yeah, you could say things are quite good between us."

Kendra and I picked out six songs, and when we turned to head back to our table, I felt a familiar brush against my body.

"Hi, Jenny."

"Oh, Hi Johnny." Kendra stood there beside me waiting patiently for her introduction.

"I thought you and Liam weren't seeing each other tonight?"

"We weren't supposed to, but he got his work done with his grandpa, so we decided to come out anyway."

"Ahem," Kendra said as she nudged her elbow into my side.

"Oh, Johnny, this is my friend Kendra Bishop. Kendra, Johnny Bryant."

"Hi, Johnny, nice to meet you."

"You too, Kendra."

I looked back at our table Liam and Tony were both walking our way. Johnny noticed immediately.

"It's good to see you again, Jenny. I'm looking forward to next week."

"Next week?"

"Yeah, that's when I start at your dad's store."

"Oh, that's right. Well, good luck. You'll like working for my dad. He's a great guy."

"I'm sure I will."

He was giving me that same smile. I found myself willing Liam to walk faster to me.

"Hey Johnny," Liam said as his arms finally found my waist.

"Hey, Liam; Hey, Tony."

"Hey, Johnny," Tony answered.

"I didn't think I would see you here tonight," Johnny said.

"Yeah, I finished early, so we decided to grab something to eat. Are you here by yourself? Do you wanna join us?" Kendra and I both gave Liam an uneasy glare, but he didn't catch it.

"Yeah, you can pull up a chair next to our booth," Tony added.

"Thanks, but maybe another time. I'm actually here with Jake Pittman. He's having a party at his house later. We're just picking up some food for it."

"I see," Liam said. "Well then, we'll see ya later."

"Sure, I'll be in touch. If you guys want to come to the party, you're more than welcome."

"Maybe." Liam and Tony both looked at each other.

"Number eighty-three," the cashier yelled.

"That's me," Johnny said. "Maybe I'll see you at the party."

He was looking straight at me. He walked by us and brushed the side of my body again. There was no way that was a mistake. We sat back down in our booth, and Kendra nudged me under the table. She had seen it too.

"What was that all about?" She whispered to me as she leaned herself practically over the table to get to me.

"You noticed it too?"

"Ahhhh, Yeah! How could you not notice it? Did you see how he was looking at you? He was flirting with you right in front of Liam!"

"Yeah, I know. It's not the first time either."

"Does Liam know?"

"No, I mentioned something to him earlier about it, but he said Johnny was just being nice. I think he wants to be more than nice though."

"What are you two girls whispering about?" Tony asked.

"Nothing, just girl talk Tony," said Kendra, a good save.

"So, do you want to go to the party at Jake's house after this?" Liam asked me.

I really didn't but didn't want to seem like a bore. "Sure, if you want to."

Tony and Kendra agreed too, so after we indulged in a large pizza eaten mostly by Liam and Tony, the four of us went to Jake Pittman's house. Jake Pittman lived on the outskirts of town in a small but nicely kept two-story house. The house was literally packed with kids from wall to wall, reminding me of the telephone booths that college kids used to pack themselves into like sardines. I didn't recognize hardly any of the people there, most were kids from the Walton area.

"Liam, Jenny, glad you guys could make it," Johnny said as we walked into the kitchen. Obviously there were no parents around. The alcohol flowed freely from one person to the next. "Grab something to drink, it's my birthday!"

"Hey dude, happy birthday. You didn't say anything."

"I know, but that's what the party is for. Jake thought we should celebrate, and I was like why the hell not." I could smell the alcohol on Johnny's breath. He had obviously been celebrating a lot.

"Do you want anything, Jen?" I saw Kendra with a beer in her hand.

"Sure, I'll have what Kendra's drinking."

Liam looked over at Kendra's drink. "A beer? Really?"

"Yeah, why not?"

"I'll be right back then." Liam walked away, leaving me alone with Johnny.

"So, do you like Spencer?" I said, trying to make idle conversation until Liam returned.

"I do. I wasn't sure about it in the beginning, but I'm beginning to like it a lot more with each new day. It's definitely growing on me." He took a step in my direction.

"So, why the move? You only have a few months before graduation. Why didn't your parents wait until after you graduated to move back?"

"Mom was anxious. She opened up a shop here in the area and wanted to move closer to it. I really didn't care, to be honest. They asked me, and I said go ahead. I actually have a lot of friends here in Spencer, and it's not like Walton's a million miles away, as you can see from the crowd here. I'm still staying in touch with them."

"So, what kind of shop does your mom own?"

"You've probably never heard of it. It's not your ordinary run of the mill shop. It's called The Spiritual Ship. She's an astrologer slash numerologist slash psychic. You know, your sign and what your number means, and what your future holds, that sort of stuff. It's crazy shit, but she gets into it. She gives readings and does spiritual maps for people."

"That's really interesting."

"Really? Most people just laugh when I tell them that. They don't really get into that kind of shit."

"I don't necessarily either, but I think that's cool that your mom's doing something she believes in." I was trying to sound appeasing, when really, I was wishing I could ask Johnny more. "So where is her shop?"

"Off the main drag going out of Spencer, past the swimming pool."

I knew exactly where it was. Johnny was giving me the same uneasy smile from earlier. Where was Liam? It shouldn't take that long to grab a couple of beers.

"So, you and Liam, huh?"

"Yeah, we're going on about three months now."

"Wow, well I definitely can understand his attraction to you. You're very pretty. If he's smart, he'll hold onto you and not let you out of his sight. You never know when somebody else might try their chances with you." Johnny had stepped closer to me.

"Johnny, I think you better back off a little."

He looked at where he was standing. "Sorry, I didn't mean anything by it. Liam and I are friends, and I have a feeling we will be too."

"Here's your beer, babe," Liam said as he came up from behind me.

"Thanks." I grabbed the beer and gulped it down.

"Whoa, slow down, Jen."

"Sorry, I guess I was thirstier than I thought."

"Apparently."

"Well, enjoy guys. I gotta go mingle with the rest of the crowd." He gave an obvious smile in my direction, and again, Liam did not notice a thing.

"See ya, Johnny."

We found Tony and Kendra and finished our beers. By eleven-thirty, the party was dwindling down, and most of the people there were either passed out from drinking too much or hooking up with someone.

"You ready to go, Jen?"

"Yeah." I had an hour before my curfew, and I really didn't want to spend it watching strangers making out. "Whenever you are."

"I'm ready too."

We didn't see Kendra or Tony anywhere. Johnny, Jake Pittman and some other guys I didn't know were talking to a bunch of girls in the kitchen. Liam waved in their direction to say goodbye. On the way out, I stopped walking and became immobilized in my spot.

"What is it? Did you forget something?" I was staring at the ground.

"Jen?"

"Huh?"

"You okay? You suddenly stopped. Did you forget something?"

"No, sorry, let's go."

It hit me like a ton of bricks though. It was Johnny Bryant's birthday today, January 11th. I couldn't believe it. We left the party, and my head was spinning with the newest coincidence. I tried desperately not to think about how Johnny was acting towards me. His intentions were almost criminal, as if he wanted to get caught flirting with me by Liam. *We're all boys from Walton as bold as he? And his birthday was on the 11th! And then his mom, a numerologist! What does this mean?* I sat quietly next to Liam as we drove off, my hand squeezing his. I needed to make sure he was real. Too much stuff was going on inside my head, and I needed Liam to bring me down from this haze. Maybe it was just the alcohol, but I needed Liam's touch. I kissed him on the cheek and continued down his neck as he drove.

"Whoa, you're going to make me wreck, babe."

I didn't stop. "Then you better pull over."

Liam pushed on the accelerator, driving as fast as he could until we had come to our spot on Brush Creek Road. We didn't waste any time. We only had an hour.

Chapter Seventeen
The Races

    The month of January flew by, bringing with it much anticipation about graduation. With less than four months until the big event, students, parents, and faculty alike were busy preparing for the momentous day. Liam and I included. Liam's plans were far different from what the colleges that were hounding him had planned for him. He was easily receiving two to three college acceptance letters a week. He pitched all of them into the trash. Many of them offered Liam full rides if he would sign with them to play football. He wasn't the least bit interested. His intent, as it had apparently always been, was to graduate from high school and take over the family farm to allow his grandpa to retire, or at least semi-retire. Liam was not the scholar type, and though most of the letters of intent promised future fame and riches, he could have cared less. Once more proving to me the sort of guy he was, not the one the school made him out to be. He wasn't about the fanfare and hype. He wanted to finish school and start his life on the farm and eventually with me.

I, on the other hand, always planned to attend college. While I was away at school, he would be preparing a life for us here in Spencer. I saw a future with Liam, and there was no doubt in my mind that he was the one for me. I wanted him to come away with me, but he strongly disagreed. It had become a sore subject between the two of us and the only time our tempers flared. We never argued with each other unless we were talking about college.

By the middle of February, Liam and I had both agreed not to discuss it anymore. It wasn't getting us anywhere. The subject was closed, at least for a while. We spent most of our time with each other and our friends. Kendra, Tony, Liam, and I had become a foursome and spent almost every Friday night together. We were joined by Parker and Kelli at times as well. There were still the drag races going on almost every Saturday night at some undisclosed location. The cops were having a field day trying to bust them, but the boys always seemed to be one step ahead. I still hadn't gone to one, and Liam had only participated in one race since the notorious race that we had a fight over. I was in Ohio to visit my sister at the time. Being the man that Liam was, he told me upfront before I left that he would be racing. Not that he needed it, but I wished him good luck and told him to kick ass! He did, winning the race in 11.1 seconds, even better than the last time. In all honesty, I actually wanted to see him race. All the rumors had aroused my curiosity.

Of course, there was still Johnny Bryant. Thankfully, he had started dating a girl, and his advances towards me had all but disappeared. I did see him from time to time at the store, but I made it a point to avoid him as much as possible.

"So, Jen, is there anything special you want to do this weekend?" We were sitting in the bleachers during our lunch break.

"No, I can't think of anything. Do you have something in mind?"

"Actually, I do," He said with a quick smirk.

"What?"

"Well, how would you like to see me race this Saturday night?" I didn't answer right away. "I don't have to race, but I really want to."

"No, you should. I would love to see it."

"Really?"

"Yeah, really!"

"Are you positive?"

"Yes, I'm positive. I want to see you race."

"That's awesome babe. You're going to love it, and I won't let you down. I'll win this one just for you." He grabbed me in his clutches and squeezed the breath out of me as Parker and Kelli walked by and sat down next to us.

"Really, you two should get a room!" Kelli said emphatically.

"That's not such a bad idea," Liam said as he continued to grope me in public.

"So, why the public display of affection?" Kelli persisted.

"I just told Liam I would go and watch him race this Saturday. I've never been to one."

"Oh, is that all. Well, bring a book. I've always found the races to be quite boring."

"Hey, that's not nice. You mean you don't watch me when I'm racing?"

Parker looked honestly hurt. Kelli kissed him lightly on the cheek to appease him. "Of course I watch when you're racing or when I'm sitting next to you."

"Better," Parker said.

"You mean you ride with him during the races, Kelli?" I never dreamed of that.

"Sometimes, if he wants me to, or if none of their other friends want to race with him."

I looked at Liam, waiting for him to respond to what I knew he was already thinking.

"I'm not asking you to ride with me, but if you want to, you can. I'm a good driver, and you'll be very safe."

"I don't know about that. Let me see you race first."

"Whatever you want," he said as he continued to nibble at my neck.

"Really, Kelli's right. You two should get a room," Parker added.

"Maybe later," Liam joked.

Liam and Parker started talking about the weekend's race and what they needed to do to prepare their trucks. Kelli and I, on the other hand, sat idly watching the crowd as they passed, making humorous comments on the outfits people were wearing. I noticed Frannie and Brenda copying each other's notes in the grassy area by the band door. Missy was sitting next to them reading a book. Aside from Kendra, I hadn't spent any time with the girls. They looked up at me at the exact same time I glanced in their direction. I would have to make a better effort to reach out to them. It seemed different now. We were growing apart, going in different directions. The final bell rang, and Liam grabbed my hand to help pull me up from my seated position.

"Come on darlin', time to get educated."

By the time Saturday came, I was second guessing my decision to watch the races. *He was right; I was nervous. Maybe if he wasn't participating I wouldn't be so on edge, but he was racing, and I am apprehensive.* Kendra tried to help me by convincing me that there was nothing to them.

"They race two or three heats, depending on how well they do. It's a straight stretch. It'll be fine. You'll see."

Her efforts were valiant, but I was still scared to death. Liam picked me up at ten that night.

"You ready to see your guy leave the others in his dust?"

"Definitely." I tried to sound positive, but it was a weak attempt.

"What's wrong?"

"I guess it's just my nerves. I'm a little more scared about this than I thought."

"Scared? There's nothing to be scared about."

"I know, but I haven't seen you race."

He gave me a reassuring kiss that lingered for what seemed like minutes. "There, does that help?"

"Well, it doesn't hurt."

"I promise you nothing will happen. You'll see. Now come on. We're going to be late if we don't get a move on."

He squeezed my leg and headed off. The races were on Ripley Road, the second choice. Someone had tipped the cops off about their first location, so in a last ditch effort not to cancel them, they changed locations. Rumor was that this was the most dangerous road. I knew that. And, of course, that would be the case with me there. *Why not worry me even more?* We drove around Devil's Bulge, a curve in the road that was known to be wicked even for everyday drivers, not to mention racing enthusiasts. We rounded the bend and saw dozens of trucks. I was amazed at the number of people that came out. There were easily thirty trucks, all shapes, and sizes, and even a few pimped out cars that rode low to the ground with the neon lighting underneath. Liam drove to a clearing at the top of a hill that apparently was the starting point for the race. He drove slow and waved to the bystanders that had already taken their seats to watch the races.

I saw Cody Hodge on the bank of a hill. "He's a look-out for us babe," Liam said.

"A look-out?"

"Yeah, we have three. Cody Hodge is one of them."

"Why three?"

"Just for security. They watch for oncoming cars and police. They have positions staked out in various locations to keep us informed. They communicate with walkie-talkies. When all is clear, they let us know so the races can begin."

"What if a car is coming? Or the cops? What happens then?"

"They have a code name for traffic. If we hear "sitting duck" we know that traffic is coming. Everyone gets in their cars or trucks and drives down Tucker's run until it's safe again."

"What about the police? You can't wait on Tucker's Run for them to drive by, can you?"

"No, definitely not. If the police are in the area, Cody or one of the other guys will radio back Blackbird. If you hear Blackbird, you know the police are on their way."

"What happens?"

"Everyone drives off. Most of the trucks go in the opposite direction of the police. We have to be careful. The police definitely know the races are going on. They just haven't caught us yet. It's not every night you see this many trucks driving at the same time, even in Spencer. It would definitely send up some red flags."

We pulled off of the road, and it looked like half the school was there.

"I'll be right back Jen. I gotta find out when I'm racing." I waited for Liam by his truck. I could see Kendra in the distance.

"So you're here to see your guy race?" I turned around to find Johnny Bryant.

"Johnny, what are you doing here?"

"I'm racing." He leaned up against Liam's truck and rested his arm above my head. "Considering I work for your dad, I sure don't see much of you at the store, Jen."

"Yeah, well, I've been kinda busy. Besides, I really don't spend much time hanging out at the store anyway."

I moved over to allow more room between us. "So you're racing?"

"Yeah, guess I'll be racing Liam in the eleventh heat." *Of course*, I thought to myself.

"Hey Johnny," Liam said as he came up behind me. "Looks like we're racing against each other."

"Looks like it, my friend. I'm out to get you this time for the last race."

"What happened?" I asked, puzzled.

"Johnny and I got paired with each other at the last race. His engine stalled on him as soon as the race started. He didn't have a chance."

"Well, that was then. I'm ready for you tonight."

"We'll see."

I could see the friendship between them and that the races were only a friendly rivalry, much like football, I was sure.

"So babe," Liam said, "looks like we've got a while before my race. You wanna watch from here, or go somewhere else?"

Since I didn't have a clue where the best seat was to watch the race, I felt inclined to leave it up to Liam. "I don't care. You're the expert here."

Liam grabbed my waist and pulled me towards him. Johnny never moved. He watched me the entire time. *How can Liam not catch on to this? I can see it. Why can't he?* I put my arms around Liam's waist, hoping Johnny would get the message.

"I guess I better go. Shanna's waiting for me."

"Okay, Johnny, see you at the finish line."

Liam opened his door and helped me in. "Why don't we go down near Devil's Bulge and watch the first few races from there. It's more exciting to see the finish than the start."

"Sounds good."

Liam found a spot right near the finish line. "Here we go babe. You're going to love this."

I snuggled closer to him. Right now I wanted to be alone with him, anywhere but here, somewhere we could lose ourselves with each other. Johnny made me uneasy, as if he was staring right through me. It was creepy, and I didn't like it. We still had some time before the races began. Cody and the other two were making sure all was clear. I stared down the road to the starting line. There were cars and people parked on both sides of Ripley Road. It looked like the bypass in downtown Spencer right before the Black Walnut parade. I was impressed that this many kids could keep the races a guarded secret. Cody Hodge was on the hill to the left of us. He was using his walkie-talkie and waiting for his signal to notify the guy at the starting line that the races were on. It was past eleven o'clock and pitch black outside except for the headlights of the first two trucks at the top of the hill. They looked like four eyes staring down at us. Metallica's Enter the Sandman was playing from someone's car. The two trucks were ready, revving their engines and trying to drown out their competition. I could feel my pulse racing, and my heart was beating a mile a minute. I hated to admit it, but I was getting excited. It was an amazing feeling. Everything from the music playing, the cars revving their engines, and the fact that this was illegal made it that much more enticing. Then, Cody's arm went up.

"It's on," Liam whispered.

Everyone who was sitting outside were on their feet, screaming at the top of their lungs for their favorite car. I saw a girl walk out into the middle of the road, right in front of the two challenging cars.

"Who's that? And what is she doing? She's going to get hit."

"That's Julia Shipman. She's from Walton. She starts the race, babe. Don't worry, the trucks are not allowed to move until her arms go down, and she goes between them."

She had something white in her hand, a flag perhaps. Then with a flick of her arm, she ran up the middle of the two trucks dropping the flag on her way. The first heat had begun. The two trucks thundered down the road, barreling at an unbelievable speed. On the right was a guy from Jackson County, and he was driving a neon yellow supped-up Ford truck. On the left was Tony Williams driving his signature all purple Chevy. The purple Chevy was moving into the lead. The Ford was close on his tail. Liam and I were both outside screaming for Tony to drive faster. I looked around for Kendra and couldn't find her anywhere. Surely she would want to meet him at the finish line.

"Come on Tony! You can do it!" Liam screamed at the top of his lungs. The two trucks were neck and neck, and then everything sped up.

The trucks were heading right for us Rick Morehead, Liam's friend, waited at the finish line to announce the winner. Both trucks hurled down the road. From our advantage point, we couldn't make out who was in the lead, but it was going to be close. We moved closer to the road so we could see past the spectators that blocked our view by standing two and three people deep. Then as fast as it had begun, it was over. The trucks rounded Devil's Bulge and crossed the finish line. Tony's purple Chevy won by inches.

"Whoo-hoo!" Liam belted out.

We ran to Tony's truck. I looked for Kendra everywhere, but she was nowhere to be found. Tony stepped down.

"Nice racing," Liam said as they gave each other a high five.

"Thanks, I was a little worried coming up to Devil's Bulge, but Kendra told me to give it all I had."

"Kendra?" I said to myself. Then I saw her appear from the purple blaze.

"Oh my God. Kendra, I can't believe you were in there. You guys were awesome. That was the best thing I've ever seen."

"I knew you'd like it. Just wait. You'll be sitting next to Liam before you know it."

Liam and Tony stepped to the side and talked about their strategies for their upcoming races.

"So, Jen, when is Liam racing?"

"Heat eleven."

"No way! That number won't leave you alone will it?"

"No, it seems to follow me wherever I go. And guess who Liam is racing against?"

"Who?"

"Johnny Bryant!"

"No, you're kidding?"

"I wish I was. Johnny told me himself."

"He did? When did you see him?"

"Earlier, before the first race. He came over to say hi."

"He did? Jenny, I'd be careful. I think he has a thing for you."

"I thought so too Kendra, but I think that's just his personality. Anyway he's with Shanna Smith."

"I know, but I also know that he stares you up and down when you're around. I've noticed it ever since that night at Lougini's. If I were you, I'd tell Liam."

"I have. That's just it. He doesn't think there's anything to it."

"I've seen that look Jen. It's the same look Liam gives you. Just be careful."

"Don't worry, I am."

Liam and Tony walked over to us. "Nice racing Tony. You were my first. I'm not a virgin anymore," I said laughing.

"Very funny, I like that one Jenny."

Liam picked me up and carried me over his shoulders.

"See ya Kendra; Bye Tony. What are you doing?"

"Girl, I'm taking you away from this. One race and you've become corrupted."

He lifted me up into the seat. He knelt over me, gazing at me with those big blue eyes. "So, you're not a virgin anymore?"

"No, haven't been one for a while. Some boy stole my heart, and I haven't been the same since."

I wrapped my legs around the lower part of his body and forced his body against mine. He ran his hands down my neck and the sides of my stomach until they found their way inside my shirt. He gingerly caressed my skin, sending a shiver throughout my body.

"Cold?" he asked.

"Not at all. As a matter of fact, I'm burning up."

He smiled as he kissed me. His hands slowly made their way from my stomach to my chest. He urgently pulled my body to his, forcing me to arch my back. My heart beat faster than ever before as he continued his sensual quest with me.

"So, who's the boy?"

"Someone very special to me, someone I love." He pulled back and looked at me intensely with those adoring eyes of his.

"We better stop before I can't stop."

"Okay," I said as I felt his warm breath on mine.

"But don't forget where we left off."

"Never," he said as he pulled me up off the seat and slid in next to me.

We waited for the next eight races before Liam thought we should drive up to the top of the hill.

"So, you like the races?"

"I do. I'm sorry I ever questioned you. It's the most fun I've ever seen. I can't believe how exciting it is."

"It's even more exciting when you're sitting behind the wheel." He looked at me with intentional eyes.

"What?"

"Race with me babe. Tonight. Just one time. By my side. Please? You'll have the time of your life. I promise. I'll take care of you. You'll never be in danger. And if you don't like it, I'll never ask you again. But please? One time, for me?" His blue eyes were like large pools of water. It was hard to resist them.

"Liam, I'm nervous. I don't know."

"Listen, there's one more heat after this. If I win the first race, which I plan on doing, promise me you'll ride with me in the second. Deal?"

I inhaled sharply. "Okay, deal. I promise."

I couldn't believe I was doing this. It was one thing to watch them, but I wasn't sure if I was ready to participate in them. Liam pulled me closer to him in reassurance. "You won't regret this."

Parker knocked on the window. "It's time, Liam. Come on."

I gave Liam a kiss for good luck and started to get out of the truck. "Heat eleven," I said to myself.

turned to face Liam. "What babe?" he asked.

"Be careful, please."

"Always Jen, don't worry."

"I know, but you're racing in heat eleven. It's that number again. Just be extra careful for me."

He could see the worry on my face. He leaned over and kissed me gently on the lips while holding my chin. "Babe, don't worry. Remember, it's a good thing. That's what we agreed upon. I'll be fine. I'll see you at the finish line." He pulled my lips to his one more time, and I didn't want to let go of him. I hesitated getting out. "You can always stay and race with me." Parker was waiting.

"No, next time. Just be careful. I love you."

"I love you too girl. Now go. I got a race to win."

Kelli was waiting for me in Parker's truck. She was going to drive us to the end of Devil's Bulge, so we could watch them cross the finish line.

"Come on Jen. They're going to start any minute."

I jumped into Parker's lime green truck. The inside looked different from when I remembered it at Christmas. Tony had been doing some decorating to his truck. It now looked like it had come from the 1970's. The seats were covered with a lime green shag covering, there was a miniature disco ball hanging from the rearview mirror, and he the steering wheel was wrapped in a lime green and black zebra stripe covering. "Nice," I said as I sat down.

Kelli laughed and gunned the gas pedal as she raced to the end of Devil's Bulge. I looked up the road. Both trucks were revving their engines, headlights staring brightly down at us. Julia Shipman walked out between the two trucks, her hand raised with the flag in it. I looked at Cody on the hill. He was nodding his head. Heat eleven was about to start. My heart pounded out of my chest as Metallica still played in the background. I could hardly breathe. The anticipation of the race was exhilarating, almost too much for me to take in. The crowd was on their feet again, some yelling for the black Ford truck and others for the white Bronco.

"Come on, babe," I whispered under my breath.

In an instant, Julia ran between the trucks and brought the flag down. I saw Liam's truck move first, but Johnny was right behind him. The two trucks flew down the road at an excessive rate of speed.

"Liam, you've got it dude! Keep it coming!" Tony yelled beside me.

I was squeezing Kelli and Kendra's hands.

"Come on babe!" I yelled. I jumped up and down. I couldn't contain myself anymore. I was caught up in the excitement. I wanted Liam to kick Johnny's ass. They barreled down the homestretch neck and neck. Then, like a bolt of lightning, Liam sped past Johnny taking Devil's Bulge. Liam won, 11.1 seconds, tying his record from last time. "He won!" I screamed. I sprinted to his truck. He was already out of it and running towards me. "Oh my God babe, that was fantastic. I'm so proud of you!" Liam swung me around, giving me a huge kiss on the lips.

"That was for you!" I jumped up into his arms and wrapped my legs around his body as he belted out a victory yell.

"Nice win, Larson," Johnny said interrupting our hug.

"Thanks man, better luck next time."

"See ya guys around."

"You're taking off?" Liam asked.

"Yeah, I guess. Shanna's wanting to leave, and since I'm out of it, there's no reason to stick around. Kick ass in the second heat, Liam." Johnny gave Liam a knuckle knock.

"See ya around Jen."

As he walked by us, he gradually touched my arm. I blew it off though; I wasn't going to let him get to me tonight. I remained focused on Liam. He won. My man won and whooped Johnny's ass. I was ecstatic!

"Babe, you were awesome!"

Parker ran over to us both. "Liam, you're in the next heat. We gotta get the truck back to the starting line."

Liam looked at me with anticipation in his eyes. "Yeah, I'll ride with you."

I was still in his arms, and he carried me to the truck and swung me into the cab. "You're gonna love this babe. Just wait. It's the next best thing to… well you know."

I hated to admit it, but I could hardly wait. Liam pulled his truck into position. His engine purred as he pushed on the gas, revving the engine. He was ready. A dark blue pickup truck pulled up next to us. I didn't recognize the driver. Liam and him both nodded to one another. Then Julia walked out in front of us. I saw her clearly, and she had long, blonde hair and a white tank dress on. Maybe she wore all white to be more noticeable, I thought. She had to be cold though. It was easily 30 degrees outside. She held the white flag in her right hand. Liam and the other driver waited in anticipation. Their eyes were glued on her. She held a walkie-talkie in her other hand, her connection to Cody Hodge.

Liam squeezed my hand tightly and then placed it back on the steering wheel. "Get ready for the ride of your life, babe."

My heart pounded. I was nervous as hell and excited all at the same time. I wanted to step on the gas for Liam. I couldn't wait. Then Julia darted past us in a flash, and the race began. Liam slammed on the gas pedal, accelerating to over fifty miles per hour in seconds.

The blue truck trailed behind. "Whoo-hoo!" Liam yelled. "Come on boy, all the way," he said as encouragement to his truck to go faster.

I wanted to close my eyes, but I couldn't take them off the road. Everything on the outside was a blur: the trees, the people, and even the houses. Within seconds, Liam was going over 80 mph. The blue truck had crept its way up though, making sure Liam knew he was still in it. We were neck and neck when Devil's Bulge was in sight. I could feel the power in Liam's truck as it seemed to take on a mind of its own. The engine roared to life as we rounded Devil's Bulge, crossing the finish line. Liam won in 10.9 seconds flat, leaving the blue truck eating our dust. The roar of the approaching crowd was thunderous. Everyone pounded on Liam's truck. In that instant, I knew exactly what it must feel like to be him. Everyone was trying to get near him, to talk to him, to touch him.

He leaned over and planted a wet, sloppy kiss on my mouth. "Because of you, I broke my old record. You're my good luck charm, babe!"

I hugged him. "That was the coolest, babe. The coolest."

"I told you that you would be safe. You'll always be safe with me around."

We got out of the car to meet his devoted fans. Parker and Tony were the first to congratulate him. Kelli and Kendra came over to me. "Oh my God, Jenny! You did it! How did it feel?"

"It was awesome Kendra I loved it!"

"I thought you would," Kelli said.

"It was so much fun. I'm really sorry I haven't been here before now."

Liam heard me. "Well, you'll never miss another one, that's for sure."

He grabbed me around the waist, and we got back into the truck. As instantly as the races had begun, they were over. The crowds of people who had come to watch were vanishing in front of our eyes. All of them gathered their belongings and drove off in a perfectly choreographed performance. Cody Hodge gave one last wave to signal that all was clear. We drove off, taking the back way to Spencer.

"Hey babe, look at the time." I glanced at Liam's clock, 12:11 in the morning.

"See, it's a good thing."

"I guess," I said.

It didn't matter though. Liam won both heats, and I had the best experience of my life, next to being with Liam, of course.

Chapter Eighteen
Secret Rendezvous

    The weekend's races had become the talk of the school. Most of the guys had agreed to have another heat as soon as possible. Parker and Rick Morehead had volunteered to make some phone calls to get the word out about the next date. It was fascinating to listen to them talk. Everything was hush-hush and behind closed doors. If you didn't know better, you would think they were planning strategies against a missile launch or something. No details were left untouched. There were spies throughout the school, and they even used code words to get the messages across. Apparently Gordon Jones, a sophomore, and a self-professed know-it-all, was the son of one of the local policemen. He had been heard telling his friends that he was trying to find out where the races were going on to help his dad out, dumb move on his part. It was the job of Cody Hodge and his friends to intentionally talk about the races around Gordon. Cody and his friends would give misleading information so that Gordon would relay it to his dad, thus leading the police on a wild goose chase. It was hilarious as well as an ingenious and foolproof plan that seemed to work.

Liam dropped me off at my house as usual. "So babe, I have to help around the farm tonight. I won't be able to call you till later."

"No problem. I'll keep my cell on."

I leaned in and gave him a kiss. Out of the corner of my eye, I could see someone walking towards my dad's office across the street.

"Love you Jen."

"Me too."

I waited for Liam to drive off before I went inside. "Mom, it's me. Mom? Where are you?"

She opened the back door carrying a couple bags of groceries.

"Here, let me help you with that."

"Thanks dear, you just get home?"

"Yeah, just a couple of minutes ago."

"Where's Liam?"

"He had to leave. He has to help his grandpa on the farm."

"Oh, that reminds me, Dad needs you to help do some inventory in the warehouse. He said there was a list in his office." I groaned in disgust.

Inventory was one of my least favorite things to do. It was tedious and monotonous, but since I wasn't going to hear from Liam anytime soon, I had nothing better to do.

"Okay, I'm going to go get started. Is Dad already there?"

"No, he's out of town for the afternoon, that's why he needed your help."

"I thought I saw him crossing the street when Liam dropped me off, must have been someone else."

"Probably. Don't worry if you can't finish it; he said just do what you can."

I grabbed an apple and headed to the warehouse. Dad's warehouse was a huge, concrete, two-story building with a basement that opened in the back, making it possible for large trucks to unload their inventory. I opened the door and surprisingly found Dad's list in plain sight. Usually, you could never find anything on his desk right away. I don't think I had seen the top of it since Mildred had retired. She was neat and organized, and Dad wasn't. I looked at the boxes that needed to be checked. There had to be over a hundred of them. At this rate, I would be here all night. I took a bite of my apple and proceeded to get started. The first half hour dragged by. I had only checked four boxes when I heard a noise from downstairs on the loading dock. It was too late for deliveries or pick-ups, and my only thought was that maybe one of the employees had forgotten to lock the back door. I went down to check it out, and like I thought, the back door was wide open. I locked the door and went to check the two other doors that were located at the back entrance as well. Both were locked. I went back to the main floor, but halfway up the steps I heard the same noise again.

"What the… hello? Is anybody down here?" There was no answer.

I stood on the steps wondering if it was my imagination or if I should be legitimately worried. I decided to check one more time. I slowly walked down the steps and looked around, All looked clear, nothing out of the ordinary and nothing out of place.

"Hmm, my imagination."

I turned around and was startled by a figure on the steps above me. I screamed.

"Jen, it's me, Johnny."

"Oh my God Johnny! You scared the living hell out of me. I thought you were an intruder."

"No, just me. What are you doing here?"

"Shouldn't I be asking that of you?"

"Remember? I work here. I'm helping your dad."

"But it's after hours."

"I know. Your dad had a late delivery last night and asked me if I wouldn't mind shelving the boxes for him. You still didn't answer my question."

"Dad asked me to do some inventory upstairs. That's when I thought I heard something. I didn't know you were here. I came down to lock the doors. I'll open them back up if you're not done."

"No, I am. I was just making one more go around to make sure I got everything." He took a step towards me.

"Well, I better get back to work before Dad gets home. Do you want me to let you out?" He was towering over me, and I felt myself cautiously backing down the steps.

"No, that's okay. Your dad left me a key. I can let myself out."

He took another step closer to me. I turned around to clear the way for him. "Well, okay. See ya later." I was uncomfortable with him there, and I wanted him to leave. His demeanor around me was unsettling, and I didn't like being alone with him.

"Jen?"

"Yeah, Johnny?"

He cornered me against the wall. "Do you feel uneasy around me?"

He read my mind. "Why do you ask?"

"I don't know. You always seem a little twitchy and nervous when I'm near you." He put his hand up against the wall, leaning over me.

"Johnny, I'm not uneasy around you. I guess I just feel that you get a little too close for your own good. You make me feel uncomfortable. You stare at me all the time. It's creepy, especially since you know I'm seeing Liam."

He had me cornered on the staircase, and his brown eyes glared down at me. "I guess you're not too off your mark."

"Huh?" What was that supposed to mean?

"I'm not going to beat around the bush. I think you're beautiful. Liam is a very lucky guy."

"Johnny, stop it. You two are friends. What you're doing here is wrong. You need to back off and remember who I am."

"And who would that be, Jenny?"

"Liam's girlfriend, Johnny!"

A malevolent grin crossed his face as he started laughing. "I don't see a ring on your finger, and to be quite honest, until I do I think I have as much right to pursue you as he does. I told you at Jake Pittman's house that Liam better watch out, that there might just be someone else interested in you."

Johnny was inches from my face, and I ducked under his arm to get away from him when he grabbed me. His grip was tight around my arm.

"Please don't go. I'm sorry I'm coming across too aggressively. It's just that I think about you a lot. Ever since I saw you in English class, I can't get you off of my mind. Why do you think I'm working here? I don't need the money, but it's to be closer to you."

"Johnny, let go of me. You're talking crazy."

He eased up on his grip allowing the circulation to return to my arm. "Jen, just think about me, that's all. I'm not going away."

I pulled my arm free. "You're a complete jackass, Johnny. Don't ever come near me again. I turned to go up the steps and stumbled backward falling on my side. "Damn it!"

"Are you okay?"

"I'm fine!"

He reached down to help me up. "Don't touch me!"

He was enjoying this too much. His body hovered over me as his arms balanced themselves on the wall behind me. "Jen, all I'm asking is that you keep your options open. You know, maybe give me a chance. Liam doesn't even have to know. It could be our little secret. Hmm... what do you say? A secret rendezvous might be fun?"

His breath was on my face. I turned away, and his hand caressed the side of my cheek. "Johnny, just leave me the hell alone."

"What are you going to do?"

My blood was boiling at this point. The nerve of him, I thought to myself. Didn't he have any scruples? Was I for the taking, like some kind of pet? He moved in even closer. "Johnny, don't you dare!" Before I could react, his lips were on mine, and without thinking, my hand came from behind and slapped the side of his face in a flash of fury.

"Ow! That's gonna leave a mark."

"You bastard! If you ever do that again, I swear..."

"Really, what, are you going to do, tell Liam? I'm one of his friends. He'll never believe you. And really, I don't think you will tell him. I know you don't want to upset him. And besides, don't tell me you didn't secretly want me to kiss you. You know you reacted there for a minute when my lips touched yours. Mmm, they are soft." He bit his lower lip. "I can tell why Liam adores you so much, but I also feel the sexual tension between us, Jen. You know it's there as well as I do."

I slapped him again. "Get out of here, you're a jackass!"

He stood up, freeing me from the confines of his trap. "Sure, I'll go, anyway, I'm done...for now at least. I think I made my point. You obviously have some thinking to do about me."

"Who do you think you are? You're a pompous, chauvinistic son of a bitch, Johnny Bryant, and I wouldn't think about you if you were the last man on earth!"

"Oh, I beg to differ. I bet you've already thought about me, whether it was good or bad. The mere fact that I am getting to you means I've already worked my way into that pretty little head of yours."

His smile was repulsive. He wasn't the least bit intimidated by me. He turned to walk away, but not before he brushed his body against mine.

"We could have some fun, Jen. You don't know what you're missing."

He turned and descended the steps. I stood there like a statue, unable to move. Then I noticed his Walton letterman's jacket. *He was number eleven too! That's right.* I had remembered his number from last season's football game. I had forgotten all about it though, not realizing the impact the number would have on my life. A flood of panic washed over my face. My head was spinning as I became sick to my stomach. *Number eleven? Liam's number.* Then I remembered Johnny's birthday party at Jake Pittman's house. *It was on the 11th too.* I was totally freaking out. A whirlwind of thoughts were deluging me. I felt like I was on the brink of a nervous breakdown. The room started spinning as I ran up the stairs and stormed out the front door. I was shaking terribly as my body heaved out of control.

What just happened? I wiped my mouth incessantly to get the vile taste of Johnny from my lips as I ran to my house and up to my room, slamming the door behind me. I was on the verge of tears, pacing the floor back and forth until I had worn a path in the carpet. *What in the hell just happened?!* I had to think. I wanted so much to see Liam right now. I had to tell him, or could I? He would literally flip out if he knew what had happened. I couldn't tell him. But what was I going to do? *Just calm down and think this through, Jenny. Be calm and rational,* I told myself. I was so upset I had bitten my nails down to the quick, a habit I hadn't done since I was a little girl.

I fell on my bed. It was only six. I probably wasn't going to hear from Liam for another couple of hours. I wanted to fall asleep and pretend it never happened. *Why was Johnny doing this to me? Why me?* My cell started buzzing. It was Liam. I hesitated to pick it up. I had to pull myself together. He always knew when I was upset.

"Hello."

"Hey babe, how's my girl?" His voice was too cheerful. He would notice my somber tone.

I made a weak attempt to sound enthusiastic. "I'm good, better now that you've called. What are you doing?"

"Nothing really. Parker's on his way over with Johnny and a couple of other guys. Grandpa and I finished early, and the guys wanted to work on our trucks together."

How in the world could Johnny go over there right after what he had done to me? I became silent. Nothing would come out of my mouth. I had become mute.

"Jen, you okay? You're being very quiet." Earth to Jen, my inner voice echoed in my ear.

"Umm, yeah Liam. I'm sorry. I guess I kinda dozed off there for a minute. You said the guys were coming over?"

"Yes, are you sure you're okay? You're acting strange. It's reminding me of a similar phone conversation."

"Sorry, babe, it's nothing. I'm just tired. I think I'm going to grab a bite to eat and go to bed early. Have fun with the guys. I'll see you tomorrow at school."

"Okay babe, love you."

"I love you too. Good night."

I exhaled sharply. My lower lip had become completely numb from the intense pressure I had put on it while biting it, a futile attempt to contain my anger at Johnny. I desperately wanted to tell Liam about his back-stabbing friend, but it would kill him. It would be an all-out war between the two of them. I had to forget about it and move on, but could Johnny? *He couldn't have meant what he said. He was just playing some sick, sadistic game with me.* I wasn't going to fall for it. I wouldn't let him think he had gotten to me. *Why did he ever have to come to Spencer High and enter my life?* I drifted off into an uneasy and restless sleep that night, yearning for answers.

I decided not to tell anyone about the Johnny incident, not even Liam, and especially not Kendra, who I could tell anything. I did approach my dad in a last ditch effort to have Johnny let go. Dad wouldn't hear of it. He said Johnny was one of the best employees he had and until I could come up with a probable reason to fire him, he was keeping him. Johnny was becoming a sore spot in my side, always nagging at me and never going away. My strategy was to forget about the incident and move on. Besides how I felt, there had been no harm done. I would act as if the incident had never occurred, a figment of my wild and sometimes cruel imagination. I would do my best to avoid Johnny, a feat harder to accomplish than I anticipated. Johnny had become part of Liam's inner-circle of friends and was more present than ever. The next few weeks of school went by without incident though.

The mundane activities of school preoccupied most of our time. We were on the countdown to graduation. Tests, papers, and school projects were taking precedence. Of course, any downtime we had, Liam and I spent together. I did my best to carry on as usual, giving Liam no reason to suspect anything. But Johnny was still in the background making me aware of him as much as possible. I still could not filter him out. He made it clear in his surreptitious ways that the incident in my dad's warehouse indeed happened. I would find hand written notes in my locker from him expressing his feelings for me. He would work late at the store, volunteering his time when he knew I would be home. I would be inundated with texts and phone calls from him at all hours of the day and night. He had become my stalker.

By mid-March, I was becoming unraveled at the seams. I had hoped that Johnny would have given up since I wouldn't even give him the time of day, but instead, his persistence grew stronger. If anything, it was me who was wearing down. I was becoming tired of his games. I needed it to be over and done with. Of course, it didn't help matters that the number eleven was more prevalent than ever. I thought I had seen my fill of it until Johnny entered the picture. It was as if Johnny knew how the number bothered me. He taunted me with it, signing his notes using '#11' as his signature. It was driving me crazy. It was time to figure this number out, come hell or high water.

I gathered all the books on numerology I could find at the library. I researched in depth, learning all I could, trying to find out anything and everything that could help reveal some information about the mystery behind this number and why it was so prevalent in my life. I came up with dead end after dead end. Most of the theories meant nothing to me. Most of them dealt with general information and how your number could guide you in your life. I didn't need that. I needed factual information that could relate to what was going on with me, and how I could understand the connection between Liam and Johnny. *Was the number a sign? A warning? Or did it even mean anything at all?* I was beginning to feel as if I was all alone in this. Even Liam had eased up on the questions, probably thinking it was just a phase I was going through. But it wasn't over, not at all. I had to find some answers and find them soon.

Then it hit me. *No, I couldn't do that. It was preposterous and crazy. But then again, she might have the answers I am seeking. She might be the one, the only one to help me... Johnny's mom.* It was a stupid thought. I might as well go to Johnny himself, for all my efforts to stay away from him would be in vain if I went to her. I knew he would take it the wrong way, as though I was seeing her to get to him. *But she might be my only hope, the only one to shed some light on this number for me.* I had to see her, but I had to be careful. I did a Siri search to find her number. *What was the name of her shop? The Spiritual Shop? No, that wasn't it, The Spirit World? No, that wasn't it either.* Maybe the shop was too new. I knew where it was though, and I would just have to drive there and hope I could do it without anyone, especially Johnny, seeing me there.

    I grabbed my coat and keys and made my escape. I saw Johnny's white Bronco parked in the employee parking lot. Good. He would be helping my dad and be too busy to notice I had left. I drove down the road past the elementary school and swimming pool. Johnny said it was near there. I looked on both sides, trying to see if anything caught my eye. Then, there it was on the left side of the road just past the park. *The Spiritual Ship.* It was a tiny shop painted in blues and purples with stars and moons sporadically placed everywhere. The sign, *The Spiritual Ship* was in the shape of a huge wooden ship with a full moon and celestial ornamentations hovering over it. Even without the name, I knew this was the right place. *How could anyone miss this?* It was sticking out like a sore thumb.

    I parked on the side of the building and walked around to the front, checking around me to make sure nobody saw me. The coast was clear. The shop looked dark and empty. Deep purple, velvet curtains covered the windows, shielding onlookers from gazing in. I approached the door slowly. The silver doorknob was in the shape of a crescent moon with a sinister face on it. Turning the knob slowly, I walked into the sounds of soothing bells echoing in my ear. The room was dimly lit and filled with astrology paraphernalia. Long colorful beads hung from the ceiling as you entered the shop. There were candles lit in every corner, all shapes and sizes, and the smell of patchouli filled the air. In the far right corner was a huge ornately decorated bookshelf, bulging with dozens of books on everything from astronomy to numerology and psychic abilities. In the middle of the room was a large table shrouded in black lace. There were two black velvet chairs facing each other. I carefully walked around, looking to see if anyone was there. I was completely alone. The room was quiet except for the sounds of my own footsteps hitting the wooden floor. I was about to leave when she appeared from behind a black velvet curtain at the back of the room.

"Hello, my dear. I didn't hear the bells chime. I'm so sorry. I hope I didn't keep you waiting."

She was beautiful, a wispy thin woman of medium height with long, black hair and porcelain white skin. Her eyes were deep brown, the same color as her son's. She wore a white, poet's shirt with a full-length paisley print, peasant skirt.

"Hello. Not to worry, I just got here. I was actually just looking around and admiring your things. Your shop is very nice; I've never seen anything quite like it."

"Thank you, my dear. Is there anything special I can do for you, anything special you're looking for?"

"Umm, I don't know. I was just driving by and saw your intriguing sign and thought I would stop in."

She looked at me skeptically as if she could read my mind. "Are you sure?"

She was reading me like a book. I sighed. "No, actually I meant to be here. I was just hoping maybe you could answer some questions for me."

She motioned me to one of the black velvet chairs. "Please sit down dear. I'm Gertie Bryant."

I extended her my hand. Hers was smooth as silk. "Thank you, I'm Jenny King. Your place is amazing."

"Thank you, it's my baby, you could say. I've put my soul into this place. So, how can I help you?"

She entwined her hands and placed them under her chin. Her fingers were laden with gold and silver rings encrusted with colorful gemstones, and her forearms were blanketed with beaded bracelets.

"I really don't know where to begin."

"How about the beginning?" She said with an endearing smile.

Her manner made me feel at home. I inhaled sharply, "maybe I should just leave. This is stupid. It's not even important, just a silly preoccupation of mine."

"No, please, tell me. If it was important enough for you to drive here, then it's important enough to talk about."

"You know a few things about numbers right? You're a numerologist?"

"Correct."

"Okay then... well I've been seeing this... number, number eleven, everywhere. At first I thought it was a coincidence because my boyfriend you see, that's his football number at school, but then the number started appearing in other places." I stopped to see her reaction. There was none.

"Go on." She said smiling.

"He would call me, and the clock would read 7:11 or 10:11, or the numbers would add up to eleven. Then I started noticing other occurrences with the number, like the fact that my address has the number eleven in it and so does my boyfriend's. I know all of this sounds trivial, but then right before Christmas Liam, that's my boyfriend, well... he and his grandpa were in an accident. It happened on Route 11, and I later found out that the call to 911 was made at 7:11 in the morning." I was rambling on and on, but once I started I was a spigot, and all the incidents just started pouring out. I continued with my story leading up to the events with the races and then Johnny, but without using his name. I did not want her to know that her son was twisted into my mess. "Well, that's about it. Pretty insane, isn't it?"

She paused. Her smile was comforting and warm. "No Jenny, not at all. I can see why you're so upset, but you shouldn't be. We're all guided by unforeseen forces. Some come in the form of angels; then there are those who are guided by special signs. That would be where I would place you. Numbers play an important role in our everyday life. Our world is run by numbers. You can't go a day without the use or help of them in your life. They're a part of us, and to ignore them would be like ignoring to breathe. You can't do it."

"I see what you're saying, but why me? And why number eleven? I mean it has happened so much that now if I don't see it I think something's wrong. I keep feeling it's trying to tell me something, a warning perhaps of something that's going to happen. It scares me."

"Have you spoken to your boyfriend about this?"

"Yes, and my sister and best friend."

"What do they say?"

"They try to tell me to be optimistic, you know like the glass is half full instead of half empty. They remind me of all the positives that were related to eleven, and I will admit there are a lot more good than bad. It's just my gut feeling that bothers me, I guess."

She placed her hands on the table. "Jen, out of all the numbers there are, eleven is one of the oldest. It dates back to the biblical era, and there are many references to it. I believe that eleven is the means to a journey. If you look at the number, it's two parallel lines moving in either direction. Because there is no end, the journey can go either way. It's up to you to decide which way to go. The direction you decide could decide your fate."

"But how do I know?"

"You don't. Use your inner feelings to help you. Let your gut instincts guide you. Become aware of them and more in tune with your body. It is your own spiritual ship you know. Our lives are a voyage, an adventure with many twists and turns in it. It's our job to become aware of the signs that are given to us. It'll help guide you down the right passage that your life is supposed to take. I do believe you and possibly your boyfriend are on some sort of journey together. You may be on this journey for some time, or you may not. I believe you should let the number be your guide. Do not be afraid of it or try to avoid it. That could cause detrimental consequences. I agree with your friends. Look at this number as a positive influence guiding you on this journey, a means to the end."

I was impressed by her knowledge. She had made more sense than I was willing to give her credit for. I got up from my seat. I needed to leave before I was missed.

"Thank you, Mrs. Bryant."

"Call me Gertie."

"Thank you, Gertie."

"You know, you're just as pretty as Johnny said you were."

"Excuse me?"

"My son, Johnny, he's mentioned you many times to me. You're just as pretty as he said you were."

I stumbled for words. "Thank you," I stuttered.

"I know you are seeing Liam. Johnny means no harm. He's always been a lady's man, ever since he was little. Please don't be offended by his feelings for you. He knows you and Liam are quite serious."

"Mrs. Bryant…"

"Remember, call me Gertie."

"Yes, of course, Gertie. Then why is he so persistent? I've made it clear that I'm not interested in him, and to be quite honest, he's made it very uncomfortable for me, especially since he is friends with Liam. If Liam was to ever find out about Johnny, well, then I'm not sure what would happen."

"Jenny… Johnny definitely has a crush on you. I won't deny you that, but you have nothing to worry about. His feelings for you are harmless. He tends to have crushes on many girls and usually at the same time. He would never interfere with your relationship with Liam."

I stood speechless to her comments. *Obviously she didn't know her son too well, or she would know that he almost used scare tactics to get his way.* There was no use to bring it up to her though. It wasn't her battle even though it was her son causing the problems.

"Well, I must be going. Thank you again for your time. You've been very helpful."

"You're welcome, come back any time."

I left feeling as if a load had been lifted from my shoulders and another one added. The comfort of having some answers regarding eleven was a relief, but it was overshadowed by Johnny. I ran to my car and took cover. Hopefully nobody noticed it was in Gertie's parking lot. I wasn't known to be the type to go for spiritual advice. I drove home just in time to hear from Liam.

"Jen, where have you been? I've been trying to reach you all afternoon."

"Hi babe, I'm sorry. I went out for a while and forgot to take my cell."

"Where? Even your mom didn't know where you were. You had me worried."

"Liam, I'm sorry." I looked at the clock. I had been gone for three hours. "I didn't realize I had been gone so long."

"I'm on my way over to pick you up. I'll be there in ten minutes." I quickly ran a brush through my hair and brushed my teeth. With a few minutes to spare, I changed my clothes and put on my favorite blue cami and jeans and a pair of flip flops. I was just in time. As I walked down the stairs, Liam entered the front door. I ran into his arms, and all the worry that had built up inside of me over Johnny's annoying persistence vanished instantly.

"What's this for?"

"I just missed you." I reached up and kissed his baby-soft lips.

"Maybe you should go missing in action more often. I like how you greet me when you finally come out of hiding." I softly chuckled at his comical statement, grabbed his hand, and pulled him out the door.

"Whoa... slow down. Where are we going?"

"Anywhere but here," I said as I noticed that Johnny's white Bronco still parked in the employee parking lot.

"Any place special?"

"Yes, let's go to our place."

A huge grin spread across Liam's face. "You read my mind." He lifted me into my seat and slid in next to me. By the time we made it to Brush Creek Road, the sun was setting on the horizon. A beautiful tangerine orange and purple haze covered the sky. I laid my head on his shoulders while George Strait played in the background. I was my most comfortable when I was with Liam. No words were needed. It was just us, being together.

"Babe, you okay?"

"Definitely, now that I'm with you." I put my hands between his legs and squeezed his upper thigh.

"Where were you this afternoon?" I looked into his crystal blue eyes. There was a look of worry in them. I took a deep breath, knowing I needed to tell him, and now was as good a time as ever.

"Liam, I need to talk to you." I put on my serious face.

He sat up, rigid in his seat. "What is it?"

"There's two things. One is about this afternoon. I did it on a whim, but I went to see Johnny Bryant's mom."

"Johnny's mom? Why?"

"Because she owns the shop down on the bypass. She's a numerologist."

"This isn't about your obsession with number eleven, is it?"

"Yes, it is. I keep seeing it everywhere. I know you say there's nothing to it, but it won't leave me alone. I needed to know if there was a reason behind it, maybe a message it was trying to convey to me. A warning or sign perhaps."

His expression softened. "Why didn't you tell me this was still bothering you? I told you, I'm always here for you." He stroked the back of my neck.

"I know, but I wanted to speak to an expert."

"Johnny's mom is an expert?" He scoffed.

"She knows more about that stuff than we do, and you know, after talking to her I feel much better about the situation."

"You do? What did she have to say?"

"Just that..." I paused. Was he going to think I was totally off my rocker, or was he going to take me seriously? "Liam... she basically said that there was a reason for the number. Maybe it is our guiding number. A path perhaps, that we were on, leading us on our journey... you and me."

I could tell he was holding his laughter inside, biting his lower lip until it had turned a deep shade of purple. "Liam? Are you going to say anything?"

He was looking in the other direction.

Finally, he spoke. "Jen, a path? A journey? Come on, babe? That's all a bunch of nonsense. You really don't believe what she says, do you?"

My heart sank. This was so important to me, and Liam was acting like a total idiot about it. "You know, I thought you of all people wouldn't laugh at this. You know how important this has been to me, and you're acting as if this was all some sort of practical joke." I scooted to the passenger side of the seat.

"Babe, come back here. I'm sorry, it's just that I know her. It's not like she went to school for this. I've known Johnny since we were little. It was always just a hobby of hers. That's why I'm not putting much truth behind it. I'm just having a hard time believing that his mom is an expert about the supernatural, or numbers or whatever." He reached over and grabbed my arm. "Come here. Don't sit over there. I'm lonely all by myself over here." He pouted his lips and winked at me as I conceded to slide back over. "If this is important to you, then it is important to me. I'm sorry for acting the way I did. You said there were two things you wanted to talk to me about. That was just number one. What's number two?" He was holding me tight, and I needed to look him in the eyes for this one.

"Well, in a way it's about the number again, but it's not about you or me."

"Okay then, what?"

"Liam..." I stared at him for a moment, trying to get my courage up and bracing myself for the inevitable.

"What, Jen?"

"Liam, did you know that Johnny Bryant's number in football was also number eleven?"

"Yeah, so what? What does he have to do with us?"

The serious look came back to my face. "Liam, a few days ago... Johnny..." Before I could continue, I felt Liam's body tightening. His eyes had glazed over. He already knew I was about to say. "Johnny hit on me."

Liam was silent. His lips pursed together tightly. There was no reaction or response except for his fist slamming into his dashboard, leaving a huge dent above the radio.

"Liam, calm down, please. I already told him to leave me alone. I've even tried to get Dad to fire him. Please, listen to me."

Liam's face turned rigid and hard. He was incoherent and in his own world. I don't think he heard a word I was said.

"Did he hurt you?"

No, no, not at all, but Liam… he's not leaving me alone."

"What? What do you mean? How long has this been going on?"

I was relieved to finally come clean. "A few days ago, in my dad's warehouse. I was doing some inventory for Dad, and when I went to the basement, I thought I had heard a noise and wanted to check on it. Johnny was down there. He cornered me. He…"

"What? Tell me!"

"He basically told me that he wanted me. I told him to get away and leave me alone, but…"

"But what, Jen?" Liam's arms were rigid and his hands were cupped together in two fists.

"But he wouldn't."

"That asshole! Wait until I get my hands on him!" He hit the side of his door so hard that the handle to his window fell off.

"Liam, please, calm down!"

"Calm down my ass! Jenny, a guy who I've considered a friend for half of my life hits on my girl, and you want me to calm down? Jenny..." His voice trailed off as he laid his face on his steering wheel.

"Liam?" I wanted to talk him down from this rage that was battling inside of him, but I was afraid I wouldn't be able to. He was more upset than I had ever seen him. "I know you're angry, and you have every right to be, but I told Johnny I love you. Please listen to me." I kissed his arm. "Liam, I love you."

He slowly raised his head and took me in his arms. "Jenny, if I ever lost you I think I would die."

"You're not going to Liam, ever."

He kissed me, and his lips pressed hard against mine with all the rage that was built up inside of him. When our lips finally parted, his eyes were on mine. "Jenny, did he kiss you?"

I hesitated, knowing that this would upset Liam more than anything. "Yes, but..."

"But what, Jenny?" Liam asked, madder than ever.

"But I pulled away. His lips were barely on mine before I slapped his face. It happened so fast. One minute he was leaning over me, and then he kissed me, but I did; I pulled away before he barely touched mine."

"You what?"

"I slapped him. I told him never to touch me again. But he won't give up."

"What are you talking about?"

"He's left notes in my locker, and I swear he schedules his hours at my dad's store so I'm there at the house. I see him watching me. I'm so sorry I didn't tell you, especially after the huge fuss I made with you and the races." My face fell into my hands as I started to cry. "I thought I could handle it. I thought I could convince him to leave me alone, but instead he persisted taunting me. I don't think he thought I would tell you. Liam, it's been awful."

"Jenny, it's going to be okay. I'm going to end this." His tone scared me.

"What... what do you mean end this? What are you going to do?"

"Don't worry, I'll handle it. I promise."

I laid my head on his chest. His heart pounded against my left temple.

"Liam, that's why I went to see his mom. He kept leaving me notes, signing it with his '#11', and then I remembered the party we went to at Jake Pittman's house, and it was his birthday. It fell on the 11th. It freaked me out. I needed to see if any of this meant anything. I needed some answers."

"I'm sorry I didn't make you feel like you could confide in me. Please don't ever keep anything like this from me again."

"I won't, Liam."

"You have to promise me you won't go back to Johnny's mom's shop either. I don't want you near him or his family."

I didn't see the need of that. Gertie had been very helpful, but I understood where Liam was coming from. It could worsen the situation.

"I won't. I promise."

He held me close. "I love you, Jenny."

"I love you too babe… so much."

The rest of the evening, we sat there quietly in the truck watching the sun slowly descend behind the horizon. The beautiful tangerine-orange and purple sky disappeared, giving way to an ominous, starless, black night.

Chapter Nineteen
The Fight

    The next few days I lived in constant fear of an impending fight between Liam and Johnny. To my surprise and Liam's, Johnny had gone missing in action at school. It was already Friday, and no one had seen hide or hair of Johnny since last weekend. Still, during school Liam barely left my side. After he would drop me off at home, I would find his truck parked in our driveway at all hours of the night. He had become not only my boyfriend but my personal bodyguard. I wondered if Grandpa Mack had any idea what was going on. I hadn't seen him for a while, and I worried about him. Surely he realized that Liam was spending a lot of time away from home. School was no different. Liam and I had become attached to the hip, not that we were ever apart that much to begin with, but I could hardly go to the bathroom without Liam being near. Most of my friends had already come to the conclusion that we were already married, but Kendra, who knew me the best, noticed the extra attention I was receiving from him.

"What is going on with you two? Did you get married and not tell me?"

"What are you talking about?" I asked.

"You and Liam, I know you two are crazy for one another, but I never see you two apart from each other. Ever! What's up?"

I looked around, making sure no one was in earshot range. Liam was in the bathroom. I knew I only had a few minutes before he would be by my side again. I had to talk quickly.

"Okay, I'll tell you. I told Liam about Johnny."

"You did? Is that what this is about?"

"Yeah, but Kendra, you wouldn't believe how worse it has gotten, more than you could ever imagine."

"Tell me!" Her voice squealed in anticipation.

"Johnny came on to me a while back."

"He what!"

"In my dad's warehouse. He told me he liked me, and…"

"Jen, stop stalling, tell me!"

"He basically cornered me in the warehouse and tried to kiss me."

"Oh my God, Jen, what did you do?"

"I slapped him and told him to stay the hell away from me."

"I can't believe this. Why didn't you tell me?"

"I don't know. I thought I had it handled, but I didn't."

"What do you mean?"

"Johnny didn't take no for an answer. He started leaving notes in my locker, and they weren't just notes that said, Hi, how's it going? They were very personal. Then his schedule at my dad's store, he's there all the time, Kendra. His shift always seems to be when I'm home. I catch him staring at me out of the corner of my eyes. He parks his truck near my car. It's creepy. It's like he's stalking me."

"Does Liam know all of this?"

"Yeah, why do you think he's become my personal bodyguard? When you said you don't see us apart, you were right on target. He never, and I mean never leaves my side. I found him asleep in my driveway the other night at two in the morning."

"Ahh, Jen, that's actually kind of sweet. He really loves you."

"I know he does. Don't get me wrong, I love the fact that he loves me enough that he would do this for me. It's just that I know he is madder than hell at Johnny. I'm just waiting for him to explode on him. It's not over."

A little grin inched its way onto Kendra's face.

"What?" Wondering why my story seemed to be amusing her so much.

"Jen, it's just that you've got two guys who are fawning over you. I mean, I should be so lucky. You have to admit that's pretty romantic."

I didn't see the humor or the romance in it at all. "You would feel differently if you were in my shoes."

Just then, I felt a familiar hand around my waist. "Ready, babe?"

"Yeah. See ya later, Kendra."

Kendra stood there, staring at us as Liam and I walked to Advanced English. She gestured with her hand to call her later. I tried to nod that I would. That is if my parole officer would allow it. This was the first time we had had Advanced English since I had told Liam about Johnny. The school had used the time slot and the classroom for freshman orientation for the past week. I had no idea what to expect since we shared this class with Johnny. Saying I was nervous was an understatement. Johnny's chair was on the right of mine. I wondered if Liam would change our seats. He did. When we entered the classroom, Liam bee-lined his way to our chairs and sat in the one I had been occupying since the beginning of the semester. If Johnny were to show, Liam would be sitting between us now. He placed my books on his old chair and gestured for me to sit down. My hands were drenched in sweat, waiting for the apocalyptic moment when Johnny and Liam would face each other.

Neither Liam nor I had seen Johnny all week, and he had missed work as well. Parker and Tony had informed Liam that word had gotten out to Johnny that Liam was looking for him. That was why he had become a no show at school and work. I didn't consider Johnny to be a coward, running away from something, especially when he seemed so bold and brash with his feelings for me. But then again, Liam and his buddies were not to be messed with, and Johnny had crossed the line. Nobody knew if Johnny was in school. If he was, he was avoiding everybody like the plague. If he was there, I was dreading the moment he walked into the classroom. Surely, Liam wouldn't start something during Advanced English, but then again, he had been waiting all week to confront Johnny. He wasn't going to let a golden opportunity pass without incident.

"Are you okay, Jen?" Liam asked as he squeezed my hand.

"Yeah babe, just nervous."

"Don't be. Nothing's going to happen in here."

The clock seemed to stand still as time barely passed. I watched the door like a hawk as student after student sauntered in. There was no Johnny. I sighed in relief when the final bell rang. He didn't show, thank God. At least we had avoided seeing him during class, and then the wooden door swung open, making a loud bang as it hit the back wall. Johnny Bryant had come to class.

"You're late, Mr. Bryant," Mrs. White said scolding him.

"Sorry." He looked straight at me with a daunting gaze as he took his seat next to Liam.

I watched Liam and waited for him to react to Johnny's presence. He sat there, quiet and still as a statue, staring off into space. His left hand was still grasping mine. I watched Liam and Johnny out of the corner of my eyes. Liam gripped his leg with his free hand. His knuckles almost popped out of their skin. I held onto Liam's left hand to remind him to stay cool and calm. I knew it was everything he could do not to pounce on Johnny there and then. English seemed to last forever. When the final bell rang, Johnny was the first to leave the class. Liam jumped out of his seat.

"Liam, where are you going?"

"You know where."

I held onto his hand. "Please don't do this," I said, fearing the worst.

"Jenny, I have to. You can't expect me to let this go. I have to take care of business."

"What does that mean? Take care of business? What are you going to do?"

"Jen, don't worry." He kissed me softly on the lips. "I love you, babe. Wait for me by my truck. This won't take long."

I stood by my chair as Liam walked out of the classroom and caught up with Parker and Tony, who were already waiting for him in the hallway. The last place I wanted to be right now was next to Liam's truck alone. I wanted to follow him, to see where he went. The hallway was crowded with a sea of enthusiastic students gathering their stuff as they headed home for the weekend. Liam and his buddies were nowhere in sight. Neither was Johnny. I saw Kendra. Maybe she would know where I could find them.

"Kendra!"

"Jen, hi, how are things going?"

"I don't know. Johnny was in class with Liam and me."

"And?"

"Nothing happened. Liam kept his cool, but that was during class. He left with Tony and Parker as soon as class was over. Did you talk to Tony? Do you know where they went?"

"No, I was hoping you would know. Tony ditched his last class. I haven't seen him since 6th period. You don't suppose they went after Johnny, do you?"

"Yes, that's exactly what they're doing. Liam told me so."

"What are they going to do?"

"I don't know, and that's what scares me."

Kendra grabbed my arm. "Come on. Let's go find them. Do you think they're still on campus?"

"Maybe, Liam asked me to wait by his truck, but that doesn't mean they didn't leave. They could have used Parker or Tony's truck."

We headed to the parking lot. If all three of the boys' trucks were in the lot, then we knew they were still there. If not, then we had a problem. We wouldn't know where to look for them. Liam's black truck was exactly where he parked it this morning, and so was Tony's and Parker's. I looked around to see if I saw Johnny's white Bronco. It was in the far corner of the lot.

"Well, looks like they're all still here."

"Yeah, Kendra, but where?"

By now, most of the kids had left the school. The ones dwindling behind were kids we didn't know. Even the faculty staff had left.

"This doesn't feel right," I said. "They should be here somewhere. The campus isn't that big."

"Let's keep looking."

We walked up the hill past the band room and towards the cliff when we heard it... a loud and the low grunt, the sound of someone being punched.

"Jenny, down there!" Kendra pointed to the football field. Johnny was being held by Tony and Parker while Liam punched him continually in the stomach.

"Oh my God, Kendra."

We ran down the bleachers as fast as possible. Two of Johnny's friends were trying to break Johnny free, but they were no match for Tony and Parker. Johnny's head was slumped over as Liam punched him over and over again.

"Liam, stop! You're killing him!"

Liam didn't look up, and he only stopped once I reached his side. Only on Liam's cue, did Tony and Parker release Johnny. Johnny fell to the ground and laid there in a fetal position holding his stomach as blood dripped from his mouth and nose.

"What the hell are you thinking?"

I bent down to Johnny's side. Kendra handed me a tissue, and I tried to wipe the blood from Johnny's lip. The cut was deep, splitting the top of his lip in two.

"Jenny, leave the scum bag alone," Liam hissed.

Tony and Parker both looked on. Jake Pittman and another friend of Johnny's, Zane Troyer, helped Johnny off the ground. I rose up and stood next to Liam. Johnny and Liam glared at one another.

"You're a lucky bastard, Bryant, that Jenny showed up, or I would have finished you off right here."

Johnny snickered at his remark, wiping the blood from his mouth. "This isn't over Larson, not by a long shot. You think a couple of punches are going to hurt me, maybe bruise my ego, you're wrong, dead wrong."

I stood there in total horror at what I was hearing. I couldn't believe that this was over me. I didn't want Johnny to bother me, but I didn't expect Liam to react in such a horrific and irrational manner.

"Come on boys, let's go," Johnny said to Zane and Jake. They started walking away, but before they left Johnny stopped in front of me, handing me the blood-soaked tissue I had given him. "Thanks, Jen."

"You bastard!" Liam screamed as he lunged towards him again. Johnny positioning himself to strike back, but this time I came between them, using myself as a human barricade between the two of them.

"STOP!" I screamed. Parker grabbed Liam's arm to hold him back. Johnny dropped his arm, laughing in a sinister manner as he brushed his hand against mine.

"See ya around, Jenny."

I was shell-shocked and couldn't breathe. I stood there while Liam, Parker, and Tony bragged about their heroic efforts.

Kendra grabbed me and tried to calm my shaking body down. "Are you okay?" she asked.

"I don't know, Kendra. I need to go. I need to be alone."

"Jenny, don't be absurd. Liam took care of it."

"Are you joking, Kendra? Did you see what he was doing? With the help of your boyfriend and Parker they could have killed him if we didn't show up when we did!"

"Nonsense, they were just trying to scare him, shake him up a little bit." I stared at her in disbelief. *Was this the same friend, trusted confidante, that I had known practically my whole life, telling me that punching someone to death was just an act of shaking some sense into someone?*

"You can't tell me you condone what just happened?" I shrugged her arms off of me.

"Jenny?" Liam had come to my side. My face was flushed and streaked from tears. "Are you okay?"

"No, Liam, I'm not. I want to go home."

"Alright, let's go."

"No Liam, by myself."

He stood there. "What?"

"Just leave me alone. I need some time."

I walked off and headed for home. I knew I had hurt Liam's feelings, especially after he defended my honor, but it bothered me how he defended it. His method was almost medieval. I never, not in a hundred years, thought he would use such scare tactics. Talking and threatening are one thing, but to actually act on those threats was totally different. I was almost home when I heard the familiar hum of his truck behind me. Liam was pulling over in front of me, forcing me to stop dead in my tracks.

"Babe, get in, please." I just stood there staring at him. "Please, Jenny." He opened the passenger door for me. I sighed sharply as I stepped into his cab. I stayed on my side of the seat with my arms crossed, looking straight ahead. "Jenny, talk to me, please. It's killing me that you're giving me the silent treatment."

"It's killing you? Just like you almost killed Johnny with your scare tactics?"

"Jenny…"

I stopped him. "Liam, do you realize you could have seriously hurt Johnny? What would have happened if Kendra and I hadn't shown up when we did? Huh?"

"Jen, you're blowing this way out of proportion. He's fine. You saw him get up."

He scooted over to me and cradled me in his arms. I shrugged him off as he continued to try and make up with me. He started kissing the top of my head and working his way down to my face until his lips were on mine.

They were soft and tender. "Stop, I'm mad at you. It's not fair for you to do this to me."

"Please don't be mad at me. I love you. Don't you know how much you mean to me? That was for you... for us. The thought of Johnny or anybody else trying to come between us kills me. I never want to lose you."

"Liam, I told you that you're never going to lose me. You were never in jeopardy of losing me. I've never wanted Johnny. I've only wanted you."

"Then why are you so mad at me?" He asked.

"I've never seen you so upset. When I saw Parker and Tony holding Johnny, and you were using him as a human punching bag, I couldn't believe my eyes. What if you did hurt him? He could press charges against you, and then what? You want to go to jail over Johnny? It's not worth it. Couldn't you just have told him to leave me alone? Did you actually have to hit him over and over again?"

"Don't you see...? I did try to talk to him. That was my intention from the very beginning."

"What happened then?"

"I wanted to scare him, Jenny. I've been a total wreck ever since you told me what he did to you in the warehouse. I wanted to let him know that I knew, and I wasn't going to stand for it. You're my girl, and if he's messing with you, then he's messing with me. That's not right; it's wrong. Plus, the fact that we were supposed to be friends, I mean come on. I went to confront him, and I found him down at the field with Zane and Jake. Tony and Parker went with me for back up, and I told him to stay away from us. He basically laughed in my face, saying that I had no hold on you and that he had as much right to pursue you as anyone. He actually swung the first punch."

"He did?"

"Yes he did. Zane and Jake were trying to pick a fight with Tony and Parker. I guess that's when it got out of hand. Johnny said until he saw a ring on your finger you were up for grabs. Babe, he was talking about you like you were some piece of meat or something. I couldn't take it. That's when it got ugly. Tony and Parker were taking care of Zane and Jake, and I was taking care of Johnny. Johnny and I actually were on the ground. Tony and Parker pulled us apart, and that's when you and Kendra showed up. They were holding Johnny while I punched him. I know it wasn't right, but it wasn't right what Johnny did at your dad's warehouse, sending you notes or any of the other stuff he's done. I was fighting for you."

"Liam, you just scared me. I never saw you so angry before. I was afraid."

"Jen, you never have to be afraid of me. But I will never let anyone come between us." We were still parked on the side of the road. "Come on. You don't really want to go home do you?" I shook my head. "Good, let's get out of here."

He slid behind the steering wheel and brought me with him. His right arm clutched my left leg. He flew to Brush Creek Road, wasting no time. Liam got out of the truck and held his hand out for me to take.

"Why are we getting out?"

"You'll see. Come on, now please take my hand."

I grabbed his hand, and he swept me into his arms. "Liam!" He carried me to the back of his truck and set me down gently.

"Now close your eyes and no peeking." I stood there in suspense as I heard Liam open the lift gate to his truck.

"What are you doing?"

"You'll find out. Be patient." After a couple of minutes, Liam took my arms and walked me over a few feet. "Okay, now be careful."

He was pushing me to sit down. "Liam, on the ground?"

"Jen, will you just trust me? You can be so stubborn." I sat down, expecting to sit on the hard, cold ground, but to my surprise I found myself sitting on something soft. "Okay, you can open your eyes."

I looked around. Liam and I were sitting on a huge blue blanket and in front of me was a bottle of red wine. "Liam, are you kidding me? When did you plan this?"

"Since last night. I've been wanting to do this for a while, I just haven't though."

"You mean this has nothing to do with what happened at school today?"

"No, but I have to admit the timing was good."

He poured me a glass of wine. "To you and me, babe, forever." Our glasses made a hollow clink as they echoed in the air. "Do you like it?"

Liam had moved in closer to me. "Yeah, a lot," I said.

"How much?"

Liam inched his way closer to me. "Very much."

"Maybe you should show me how much."

Liam leaned down, and his lips hovered over mine. "I don't know about this. I should still be mad at you."

"You can't punish me for fighting for you."

I hesitated, contemplating my next move. "Come here then." I pulled his shirt to me, planting my wine-soaked lips on his. We both dropped our glasses and spilled the wine on the blanket.

"So are you still upset with me?"

"Maybe a little bit, but I'm a firm believer in forgiveness."

"Jen, I love you."

"I know."

"I thought... you might..."

"What?"

"I don't know. I just thought that maybe you liked the attention from Johnny. I was worried you might have wanted him, maybe more than me. I've been really scared thinking I might lose you to him."

"Are you crazy? I've never wanted Johnny. It's always been you. Why do you think I was so upset? I wanted Johnny to leave me alone. I wanted him out of my life."

"Are you sure?"

I pulled him to me and kissed him as hard as I could. "I'm positive. I'm in love with you."

"That's all I needed to hear."

There was a definite chill in the air, but I couldn't have cared less. Liam and I were wrapped in each other's embrace. The blue blanket sheltered both of us from the wind, and the wine had numbed me as well.

"Do you want to get back into the truck?" he asked

"Maybe in a little bit." I was focused on the star-lit night. "It's gorgeous up here. I never want to leave."

"Don't you think we would be missed after a while?"

"Maybe, but I don't care. I have everything I want right here. Let them send out a search party if they want. I dare them to find us."

"Jenny, I'm sorry you had to see me hitting Johnny today."

"Me too. I just don't understand why Johnny won't give up. I'm still nervous. What if he doesn't stop? Then what?"

"Don't worry," he said. "It'll be fine. Let's deal with it as it comes. He knows to stay away, and if he's smart, he will. Not only does he have me to worry about but everyone else in the school too. He's not making many friends."

"I don't think he's going to give up so easy. And what about work? I've got to convince Dad to let him go."

"Do you want me to talk to him?"

"I don't know, maybe I should explain to him what happened? I wish this never happened. I thought you guys were friends. I don't get why he would want to do this and ruin your friendship."

"Johnny's always been a player, a teaser. He always wants what he doesn't have. He feels it's his for the taking, even if it is you. Although I will say, it's usually been sports that have been his challenge. Never known him to stoop this low and try to take another guy's girl."

"But doesn't he take no for an answer?"

"Not always." Liam laid his head on my lap. I played with the curls in his hair. "Promise me you'll stay away from him, okay?"

"I will." Easier said than done, I thought as I wondered how I would avoid him while he still worked for my dad.

I played with Liam's curls, letting them fall in between my fingers. "You know, I love your hair."

"What? Where did that come from?"

"I don't know. I just thought you should know." He rolled over to face me with a sinister grin creeping onto his face. "What are you thinking?" I asked. He started moving in closer to me. He let out a wicked chuckle. "Liam, what are you thinking?" I tried to move, but I was trapped under his body. His left hand found its way under my shirt and he gently caressed my stomach. His wicked grin told me this wasn't foreplay. "Liam, please don't." I knew exactly what he was thinking, and then without warning, he started tickling me incessantly. I screamed in desperation for him to stop, but the more I screamed the more obsessed he became.

"Say I'm the greatest." I was laughing so hard that I couldn't hardly breathe, much less speak. He tickled me faster. "Say it, babe, or I won't stop. Say I'm the greatest."

"I'm the greatest!" I blurted out.

"Wrong answer." I was still laughing uncontrollably.

Liam was holding onto the sides of my stomach as his tickling rampage continued. "You're the greatest Liam. You're the greatest!" I screamed.

"That's much better." He let up his hold. "You know, actually in my eyes, you're the greatest," he whispered.

"Do you think it will always be like this?" I asked as I gazed at the stars.

"What do you mean?"

"This, us, here. Will it always be this great? Will you always want to tickle me, caress me, you know…want me? Will this feeling always be here? I mean, you're not going to grow tired of me, are you? Or bored? Are we still going to come here five, ten years from now, and will it still feel this special?"

He sat up and looked me straight in the eye. "Jen, this won't be the same."

"It won't?"

"No. If anything, it's going to get better. My feelings for you grow stronger every day. I love you more today than yesterday, and I'll love you more tomorrow than today. I've meant every word I've ever said. You know when you told me that your heart skips a beat when I'm near?"

"Yeah."

"That's only a part of what you do to me. When you're near, I can't breathe; you literally take my breath away."

"Even my silly fetishes? You don't mind them?"

"Jen, even your silly obsession with the number eleven. It's a part of you, and I love every part of you. I'm always going to be here. I'm not going anywhere. I want to be here for you always. Don't ever doubt my feelings for you or think otherwise. Okay?"

"Okay."

We left Brush Creek that night and headed to my house. Liam walked me in and exchanged some pleasantries with my parents before leaving. He needed to get home and get to bed. He was meeting Parker and Tony early Saturday morning at Joe Michael's auto shop with their trucks. Joe was three years older than us and a football jock that played with Liam before he graduated. He had a promising career in front of him after being accepted at WVU on a full-ride football scholarship, only he broke his hip and pelvis in a drag race three days after graduation. His car blew a tire and flipped over four times, trapping Joe inside. He spent two months in the hospital and had to have six months of rehab. Joe's dream to play college ball ended that night. Instead, he opened an auto shop and has turned a hobby of pimping out cars and trucks into a full-time profession. Liam said he was the best in the area. Half of the muscle cars and trucks around here are due to the handy work of Joe. Liam was determined to have the best truck for the upcoming race, knowing full well that he might be up against Johnny again. There was no way he was going to chance this race without Joe's help.

"I'll talk to you tomorrow. I don't know when I'll be home. Me and the boys plan to spend most of the day and maybe Sunday at Joe's, but I'll be in touch, okay?"

"Sure, love you."

"Love you more." He gave me his wink and drove off.

I spent the rest of the night on the phone with Kendra, both of us going over the events that led to Liam and Johnny fighting. Tony was hopping mad at Johnny too and wanted as much of a piece of him as Liam did.

"What are your plans this weekend?" Kendra asked.

"I don't know. I'm going to play it by ear. Sounds like I won't be seeing much of Liam though."

"Yeah, I know what you mean. I think they're planning on spending the weekend at Joe's shop. Anyway, that's fine. I'm going to Charleston for the weekend with my parents. It's my aunt's 70th birthday, and she lives by herself, so we're spending the whole weekend with her. You wanna come with us? It'll give you something to do since the boys will be busy with their trucks."

"Nah, thanks though. Mom and Dad need help around the store. They're still doing inventory, and Dad is short a couple of guys this weekend. But thanks for asking. Have fun."

"Yeah, it's always fun to spend your weekend away from your boyfriend and hang out with people more than 3x your age. I can't wait!"

"Well, try to have a good time, at least for your aunt's sake. I'll see you at school."

The weekend dragged on, and by Sunday I was bored out of my mind. I hadn't seen Liam all weekend and only talked to him a few times when he would check in to see how I was doing. I could hear the excitement in his voice when he talked about his truck and how Joe was helping him get it in tip-top shape. I was happy for him, but I was miserable for myself. There was nothing to do, I had even called Missy, Shauna, and the rest of the girls, and all of them were busy with their boyfriends and lives. I was totally out of their loop now. I felt like kicking myself for not accepting Kendra's invitation to her aunt's birthday. *At least it would have been something to do.* I hated doing inventory and had gotten out of it until Sunday. Sundays were usually short days for the store, and Dad decided to close the store altogether in order to finish it. I moped around while I tried to neglect my duties. Dad had left me specific instructions to count all the canned goods and categorize them in alphabetical order. More inventory; I couldn't stand it. I was basically on my own to do the inventory in the store while my dad worked in the warehouse. Besides the manager Vernon Phillips, who was busy with payroll in dad's office on the 2nd floor, I was the only one in the supermarket. A welcome relief. I could take my good ole time without my parents looking over my shoulder constantly. After two hours of tedious, mundane work, I had only made it to the C's... creamed corn. I jumped when the door slammed and looked out the back window of the door. Vernon's car was still there. Maybe Mom and Dad had come in. I walked upstairs to Dad's office. The room was completely vacant.

    I turned to go back downstairs.

    "Hi, Jenny," Johnny said.

    "Johnny, what are you doing here? You seem to have an uncanny knack for sneaking up behind me." I backed up and walked behind dad's desk, keeping a good distance between the two of us.

    "I came for my check. Your dad said Vernon was doing payroll and I could pick it up today. Surprised to see me?"

    "Uhh, yeah. That's the understatement of the year." I was still baffled that he was standing in the same room with me.

    "Jen, don't worry. I'm not here to bother you, just to get my check. Do you know where it is?"

    I looked around. The only place I knew Dad to keep payroll checks was in his vault, but it was locked, and I didn't know the combination. "Umm... no Johnny, I don't. Vernon must have just left. If you want to come back later or I could have Dad mail it to you."

    "No, that's not necessary." He sat down in the chair across from me. "I'll wait."

"But I don't know how long Vernon will be, or if he's even coming back. It would be better if I could have Dad mail it to you, Johnny."

He put his feet up on Dad's desk, making himself right at home in his chair. "I saw Vernon talking to your dad. He said you could give it to me."

He wasn't going to budge. I noticed the cut on his lip required stitches, and the corner of his left eye was bloodshot, obviously a result of Liam's fist. I shuffled papers on Dad's desk, pretending to look for Johnny's check, knowing full well it wasn't here. "Johnny, I'm not seeing it."

He sat up and leaned towards the desk. He placed his hand on top of mine. "That's okay, Jen. I'll wait for your dad. He said he would be up eventually. I need to talk to him anyway."

I realized my hand was still under his and instantly moved it. "Oh?" I said, trying to sound indifferent.

"Yeah, this is my final check. After what happened at school on Friday I thought it was best that I didn't work here anymore, you know, with everything that went down."

I stared at him, almost intimidated but relieved by his statement. "Johnny... it's just that, you have to realize that there couldn't be anything between you and me. It never was going to happen."

"Are you sure about that? I mean... absolutely sure?" He spoke as if he knew something I didn't.

"Yes, of course, I'm sure, Johnny. Why would you ask that? Look, it doesn't matter why you asked it. I know there's nothing between us, and that's all that matters. I will say, that I am sorry about Friday. I never meant for you to get hurt, especially over me.

But, Liam was upset. You have to understand where he was coming from."

Johnny inhaled deeply. "Yeah, I guess, but it doesn't change how I feel about you."

"You don't even know me, Johnny. Why do you keep saying stuff like that? I think you just better go. I'll be sure to tell Dad to mail you your check. I just don't think you should be here right now."

"Why? Because you're here? Because we're alone? Are you worried I might try to corner you again?"

"Never mind, you stay. I'll go. This is ridiculous."

I began to walk out when Johnny rose to his feet and caught me by my arm. "Jen, I'm sorry. I didn't mean to make you upset. I seem to do that a lot lately. It's just that I never get the chance to talk to you alone, and when I do, I still seem to louse things up. I know you want nothing to do with me, but I would like the chance to convince you otherwise. I know what you're going to say. You're with Liam. I get that. Believe me. But if you would just give me the opportunity for us to get to know one another, then that's all I ask, no commitments. Maybe just friends or hopefully better friends than what we are now."

Did he think that it was easy as that? All I had to do was just to get to know him better? As if Liam was not in the picture.

"Johnny, you're asking something of me that I can't do. What about Liam? You seem to forget that I'm with him."

"Jen, he doesn't have to know."

"The fact that you even said that Johnny repulses me. Why would I want to risk the best thing that's ever happened to me just because you want to have a little fling?"

"Maybe you'll realize that he's not the best thing that's ever happened to you. Maybe you'll realize that there are other fish in the sea."

"You're an arrogant son of a bitch, Johnny!" My hand swung around and hit his face before I even realized I had slapped him again.

He grabbed my hand instantly in his. "You're getting good at this. I think this one will definitely leave a mark."

He moved in within inches of my face, holding tight to my hand. "Johnny, please let go of me." He didn't listen. Why should he? He never listened to anything I had to say. He brought my hand to his chest, keeping it cupped in his. I could feel his heart beating against my palm. "Johnny, please… I've got to go." I wanted to tell him to stop playing with me, to leave me alone, find someone else, but nothing came out. Instead, I stood there while he held my arm in his grasp. His brown eyes crept closer to mine, and when I thought he couldn't get any closer, he kissed me. The strangest feeling came over me. I wanted him to stop, but for the life of me I didn't resist him this time. He was being tender, and the threads of his stitches were tickling the corner of my mouth as his lips gently molded to mine.

Coming to my senses, I jerked myself from his grip. "Damn you!" I screamed while wiping my mouth in disgust. "Why are you doing this to me?"

"I thought you should see what a real kiss is like, and by your reaction, I think you might have enjoyed it."

"Stop it, Johnny. Please, just leave me alone. Why are you doing this to me? And to Liam? He was supposed to be your friend? Can't you just take no for an answer?"

"No, I can't because deep down I think you might feel differently about me. I told you I wasn't going anywhere. Do you think what happened Friday is enough to scare me off? Give me a little credit. It's not over, and it won't be until I have my chance with you."

"Dream on. You're a complete ass, Johnny!"

"Come on, Jen, you know I've gotten to you a little bit."

I scoffed at his egotistical remark. "You're crazy."

"Yeah, maybe. Mom calls it a stubborn streak. Oh, which reminds me, she said she had a very nice time when you came by her shop. She wanted me to tell you hi. Are you sure you weren't there to maybe see if I would be? Huh?"

"Do you think the world revolves around you or something? I had my own reasons to see her, and they're none of your damn business." He was standing so close to me I could count the stitches in his upper lip.

"Well, maybe not…" His voice trailed off as he stared at the ground, contemplating his thoughts. "Jen," he paused and took a deep breath. "I never meant for this to happen. I mean, I tried not to like you. I went out with other girls, hung out with my friends, but I couldn't erase you from my thoughts. I cringe when I see you with Liam. When his arms are around you, I want them to be mine instead of his. So… I saw no other option but to be truthful with you. Maybe I went about it the wrong way at the warehouse, but at least I'm not hiding my feelings for you anymore. I guess I thought if you knew how I felt, maybe you would consider me."

"Save your breath. There's nothing you can say or do that's going to change my mind about you. Do me a favor and just leave it alone. You act as if this is just about you and me. It's not. This involves Liam too. I love him, and nothing's going to change that." I turned away from him and ran down the steps, almost knocking down my dad.

"Jenny, honey, are you okay?"

"I'm fine, Dad. It's nothing."

I ran home and grabbed my car keys, not knowing where I would end up, but I knew I needed to get as far out of Dodge as possible. I drove for over an hour just meandering through the countryside when I finally came to a hilltop clearing and pulled over. *Why was this happening to me? Why couldn't things just be easy and normal again?* I felt like the whole world was crashing in on me. Everything seemed to be spiraling out of control and into oblivion. I sunk into my seat and prayed for an answer as I cried my heart out. I wanted Liam and just as God had heard my prayer, I heard a thunderous noise coming up the hill.

"What the hell?" I could see the dust billowing up in the air, but could not make out who or what was causing the commotion. And then I saw Liam's truck. He sped towards me at an exponential rate, swerving to a stop next to my car, missing me by inches. I sat there as Liam rushed to my side.

"Jenny, are you alright? What happened?"

"Liam, how in the world did you find me?"

"Never mind that, are you okay?" My red, swollen eyes were a dead giveaway. I tried to shrug it off, not wanting to upset Liam anymore.

"Liam, it's nothing. I just needed to get away, that's all."

"Jen, tell me the truth." He had opened my door and pulled me out. "I called your house. Your dad said you left crying. I've been looking for you ever since. Does this have anything to do with Johnny?" I didn't speak. I didn't have to. Liam knew right away. "What happened, Jen?"

"I just had another run in with Johnny. He came by the store to pick up his check while I was there. He..."

"What, Jen?"

Liam's face was blazing red. His hands tightened on my arms. "Liam, he's... he's not giving up. He said he won't stop until I'm his."

"That son of a bitch! This time I am going to kill him. Did he not get the message on Friday?"

"Please, I just want to forget about this. I'm so tired of it." I was crying uncontrollably, and my whole body trembled. "I'm afraid. I don't want you to fight him anymore. It's going to get worse. Can't we just forget about him, try to just to ignore him, please, for my sake?"

"Jenny, I'm sorry, I can't. You can't ask that of me."

He was right. I knew that. This wasn't going to be over until someone got hurt, or worse, maybe killed. There was nothing I could say or do to change the path that we were on. I thought back to Johnny's mom telling me that we were all on a path, a journey. I wondered if this was what our journey was. *Was this what the number eleven was trying to tell me, that I would have to choose, and if I didn't, the choice would be made for me?* I was scared beyond belief. I couldn't bear the thought of Liam getting hurt because of me, and I couldn't bear the thought of Johnny getting hurt either. I wanted to run away and leave all this behind me. I wanted Liam and I to be where we were before Johnny entered the picture, but it would never be that way again. Liam and Johnny were going to have it out over me. I had to do something, but I didn't know what. It wasn't about just me anymore. This was about all three of us.

I closed my eyes and pressed myself against Liam's body. I fell into his arms, exhausted from the turmoil. We didn't do much talking the rest of the afternoon. Liam wasn't in the mood, and I was too emotionally drained to care. All I wanted to do was go home, so Liam followed me back to my house. I was cautious as I drove in, looking everywhere for the white Bronco. I knew, or at least I thought I knew, that Johnny would be smart enough to not stick around. After everything that has happened, I didn't put much past him. I didn't want to go inside and be interrogated by Mom and Dad, so I waited until after Liam left. That way when they did ask me questions, I could make my story short and sweet without Liam adding his two cents worth. Liam and I ended up sitting on the porch for the rest of the evening until it was time for him to leave. I was mentally exhausted from the entire weekend, and sleep was going to be a welcome refuge.

"I'll stay if you want me to. Just say the word," he said.

"Be realistic. You can't. Grandpa Mack has enough to worry about without worrying where you are at all hours of the night. I'll be fine. I promise. I'm just going to bed after you leave anyway. I'm not worried. I just want this whole thing to be over."

"Don't worry, Jen. It will be."

We kissed goodnight. I stood on the porch as he walked away, wondering if I would find him sitting in my driveway in a few hours.

Chapter Twenty
The Promise

    Word spread quickly of the fight between Liam and Johnny. Faculty and students alike were talking about it, and by lunchtime so many versions of the story had erupted, I was even questioning myself what really happened, and I had seen most of it. I was bombarded with questions from everyone wanting to know the scoop. I found myself hiding in the bathroom to avoid the frenzy. It didn't help matters that Johnny was doing his best not to avoid me. I had found a lavender rose in my locker that I thought had come from Liam. When I approached Liam to thank him, he didn't have a clue what I was talking about. It didn't take either of us long to figure out who it was from. It took both Tony and Parker to hold Liam back from going after Johnny again.

    It was as if Johnny was trying to push Liam over the edge, to see how far he would go before breaking. The only good thing was that Johnny switched his Advanced English class to another period. I can't even begin to think of the bloodbath that would have taken place during Mrs. White's theory of synonyms if he hadn't. Liam was at his breaking point, having had enough of Johnny's bold and brazen behavior. Liam, of course, continued to stay by my side, becoming my shadow wherever I went. If he couldn't be with me, he made sure one of his friends was. I couldn't pee without having someone do a bathroom check first.

Of course, the other tidbit of news that was burning everyone's ears was that there would be a race between Liam and Johnny. Liam and his buddies talked strategies constantly. They were on the phone regularly with Joe's shop, scheming and devising their plans. By the end of the school day, Liam and Johnny had mutually agreed to a date, Saturday April 11th on Ripley Road at eleven o'clock in the evening. To keep the race a secret, no one was to speak a word of it. This way there wouldn't be any attention drawn to it. Of course, that's exactly what didn't happen. The only good thing was that the date had not been divulged.

Liam and Johnny had decided that there would only be one heat. But instead of the usual heat where the winner was decided at the end of Devil's Bulge, they decided to make it a little more interesting. This time they would turn around at Devil's Bulge and drive back to the starting point, a very dangerous maneuver. Devil's Bulge had one of the sharpest hairpin turns in the county. It was hard enough to make the turn driving normally, much less going over eighty miles per hour. It would be a death race.

I met Liam outside of the band room after the final bell. He had skipped our last class together, and this was the first time I had seen him since word had gotten out about the race with Johnny. I was livid with him. I walked to his truck in silence.

"Jen, are you mad about something?" I remained quiet, walking with my arms crossed. "This is about the race isn't it?" I kept walking. "I thought so. I know you're not happy about this, but Johnny agreed to it also. It's between me and him now."

I abruptly stopped walking. "Are you joking, Liam? This is about all three of us. None of this would even be happening if it wasn't for me. Maybe I should have given into Johnny. At least you'd both be alive after all of this is over."

Liam grabbed my arms and pulled me close to him. "You don't mean that." I looked at him apologetically. I didn't mean it.

I grabbed his hands and squeezed them in mine. "No, of course not. You know that. I want you, but that's just it. There's never been a choice for me. It's always been you, but because Johnny won't give up you two now have to race over me? What if Johnny wins the race, Liam?"

"He's not going to." He sounded offended.

"You don't know that. Am I supposed to run into his arms because he won my virtues? Huh? This whole damn thing is absolutely insane. Even if he does win, it's not going to change anything. My feelings for you will remain the same. You're not going to lose me over him, but I could lose you. You could be killed in this stupid race! Is this really worth it?" I was shouting so loud that a crowd had gathered around us.

Liam grabbed my hand. "Come on."

This time he was being the silent one. "Liam, talk to me, now!"

We reached his truck and opened the driver's side of the door. "Get in," he demanded. I immediately got in and slid over to make room for him. He just sat there, not saying a word.

"Okay, if this is how it's going to be then just take me home."

Liam's hands were grasping his steering wheel as he stared straight ahead. "Jenny…"

"Oh, he speaks!" I said sarcastically.

He turned in my direction. "Tell me something? Am I worth it?"

"What?"

"Am I worth it? Do you love me enough that you would lay your life on the line for me?"

"What a thing to ask of me. Why are you talking like this?"

"Because you are worth it, to me at least. There's nothing in this world that I wouldn't do for you. I've meant every word I've said to you from day one. My feelings for you haven't changed, if anything they've only grown stronger. I know in my heart that you're the one. You're the one I want to spend the rest of my days with. You're the one I want to take care of, to love, to laugh with, to have my children, and to grow old with. I would die for you in a heartbeat. I know we're both young, but I know I've found the girl I want to spend the rest of my God-given days with. I don't need to look anymore. You're my life, my future, and I'm fighting for it. I want you to be a part of mine, and I won't let anyone come between us.

"And right now Johnny Bryant is coming between us. Whether you think so or not. I know how you feel about me, and I know that you don't care about what Johnny says or how he feels about you, but I do. He's trying to take my everything away from me, and I can't let him do that, Jen. I'm scared to death of losing you to him. He's playing a game, a game he wants to win. This is so much bigger than what it was before. This whole thing has grown out of proportion. It's between Johnny and me now, and the only way to settle this thing between us is by racing him on the 11th. You've got to trust me, Jen. I'm not planning on losing the race, and even if I do, we're not losing each other. You're my soul mate. Something brought us together. I don't know what it was, maybe your number eleven did have a part in it, maybe it's kismet, fate, luck, I don't know, but I do know we're meant to be together. That's why I'm doing this, Jen because you're worth it."

I sat not knowing what to do or say. Liam loved me enough that he would die for me. I hugged him tighter than I ever had before.

"Jenny, this race is beyond us, but I'm going to win it for us."

"I know. I'm just scared. You have to promise me that you won't let anything happen to you. You've got to come back to me unharmed. Promise me, Liam!"

"I promise, babe."

Chapter Twenty-One
The Ring

I was relieved and still nervous as hell. What used to be butterflies in my stomach had grown into full-size moths. Over the days that followed, I turned into a complete mess. My every conscious thought was consumed by thoughts of the impending race. I couldn't eat or sleep. I tossed and turned all night, praying for daylight so I had a legitimate excuse to get out of bed. Liam was spending most of his free time at Joe's with the rest of the guys. With less than a week and a half before the race, he didn't want to leave anything to chance.

While Liam was at Joe's, I spent most of my time with Kendra. She was just as worried about the race as I was. Apparently Tony had decided to ride with Liam, giving him moral and technical support. Misery loves company, so Kendra and I were both great for each other, leaning on each other more than ever for moral support. School had become an afterthought. Being that we were seniors, we were just going through the motions until graduation. Most of our fellow classmates were caught up in what they were going to be doing after graduation. Some were getting jobs. Some were skipping college altogether. Others were leaving for the college of their choice. College was still up in the air for Liam and me. We had both been accepted to WVU, Liam receiving a full ride to play football. It was a dream come true, but unfortunately it wasn't Liam's dream. His mind was still made up. He was going to remain on the farm to help his grandpa. Joe had asked him to become a partner with him at the auto shop. This, in Liam's eyes, was much better than a full ride to play college ball. He loved working on his truck, and the thought of doing something like that every day was too much for him to pass up. He hadn't said yes yet, but we both knew he would.

I couldn't bear the thought of leaving for college without Liam, and since he wasn't going with me, I was staying too. That was a decision that hadn't gone over well with my parents. Although Liam was ecstatic over my decision, he didn't want me to give up my dream because of him. But Liam was my dream. I could still go to a community college and stay in town and help out with my parent's business. It was a win-win situation for everyone, at least in my eyes.

So, while the rest of the senior class was immersed in the day to day activities that would lead to the rest of their lives, Liam, Johnny, and I were concentrating on April 11th, a date which would decide our fates. As the date approached, I became more aware of how dangerous this race was going to be. It wasn't uncommon for me to walk past fellow students and hear them whispering about the upcoming event. 'Poor, Jen, she looks a wreck', or 'I hope Liam doesn't get hurt in this race or worse... die'. 'What a shame that it has come to this.' Comments like this were abundant. I shrugged them off as best as I could, but it became increasingly harder to do as the race grew closer. It was the talk of the school, and although we did our best to keep the venue a secret, the location still leaked out. Everyone planned on being there. It was the last thing any of us wanted.

This was supposed to be a private race between Liam and Johnny, two turns on the road, the winner claiming victory, not over me anymore but over who the better man was. It had turned into a contest of who had the biggest balls, an immature game that could cost me the love of my life, but I had no control over it. Instead, I supported Liam and hoped and prayed for the best. More importantly, with word spreading so quickly about the race, all of us involved were worried that the police would definitely find out about the location.

Gordon Jones was still on our trail, so Tony and Parker had devised a scheme to throw him off our track. They spread the word that the race would take place on April 18th instead and at Steele Hollow Road. This would be exactly one week after the real race, hopefully by the time the fabricated story hit the rumor mill the race would be over. With the help of the gossiping skills of the student body, Gordon would take the bait. It worked. The time and date spread like wildfire, and by the end of the week, Liam had heard that the police were planning a stake out on the 18th near Steele Hollow Road. Everything was falling into place.

I was mentally drained by the weekend. Liam was still spending most of his time at Joe's shop with Tony and Parker. His truck was in excellent condition. The paw-wows now consisted of driving techniques for the race. This had turned into a twenty-four-seven obsession with them. I had to wonder if Johnny was putting as much effort into the race as they were. By Saturday night, one week before the illicit race, Kendra and I had forged a new relationship between girlfriend widows. With our guys spending their evenings with Joe instead of us, we rekindled our relationship that had gotten sidelined when we both started dating.

"So, has Liam talked anymore about the race?" she asked me.

"No. Nothing new at least. He doesn't want me to be there though."

"Why?"

"I don't know. He thinks it would be safer if I stayed home."

"Are you?"

"Hell no. This all started over me. There's nothing that's keeping me away from Ripley Road next Saturday."

"I don't blame you, but I understand why Liam wants you to stay away."

"I know, but I will be there Kendra. I have to. Do you mind if we change the subject? I'm tired of talking about it. It seems that's all I hear anymore. Do you want to go the movies or something?" I was bored out of my mind and needed to get out of the house.

"No, I can't. Tony is actually coming over tonight."

"He is? You mean he's not spending his free time at Joe's?"

"Not tonight. He called me earlier and told me he would be over at seven."

"You better go then; it's six-forty-one now."

"It is? I totally lost track of time. I'll talk to you later. Are you supposed to see Liam tonight?"

"I don't know. He hasn't called me yet."

"Well, don't worry, Jen. You know he's doing this for you."

"Yeah, I know."

I walked outside and watched Kendra speed away. I was jealous. She was at least going to be with her guy tonight. I on the other hand just waited for a phone call. I was feeling sorry for myself when I saw headlights turn down my driveway. My heart jumped. Liam, I thought. I ran to the end of my driveway to meet him, but to my dismay it was a white Bronco.

Johnny pulled up next to me. "Hi, Jen. Glad to see me?"

"Oh, it's you. What do you want?"

"To see you."

"I can't believe you're even here Johnny. Do you have a death wish or something? If Liam knew you were here…"

"But he doesn't. He's at Joe's shop, and by the looks of things when I drove by, he's going to be busy the rest of the night."

"So what? I don't have to see him every night."

"It looks like you've been spending a lot of nights without seeing him. Do you want to take a ride?"

"With you?" Not a chance."

As I turned to walk away, Johnny jumped out of his Bronco and caught up with me. I whirled on him. "Johnny, please. Can't you just take no for an answer? I'm not interested."

"But I am, Jenny."

"Liam could show up at any moment."

"I'll take my chances."

I felt as if I was battling a losing war. I continued walking, and Johnny kept in step with me. "I'm going inside Johnny, and I want you to leave."

"Can't you just sit here and talk to me? I promise I won't try anything. I won't even try to kiss you anymore. Please? Scouts Honor."

He motioned to the porch swing as he made an x over his chest. "I'll sit on one end and you on the other," I said. I knew better, but I thought maybe if I could talk rationally with him I could convince him to really leave me alone or better yet, to call off the race. I grudgingly walked to the swing and sat as far away from him as possible. "So, what do you want to talk about?"

"Anything. Whatever you want."

I could see this wasn't going anywhere. "Listen Johnny, I do commend you for being persistent, but your efforts to win my affection are pointless. My feelings for you are not going to change. You really need to accept that and move on."

"Are you positive, Jen? 100% positive?"

"Yes, and furthermore, this race between you and Liam is stupid. Call it off. If you care for me like you keep saying, call it off. It's scaring me to death that something might happen."

"Are you worried about me?"

"Johnny come on. That's not fair, of course, I don't want either one of you to get hurt, especially over me, but I definitely don't want anything to happen to Liam. You have the power to call it off. This all started because of you. Tell Liam you're over it, and the race doesn't have to happen. Do it for me, please." I found myself facing him, my eyes pleading with him. He leaned over to me and pulled my chin closer to his face. "Johnny, please don't do this again."

"Jen, I would do almost anything for you." I felt victory at hand. "But I can't do that. This race started out over you, I agree, but it's between Liam and me. We have a score to settle, and I'm not backing down." His eyes were serious as they stared into mine.

"Then leave Johnny. We have nothing more to say to one another." A crooked smile crept onto his face. He leaned as if he was going to try and kiss me, and I quickly moved backward. "No, Johnny."

"Well, you can't blame a guy for trying." He immediately jerked his head towards the street. "Looks like this is my cue to leave anyway." He blew me a kiss with his fingers. "See ya around, Jenny."

Liam pulled up to the curb just seconds after Johnny drove off. For a minute I thought Liam wasn't going to stop, his engine revving as he sat in his truck watching the white Bronco turn the corner.

I walked to his side. "Hey babe, perfect timing."

"What the hell was he doing here?"

"One last vain attempt to win my heart." There was no use lying to the fact why he was here, and Liam wouldn't have believed it anyway.

"Is everything okay?"

There seemed to be a double meaning behind his question. "Yeah, I told him to go. I think he's going to leave me alone now." I could tell Liam still wasn't convinced; and, to be honest, neither was I. Why would Johnny honor my wishes this time? Only time would tell.

"You want to go back to my place? Grandpa is out of town for the night. We can finally be alone."

"Definitely, let me grab my jacket. I'll be right back."

It had been awhile since I had been at Liam's house. I missed it there. I felt more at home there at times than my own house. Liam drove quickly there as though we would miss something if he drove any slower. He pulled the truck to an abrupt stop and guided me out on his side. We walked into the living room where he ordered me to sit down.

"Stay here. I'll be right back."

"Where are you going?"

Liam vanished behind the kitchen door without answering. I made myself comfortable on the floral sofa and proceeded to pet Blue while I waited for his return. Liam appeared a few minutes later wearing new clothes with his hair hanging down. He kept one arm behind his back and walked directly towards me making it impossible to see what was behind him.

"What do you have behind your back?"

He said nothing but proceeded to sit down next to me, grabbed my neck with his free hand, and kissed me like there was no tomorrow.

"I'm sorry I've been spending so much time away from you."

"That's okay. I understand."

"No, it's not okay."

He pulled his arm from around his back. In his hand was a group of lavender roses. "Liam, they're beautiful!"

"Not half as beautiful as you."

"What did you do, corner the market on lavender roses?" I didn't wait for an answer. My eyes transfixed on a pale blue ribbon that was tied to one of the stems with a small purple bag dangling from it.

"What's this?"

"Open it."

"What did you do?" I asked.

I took the ribbon and carefully untied the bow, making sure not to drop the delicate bag. I was so nervous that my attempt not to drop the bag made the bag slip through my hands and fall into my lap. I stared at it and then at Liam. My eyes darted back and forth to both of them for minutes.

"Well, are you going to open it or do I have to do it for you?" Liam asked anxiously.

"No, I'll do it." I carefully pulled the purple cord and placed my hand inside. My heart was racing as I felt a tiny object in the palm of my hand. I pulled it out hesitantly and kept my hand closed. I was scared to death to open it. Finally, with a deep breath I opened the palm of my hand. In the middle of it laid a silver ring with a beautifully heart-shaped diamond perched on top of it. It took my breath away. "Liam? Is this what I think it is?"

He took the ring in his hand. "Jen, I love you more than anything. This ring represents my heart and my love for you. I want to marry you."

I stared in disbelief as the ring glistened under the light of the lamp. I couldn't believe what was happening.

"I know you might think this is too soon. Hell, we're only seventeen, but we both turn eighteen next month, and we'll be graduating in less than six weeks. You know I've loved you from the moment I first laid eyes on you. Please, baby." He went down on bended knee. "Make me the happiest guy in the world. Marry me."

I held out my trembling left hand as he placed the ring on my third finger. I was shaking so much that I didn't know if I could answer him. My head nodded up and down as I finally found my voice. "Yes, Liam, yes!" I exclaimed.

"Whoo-hoo!" Liam shouted as he swept me up in his arms. "I love you, Jenny!" He twirled me around the living room as we kissed. "Thank you, thank you." He sat me down again.

"Liam, I can't believe you did this."

"I told you I wanted you forever."

"I know; I just never expected it so soon."

"Jenny, I've had this ring for a couple of months. I was planning on giving it to you after graduation, but I couldn't wait any longer. I want the world to know you're mine. I want Johnny to know you're mine. That he can't come between us. Let him tell you now that there's no ring on your finger."

"Liam, you never had to worry about that." I brought his face to mine and kissed his lips over and over again. I stared at the ring as the facets in the diamond twinkled under the light. "It's the prettiest ring I've ever seen. Does Grandpa Mack know about this?"

"Yeah, this ring has been in my family for a long time. It belonged to my grandma and then my mom."

I was in awe. "Are you sure you want me to have it? I mean…."

"Jen, there's no other place for this ring to be except on your finger."

"It means even more to me now." We sat on the sofa with Liam cradling me his arms. "Liam?"

"Yeah?"

"There's something I've got to tell you."

"What is it?"

"Tonight, when Johnny stopped by..."

"Yeah?"

I could feel the muscles in Liam's arms contracting. "I told him to call off the race."

"You what? Why?"

"Because I don't want you to race. I'm scared to death something might happen, and now I especially don't want you to do it. There's no reason for the race to go on."

"What did Johnny say?"

"He said no. He said that you two had a score to settle, that it wasn't just about me anymore."

"He's right. The race has to happen. Why was Johnny really at your house tonight?"

"I told you, he wanted to see if I had changed my feelings for him, but I told him as I always have, that I love you and he needs to move on. I think he's going to leave me alone now. I don't think we have to worry about him anymore."

Liam squeezed me, pulling me tighter to him. "Let's hope not, babe." He kissed the top of my head, making a path down my neck. His breath was warm against my skin. "You know, Grandpa won't be home until tomorrow night."

"Really?"

"Uh-huh. We have the whole house to ourselves."

He continued kissing me and moved down my left arm. "Well, I still have a curfew you know. I have to be home by 12:30."

"No you don't."

"I don't?"

His blue eyes were sparkling as a wicked grin came across his face. "No. You're spending the night with Kendra. Well, at least that's what your parents think."

"Liam Larson, what did you do?"

"I called Kendra and arranged it with her. She told your parents that I was dropping you off at her house and the two of you were going to Charleston to see a movie. Then you were just going back to her house to spend the night."

"And they bought it?"

"Hook, line, and sinker. All you have to do is check in with them when you get back from Charleston. Say around eleven o'clock."

"You mean I... we... can have the whole night to be together?"

"The whole night, and some of tomorrow if you like."

"You're a genius, babe."

"I know."

I pulled him to me and tangled my hands in his hair kissing him over and over again. "I love your hair, babe," I said as I giggled between kisses.

"I know you do, that's why I took it down, Jenny Larson."

The sound of my future last name sounded so good coming from Liam's mouth. "I like the sound of that."

"Me too."

Liam carried me in his arms to his room. We spent the rest of the evening behind closed doors. By morning, I was still fixated with the jewelry that embraced my ring finger.

"Do you love it, babe?"

"I do! I can't keep my eyes off it."

Liam grabbed my hand. "Now you know how I feel when I look at you."

"Liam, promise me it will always be like this."

"Like I said, it'll only get better."

I exhaled sharply. The elated feeling of becoming Mrs. Liam Larson was overshadowed by a sobering thought. I was going to have to tell my parents. They were over the moon for Liam, but I don't think they were expecting I would be engaged before I graduated from high school.

"What's wrong, Jen?"

"My parents. They love you, Liam, but I don't know how they're going to take this. I don't think they're expecting me to come home with an engagement ring on my finger."

Liam pulled me to him. "Jen, I think they might already be expecting it. Grandpa told them I was going to give you the ring after graduation."

"He did?"

"Grandpa had a long talk with them. He's a very good communicator you know. I think you're going to be surprised by your parents' response."

I was astounded but still nervous. "Liam, please, you'll be with me when we tell them won't you?"

"Where else would I be?"

"Good, then let's go and tell them now. I don't want to put this off."

We drove straight to my house and spent the rest of the afternoon with my parents. Liam was about half right with their reaction. They did see it coming, but they didn't see it coming so soon. After a full Sunday afternoon of convincing them that this was what we both wanted and that we knew what we were doing; Mom and Dad gave us their guarded blessing with two conditions. We had to graduate from high school, and I still had to consider college. We promised, with Liam adding that he would make sure that I didn't give up any of my dreams. How could I, when the dream of becoming his wife was going to come true.

Chapter Twenty-Two
Fade to Black

The next week of school flew by in a blur. I don't know if it was because I was caught up in the concept of becoming the future Mrs. Liam Larson or the fact that the race was looming. By Saturday, I had become a total wreck. All I could think about was that in a few short hours, Liam would be risking his life for nothing. We were engaged, and more than ever, I didn't understand the premises for the race. In my mind, Liam and Johnny were just trying to prove who had the biggest balls, which I thought was absurd and ridiculous. Luckily for me, I was inundated with phone calls all day that kept me distracted from thinking about the impending race.

Liam was picking me up at nine-thirty, and as far as Mom and Dad were concerned, he was taking me to Kendra's after our date. I was spending the night with her again. I was becoming an expert in devising fail proof ruses. Besides, since our engagement Mom and Dad had let up on the reins a bit. I wasn't sure if they had caught on to some of our schemes, but if they had they were playing along with them brilliantly. By eight-thirty, I was ready to leave and a total mess. I had worried so much about this stupid race that I had become literally sick, throwing up three times in the bathroom and once in my waste paper basket. When Liam did pick me up, I looked like death warmed over.

"Are you okay?"

"No. I've had an upset stomach all day. I can't keep food down, and I'm dizzy. I know it's because of this stupid race."

"Babe, you have to pull yourself together. I told you everything is going to be fine. I've raced lots of times. Why would this race be affecting you like this now? You've known about the race for weeks."

"I don't know, maybe because it's the 11th; you're racing at eleven o'clock at night; it's raining; and you and Johnny seem to be hell bent on proving who's faster and better!"

"Calm down girl. No wonder you've made yourself sick."

I didn't answer him; I just sat there sipping club soda as we drove to Ripley Road. We arrived at our destination to find an incredible sight in front of us. There had to be at least fifty cars lined up along both sides of the road to watch the race.

"I can't believe this!" I said as we passed the cars.

Liam slowly drove up the hill to where the race would begin. Kids were yelling Liam's name as we passed them. Over half of the school was there. Everyone waved and cheered to show their support. Some had even made signs. "Make him eat dirt!" "Liam all the way!" "Number Eleven Rocks!" Johnny had a few supporters cheering him on as well. "Johnny Bryant has what it takes!" "Broncos do it better!" "Johnny Bryant, Number Eleven!"

"Liam, I'm worried. If all these people are here, then surely the police must know."

"We're just going to have to take our chances. It's too late to call it off now. Besides, Johnny's already here."

At the hill top, Johnny's white Bronco was parked sideways to the road. He stood there with Zane Troyer and Shanna Smith. Her arm secured tightly around his waist. Parker and Tony, along with Kelli and Kendra, were waiting for us as well.

"Hey guys, ready?" Tony asked.

"Hell yes!" Liam responded confidently.

I walked over to Kelli and Kendra. "You look awful, Jen. What's wrong?" Kendra asked.

"I feel awful. It's this race; my stomach has been in knots all day. I just want to get this over with. I'm tired of thinking about it. Where did all these people come from? I thought we had kept this to a minimal secret? What happened?"

"It was Shanna," Kelli answered.

"What? Why?"

"It's just her way, Jen. She's really turning into a mean, vindictive bitch."

"Those are some harsh words coming from her best friend," I said.

"Well, the past couple of months I've seen a side of her I don't really care for. She's fake, and I don't like it. Besides, she still holds a grudge against you. She needs to get over it. You and Liam are great together. I'm sorry I ever doubted it. I just wish she could see that. Instead, she would rather play games. That's why she's on Johnny's side."

"Then she's on the right side. Johnny likes to play games too. They're perfect for one another."

I knew it was almost time for the race. Julia Shipman was on the walkie-talkie getting her instructions from Cody. I felt myself becoming sick again. "I'll be right back, guys." I quickly made my exit and ran behind a grouping of tall trees and bushes. All the club soda I had nursed so gingerly on the drive here came right back up.

"Are you alright, Jen?" Johnny said stepping out from behind a tree.

"Johnny, what are you doing here?"

"I'm in the race, remember?"

"You know what I mean. Are you wanting to get killed? Liam's right over there."

"I'm not worried. You don't look so good. Are you feeling okay?"

"I'll be fine."

I started walking back to Liam when he grabbed my left hand. "So it's true?" As he held my ring finger in his hand.

"You mean the ring? Yes, it is."

"It's nice. Are you sure about this?"

"Johnny, would you please just give it a rest. I'm tired of your head games. You promised to leave me alone."

"I said I wouldn't try to persuade you anymore. We can still be friends can't we?"

I took my hand back. "I've got to go."

"Well, I hope you feel better. See you after the race."

"I don't think so," I said and abruptly walked away from him.

"I've been looking all over for you. Where have you been?" Liam asked.

"I got sick again."

"Are you okay?"

"I'm fine. Don't worry about it. What's going on?"

"It's time. Me and the boys are doing one final check on the truck, and then the race will begin." I felt my heart pounding in my chest.

"Liam, please, please be careful. I have this awful feeling in the pit of my stomach that something bad is going to happen."

"I will be careful, trust me."

I could feel tears welling up in my eyes. "Babe, come here," he said. "Please don't cry. This will all be over in minutes." He pulled me to him and gave me the longest and softest kiss I could remember. "I love you Jen."

"I love you too."

"Liam, it's time," Tony said and handed Liam his keys.

"Wait for me right here. I'll be back before you know it."

I sighed heavily and put on the best fake smile that I could. "Okay, good luck."

"Drivers to your gate!" Julia yelled. She was dressed all in white again, wearing a sleeveless white tank top, white shorts, and knee-high white boots.

Kendra and Kelli walked over to me. "It's going to be fine, Jen. Liam's a great driver." Kendra's vain attempt of reassurance did little to help me.

"I can't do this, Kendra."

"What are you talking about, Jen?"

"I can't stand by and watch Liam race. I've got to be with him."

"Are you crazy?"

I ran off before I could answer her. Johnny and Zane had already driven to their starting point, Liam and Tony were getting in the truck.

"Wait, Liam!" I yelled as loud as I could.

"What is it, Jen?"

"I can't let you do this without me. This all started with me, and it's going to end with me too. If you race, then I race."

"Don't talk crazy. I'm not letting you ride with me this time."

"Yes you are. You said everything would be fine. There's nothing to worry about. If that's the case, then there should be no problem. Right?"

I looked at Tony, and he shrugged his shoulders. "It's your call, Liam."

Liam's eyes moved from mine to Tony's. "Jen..."

"No, Liam, you can't change my mind. I'm riding with you."

He knew I was serious. "Get in then."

I stepped up into the truck and took my seat. Kendra and Kelli stared at me in disbelief.

"Are you sure about this?" Liam asked.

"Absolutely, we're a team. You and me all the way."

He squeezed my hand and then slowly drove his truck to his spot, paralleling his black Ford pickup to the white Bronco. I looked at the stretch of road in front of us. The rain beat down on the windshield making it hard to see. I could barely make out the spectators that were lining both sides of the road. Some of them were drenched to the bone while they held their signs high in the air. Others waited patiently in the confines of their cars for the race to begin. An ominous feeling came over me while we waited for Julia's cue. I stared at the road.

Suddenly, everything made sense. The path in front of me was the road that Liam and I had been on from the beginning. The double yellow lines that separated the two lanes instantly became the number eleven. The start of the race signified the beginning of our relationship, the journey to the end of the race was our time up until this point. *Was the ending to be determined by the outcome of this race?* I became more petrified than I had ever been. My gut told me to scream at the top of my lungs and to tell Liam to stop and get out. But there was no time; we were only moments from the race. My head spun. Liam, Johnny, and even Julia became distant to me. I felt that I wasn't even in control of my own body. *Was I getting sick again? I have to calm down and rationalize this.*

The thoughts swam in my head of what my family and friends said about eleven. "It's nothing Jen, just a coincidence. Look at it as the glass half full not half empty. It has to be good if it brought you and Liam together." Over and over I heard the voices talking to me. I heard Gertie repeating that Liam and I were on a journey together, our path, and in front of me I saw the path. *Do I finally understand the meaning behind this maddening number?* Instead of fighting it, I embraced it, welcomed it, let it guide me and Liam to our destination. But how could I? I still didn't understand. I wanted someone to help me, to answer my questions, *please before it's too late.* I screamed from the inside out, but no one could hear me. Liam still stared straight ahead, waiting for Julia's cue. Then as Liam's clock changed to 11:01, it happened. Julia's hands came down. "No!" I finally belted out from the depths of my soul, but it came too late. Liam slammed on the gas and flew down the road, passing Johnny instantaneously. The race had begun.

"Hold on babe, this is it!" Liam screamed with enthusiasm.

He was enjoying this, but how when I was clearly not? He zoomed down the wet, black pavement, shifting gears as we passed the exuberant spectators that were cheering us on. Liam looked calm but determined. His eyes were focused on the turn up ahead. I saw Johnny's white Bronco coming up from behind us. He was gaining momentum as Liam continued to stay ahead of him. We barreled down the stretch of road that became nothing more than a black streak in the pouring rain. Liam and Johnny were neck and neck, neither one letting the other have a chance to take the lead. The spectators were nothing but a blur, but it was weird. I could make out each one of them as if we were passing them in slow motion.

There was Mike and Marty Skinner on top of their mom's minivan cheering us on while they beat on their snare drums. Frannie and Shauna with Steve and Drew were holding a sign with #11 in blue and gold. Brenda Benson clapped her hands feverishly and many others, too numerous to count. But it didn't make sense.

We seemed to be going so slow, but Liam's odometer begged me to think different. The gauge was inching its way past the seventy mile per hour mark. We were gaining speed instead of slowing. I closed my eyes. Devil's Bulge was in sight. Liam and Johnny were still neck and neck. *How in the hell were they both going to make the one hundred eighty degree turn without hitting one another?* I braced myself for the inevitable and prayed to God to get us through this.

Liam was more driven than I had ever seen him. "Here we go, Jen," he exclaimed as we approached the turn. Liam was only millimeters ahead of Johnny when he slammed on his brakes, instantly causing Johnny's Bronco to zoom past us. Liam took the turn as he spun the truck around, forcing the truck to make the one hundred eighty degree turn effortlessly. He didn't break a sweat. It was incredible! A professional race car driver couldn't have handled the turn better. We were facing the homestretch, and Liam was minutes from victory. He slammed on the gas again, and his black Ford pick-up roared to life, becoming a savage beast right before our eyes, gripping the wet road with its claws. It seemed to take on a mind of its own, knowing exactly what Liam wanted it to do. It roared up the road approaching the hill, accelerating at an unbelievable speed as the odometer passed the eighty mile per hour mark.

The beast devoured the road beneath it as it clawed its way to the finish line. A rush of adrenaline came over me. All the fear and anxiety that I felt up to this point dissipated. I found myself screaming at the top of my lungs, not for Liam to stop but for him to go faster! "Go, babe go!" I looked behind me. Johnny was easily two to three car lengths behind us. Liam had this race. It belonged to him; he owned it. Liam and I screamed as we raced up the hill to the finish line. I could see Kendra, Tony, Parker, and Kelli cheering us on.

"Go Liam! You've got it!"

"We're doing it, Jen!" Liam glanced at me with a huge smile. Victory seemed imminent and only moments away.

And then from the corner of my eye I saw it. A brown flash streaked across the road right in front of Liam's truck. "Liam, watch out!" I screamed, but it was too late. He tried to swerve the truck to miss the huge deer that stopped in the middle of the road, right in our path. The left front corner of Liam's truck clipped the deer, causing the truck to spin out of control. Liam frantically tried to regain control, turning the steering wheel back and forth, over-correcting it as he desperately tried to negotiate the out of control beast. It was useless. The truck spun out of control, turning on its side, flipping over and over again. I could feel Liam and I being bounced around from side to side inside the cab, our bodies becoming mere targets to all the objects falling on us. I could hear Liam's sweet voice screaming my name, but I couldn't find him. I tried to respond, but nothing would come out. I became hysterical, desperately trying to get my bearings, but the beast continued to roll over and over again, bouncing like a rubber ball.

Finally, it came to a stop, exhausted from the beating it had taken. I could hear Liam groaning near me, whispering my name. I tried to call for him, but my voice failed me. My ears rang with the echoes of voices outside, yelling for Liam and myself. I lay there helpless, unable to move. The voices I heard became weaker. *Where were they going? Come back! Help us! Don't leave us here,* but the voices were fading. "Liam, Liam!" I screamed, but there was no response. I couldn't hear his voice anymore. I was panicking. My whole body was cold and numb. I felt something wet dripping down from my face. "Liam, where are you?" I fought to stay awake, but I was so sleepy, so tired. "Liam?" There was still no answer, only the faint sound of footsteps rushing to the truck. I needed to close my eyes, if only for a moment. I was just so tired, too tired to fight this off anymore. *Surely someone was coming to help us,* and then everything faded into black.

Chapter Twenty-Three
Vivid Dreams

I must have been dreaming; there was no other explanation for it. I was looking down at a girl. She was laying peacefully in a hospital bed, her head wrapped in bandages, her face swollen, and her body broken, battered, and bruised. Her right arm was in a cast from the tips of her fingers to her shoulder. Her left leg was cradled in a less severe form of a cast that kept her leg elevated off the bed. An IV dripped a foreign liquid into her arm while a monitor kept tabs on her vitals. I didn't recognize her, but how could I? Her face was distorted from the swelling and bruising. My heart panged for her, the poor thing. *What happened to her? How did she end up here in such an awful state? She must be loved though.* There were dozens of get-well cards, handmade posters, and flowers inundating her room. But the most touching sight was the boy who kept a vigil by her side. His head bowed down on her bed as if he was praying. He held her left hand and gently caressed it back and forth, playing with a shiny trinket that protruded from her one finger, a beautiful object that sparkled as he played with it.

He was sad, very sad. His crystal-blue eyes were red and swollen. I wanted to reach out to him. He looked so familiar to me. I wanted to help him, to let him know everything was going to be okay, but I couldn't. I just hovered above them and watched as he sat next to her motionless body. He was talking to her, perhaps telling her stories. I couldn't make it out though. His voice was nothing more than a whisper, hardly audible above the noise of the machines that surrounded this helpless girl. He obviously cared for her deeply, perhaps even loved her. He seemed to be calling her name, trying to wake her up perhaps, but she didn't respond, only lying there peacefully in her dream-like state.

I wanted to take the sadness and grief away from him, to make things right. I felt the grief that engulfed him. He was carrying a burden almost too much for him to bear. He was barely holding on, and I could feel him slipping away. His strength was diminishing quickly. I pleaded with the girl. "Please wake up. He is so sad without you. He can't hold on much longer. You need to wake up." She couldn't hear me, though. I looked at the boy. "Keep talking to her. She hears you. You mustn't give up!" He didn't even flinch. *How can I hear him, but he can't hear me?* "Please, wake up." I stretched my hand out to touch the young man's shoulder, a familiar sensation ran through my body. He sat there unscathed. *How can he not tell I am here?* His red, swollen eyes could only see the young girl lying in the bed. He stood up sweetly kissing her hand as he walked to the window. He walked with an unusual gait, limping as he braced a brown wooden cane for support. The boy was hurt too.

He stood at the window gazing up at the sky as he pleaded for mercy, his eyes full of pain and despair. "Dear God, please bring my Jenny back to me. I will do anything. Please don't take her from me. I beg of you. Take me instead. Please save her soul."

I could feel the love he had for her. He loved her so very much. I went to reach for him again, to touch him, to console him, but he was out of my grasp. He went back to his seat next to her, taking her hand into his again, pleading with her to wake up. My heart felt ripped in two as if someone had taken all the goodness and happiness from me and replaced it with sadness and grief.

"Jenny, I love you. Please baby, wake up for me. It's Liam."

Liam? I know that name, don't I? It sounds so familiar.

"Jenny, please, for me, I'm so sorry."

Is that her name? But that's my name, isn't it?

"Jenny, please come back to me. Don't leave me, baby. I need you."

I had to pray for them. I wanted to stay with them, to try and comfort them, but I was being pulled away. I tried desperately to fight it, but the pull was too strong. They were slipping from my sight, becoming nothing more than mere dots in my vision. I had to go. The room was becoming dark and cloudy, as though I was looking through a tunnel. I couldn't make them out anymore. "Please don't leave!" I begged, but they were vanishing. A voice was calling for me. I had to go towards it, towards him. I looked towards the tunnel, and then quickly back again. They were gone. I was all alone again, floating in complete darkness. I felt scared and alone. I heard the voice calling me again.

I searched for the voice, following it as it called my name. "I'm here, right here. Where are you?"

"Jenny, please Jenny come to me!" The voice was so familiar.

"I'm here. I'm so scared. Please help me. I can't see you. I can't find my way to you! You need to show me the way!" I cried out. I followed the voice, and it became stronger.

"Jenny!"

"I'm coming, I'm coming! Please don't leave me," I screamed. I felt myself falling, and the voice became stronger and faster as I fell. The voice became closer and closer. I saw a light below me, and I couldn't stop myself from descending to it. I wanted to go to it. "I'm coming, please keep talking!" I continued my descent, and the voice sounded like it was right next to me now.

"Jenny, I love you, please come back to me." And then I hit the light, falling softly onto a blanket of white.

"I'm here. I'm here. I'm right here, Liam." I struggled to find him. It was Liam's voice I had heard, but everything was so dark. "Liam, where are you?"

I heard him again, "Baby, please!" I could feel him near me, but everything around me was a shroud of darkness. I struggled to see him, searching for the light that had brought me to him. Then, there in the distance I saw it: the light, his voice was coming from the light.

"Liam!"

"Jenny, please wake up baby!" I ran towards his voice, running to him as he called me. Then I saw him sitting next to me, his warm face buried on the side of my left arm.

"Liam," I faintly whispered. My throat screamed in pain. It felt raw and sore. I struggled to say his name again, "Liam." I hardly heard myself. He sat with his head still concealed in my arm. *He is crying; why is he crying? Is this a dream?* I had been away from him for so long that it seemed his image was nothing more than a vapor, an image of my distorted dreams. *What happened to make him so sad?* I earnestly tried to get his attention, to reach out to him. I went to touch him when the pain shot through my body like a cannon. I screamed in agony, but Liam couldn't hear me. I looked down at my body. It was foreign to me. Fear engulfed me. *What happened to me?* I couldn't remember anything. "Liam!" I screamed, but it was only heard by my own ears. I said his name again to no avail. I noticed his hands were cupping my left hand. I tried to move it, but my body seemed so tired and weak. The smallest effort to move took my breath away in exhaustion. *Why am I like this? I don't understand.* I had to keep trying though. The frustration was overtaking me as I slipped away again.

I struggled to keep my eyes on Liam, staring at him. I had found him or was this still part of my vivid dream? He looked so real. If I could only touch him to make sure, but my body was so weak. I was fighting to just keep my eyes open. I reached for him, a pain of unimaginable intensity corralled through me as my body stiffened. My whole insides felt whipped and beaten. *How could this be when I have barely moved my hand?* "Keep trying, Jenny. You can do it!" I told myself. Liam's head was still bent down next to me on the bed rail; I futilely maneuvered my left fingers around Liam's hand. "Squeeze his hand, harder! Damn it! Squeeze!" Every part of my body screamed in agony. The pain was too much for me to bear. A scream from the depths of my inner soul came bellowing out of me, burning the interior of my throat.

He lifted his head and looked at me. He had heard me. "Jenny! Oh My God, baby! You're awake!" He was crying, and the tears streamed down his face. I fixated on his eyes, those gorgeous crystal blue eyes that were now swollen and bloodshot. My head was pounding. *What is going on with me?* Nothing was making sense. *What had happened to me? Why can't I speak without it hurting? Why is my entire body in agony every time I move? Why am I lying here in what must be a hospital bed?*

I scoured the room. There were dozens of cards and flower arrangements littering the walls and tables in my room. I tried to remember, racking my brain for any information that could explain what had happened to me and why I was here, but nothing. The frustration was overwhelming, causing my head to pound even harder. I couldn't remember anything, and nothing was filtering through. I wanted to cry, but I was too afraid that it would bring me more excruciating pain. Liam was crying harder than I had ever seen him. His hands cupped mine, squeezing them as he thanked God over and over again for sparing my life. *Sparing my life?! Isn't that what you say when someone has almost lost their life... almost died? But not me? I couldn't have been in any mortal danger? But was I? Did I die... was that me in my dream? Was the young man Liam? But my body was beyond recognition? The bruises and swelling, the bandages, the casts? Something horrible had happened to that girl. It couldn't have been me!* I frantically tried to look down at my body. The tubes and bandages restricted my movement as I gasped in horror at what I saw! *It was me! What happened?* I squeezed Liam's hands. I couldn't hold back the tears, pain or no pain, I couldn't control them. I was too scared. Liam kissed me gingerly on my left hand, the only part of my body that seemed to be normal.

"Baby, don't cry," he whispered as he wiped the tears from my swollen and battered face. I had to speak to him. I had to ignore the pain that gripped the inside of my throat like a vice.

"Liam," I said, but I could hardly hear it myself.

"Jenny, it's okay. Don't try to speak. Just rest." But I had to. I needed answers.

We stared at one another, and he looked so sad and tired but relieved, as though he had just been to hell and back. I tried to wipe the tears from his face with my hand, but he grabbed it and brought it to his lips. My hand caught the tears as they fell onto my fingers. They were warm to the touch.

"I love you, Jenny. I love you so much."

"I love you too." My lips moved, but the words seemed inaudible, only a whisper, but Liam knew. He knew what I said.

I felt my body giving in to the pain again, weakened by the effort to stay awake. I was so tired. I had to close my eyes just for a moment, but I didn't want to take them off Liam. I had just found him again. I was too afraid I would lose him again in the darkness, but I couldn't fight the sleep. My eyes were closing. Liam's face faded from view.

"Sleep, Jenny, just sleep. I'll be right here, baby. I promise. I love you so much," I faintly heard him say, as I felt his soft lips on my hand again.

The familiar darkness that I had been so accustomed to was waiting for me. I had to go to it, unable to fight it anymore. I was so tired. I let my eyes close as Liam faded away from my sight, and I welcomed back my dark friend.

Chapter Twenty-Four
Déjà Vu

Did you ever feel like someone was staring at you while you were sleeping? Well, that's exactly how I felt. I felt myself trying to wake from what felt like a long and much-needed rest. My body felt stiff and sore and every time I moved a sharp pain shot through my entire body as if someone had hit me with a sledgehammer. It was Déjà Vu. I recalled having this feeling before but could not remember when or where. I groaned in agony as I tried to shift positions.

"Jenny?" I heard someone say. I felt a warm touch on my left hand, a familiar caress that seemed to have been absent from my memory for a very long time. "Jenny?" he said again. I knew that voice. I grumbled trying to find mine.

A searing pain embraced my raw throat. "Ow!" I bellowed.

"Jenny, careful. Don't try to talk," he said again. I slowly opened my eyes which fought to remain closed. My whole world seemed to be a black veil. I could see prisms of light as I forced my eyelids open. "Jenny, baby." I locked in on the voice that had been saying my name. My eyes adjusted to the bright light that blanketed them. Everything was out of focus.

I tried to rub my eyes to help them adjust to the unusual brightness. "Ow!" I bellowed again. My right arm throbbed in pain. I couldn't move it. My eyes came into focus, and I noticed that a white cast covered my entire right arm. I felt the same touch on my left hand again, and I glanced quickly at it.

"Jenny, baby, it's me, Liam."

"Liam?" I whispered. He was sitting next to my bed, holding onto my left hand tightly in his. "Liam," I said again. I felt this overwhelming urge to touch him, but I was confined by tubes and machines that held me prone in the bed.

"Jenny, don't move. It's okay."

"Why am I here? What happened?" I was confused, and I didn't understand why I was lying in a hospital bed. I remembered a dream that was just like this, but it was a dream, right?

"You don't remember the accident?"

"Accident? What accident?" Liam's tear-stained face was overcome with emotion. "Liam, what happened? What accident are you talking about?"

He didn't speak, only stared at me, searching to find a way to explain to me why my body was so broken. "Jenny, the night of the race between Johnny and me on Ripley Road, do you remember that night?" I racked my brain trying to remember what he was talking about. I shook my head frantically, causing a numbing sensation to travel from one end of my temple to the other. He gently rubbed my left hand with his. "You were in the accident that night with me. We were racing against Johnny Bryant on Ripley Road. It was raining. It was dark and...and a deer darted out in front of my truck. I... I..." His hands gripped my hand tightly, and he was shaking.

"What?" I whispered.

Liam locked his eyes on mine. "I tried to miss the deer, but he came right out of nowhere in front of the truck. He wouldn't move, just stood there looking at us. I swerved to miss him, but it was too late. The truck spun out of control. It flipped and rolled before finally landing on its roof. I tried to get you out, but my legs were pinned under the steering wheel. You had me so scared, babe. I screamed for you over and over again, but you just laid there unresponsive. I thought I had lost you. I've never been so scared in my life. Baby, I never meant to hurt you. I'm so sorry." He lowered his head as his voice trailed off.

"Liam, it's not your fault. It's nobody's, please. It's okay."

"I tried so hard to help you. You kept mumbling my name, but I couldn't get to you. I couldn't move..." Liam's face became somber. "If it hadn't been for Johnny..."

"Johnny? Johnny Bryant?"

"Yeah, Jen. He was the first one to the truck. He saw the whole thing happen because he was behind us. He almost hit us, but he was able to swerve out of the way. He pulled you out. You were bleeding pretty badly from your head, and the dashboard was pressed against your stomach. If it wasn't for Johnny... well, he probably saved your life. He's been here a few times to check in on you." I watched Liam as he spoke gratefully about Johnny. It seemed so ironic considering how much he hated him.

"What about you? Did he help you?"

"He tried, but the steering wheel was bent against me, pinning me in. The paramedics had to get me out, but I'm fine compared to what happened to you." He held up the wooden cane.

"I'm sorry, Liam."

"Jen, please don't say that. You have no reason to feel sorry for me. I'm the one responsible for this, responsible for you being in here." He hung his head down again.

"Please don't." But looking down I noticed my body and wondered what exactly was wrong with me. "What happened to me?" I was almost too scared to hear the answer.

"You were banged up pretty bad. You've been in the hospital for over two months."

"Two months? What month is it?"

"June, Jenny."

"June? You mean I've missed graduation, my birthday, your birthday?"

"Yeah, Jen, you've been in a coma. You suffered a concussion, and you have a deep cut on the side of your head. And as you can see, your right arm and left leg are broken."

There was a long pause before he spoke again. The silence was deafening.

"Liam?"

"You had some internal injuries too."

My stomach tightened. "I did?"

"There was some internal bleeding. It was pretty bad…" His voice quivered.

"What Liam?"

He sighed heavily as his tone shifted. "Jen, you were pregnant."

"What?" My mind wasn't registering his last comment. I felt my heart sink to my stomach. "What did you just say?"

"You were pregnant, about three months. They couldn't save the baby... your injuries were too severe."

My lips started quivering. I felt sick to my stomach. I clenched it, and it felt so hollow and empty. How could all of this have happened to me? Was it not enough that I was lying here with a broken body, did my soul have to be ripped from me as well? I felt Liam's soft touch against my face wiping away the tears that I didn't realize were falling.

"Jenny, I'm so sorry. They tried everything in their power to save the baby, but... they just couldn't. You were dying... they had to save you."

I laid there staring at the ceiling. "I was pregnant." Past tense.

I felt the world on my shoulders right then and there. The pain became a heavy weight, smashing me down, burying me in grief. This was too much for me to take. I literally wanted to die at that very moment. Maybe I should have. Then this feeling of loss and emptiness wouldn't be here. I felt weak and nauseous, just like I did the night of the races. "The night of the races...Oh my God, I remembered. I remembered feeling sick to my stomach, the overwhelming feeling of nausea that made me throw up over and over again throughout the day. And then... the race..."

I grasped Liam's arm. "Liam, I remember. Oh my God, I remember the race. You were winning. We were on the homestretch. I remember seeing Tony, Kendra, Joe, and Parker;

they were waving us on...but it was raining so hard, and then out of nowhere, the deer."

"That's right, Jenny. I tried so hard to miss the deer. But..."

"I know, Liam, but you couldn't avoid him. He came out of nowhere. I remember the truck spinning out of control, and then I just remember people running towards us, screaming. I remember, Liam. Oh my God, was that really two months ago? Have I really been here that long?"

"You have."

"What's the date?

"June 11th."

"The 11th? Wasn't the race on the 11th?"

"Uh-huh, Jen. I know. It's that damn number again."

There was so much to take in, to absorb. I ached, mentally and physically. I was still so tired. I closed my eyes, hoping when I opened them again all this would be just a terrible bad dream. But I knew it wasn't. It was all too real: the hospital room, my broken body and spirit, Liam sitting next to me while I lay helpless, and the number eleven.

"Jenny, if I could take this away from you I would in a heartbeat. You don't know how many times I've prayed to God for me to change places with you. I should have listened to you in the beginning. I should have never raced. If I had just listened to you, none of this would have happened." He was falling apart in front of me, breaking down. The guilt and grief he had been carrying with him while I was here was finally tearing him apart. His will and endurance dissipated beneath him.

I clutched his hand as he turned to look away. "Liam, look at me. I don't know why this happened to us, but it hasn't changed me. My body might be broken, but my heart isn't. My feelings haven't changed. You are why I'm here, why I woke up. I heard you when I was away. It was so dark, but it was your voice that I heard. I followed it until I saw you. I came back because of you. You brought me back. That has to mean something."

The blue of Liam's eyes were covered in a shroud of tears. "Jenny, I just can't believe that. I can't get over the fact that I got away with a bad leg, but you... that I...that I almost lost you. And you were pregnant. You were carrying our baby, Jenny. If I had just..."

"Stop it, Liam, please. I can't take this anymore. My head is reeling from trying to absorb everything that's happened. Stop blaming yourself for something that you had no control over. What happened, happened. I'm really tired Liam. Can you go call my parents? I want to see them."

He kissed me tenderly on my bandaged forehead. "Sure, Jenny. I'll be back later."

The next few weeks were the most grueling of my entire life. I had been laying in a bed for over two and half months with hardly any body movement. I had become weak and feeble. The littlest effort to try and walk wore me out. I wanted to give up and give in to the pain and misery that I had become so accustomed to, but my doctors and family wouldn't allow me to do that. Day in and day out, I diligently got out of bed and tried to walk, being constantly pushed by my therapist.

My parents came every day to help as well as Liam, cheering me on and lending their support as I struggled to regain the use of my crippled body. I was making great strides, and by the end of June, I was able to walk on my own with the help of a walking cast. Most of my physical pain was gone, of course there were some grim reminders of the accident like the countless scars that covered my body, a result of me laying in a bed of broken glass at the scene of the accident.

Liam also had some reminders of that fateful night as well: a permanent limp from the severity of his dislocated hip and broken leg. Any hopes that he may have had to play college football had been dashed away on April 11th, not that he cared. As he said, his future never included playing football past high school. But to those who thought differently, it was a crushing blow to their hopes and dreams for him, especially mine and Grandpa Mack's.

On a different note, one of the positives from the accident was the outpouring of support from friends and the community. Not one day went by while I was in the hospital that I didn't receive some sort of token of support from somebody. Even Shanna Smith, the last person on Earth who I thought I would ever hear from sent me a bouquet of flowers, maybe her way of burying the hatchet. The only person I did not hear from but had hoped to was Johnny. He apparently had visited me on numerous occasions when I was in a coma, even sharing time with Liam, but now that I was awake and coherent, he had become a no show. Not even a card or a phone call. After weeks with no word from him, I had given up hope that I would hear from him. He obviously had been able to move on from this. But deep down, I hoped that out of all of this, out of all the trials and tribulations that we had endured, we could have come out at least as friends, but maybe it was for the best. I wished he would have allowed me to help make that decision for us.

Liam and I also tried to move on from the accident. He carried so much guilt, blaming himself for everything that had happened that fateful night. He said he should have read the signs, listened to me. Even the number eleven weighed down on him. The deer that ran out on the road that night had an eleven-point rack. Another reminder of how that number played a vital role in our lives. I tried to talk to him, to have him open up to me about the accident, but the guilt he carried was bigger than the both of us. I had missed out on over two months of my life. I should be the angry and upset one. I was the one that came out on the worst end of the deal with all of it, but for some reason, Liam couldn't get past that all of this would never have happened if it weren't for him.

I tried in vain to talk to him, but the more I tried the more withdrawn he became. He would talk about certain things, like events that had happened or that I had missed. There was the prom, Liam stayed with me that night, bringing me a corsage and playing the guitar for me. There was also my 18th birthday and Liam's 18th birthday that I had missed. And of course, there was graduation, my cap and gown hung in my hospital closet, along with my diploma. The graduation class wore blue ribbons on their sleeves in recognition of me, but as far as the accident, Liam clammed up every time I tried to discuss it.

By the time I was released from the hospital, almost three months after the accident, Liam had drifted into a deep depression, not that he hadn't already been in one. It was hurting me worse than any of the injuries I had sustained from that night. He couldn't let it go, and there seemed to be nothing I could do to convince him otherwise. He came to my house every night and helped me with my therapy and waited on me hand and foot. It was his way of trying to make up for what had happened. Even though I tried to convince him that it wasn't his fault, there was nothing I could say or do to change his mind. Everyone, including Grandpa Mack, Mom, Dad, Tony, and Parker, all tried to bring him out of this funk he had put himself in, but Liam continued to act like some sort of servant to me. A robot, if you will.

The Liam that I loved, the fun-loving, crazy, wonderful boy with the crystal blue eyes, had been replaced by some sort of Stepford robot with soulless eyes. It was driving me crazy, and I needed my Liam back, but he was gone.

After a few weeks at home, I had made great progress in returning to normal. My arm was moved to a brace, and I was able to walk on my own accord with the help of the walking cast. I still hadn't heard anything from Johnny, and although I had come to the conclusion that I wouldn't, deep down I kept hoping. I needed to thank him for his bravery that night, so I decided to take matters into my own hands.

It was Friday evening, and I was expecting Liam in a little bit. I had about an hour before he arrived. I dialed Johnny's number, hesitating between each number. I was scared, maybe because of the not knowing: not knowing how he would react to my voice, and not knowing if I was doing the right thing. It had been over three months since I had seen or talked to him, and I didn't know what to expect. This whole accident could have changed his demeanor like it did Liam's. I took a deep breath as I called his number. The phone began to ring. The thought crossed my mind to hang up after the first ring. *Then at least I could say I tried, and he just didn't answer, but that was the coward's way out.* I let the phone continue to ring.

"Hello?" said a woman's voice.

"Hello, is this Gertie?"

"Yes it is. Who's this?"

"Hello Gertie. I don't know if you remember me. It's Jenny King. I came into your shop a few months ago."

"Yes, yes, dear. Of course I remember you. How are you doing? You know we've been so worried about you."

"Thank you. Slowly but surely, I'm doing better."

"I'm so glad to hear that. You know Johnny has been worried sick over what happened."

"Well that's why I was calling. I wanted to speak to Johnny. Liam told me that Johnny played a big part in saving me. He was the one that pulled me from the truck. I wanted to thank him. I haven't heard from him since the accident. Is he around?"

There was a long, silent pause on Gertie's end of the phone. "Jenny, I'm sorry. Johnny isn't here."

"Well do you know when he'll be back?"

"No, you don't understand, Jenny. He's moved out."

"Moved out? When?"

"About a month ago. He's living with a friend of his."

"Where? Is he still in town?"

"Yes, he's living with Jake Pittman for the time being. After the accident, he needed some time away. He's been trying to deal with what happened. After graduation, he was sitting around, and it was actually Jake's idea for him to move in with him. I guess he was hoping he could bring him out of this slump he was in."

"Oh, I see. Well, if you do hear from Johnny, would you please tell him I tried to reach him."

"Sure, Jenny."

"Bye Gertie."

"Bye, dear."

What do I do now? I thought to myself.

But before I could answer, the phone rang. I picked it up on the half ring. "Hello?"

"Hey babe, it's me."

"Hi."

"Hey, do you mind if I come over a little later than I said?"

"No, not at all. I'm not going anywhere," I said, feeling somewhat slighted. "Is anything wrong?"

"No, it's just that I'm in the middle of a couple of things and would like to finish it before I come to your house."

"Oh, no problem. Like I said, I'm not going anywhere."

"You okay, Jen?"

"I'm fine. I'll see you when you get here."

"Alright, bye."

"Bye."

I should have been wondering why Liam was being so vague but my thoughts were preoccupied with Johnny. I really wanted to talk to him, to at least thank him, but until I was capable to drive again, I was stuck. My only hope was Gertie. Maybe she would convince him to see me, or at least call me.

Chapter Twenty-Five
An Unexpected Surprise

I had my eyes closed while swinging on the porch swing. The warm summer breeze blew across my face and hair, and it felt nice and comforting. I began to shift my position on the swing, trying to get as comfortable as I could with a walking cast weighing my leg down when I felt the touch of a hand on my cheek.

"Hi there."

I opened my eyes to find Johnny standing over me. "Johnny!" I rubbed my eyes to make sure he wasn't a figment of my imagination. "You're here!"

"You seem surprised to see me?"

"I am. I really didn't think I would ever see you again."

"Well, that was my plan, but I got a message from Mom saying you had been asking for me."

"Yeah, I have. Why didn't you come see me in the hospital?"

"I did. I was there almost every day the first few weeks you and Liam were there. I would come by and just sit with you. You were a mess Jenny, I must say, you heal up nicely."

I felt myself beginning to blush. "Thanks, Johnny."

"You're very welcome. Anyway, as I said, I did come by a lot to see you guys. I hope Liam told you that we are on speaking terms again. We decided to put the past behind us and move on. That accident made us both realize how stupid we had been acting. I'm sorry for what I did. It was wrong."

"Johnny, really it's okay. It's over with. I've learned not to dwell in the past anymore, just to move on. That's my new philosophy on life."

"Well, it's a good one to practice. Was there a reason you were trying to reach me?"

"Uh, yeah, Johnny, there was. You know while I was in the hospital I was out of it for a while. After I came out of the coma, I really didn't remember much about the accident. I still don't remember everything. There are a lot of gray areas, but Liam tries to fill me in as best as possible. Johnny, he told me that it was you who pulled me from the truck. It was you who saved me from being crushed to death."

"Jenny, everyone was helping that night, not just me."

"I know, but you were the one that pulled me out, weren't you?"

"Yes, I did. I had to; I had to help you. When I saw you there, trapped and helpless, I couldn't stand there and do nothing."

"Well, I just wanted to say thank you."

"You don't have to thank me. Jenny, anyone would have done the same thing, including you if you were put in that situation."

"Yeah, maybe, but it wasn't me or anybody else. It was you, and I just want you to know how much it means to me that you did that for me."

Johnny stared at me with an endearing smile. I felt an inner calming come over me. I leaned over to him and kissed him softly on his lips. Leaning back, I saw the small scar from where Liam had punched him. Johnny too carried a reminder of our past.

"A kiss? Without being cornered or slapped in the face? How bold of you!"

"Very funny, accept it as a token of my appreciation. It's the least I could do after you saved my life." I sighed heavily.

"What is it, Jen?"

"Do you think it will be possible for us to be friends?"

Johnny bit his lower lip. "Yeah, I don't see why not. I would really like that actually."

"Me too."

He leaned and hugged me, being careful of my arm and leg. "I'm glad to see you're not breakable."

I laughed. "Yeah, I heal up pretty nicely."

"Definitely. So... where's Liam? I'm surprised he's not here."

"He will be. He's coming later."

"Are you guys doing okay? You know, Jenny...I heard about the baby. I'm really sorry."

"Thanks, Johnny, it's okay. Actually, I think being in a coma was therapeutic for me. I've been able to handle things and process them better because of it."

"What about Liam?"

"I don't know. Sometimes I think he's doing okay with what happened, and then there are times when he seems withdrawn and distant. I've tried to reach out to him, but he just doesn't seem to want me to."

"Give him time. He's going through his own personal hell right now. He's blaming himself. He loves you; I know that. He almost died with you in the hospital. It killed him to see you lying there. I was witness to it. You just need to be there for him and let him work through this. You know, I can feel for him, because I was blaming myself also."

"You were?"

"Yeah, I felt I had brought all that on. If I hadn't made a complete ass out of myself and tried to go after you, Liam and I never would have been fighting and the race never would have happened."

"But you guys race all the time. It could have happened no matter what."

"Yeah, but the race would have ended at Devil's Bulge. We should have never added another lap. Just give him time, Jenny. That's what I had to do. That's why I moved out. I needed to get away, even from my family. Even my mom was a reminder of you. She really thinks highly of you and was always asking me about you. And your number thing, she was always reading cards and shit. She knew you'd be okay. Your number eleven, it's a good omen; she truly believes that."

"Even with everything that happened, Johnny? I mean the accident happened on the 11th. I almost died, Liam got hurt, and we lost the baby. How could it be good?"

"I don't get it, Jenny, but Mom says that the number was significant in shaping your path. You didn't die. You lived, and so did Liam, and for the other stuff, I guess it's a learning experience on the road of life. At least that's what Mom says. You have to have some bumps along the way to find out your destiny."

"Those were some pretty nasty bumps."

He snickered. "Yeah, but Mom believes that out of the negative comes positive. Look at us, we're here now as friends, and so are Liam and I. He's still going down the path, finding his way, but his path will lead him to you. You just need to give him some time. He'll come around. Believe me, he needs you. He just has to work this out himself. You can't expect him or any of us for that matter to be unscathed by the turn of events from that night."

"But Liam acts different, like he's changed or something."

"We've all changed. Just be patient, you'll see."

"I think I underestimated you. You're really a good friend, Johnny."

"I know, that's what I have been trying to tell you all along," he said confidently.

He then pulled out a pen and bent down next to my leg. "What are you doing?" I asked.

"I'm going to sign your cast. You don't have any signatures on it."

"It's because it's a walking cast, Johnny, you know the soft kind. I've had the hard cast off for weeks."

"Well, I still want to sign it." He took the pen and began to scribble on part of the hard plastic. "There," he said as he finished writing.

The writing was upside down to me. "What does it say? I can't make it out."

"To Jenny, for having an unbreakable heart. You will always hold a place in mine, with love, Johnny."

"Ah Johnny...that's really sweet, thank you."

"I mean it Jenny. I know there will never be a you-and-me the way I had hoped, but I do want this...you and me as friends, and I'll always be here for you if you ever need anything."

"I know that, Johnny."

He leaned down and kissed me. "Liam's a lucky man, Jenny. You have a great kiss."

I looked at him as if I was losing something very important to me. "Johnny..." He wouldn't let me finish.

"Well, I better go. I'll be in touch, Jenny."

"I'm counting on it."

"See ya around."

Johnny walked away without looking back once. I wanted him to. I wanted him to look at me. Something inside of me was screaming out to stop him, but I didn't. I just watched as he drove off in his Bronco. A feeling of regret deluged me, as if by him leaving I was losing something I could never get back. I wanted to run after him. *Maybe I was too quick to judge him. Maybe there was more to us than just being friends, but what about Liam?* I loved Liam. Johnny was right, there could never be a Johnny and me the way there was between Liam and me. I knew I would always have Johnny as a friend, and for now, that would have to do. Maybe for always, but it was Liam that I needed, who needed me.

The regret slowly dwindled away, and an overwhelming feeling of anxiousness replaced it. I had to see Liam, and I had to fix the rift this accident had caused between us. It was eleven minutes after eight, *another sign perhaps.* I hobbled my way into the kitchen and grabbed my keys. *Come hell or high water, I am going to Liam, even if it means driving myself.*

Mom and Dad were both asleep in the back room, taking a break from all the activity that had surrounded us since I had gotten home. It was my perfect escape. By the time they awoke, I would be long gone to Liam's, and I could escape the argument about driving with a broken arm and leg.

I sat stiffly in my car, trying to become as comfortable as possible considering my predicaments. Luckily, it was my left leg with the cast, making it easy for me to control the gas and brake with my right leg. My right arm still bothered me to some degree, but it was nothing that I couldn't handle. I looked around before I backed out. This was going to be too easy, I thought. I slowly crept out of the driveway and drove off. Destination: Liam.

Chapter Twenty-Six
Goodbye

Liam's house was usually a twenty minute drive for me, but because of my impediments, the trip took much longer. His driveway was long and winding, and I took my time maneuvering the curves. There was more foliage than I remembered. It was mid-July, and everything was in full bloom. The last time I had been here was right before the race in early April when the trees were still bare. The trees now shrouded the view of Liam's house with its abundant greenery. As I made the final turn, the house come into sight. There was no sign of Liam's truck or Grandpa Mack's. The place looked completely deserted except for Blue who came to greet me as I exited my car.

"Hello, friend, you here by yourself? Huh? Where's Liam? Do you know?" Blue wagged his tail frantically as I waited for him to answer me. "Hello? Liam? Grandpa Mack?" There was no answer.

I went to the front door, turned the knob, and it opened effortlessly. The house smelled of fresh coffee. I made my way to the kitchen in hopes of finding them there. The kitchen was empty though, just like the house seemed to be. I took a seat and contemplated my next move. My leg was throbbing, and I was sure I over did it by driving. *I had no choice; I had to see Liam, but now that I am here, where was he? Maybe I should have waited for Liam to show up at my house. That's probably where he is now, and I was here. I didn't even leave a note letting anyone know where I was going.* I was so sure that Liam would be here. *Oh well, I better go before Mom and Dad have the police looking for me,* I thought. I left Liam a note by the kitchen sink to call me, and I headed to my car.

"What are you doing here?" Liam asked coming up from behind me.

"Liam!"

"How did you get here, Jenny? Did you drive here yourself?"

"Yes, I had to see you, and I couldn't wait."

"I told you I was coming over."

"I know, but I needed to see you now."

"Jenny, are you okay?"

"I'm fine... actually... Liam, no I'm not. It's just that I don't know what's going on with you anymore. You seem different. You act different when you're with me. You seem to be making excuses not to see me, and every time I try to ask you what's wrong, you say nothing and you've become so distant. I feel like... like I'm losing you."

"Ahhh, Jenny, baby, I'm sorry. Come here and sit down."

He took my hand and helped me to the steps. Sitting down, he looked at the ground taking back his hand and intertwining his fingers. He didn't say a word for the longest time, only taking deep breaths as he continued to avoid eye contact with me. Finally, after what seemed like hours but in reality was only a few short minutes, he directed his blue eyes to mine.

"Jenny, it's just that I still feel so guilty over everything that's happened."

"Liam, you know when I woke up in the hospital I thought that the worst of this horrible ordeal was over, but this, having you act this way towards me, it's even worse than the accident."

"I'm sorry, but I can't get over the fact that this is all my fault. And it doesn't matter what anyone says, Jenny. I blame myself. I could have lost you. Hell, I almost did. And the baby, Jenny, our baby... I just... I don't know, Jenny. It's not that I'm trying to avoid you. I love you. But, every time I see you, see your broken leg, your arm in a cast, it reminds me of that night. I swore to you that I would always be there for you, to take care of you, that I would never hurt you and look what I did. I can never forgive myself."

"But don't you see, Liam, there's nothing to forgive. It was an accident, and that's all. I mean... I'm ready to move on, and I'm the one that was laid up in the hospital for almost three months. I lost three months of my life that I can never get back. And it's not because of you... it's just what happened. You didn't force me into the truck. I got in under my own will. It was my decision to be with you, to ride with you, and if I had to do it all over again, I still would. I thought we were a team, are a team? Liam I need you to move on too... I need you here for me. I need you back, the way you were, my Liam, the guy who likes to laugh with me, tease me, chase me around, the guy I met last October. You promised me those things would never change." Liam said nothing. "You know... I saw Johnny today."

"You did?"

"Yeah, he stopped by the house today to see how I was. Actually I had been trying to reach him."

"What did you want to see him for?"

"To tell him thank you. To tell him how much it meant to me for what he did the night of the accident. You know he never saw me after I came out of the coma. I needed to know why."

"Oh. So you guys are..."

"Friends. We're friends, Liam, just like you two are. I told him I wanted to be friends with him, but I loved you. Like I've always loved you, maybe even more. We share something that bonds us even more closely together."

"But the baby, you lost the baby."

"I know I did, and it hurts me to no end, but it's killing me that I'm losing you too, Liam."

"So you and Johnny are just friends?"

"What else would we be?"

"I thought maybe you would think differently of him...I mean he did pull you out of the truck. I couldn't do that for you."

"Yes he did, but it was you who pulled me out of the darkness when I was in the coma; it was your voice that kept me going, Liam. It was you and only you. Our paths are meant to be together, don't you see that? You and me, we're a team, the Larson/King team, and one day it'll be just the Larson team," I said as I played with the ring on my finger. "What does this ring represent Liam? Have your feelings changed so drastically for me? Should I give this back to you?"

"Jenny, no."

"Then tell me what the hell is going on? I'm tired of this."

"It's just that I feel that this should have never happened. You're right, there were signs, and I didn't pay attention to them. I ignored them. I was so caught up in being the Liam Larson that I almost lost the most important thing in my life. I'm not good enough for you, Jenny. You can do better than me. Maybe you should be with Johnny."

"Is that what you think? You think that I should be with Johnny? That you're not good enough for me? That I should just throw the past nine months of our time together out the window because of that stupid accident? You're giving up on us so easily? Just like that?"

"Jenny, that's not what I meant."

"Then tell me what do you mean? I'm listening. I've got all night. Blurt it out, Liam. I want to know!"

"You know when I saw you lying in the hospital bed, I stayed with you day and night. I watched you. I would talk to you, and you just laid there like you were sleeping, except you were hooked up to every machine possible. Tubes were coming out of your throat and nose. It was so surreal, like some sort of dream or more like a nightmare. I thought you would open your eyes and everything would be great, the way it was before the accident. I couldn't bear to see you so hurt and damaged, and the thought kept crossing my mind that I did this to you, I put you in there. It was too much for me to handle. I just wanted you back, Jenny. My world was collapsing in front of me, and I had no control over it."

"But don't you see? Liam, I did come back. When I was on the brink of dying, between here and there, it was you who brought me back. Doesn't that count for something? I mean, why did I come back if this is what was waiting for me? If you're not sure about me, about us, then I should have just slipped away."

"Don't ever talk like that. One of the happiest days of my life was when you woke up from that coma."

"Then what's going on, Liam? We should be celebrating that we're both alive and together and just move on from this. No one is blaming you."

"I know, Jen. It's just that I should have been more responsible. You know your number eleven? I should have listened to it. Maybe you did have something there. I mean the accident happened on the 11th, my number is eleven, and even Johnny is associated with it. Nothing but bad has come from it when it concerns us."

"You're right, the accident did happen on the 11th, and your jersey number was eleven, but did you forget that I came out of the coma on June 11th? You are the best thing that's ever happened to me. The eleven represents good stuff."

"But I should have paid closer attention to the warnings. The signs, they were there if I would have just got my head out of my ass."

"Liam, you said it. The number was there giving us a sign, but sometimes we have to take the sign as just that, a sign. I know now that you're the one, that we're meant for one another. There's always going to be obstacles along the way, but if we have each other then we can get through them. I mean, if we can come out of this, then there's nothing that can stop us. You know when I saw Johnny's mom, Gertie? She told me that our numbers are our guides. They can lead us on the journey, but when we come to a fork in the road, it's up to us to decide which road to take. I was looking at the number as a negative, always looking for something bad to happen. I was scared, even the night of the race, but now I know that it was there for reassurance. Everything about the number has only been good. If anything it's protected us from the bad things. It brought us together, you and your grandpa are alive, we're alive, everything about the number is good. Our path is together. I want you, not Johnny. I want my journey to be with you."

Liam was quiet, holding my hand in his as he moved the ring around my finger. "I love you, babe. I've always loved you."

There was still nothing. Liam might as well have been in outer space. I just couldn't reach him.

Then in desperation I took the ring off my finger and handed it back to him.

"What are you doing?"

"I want you to give this to me when you're 100% percent sure that you want me. I've told you how I felt. I need you back, but only if you can get past this and move on with me. I don't want to dwell in the past. We wouldn't be here if it weren't for the events that shaped our past, but I'm ready to look at the future. I need you to be ready as well." I ran my fingers through Liam's hair. It was longer, and the curls descended into dirty-blonde waves that fell on his shoulders.

He leaned into me, wrapping his strong arms around me. "I don't ever want to hurt you again, Jenny."

"Liam, you never did hurt me. This is what hurts me, you being distant to me."

He closed in on me, his lips gently brushing mine. "I love you, Jenny." He then pressed his lips on mine, kissing me. It was the most passionate and loving kiss he had ever given me. I held onto it as if it were our last. "Jenny," he finally said, "I don't want to lose you either. I just don't know how I can move on from this.

What if something else happens? How can I live with myself knowing that I've put you in danger again?"

"Damn it, Liam! Can't you get over this! You're not at fault. My God, even Johnny is moving on, and he was as much a part of that fiasco as anyone!"

I was at my wit's end and willing to try anything to shake some sense into him, but the remark had no effect. He sat there with a blank expression on his face. Fine then, I thought to myself, if that's how he wants it. I bolted from the steps almost falling over at the same time. My leg gave under the immense pressure that I had put on it.

"Jenny, are you okay?" Liam asked, grabbing my arm.

"I'm fine," I said as I jerked my arm out of his grip.

"Jenny, please don't do this. Try to understand where I'm coming from. Please don't give up on me. I just need some time."

"I've never given up on you. It's you who has given up on yourself. I am not going to stand here and watch you give up on us, and that's exactly what you're doing. What happened to the boy who wouldn't leave me alone, who said he couldn't live without me? Huh?"

"Jenny..."

"I've gotta go. Goodbye, Liam."

I turned and walked away, trying to be as graceful as I could as I hobbled to my car. I anxiously anticipated that Liam would pull me around and stop me before I left, but he didn't. "Please come after me, Liam. Please stop this stupid nonsense and just come after me. Stop me from leaving, please," I pleaded to myself. But he didn't. Instead he sat there with his head hanging. I got in my car and stared at him as he sat in self-pity. I hoped he would come to his senses and stop me from driving away, but the more I sat there the more I realized he wasn't going to budge. I drove away feeling like my soul had been ripped from my very body. The drive to my house was long and slow, partially because I didn't want to go home and also partially because my leg ached from using it so much. I kept a watchful eye on my rearview mirror to see if I could see Liam's newly restored black Ford truck following me, but it was nowhere in sight. I wanted to cry, or better yet scream, but there seemed to be no voice inside of me left. I was completely empty of tears. Upon arriving home, I was glad to find that my parents weren't outside with a search team looking for me. I carefully snuck inside only to find them waiting in the living room.

"Hi, guys," I said trying to act nonchalant. "I guess you're wondering where I've been."

"Well, Jen, at first we were. You know a note would have been nice. You had us worried sick. Where in the world did you get the idea that it would be okay to take the car for a drive in your condition?"

I looked at Dad for support. "I'm sorry, but you don't understand. There was something going on with Liam, and I had to see him. It couldn't wait." My voice quivered as I spoke.

"Honey," Dad's voice always reassured me. "You could have asked us to take you to Liam's. You could have wrecked, do you understand that?"

"But I didn't. I was real careful driving, and as you can see, I'm no worse for the wear. I'm perfectly fine. So, unless there's something else you want to say to me, I would like to go to my room now."

"Jenny, is something wrong? Is something going on between you and Liam?" Mom asked with concern.

"I don't know, Mom. I really don't know, but I don't feel like talking about it right now."

"Sure sweetheart, we're sorry for the third degree. We'll give you some space. Everything will work its self out. You'll see. You just have to give it time, but please understand how we felt when we found you and the car gone."

"I know. I'm sorry."

I feebly walked to my room, taking my time. The pain in my leg was almost unbearable, and all I wanted to do was lie down. I took a quick glimpse out the front window hoping I would see a black truck. Nothing. "I guess he had made his decision." I checked my phone for missed calls. There was nothing from Liam but six from Kendra. She would want to know everything, and I wasn't in the frame of mind to tell her. Right now, I wanted to bury myself in my bed and go back to that place of darkness that had befriended me while I was in the coma. After everything that had happened today, sleep was going to be a welcome refuge.

Chapter Twenty-Seven
Eleven Minutes After Seven

I didn't hear from Liam that night. As a matter of fact, I didn't hear from Liam for the next few days. I had become fixated with staring at my phone and sitting on the front porch, hoping he would call me or show up at my doorstep. The little trip that I took to Liam's house had played a toll on my leg. I was on strict orders from Dr. Garrett that I was not allowed in a car unless I was the passenger. So now, no matter what, the ball was in Liam's court. It was out of my control to go to him. He would have to come to me.

After a week of not hearing a word, I had become perplexed with a myriad of emotions. I began to have feelings for him that I had not felt since the beginning of last year when he bombarded me with his presence. I felt disgust and hatred, only because I was mad at him for obviously giving up so easily on us. I loved him desperately and missed him more than I could believe. *How could someone feel so strongly about another human being and then be so quick to drop them?* I made countless phone calls to his house and cell, but all were made in vain. He never answered. Grandpa Mack tried to reassure me that Liam was okay but just needed some more time. This was why I was so mad at him, for lying to me, for telling me he would never leave me, that he couldn't live without me, for leading me on, for making me fall so desperately in love with him. I had been fine without him, but he had convinced me otherwise. *Had this all been a game with him, stringing me along like a puppet and then letting me go on his own free will?* It was so cruel and unfair.

This wasn't the Liam I had grown to know and love, not even a phone call to see how I was doing. I was breaking inside. I would much rather endure the agony of the accident again than this. I was sinking into an unbelievable pit of self-pity and depression. I began placing the blame on myself for that night. *I should never have gotten into the truck. If I had stayed on the sidelines with Kendra and the rest of them none of this would be going on.*

I spoke with Kendra on numerous occasions, hoping she could shed some light on the situation, hoping Tony was telling her about Liam, but it was like breaking into Fort Knox. He wouldn't divulge anything. He only said Liam didn't want to talk about it. Days and weeks ran together, one into the next. Before I knew it, July was gone, and the hot days of August were upon us. The old saying that time heals all wounds was a huge misinterpretation. If anything, time made things worse, at least in my case. I tried to keep busy by helping out at the store when needed or helping Mom with her baking. It had become a business in itself, but the diversions of normal life did nothing for me at night.

That's when it was the worst, when I was alone in my room. I missed Liam the most then. I couldn't sleep and desperately sought it. Only when I was in an unconscious state of mind and my world was black again did I feel comfort. There, in the oblivion, I could hear and see Liam. There we were together again. During the day, I spent time with my old girlfriends, trying to become reacquainted with them before they left for school. Except for Shauna, who was taking a year to travel the countryside, all were headed for college. Even Kendra was finalizing her plans. At one point, long before Liam was in the picture, we had planned to room together, but all that changed, especially after the proposal. I was in limbo, waiting for Liam to make up his mind, to clear his head and move on. We had decided that I would commute and go to a local college, but did that even matter now? It looked like I was free to do as I pleased and go where I pleased, college included. I moped around while Kendra packed some of her stuff.

"Jenny, please, you have to bounce out of this. Here, help me pack my suitcase."

I half-heartedly took a sweater that Kendra handed me. "That's easier said than done, Kendra."

"Look I can't explain what's going on with Liam. Nobody knows except him. I do know that a part of him almost died with you that night, and it's just taking him longer to move on from it. It's not helping you to mope around. I know he loves you. That's why he's taking this so hard."

"But don't you think he would want me to help him through it? Didn't he think I might need him too, a shoulder to cry on, too? He's not the only one that was affected by the accident. Damn it, Kendra, he hasn't even called me in over a month. What's up with that? He said he loved me, that he never would hurt me, what does he think he's doing to me now? This can't be for my own good."

Kendra stared at me as I vented. "Jenny, I know you're going through hell right now, and all I can say is that you need to keep moving on and things will work out. If Liam cares for you like everyone in this town knows he does, he'll come around. He's had a much harder life than you. Maybe this was just one more blow that he wasn't ready to deal with."

She had a point. He had lost his Mom, Dad, and Grandma, and almost his grandpa. Losing me could have been the last straw.

"Kendra, that's even more reason why I should be with him. I can help him through this, and if does care for me, why isn't he at least calling me?"

"Look, Jenny, I can't answer that, but I do know Tony says you're all he talks about. Just don't give up on him."

It was hard to believe Kendra when I felt so awful, but I had nothing else to cling to, and I needed Liam back. I just hoped that this little vacation he took from us wasn't his way of leaving me.

"Well, I guess that's that." We sat on her suitcase trying to close it.

"What did you put in here, the kitchen sink?"

"Ha ha, very funny. I'm taking that next time."

"I'm going to miss you. Who am I going to talk to?"

"We have each other's numbers, and I'm only going to be an hour away. We'll get together. I'm going to miss you too, Jenny."

"When do you leave?"

"I'm supposed to leave tomorrow, but I'm waiting until Friday. Tony is taking me out tomorrow night before he leaves for school." Her phone started ringing. "Speak of the devil."

"I'm going to go. If I don't see you before Friday, you better call me. Love you, girlfriend."

Kendra gave me a huge hug. "Love you too, dawg!"

I left quickly after Kendra answered her cell. I was already emotional enough, and I didn't need to make it worse by overhearing her and Tony talk. It was a reminder of Liam that I couldn't handle. I took my time getting home. There was nowhere to go and no one to see. Suddenly, I felt so alone.

Normally I would head out to Liam's, or I would be waiting for him to pick me up. But not today. Today, with all my friends busy with their college plans, I was by myself. A sinking, hollow feeling hit me. I turned the corner to my street. I must have been so caught up in my own self-pity that I didn't notice the black Ford pick-up truck parked in my driveway. *Liam,* I whispered. The truck looked surreal to me. I hadn't seen it in so long that I thought it was a dream. My heart started beating rapidly. "What is he doing here?" I was scared, almost too scared to move. *What if this is it, he came to say goodbye, to say it is over in person?*

I stayed in my spot, contemplating on whether I should stay in my car and drive away, avoiding the whole confrontation. I might be able to handle it better if I didn't face him. *What a coward I am turning into. All this time I scrutinized him for not showing up, and when he does, I can't bear the thought of seeing him because I was too afraid of the outcome.*

I squeezed the handle of my door, but before I could move, Liam walked over. He looked different, better than the last time I saw him. His hair was shorter but still fell around his handsome face, framing those beautiful blue eyes that God had bestowed upon him. I took a deep breath, unable to exhale, and I watched as Liam walked my way. My grip tightened on the door handle. I finally exhaled as Liam stopped in front of me. He was only a foot away from me, and his face was even more magnificent than I had remembered. The stubble that he had grown over the summer was gone, giving way to his masculine jaw line. I stared at him, wondering if he was just an illusion. It had seemed so long since I had seen him that I was having a problem grasping that he was standing in front of me.

"Hi," he said calmly.

"Hi." It was as if we were meeting for the first time.

"You look good, Jenny. No more crutches?"

"No, all gone."

He looked around, finally gazing at the pavement as he kicked a rock between his boots. "Look, I'm really sorry for how I've been behaving, especially this past month." I remained quiet. "Would you like to take a ride with me, maybe go someplace where we can talk in private?"

He looked back at my house. My parents were standing on the front porch.

"Sure."

He opened my car door, took my hand in his, and led me to his side of the truck. With an easy effort, he lifted me into the cab, and I slid over to the passenger side, not knowing if he wanted me next to him or not.

"What are you doing over there?"

"Sitting."

He pulled me back to his side. I was relieved and cautious at the same time. His actions made me think things were going to be okay, but after a month of not hearing from him, I wasn't sure. My heart was on the verge of breaking in half. I had to be on guard.

"You belong here, Jenny, next to me."

He stared intently into my eyes. There were no words spoken, but I could hear everything his heart was saying to me. As we drove off, I noticed my parents smiling arm in arm. "Funny," I thought, "they normally don't stand there as I leave." The drive was quiet with Liam and I not speaking. He kept his right hand tight around my left hand, squeezing it as if he was afraid I might fall out of the truck if he let go. He didn't say where we were going, but I was familiar with the route and knew exactly where the truck was heading: Liam's house. The winding drive that led to his house was barely visible now. The trees and shrubbery were thick and abundant with greenery, causing a tunnel effect that covered part of the drive. Liam came to his house and parked the truck. I looked around for Grandpa Mack. His truck was missing. It looked like we were alone.

"Here," he said as he climbed down and held out his hand for mine. I started climbing out of my seat when Liam picked me up in his arms.

"Liam what are you doing? What about your leg?"

"My leg is fine. It's not going to keep me from holding you in my arms. Anyway, this is something that I should have done a long time ago." He led me inside and into the living room, not once took his eyes off me.

I looked around to find the living room completely filled with lavender roses. "Oh my God, Liam. They're gorgeous."

"Just for you, Jenny." Liam sat me down on the sofa. He in turn knelt down in front of me on bended knee.

"Liam," I whispered as my heart started pounding out of my chest.

"Jenny, I can't expect you to forgive me for how I've acted over these past few months. I can only hope that me telling you here in front of you, on bended knee how sorry I am will be enough. I love you more than life itself, and I'm so sorry for the hell and torture I have put you through. I was being selfish and stupid and clearly not acting myself. I promise to you that I will never act that way again. I was wrong to shut you out. I thought that you would be better off without me, but I'm not better off without you. I still can't live without you, Jenny. These last few months have been a living hell for me, and I need you back in my life today, tomorrow, and forever. And whatever the future holds for us, as long as we're together, side by side, I'll know we'll make it. Our journey is together, and I'm ready to pay attention to the signs, whether they are an eleven or something else. I now know that is what brought us together in the beginning and that's what brought me back to you today. We can do anything, as long as we have each other. Please, Jenny, will you have me back?" In his hand he held a small black velvet box that held in it my ring. "Please, baby, will you marry me?" he asked again. He took the ring out and slipped it back on my left ring finger. "This is where it belongs, babe."

    I sat there staring at him, in total awe. "Are you sure Liam, absolutely sure, that you want me, the way I am, the way we were?"

    "More than ever. But not the way we were. You're right, our past shapes our future, and what happened, the accident, well, that's a part of us, and I know that now. I know that you don't blame me. I know that I can't change it, but I don't want to. It's made me realize what's really important in life, you, us."

    A contented feeling swept over me. I knew Liam was ready to move on and to move on with me. I swung my arms around him, giving him my answer. "Yes, baby, yes!"

    He grabbed me back, lifting me up in his arms. I wrapped my legs tightly around his waist as we found each other's lips. We kissed each other passionately, the way it used to be, the way it should always be.

    "I missed you, Jenny. I love you so much."

    "I love you too, Liam."

I stared at my ring. "What are you thinking about?" Liam asked.

"Just you and me."

"You mean Mr. and Mrs. Liam Larson?"

"Yeah, Mr. and Mrs. Liam Larson." I liked very much how that sounded.

I then knew why Mom and Dad were standing on the porch smiling. They knew before I did. Liam had talked to them. My body ached, this time not from the agony and pain that I had endured over the past few months, but now for the love that I had, that Liam and I had for each other. Liam carried me upstairs. The grandfather clock read eleven minutes after seven. How appropriate.

"We have a wedding to plan," he said softly in my ear.

"I know. We should start planning it soon."

"Yeah, we should." He kicked his bedroom door open. "But not right now. Right now we have some catching up to do." He softly kissed me as he closed the door behind us.

I stared at my ring. "What are you thinking about?" Liam asked.

"Just you and me."

"You mean Mr. and Mrs. Liam Larson?"

"Yeah, Mr. and Mrs. Liam Larson." I liked very much how that sounded.

I then knew why Mom and Dad were standing on the porch smiling. They knew before I did. Liam had talked to them. My body ached, this time not from the agony and pain that I had endured over the past few months, but now for the love that I had, that Liam and I had for each other. Liam carried me upstairs. The grandfather clock read eleven minutes after seven. How appropriate.

"We have a wedding to plan," he said softly in my ear.

"I know. We should start planning it soon."

"Yeah, we should." He kicked his bedroom door open. "But not right now. Right now we have some catching up to do." He softly kissed me as he closed the door behind us.

Jamie Kincaid

Jamie Kincaid grew up in Spencer, West Virginia. She has been a lover of words and a storyteller since she was a little girl. And although she carries two degrees, one in Marketing from Glenville State College in Glenville, West Virginia and the other in Education from Buffalo State College, in Buffalo, New York, her affair with writing always remained. She has traveled and lived in many areas but if you were to ask her where her home is, she would tell you in a heartbeat that it is and always will be Spencer.

In her spare time, when she is not writing and taking care of her family, you can find her running miles and miles. She lives in Ohio with her husband and their three beautiful children and her golden retriever who remains faithfully by her side while she continues to write her next tale.

She would like to thank her family and friends for their love, support and belief in her. And for those wonderful friends who always came to her rescue to help her out of computer situations, (you know who you are!) And for Him, who lifted me up and made me realize this is who I am and that it was only a matter of time before the world would know that too, seeing her stories in print can only be described as epic for her, a dream come true.

Liam and Jenny... they are in each and every one of us, believe in fate, true love, kismet... pickles, wild horses, silly jokes, sweet tea, endless talks, endless nights, drives to nowhere, heart and soul, you 'n me, always here, always and forever, destiny 831.

Made in the USA
Lexington, KY
06 December 2016